PRAISE
THE LAST T

"*The Last Treasure* is a true gift, delivering delicious r
balanced with serious emotional depth. Erika Marks has written an exhilarating tale of passion reignited."

—Kathleen Grissom, *New York Times* bestselling author of *The Kitchen House* and *Glory over Everything*

"Powerful, intimate, and beautifully written. A treasure of a story peopled with complex and compelling characters. I loved this book!"

—Wendy Wax, *USA Today* bestselling author of *Sunshine Beach*

PRAISE FOR THE OTHER NOVELS OF ERIKA MARKS

"Erika Marks creates an intoxicating blend of love, lost and found, and confronting the ghosts that lurk in our pasts. I highly recommend this beautiful story of growing up, growing older, building up walls, and knocking them down."

—Karen White, *New York Times* bestselling author of *Flight Patterns*

continued . . .

"A deftly woven tapestry of love, loss, and family loyalties. Erika Marks's modern-day *Romeo and Juliet* is pitch-perfect."

—*USA Today* bestselling author Wendy Wax

"The plot is heartwarming and engaging, stirring up a depth of emotion that makes this novel the perfect summer read."

—*RT Book Reviews* (4½ stars)

"An elegant and enchanting story about rescuing ourselves by saving each other, and a beautiful reminder of the magic and mystery we hold in our hearts."

—Eleanor Brown, *New York Times* bestselling author of *The Weird Sisters*

"A fascinating novel about the love and loss of relationships. . . . With Marks exercising great skills as a writer, you can feel the sand between your toes as you explore the beach and its byways, peopled by enjoyable and interesting characters." —The Huffington Post

"An awesome story of love, forgiveness, and letting go of the past . . . filled with secrets and heartbreak." —Fresh Fiction

"Magical! *The Mermaid Collector* had me immediately transported to the windswept cove at Cradle Harbor, feeling the mist on my face and the sand under my feet—and looking for mermaids at every turn."

—Sarah Jio, *New York Times* bestselling author of *Goodnight June*

"Spicy, delicious, and filled with surprises, *Little Gale Gumbo* is a wonderful stew, a debut novel that will fill you with joy. Put it on your reading menu and enjoy!"

—Adriana Trigiani, New York Times bestselling author of *All the Stars in the Heavens*

"Women's fiction to be savored . . . a winner."

—*Library Journal* (starred review)

Also by Erika Marks

It Comes in Waves

The Guest House

The Mermaid Collector

Little Gale Gumbo

The Last Treasure

Erika Marks

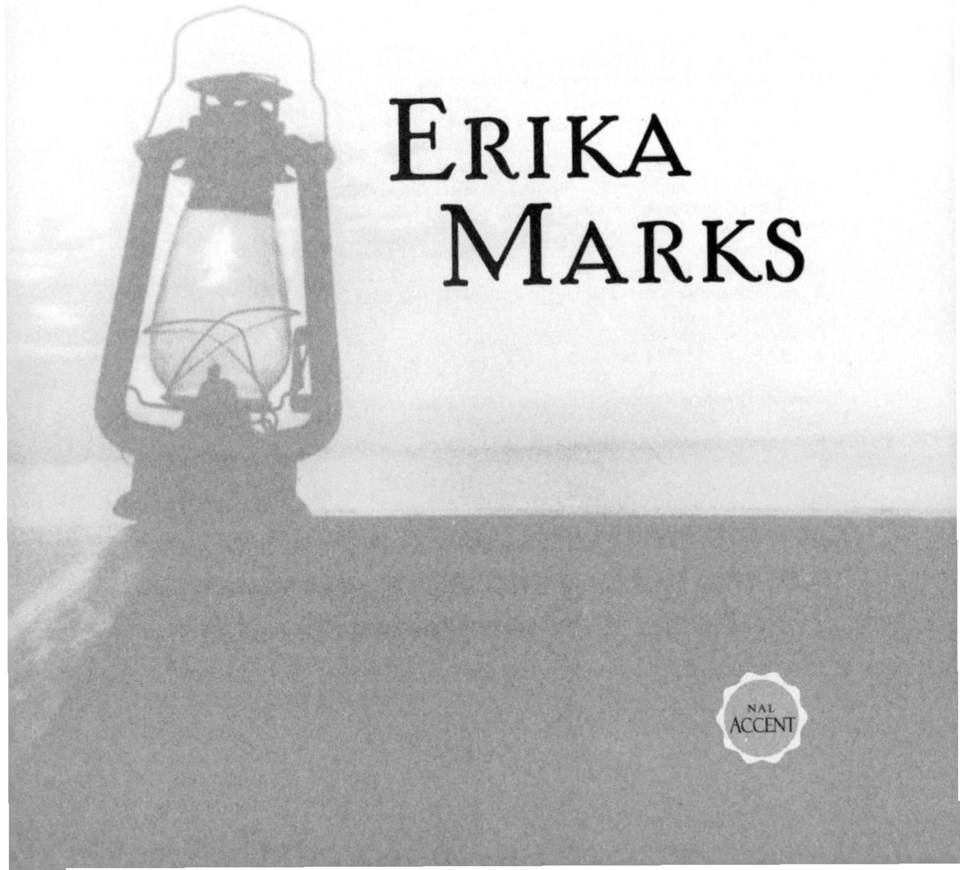

NAL Accent

NEW AMERICAN LIBRARY
Published by the Berkley Group,
an imprint of Penguin Random House LLC
375 Hudson Street, New York, New York 10014

This book is an original publication of New American Library.

First NAL Accent Printing, August 2016

For more information about Penguin Random House, visit penguin.com.

LIBRARY OF CONGRESS CATALOGING-IN-PUBLICATION DATA:

Names: Marks, Erika, author.
Title: The last treasure/Erika Marks.
Description: New York: New American Library, [2016]
Identifiers: LCCN 2016008847 (print) | LCCN 2016015910 (ebook) |
ISBN 9781101990841 (softcover) | ISBN 9781101990858 (ebook)
Subjects: LCSH: Triangles (Interpersonal relations)—Fiction. | Man-woman
Relationships—Fiction. | Underwater exploration—Fiction. |
Shipwrecks—Fiction. | Salvage—Fiction. | Domestic fiction. | BISAC:
FICTION / Contemporary Women. | FICTION/Family Life. | FICTION/Sea
Stories. | GSAFD: Love stories. | Sea stories.
Classification: LCC PS3613.A754525 L37 2016 (print) | LCC PS3613.A754525
(ebook) | DDC 813/.6—dc23
LC record available at https://lccn.loc.gov/201608847

Printed in the United States of America
10 9 8 7 6 5 4 3 2 1

Cover art: Evening at Kalahari © plainpicture/KNSY Bande; sunset © Craig Aurness/Fuse/Thinkstock Images
Cover design by Sarah Oberrender

PUBLISHER'S NOTE
This is a work of fiction. Names, characters, places, events and incidents are either the product of the author's imagination or are used fictitiously. The author's use of names of historical figures, places or events is not intended to change the entirely fictional character of the work. In all other respects, any resemblance to persons living or dead is entirely coincidental.

Penguin Random House

To my mother, a poet at heart,
who gave me my love for words and waves.

A woman knows the face of the man she loves as a sailor knows the open sea.

—HONORÉ DE BALZAC

Each man makes his own shipwreck.

—MARCUS ANNAEUS LUCANUS

The *Last* Treasure

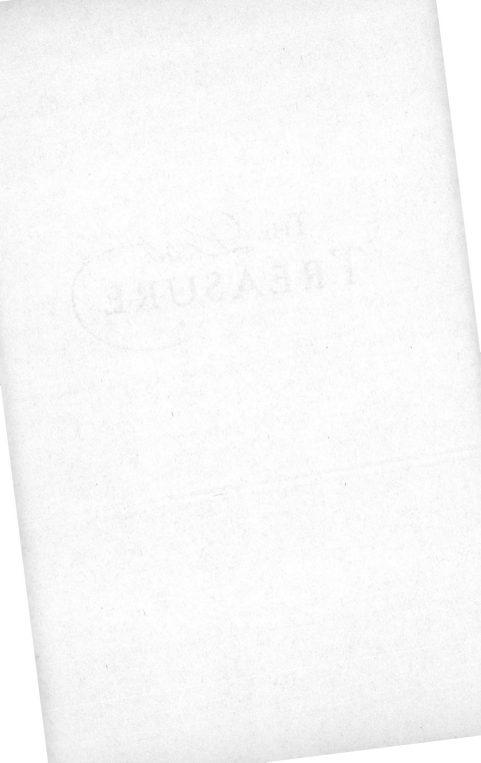

TO: Sam Felder <sfelder76@gomail.com>

FROM: Beth Henson <bhenson@obshipwreckmuseum.org>

Sam:

I hope this e-mail finds you, and finds you well.

Last week, our curator discovered a logbook in the home of a Buxton collector. It appears the last few entries were written by Theodosia Burr Alston in the months following the *Patriot*'s disappearance, so of course I thought of you right away.

I don't know if you are still entertaining your investigation of the mystery, but I did want to let you know in the event you might wish to come to the museum to have a look. If you do, I'll gladly reserve any announcements to the press until you've had a chance to see the journal for yourself. We are, as you can imagine, excited beyond words at this acquisition.

Also, I have an extra bedroom if you need a place to stay.

It would be lovely to catch up.

Fondly,

Beth

BETHANY HENSON
DIRECTOR, OUTER BANKS SHIPWRECK MUSEUM
NAGS HEAD, NC

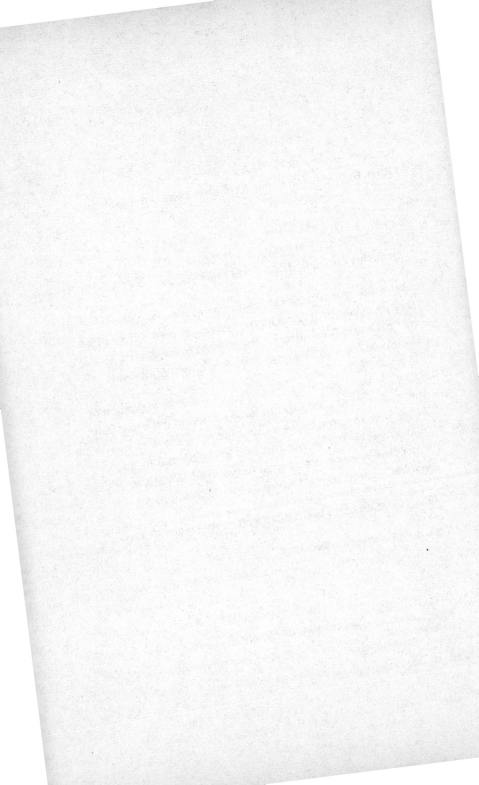

She descends through the mist, the weight of her tank rolling along her spine, the smooth motor of her fins cutting silently through the water.

She is looking for the wreck's debris field, the pieces of its battered puzzle emerging through the murky haze, and the clouds of sand and silt that have kept the ship's bones hidden for so long will part like smoke.

But something is wrong.

The strange color of the water is her first warning—a purplish black, bearing no resemblance to any ocean she has ever dived beneath. When she slides her hands through this water, it feels thick and warm, which the sea never is at such depths. She swims on, diving deeper, her weight belt fighting her body's natural buoyancy. Where is the bottom? She should have reached it by now. Her bearings lost, she looks the only way she can, side to side, her vision restricted by the small window of her mask. She is desperate for some marker to ground her, the towline to the boat or telltale bumps to signal the ocean floor. It is as if she has been set adrift in space, an eternity of nothingness around her, no edges, no corners, just endless dark and the curdling certainty that she is alone in the universe.

She reaches for her gauge to check her oxygen and sees the impossible—only a hundred pounds left; just a few minutes in the water and the tank is nearly drained. Blood rushes to her scalp; panic surges. She has to turn around, go back, go up.

Rising, she is relieved for a glorious second to feel her body obey; then fear returns. She swims harder, hands clawing as they race toward the glowing surface, as if she is buried in dirt and trying to dig out.

But she knows she swims too fast. Her joints ache. She has to slow down, but still her arms and legs continue to fight, even as excruciating pain tears through her elbows and wrists.

If she can just get back to the boat, back to the top.

If she can just breathe.

1

KEY LARGO, FLORIDA
June 25

Liv bolts upright, her chest squeezed like a fist. She needs a breath, just one, but there's no air, only hollow wheezing. She reaches into the dark and slaps at the nightstand, finding the drawer pull and tugging hard, sending the clutter of shells and hair clips inside it skidding to the edge like unbelted children in a swerving car. When her fingers finally land on her inhaler, she shoves the cylinder into her mouth and sucks in as she depresses the top, relief shuddering through her to feel the rescue of air.

Safe.

She falls back against the headboard, blinking into the black, and waits for her breathing to slow.

Stupid, awful dream. Third time this week. Whit would

surely blame the leftover Thai she devoured shortly before ten, or the cup of mocha chip she indulged in afterward.

Whit.

She reaches out for the long compass of her husband's sleeping body, but her fingers land on the empty mattress.

She feels for her phone and clicks it to life.

Three thirty-two.

He did return from dinner with Phil Edwards, didn't he?

Or did she just dream the crash of him coming into their bedroom, the groan of the bed when he fell on it, still dressed, the two thumps of his shoes hitting the floor? What about when he rolled against her and reached up under her T-shirt, wanting to make love, then falling asleep before he could get her underwear off?

She scans the dark, listening. The familiar clanging of metal blows through the screens, the telltale clamoring of movement on the boat, then the frothy growl of *Theo*'s propellers spinning to life.

Oh God.

She kicks herself free of the sheet and lands on the cool Mexican tile of their bedroom floor, knotting her red hair as she rushes down the hall to the living room. Through the sliders, beyond the line of palms that separate the lanai from the concrete of the dock, she can see him on the upper deck of their thirty-foot dive boat.

She yanks the door open, no time to close it behind her. The humid air clings to her bare legs, a curtain of moisture, as if she's stepped through a giant spiderweb.

"Whit!" she yells as she runs down the steps, terrified he won't hear her over the whir of the motor. *"Whit!"*

Miraculously he turns and sees her, a drowsy, pleased smile spreading across his face. He's wearing only a pair of boxers. Her immediate thought: *Please, God, don't let him fall in*. Sober, he is the strongest, surest swimmer she knows; drunk, he will sink like a stone, and with his six-three and two hundred twenty pounds, his rescue will be impossible for her small frame.

"Avast, me beauty!" He swings his glass high, sending a necklace of liquor arching through the dock lights, and her pulse quickens.

He only speaks pirate when there's bad news.

The concrete is damp and prickly under her bare feet. "Whit, what are you doing?"

"I thought I'd take the old girl out for a moonlight ride. Join me?" His blue eyes are wild, wolfish.

"There's no moon," she says, as if the correction might deter him. "And you're not even dressed."

"Right you are, lass." He tugs a faded Marlins cap off the throttle handle and snaps it over his tousled blond hair, giving her a satisfied grin. "Better?"

Terrific.

She rushes onto the boat and climbs the ladder to the flybridge, feeling the tremors of panic soften when she arrives at the helm. This close, she could lunge for the ignition if she had to—but the current of dread still sizzles in the muggy air. A nearly drained bottle of scotch sits by the wheel, the amber liquid shuddering with the vibration of the engine. He's done something foolish, but what? The possible transgressions race through her: *An impulsive purchase they don't need? The coltish blonde he flirted with at Rachel and Daniel's solstice party? Has he totaled the van . . . ?*

Despite his height and sturdy build, her husband looks fragile, like something glued and not yet dried, and it scares her.

She can hear the tremble of uncertainty in her voice. "Love, shut her down and come back to bed. You need sleep."

"God, I love this boat." He drops into the captain's chair and swivels around, his expression wistful as he scans the controls. "Do you realize that we could chart our entire life together on this boat, Red? That every moment of significance for us happened right here?"

She nods, nostalgia falling like a shawl over her too, snug and warm. Even now, beneath the diesel fumes, she can still find the scent of rusted metal and warm rubber, the intoxicating smells of a perfect dive.

But when Whit lifts his gaze to find hers, his eyes crackle with lust—it's not their early memories of treasure hunting that he's recalling.

"The first time I kissed you was on this boat," he says. "The first time I held that gorgeous hair in my hands." He opens his huge hands and closes them in fists. "Christ, I couldn't get deep enough inside you."

His eyes slide down her body, drinking her in, and the familiar tug of longing pulls at the space below her stomach, the weight of wanting his words could always coax from her like a fever.

But despite desire, impatience burns. She just wants it over with—wants to know what he's done. Let it be something small, something easily and quickly repairable. They have only two weeks before they are scheduled to begin their next mission in North Carolina, the one Whit has promised will bring them the success their recent salvage missions haven't.

"Whit, *please*." She's begging now. "What's wrong?"

He spins the chair back around and lands under the glare of the spotlight. For a blissful moment, she thinks the crescent of purple under his right eye is a trick of the night, a reflection from the surface of the canal, and her heart holds for a second before it crashes.

"My God, your face!"

"It's not so bad," he says cheerfully. "Feel worse for the table."

"You should be putting ice on it."

"Good idea." He slams his tumbler against his eye and winces. "Shit."

She tries to help guide the glass to the worst of the bruise, but he waves her off. "It was all a big misunderstanding." His voice is conversational, as if she might actually enjoy this story. "Phil and I were waiting for our beers, and this knucklehead next to us accuses Phil of stealing his seat, so I tried to—"

Phil? Blood rushes to her forehead. "Whit, please just tell me you didn't let our project archaeologist see you get into a bar fight."

He squints his uninjured eye. "I don't think he saw much after that unfortunate pop to the side of his face."

"He got *hit*?"

"It was just a tap, really. I doubt he'll need more than a couple stitches. Serves him right for having such a lousy swing."

"Whit!" Liv claps both hands over her mouth, sure if she doesn't she will let go a scream that will draw every one of their neighbors out of bed.

They have spent months putting together this salvage project of the *Siren,* a blockade runner buried off the coast of Wilmington that sank with a fortune in her hold, and he has blown it up in a single night. All the pieces they've secured, the beach house in Topsail that is to be their base of operations, already rented. A seventy-eight-foot commercial dive boat, already chartered.

Panic sends her heart into a gallop, thumping hard against her ribs. "What are we supposed to do without an on-site archaeologist?"

Whit tugs off his cap and tosses it behind him. "We'll just hire someone else."

"Who? There isn't anyone left on the planet who'll put up with you!"

"Then you're stuck with me, lass." His eyes flash wickedly. "Let's go below and I'll shiver your timbers."

"Whit—I'm serious!"

"Aye, so be I," he growls playfully, yanking her into his lap and getting a bite on her neck before she wriggles free and moves for the ladder. "Red, wait."

She hears the engine go quiet, but she is already back down and across the deck, training her eyes on the water and trying to find focus in the calm surface.

Two weeks. Maybe there is still a chance they can find

someone else to take over the PA role in that time, even on such short notice. It would have to be someone familiar, with a good reputation. Someone who could step right in, no hand-holding. Someone who could keep Whit straight, keep him coloring in the lines, as Sam used to say—

Sam.

Gooseflesh flares up her bare arms. She grabs herself and rubs hard, afraid Whit will see the tiny traitorous bumps.

She takes a seat on the bench and waits for him to descend the ladder. "What about Sam?" she asks.

Whit's eyes cool, the teasing cornflower blue darkening to pewter.

"He used to be one of the best marine archaeologists out there, Whit."

"Until he went back to law school."

"That doesn't mean he's washed his hands of the field completely."

Whit stares down at her with disbelief. "Felder left, Red. He left you—he left *us*. He made it clear he wanted out."

"That was nine years ago. Maybe he's let that all go."

No wonder he continues to look at her as if she's lost her mind. Sam who believed sentimentality was a character flaw; Sam who could—and *did*—turn off emotions like car engines?

Still she presses on. "Maybe he's forgiven us."

"Forgiven us?" Whit frowns at her. "What the hell did we ever do to need his forgiveness?"

We fell in love, Liv wants to say but doesn't—and she doesn't need to. Whit's eyes find hers and flash with understanding.

"We have to at least consider asking him," Liv says calmly.

"Scrapping this project isn't an option. Not when we're so dangerously close to being in debt."

Close? God, who is she kidding? They're already sunk. The fortune they made from the recovery of the *Bella Donna* six years earlier has been bled—not to mention the legal fees they incurred fighting for their fair share of the valuables—and they are hemorrhaging with the cost of this new mission. The *Siren* may have held millions in gold when she sank on her way to Charleston—or so Whit insists. Even if they recover only a piece of that fortune, they'd be on firm ground again.

Whit blows out a hard breath and joins her on the bench, swinging his nearly drained bottle between his knees. "I don't know, Red. There's too much history there."

"This time would be different," she says. "This wouldn't be about the *Patriot*."

"Wouldn't it?" Whit's eyes hold hers, demanding truth. The mystery of the *Patriot*'s 1813 disappearance was the thread that had always stitched their lives together—hers, Whit's, and Sam's—from the moment they united as students to find the elusive shipwreck until the day they each went their separate way.

Whit promised her that he'd find the answers Sam couldn't. It had been a fierce and heartfelt vow—the only kind Whit could ever make. He'd even renamed their boat *Theo's Wish* for the wreck's most famous passenger, Theodosia Burr Alston, knowing how attached Liv had become to the lost woman. Whit had sworn not to quit until he and Liv solved the mystery, and proved what they'd always believed, that pirates had seized the *Patriot* and taken Theodosia captive. But thirteen years after their first expedition to search for the lost schooner, life and the pursuit of treasure have taken them far from their precious investigation, and Liv still doesn't have her answer.

Tears sting the insides of her cheeks. She could tell Whit about her nightmare, make him feel especially guilty for putting all this at risk when he knows she has promised her doctor this will be her last deep dive, but she doesn't want to relive it. And she doesn't have to confess her dream to convince him.

He downs the last of his scotch, wincing as if he's swallowing nails. Around them, the music of night animals stirs in the quiet, the buzz of insect wings, the trill of frogs. Whit's phone sits on the hatch—he scoops it up and begins to type.

"You won't find him that way," Liv says.

"Watch me."

She shivers, her hands clasped, toes clenched. She considered searches like this a hundred times, curious as to where life took Sam in the years after he left her. It is the ease that has kept her from looking—knowing how much she could find out, and how quickly.

"He's on the cape," Whit announces, holding out the phone to show her. "Captain of a dive charter boat."

Liv takes it, startled. Sam back to dive charters? Is Whit sure it's the same Sam Felder? What happened to his pursuit of maritime law? She scrolls to read all about the captain of the *Flotsam*. There isn't a picture, but there's no question Whit's found him.

She hands back the phone quickly, as if she couldn't care less what has become of Sam Felder, only whether he'll accept their offer, and Whit begins to dial.

"You're calling him now?" she says.

"Why not?"

Her skin warms again, regret surging. She stands, too quickly, and feels light-headed. A wave of guilt quickly steadies her.

In all her disappointment and fear, she's been neglectful too.

"Maybe we should see if there's another time, a *better* time," she says sheepishly. "Maybe wait till the fall now."

When she glances back at Whit, he is frowning at her. "What are you talking about?"

She shrugs. "I'm just saying, why rush? We've hit a bump—it happens. Maybe the best thing to do is step back and see if we can't reschedule the project."

"Red . . ." His voice deepens. "If this is about your father . . ."

She shakes her head and looks away. "It's a long time to leave him."

Whit groans. "For Christ's sake, you're not *leaving* him—you're going away for a few weeks. For work. Besides, he won't even know you're gone."

She closes her eyes, the reminder terribly painful though she knows Whit doesn't mean to hurt her.

"Baby, he has people there to take care of him." His tone has turned tender, all reproach gone.

But still she can't relent. "People," she says. "Not his daughter."

"At some point, you're going to have to let yourself off this cross, you know." He reaches out to stroke her cheek, but she turns away and rises. There's no point in this argument—it's always been so simple for him. But then Whit was the one who'd convinced her to move out of her father's house into the dorms, when Sam had cautioned her to use patience, to live at home a while longer. Sam who promised her there would be a reward for propping up her overly dependent father—Whit who'd urged her to cast aside duty and spread her wings, to soar the way her mother never had the chance to do.

"I'm going in," she says.

"Red." Whit's call stops her at the edge of the boat. She turns back, seeing a flash of trepidation spark in his eyes. He levels a hard look at her, those silver-blue pools like two whitecapped seas, swirling and deep and blowing right through her. His appeal is a force of nature—as unyielding as the tide.

"She's still out there somewhere and we'll find her," he says. "I intend to keep my promise."

She blinks back tears as she turns for the house. "You always do."

Damn.

Whit climbs back up to the flybridge and stares out at the canal. He never meant to finish the bottle. He never meant to start that fight in the bar—or lose them their PA.

He never means any of it.

Dueling points of pain pierce his temples. He squeezes his eyes shut.

Livy.

She can look at him, flutter those long red lashes, and wreck him. Whit tells himself he's made her happy all these years and most days he believes it. Then there are nights like this one, black nights so silent you have to remind yourself you're not underwater—and how do you know you're not? When you breathe, which sometimes you have to remind yourself to do too—and then you're full of doubt, fat and bloated with it like a tick.

He worries about her diving. The *Siren* is deep: nearly a hundred and fifty feet down—the deepest she's ever dared to go. But how can he forbid her now, when he was the one who'd convinced her to learn to dive in the first place, teaching her that weekend Sam was out of town and she'd nearly drowned in the process?

Jesus, he'd been so scared of losing her that day. And she hadn't even been his to lose yet.

If he weren't so drunk, Whit knows he could untangle his thoughts, but maybe it's best they stay all knotted up. He's not dumb—not even when he's drunk. Sometimes he thinks he might just be sharper this way. People get lazy when they know you're drunk, unguarded and loose, sure you won't remember their confessions or even hear them. He's learned a lot at the bottom of a bottle.

And now he has to ask Sam Felder to save his skin. And Sam will see that Whit hasn't kept his promise to Liv—the only one she ever really cared about: to find out what happened to the *Patriot,* and, more important, to Theodosia. Theo.

Maybe Liv's right—Sam never hung on to the past. Of course Sam's probably given up the mystery of the *Patriot*. Whit has nothing to prove—especially not to Sam Felder. Only to Liv. Only her. He just hopes she can forgive him one last time.

The light in their bedroom blinks out. Whit stares at the

dark rectangle of glass, imagining Livy lying in her usual pose: one leg long, the other bent. His flamingo. Just like the one he'd had tattooed on his shoulder three years ago after he lost their wreck claim in a poker game on Wes's boat. Still furious, she'd told him the tattoo looked like a mutant crawfish, but she'd kept them in bed until noon the next day, admiring it until she teared up. *"I thought flamingos were supposed to be pink,"* she said. *"Not mine,"* he told her.

Yes, maybe it's better that he's plastered, he thinks as he rolls his thumb over the screen to find Sam's number. Maybe numb like this, he can pretend he doesn't care. He's done it before.

Provincetown, Massachusetts

"Yours."

Justine's voice purrs through the darkness, so effortlessly Sam thinks he dreams the word, but the chimes continue, growing louder.

He turns his head, disparate pieces of information coming together in sharp focus. His ring. His phone. He reaches across her naked body for his cell, squinting to read the screen. He doesn't recognize the number, so he lets the call go to voice mail, dropping the phone back on the shelf and blinking up into the watery blue-black, listening to the familiar sounds of the sea at rest all around him, the slap and suck of waves against the hull. The lullaby of the tide. He was dreaming of a coral reef, curtains of fish like stained glass, and he wants to get back there.

He throws an arm over his eyes and sleep returns.

• • •

Justine is already dressed when he gets to the galley to make coffee at six thirty.

Her blue eyes ice over. "I'm not sleeping here anymore. My back can't take it."

She made the same ultimatum the last time he met her for dinner. After all, she argued, she has a beautiful town house with windows instead of portholes, and sheets that don't smell like salt and rust. She should have known him three years ago when he was still at the firm and living in a condo with a tenth-floor view of the Chicago River. She would have liked his digs just fine then.

He knocks the old grounds out and gives the basket a rough rinse.

"You could rent a real place, you know," she says. "God knows you could afford it." Her face softens slightly when she reaches out to touch his short beard. "The office gets new listings in every day. I could show you some."

"This *is* a real place."

"I mean a real place on the *ground*."

He pops the top off the coffee can.

"So, who was that who called last night?" she asks. "And please don't tell me you're married."

The phone. Sam walks back to the berth and picks up his cell, seeing the telltale envelope in the corner of the screen. He listens to the message as he returns to the galley. The man's voice is rough, tentative, familiar.

"Sam, it's Whit . . . Yeah, *that* Whit . . ."

After that he hears only pieces.

"—need a new project archaeologist—

"—I screwed the pooch—

"—kind of last minute, I know—"

An interminable rambling minute later, Sam hangs up.

Justine studies him as he returns to the galley. "Everything okay?"

"Fine."

"Who was it?"

"Wrong number."

He returns to the coffeemaker and frees the empty carafe. Justine slides in between him and the counter, blocking him, her eyes trying to hold his. Her fingers dance up his bare chest. "My first showing canceled," she says. "Maybe we could give that awful bed of yours another try?"

Sam reaches around her to push the pot back onto the plate. It's almost seven. He doesn't have time for coffee—what was he thinking?

"I need to get the boat ready," he says. "It's late."

Justine steps aside. "Wow, someone woke up on the wrong side of the bunk, *Captain*." She sweeps up her purse and moves to the ladder.

Sam watches her exit the cabin, thinking he could stop her if he wanted, say something kind, but his thoughts are already a million miles, another lifetime, away.

Today's passengers are a bachelor party, three men from Boston, all in their late twenties. Cape Cod is loaded with wrecks, several of which are in the harbor and easily accessible—others, such as the famous pirate ship *Whydah*, lay just outside park waters. Sam has chartered to those sites on occasion, but since today's tour members have requested an easier dive, he will take them to *Marisol*, a trawler not far from shore that sank in forty feet of water, her pilothouse still intact and covered in a colorful rug of anemones.

His first mate, a good kid named Pete, helps the men set up on the deck. Sam watches them carefully as they strap in. Often divers inflate their experience to be allowed down without a guide, and Sam fears these men have done just that. Two stumble with their gear—and though Sam can't know if it is the effect of too much partying the night before or a general lack of skill, it doesn't matter. Even an easy dive comes with risks, and he is not a betting man. Sam has dived and crewed with careless men and he knows the ripple effect of one poor decision when you're under.

He tells Pete to suit up and follow them down as a guide. The ringleader, a cocky, doughy-faced blond, is insulted and resistant, insisting the charter company assured them they could dive on their own, but Sam is feeling especially agitated this morning and he doesn't care. The guy can agree to a guide, or they can all go back to the marina. There are a few tense moments of indecision, but the man finally consents. Minutes later, the four take their giant strides off the swim platform and descend, leaving Sam on board to watch the water and the horizon. Bad weather can appear without warning and churn the sea in a heartbeat. Still it will be a good dive for them, he thinks as he walks the deck. Good visibility.

If it was a tougher dive, he might have considered joining

them. The water seems too quiet up top. Or maybe his thoughts are too loud.

An hour later, the group surfaces, and just in time too. Clouds have gathered and the sea is building a steady chop. Out of their gear, the men congregate on the benches and drain sodas.

The blond cowboy makes his way over to Sam at the bridge, wearing an admonished smile.

"Sorry about that earlier," the younger man says. "I was thinking maybe we'd find ourselves a little luck down there. A few gold coins, you know?"

"Not likely on a fishing boat," Sam reminds him.

"You ever find treasure around here?"

"Not here, no."

The man's eyes brighten. "But somewhere, right?"

Sam shrugs, his patience thinning again. "Somewhere, yeah," he says, turning his attention to the wheel.

Back at the marina, the men pile into their cars and head into town for their last night of debauchery. Sam tells Pete he can take off early, that he's more than paid his dues for the day, and the young man is grateful. More than anything, Sam just wants the boat to himself again.

Night arrives while he works, putting away gear, refilling tanks. Around him, the marina hums, the other charter boats winding down for the night too, last-minute maintenance and cleaning, shouts between decks, a few muffled televisions. The village of water homes. Lives clocked by the tide, as easily untethered as their boats.

All day he's had distractions, reasons to keep his mind and hands off the ghost call from his past and the sneaking curiosities it brought with it, but now the night stretches out before him as vast and quiet as the sea.

Now when the question knocks again, he will have no choice but to answer.

Might as well let it in, he thinks as he slips belowdecks.

He has to move two file boxes out of the hanging locker beside the berth to get to it, but the map is right where he remembers.

He takes the roll to the table and uncurls the heavy paper, securing the corners to keep it flat—if the four ends can still be called corners, as speckled with tack holes as they are, reminding him of those target papers at shooting ranges. He's not sure there's even enough paper left to attach it to a wall anymore.

The haphazard scribbles of their years of notes swim over the yellowed map, Liv's handwriting and his. He finds himself reading them and smiles, remembering when they added each one, especially the first few: the labels Liv set down with feverish speed that night in Hatteras, spilling everything she knew about the *Patriot*'s disappearance while she wrote, explaining that she wanted to know where the schooner sank so she could find out what happened to her most famous passenger, Theodosia Burr Alston—an interest Sam marveled at, even if he didn't entirely understand Liv's passion at the time. How quickly and completely he'd found himself transfixed, watching her slide her pencil all over the coastline that night, the determined way she'd sucked on her lower lip. He'd wanted to suck on it too.

He's nearly thrown the chart away a dozen times. Life on a boat requires a maniacal degree of downsizing. Must-haves are priority: clothes, food, a modest library of only one's most treasured books. And yet he found room for the chart.

He still isn't entirely sure why he took it when he moved out of their apartment, knowing how much the map meant to Liv, knowing how many years of research she'd collected on its thick crackled surface—much of which they'd collected *together,* he reminds himself. It wasn't as if he didn't have a right to the chart—it had belonged to them equally, hadn't it? Had he taken it to punish her for not wanting to go to Chicago with him? Maybe. Or was it because he wanted to be the one to deliver her the answer to the mystery? He wonders if Liv even cares anymore about the *Patriot,* about Theodosia—Theo, as Liv had always called her, as if the lost woman was a dear friend.

When Sam learned that Liv had married Whit Crosby, he'd found it wholly impossible to believe. It didn't make sense. Whit and his reckless methods, his total lack of self-control or regard for rules. Even now his mind still can't form the image of the two of them together—and he avoids trying.

He slides his hands over the dry paper, the heat of his palms drawing out the salty smell of age and wear.

He forgot how Liv never bothered to dot her i's.

There are seamen who believe they can hear the cries of the lost when they near a deadly stretch of water, fiercely superstitious men who live and breathe by signs when they cross an ocean. Sam traveled with one on the salvage mission of a submarine: a wiry man with milky blue eyes who went belowdecks when they anchored, shaking because he claimed to see the ghosts of drowned soldiers rising from the sea.

If Sam were one of those men—which he isn't—he might decide the universe has aligned his stars. Because just the week before, out of the blue, he received an e-mail from Beth Henson—a former classmate from ECU he hasn't heard from in years—telling him of curious news: a diary, believed to be written by Theodosia Burr Alston, and dated after the *Patriot*'s disappearance, had just been acquired by the Outer Banks Shipwreck Museum where Beth is now the director. Maybe Sam would like to come down and have a look through it—that is, if he was still interested in the mystery?

Truthfully he hadn't been. Not anymore. He'd put the *Patriot* and Theodosia away when he and Liv broke up. Sure, he thought about it from time to time, casually following any leads that cropped up in his news feeds about unidentified shipwrecks, especially those found around the Outer Banks, but now . . .

Whit's message. The chance to see Liv again.

Beautiful, stubborn Liv.

Sam won't lie—he's curious. Not about the journal, not that. About Liv. He's curious to know how the years have treated her—if living with Crosby has changed her, if she ever wishes things had turned out differently. He wonders if she's surprised he left his father's law firm and returned to the water. If Sam saw her again, if she saw him, would she wish they'd never said good-bye?

And yes, maybe it turns him on to think he could return with news of a diary. That he could give Liv the one thing she always wanted: to know what really happened to Theodosia.

Challenge—hot and ferocious—charges through him; memories spill like water from an overturned glass.

Sam could wait to call them back, he supposes as he picks up his phone and retrieves Whit's number. Make them wonder, maybe even make them sweat—but it's a waste of time.

Already he can see the flash of excitement in Liv's eyes when he tells her about Theodosia's diary, the grateful wash of salmon that will flood her cheeks, swallowing the starry map of her freckles.

He closes his eyes and pulls in a hard breath.

Already he can feel the heat of her body under his.

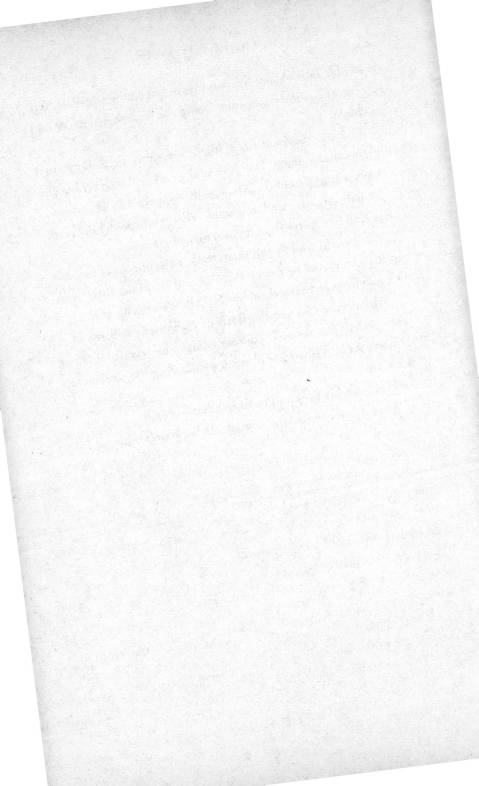

2

TOPSAIL ISLAND, NORTH CAROLINA

Two weeks later

Tuesday

When Whit turns the van into the driveway of the three-story Caribbean-style castle just before noon, Liv is certain it is the largest, most ostentatious house she has ever seen. Palms flank the arched entryway like palace guards, bright blue hurricane shutters swing out, and decks wrap around all three floors, not including the top story, which appears to be made entirely of glass.

"Now, I know we said we wouldn't go crazy this mission, Red—"

"We?" She spins in her seat. "You promised me something cozy, something *small*."

"This is small . . . *ish*."

"Compared to what? Buckingham Palace?"

"Exactly." Two weeks after his row, the curl of navy and purple that circled his right eye has finally softened to a yellowish green. He gives her his very best smoldering smile, which he knows damn well can absolve him of practically anything, short of murder—and very well maybe that too, though she hopes they never have to find out—but today she's determined not to give in to his charms.

"Maybe it only looks big on the outside," he says.

She closes her eyes.

"We've got a crew of eleven, Red. Did you think we'd all share one big bed?" His grin widens. "Kinky girl."

He reaches across the seat to grab her thigh, but she twists away from him, not yet ready to let him off the hook.

A warm breeze drifts through the window, salted and feathery and so achingly familiar she thinks she could cry. It's been almost a decade since she left North Carolina. Standing at the rental car counter at the Wilmington Airport that morning, she waited for the sensation of her return to settle into her bones, sure it would the minute she and Whit stepped off the plane or walked through the sliding doors to find their shuttle—it didn't. And now she understands why.

Until she arrived at the water's edge, she wasn't yet back.

Whit rubs his jaw. "Okay, maybe the elevator is a little over-the-top."

"There's an *elevator*?"

He leans over and kisses her hard on her gaping mouth, the way he always does when he knows he can't win an argument or change her mind and he is simply too impatient to keep trying.

Then he yanks the handle and kicks open the door. "Last one in has to scrub all six heads."

Eight, actually. Counting the two outdoor showers, which Liv does as she tours the three floors, finding a view of the Atlantic in nearly every room, and decks scaled for cruise ships, which makes perfect sense, really, when the polished wooden ceilings look like upside-down ships, their laminated beams curved like ribs. Madness.

The first crew members arrive shortly after one. Four men in their twenties climb out of an enormous white truck—one with a completely shaved head and sleeves of tattoos, another with a ponytail, all with deep, even tans. They unload their gear and a ridiculous amount of beer. Whit has promised not to partake, but Liv isn't holding her breath. She knows how the spell of preproject euphoria can take over, how small toasts can lead to drained bottles, shots to tumblers. She just hopes everyone gets along. Emotions can run high on the water—and *under* it.

An hour later, four more crew members arrive, these men much older than the first group, their skin leathery, their thin lips chapped. Two of them, Chuck and Dennis, Liv knows from their work on the *Bella Donna*. They smell so strongly of diesel when they hug her that Liv wonders if they have bathed in fuel. Whit whisks them inside, where they complain of the traffic and the crappy roads before dropping their gear in the foyer and demanding a bathroom and a beer before any further interaction. By four, the men are all downstairs in the game room playing pool, and the pristine kitchen has been turned into a mess hall. Bags of potato chips and empty beer and soda cans litter the huge granite island; the Sub-Zero fridge is packed with stacks of meat and bags of shrimp bound for the home's outdoor grilling station later that night. Liv doesn't dare ask how much it all cost.

By five, still no Sam. It would serve her right, Liv thinks as she steps out onto the deck and sinks into one of the Adirondack chairs that line the back of the house, if she pushed so hard to get Sam here only to have him leave them hanging—the very thing he always used to claim Whit did to them, which Whit did, on more than one occasion.

Maybe this will be Sam's final chance at tit for tat.

Or maybe she's just nervous and paranoid.

A quartet of pelicans glides across the sky. She watches them descend, smiling at their wobbly landing on the water. The breeze that brushes past her is fragrant with the dry, herby smell of sunbaked dune grass. The water is calm today, at least on the surface, part of the stretch of sea known as the Graveyard of the Atlantic. Liv traveled its length like a highway when she and Sam and Whit ran their treasure-hunting charter.

Looking out at the water now, she finds it hard not to think of Theodosia or the *Patriot,* but she can't allow herself to get caught up in the search again. They are here to recover the *Siren*. But God, it's hard, really, to look at *any* part of this view and not think about those early days, when she and Whit and Sam believed themselves clever enough to find the *Patriot* on their own. When the mystery of Theodosia Burr Alston's fate had consumed her—only slightly more than her need to belong to Sam Felder.

Behind her, through the high wall of windows, the rise and fall of the men's loud voices draw her out of her memories. She is sure it must just be the excitement of a victorious billiard match, but then the deck door swings open and Whit appears with his hands on his hips.

He can flash that smile all he wants—she's still pissed about this ridiculous house.

She leans back in the chair. "I'm still not speaking to you, you know."

He grins. "Fine, don't speak to me. Just come inside. You're going to want to see this."

In the living room, she finds the crew huddled around Whit's computer, their voices climbing over one another's. He shouts for them to move out of the way and plants Liv in front of the screen, his hands heavy on her shoulders. Even before she sees the blurry image of the seafloor, she can feel his pulse thrumming through his palms, and her own heartbeat hastens.

He's found something.

Something *big*.

"What does that look like to you?" He points to the lower right corner of the gray image, tapping his finger on the faint edge of a crescent shape that pokes out of the gray bottom.

She twists to look up at him; his eyes flash knowingly, but he won't say a word. And she doesn't want any hints. Identifying artifacts from scans, figuring out what is treasure and what is just rubble, is one of her favorite parts of the hunt. It *could* be the lip of a medicinal jar, she thinks, studying the image again—after all, medicine was one of the more popular contrabands blockade runners delivered—or maybe a porthole. Or maybe . . . Liv tilts her head. Is that the bottom of a letter just above the ridge? Maybe an *N* or an *R*? It could be, and looking closer she thinks there might be more letters. And the edge of the curve looks flat, not rounded. Tapered, like a—

Her cheeks flush hot. She spins around to face him. "You found the bell!"

Whit lifts her off the floor and kisses her deeply, managing to swing her a half turn in the thick of the huddle. Another round of victory cheers and high fives; Liv wants in too, demanding they slap their meaty palms against her small hand. It's tremendous news. If they've located the ship's bell, they can prove the wreck is the *Siren* even before they bring up a single artifact. Whit orders them all into the kitchen to celebrate and tears into a bottle of champagne he vowed to save for their first day on the water, but Liv knows better than to remind him. She searches the high cabinets for flutes but is too late. The men are already passing the bottle around and swigging from it. When it is her turn, she takes her sip and tips her face up when Whit swoops in to deliver her a champagne-soaked kiss.

They are still emptying the bottle when Liv sees Dennis cock his head strangely, as if he's heard something. He raises his hand to quiet their noise and in the next instant, the chime of the doorbell comes.

Sam.

Liv meets Whit's eyes, and a chill flutters the hairs on the back of her neck, like a scarf being pulled off in winter, skin covered now exposed to the elements again.

It is Whit who greets him, recruiting a few of the crew to join him in the foyer for introductions.

Liv flees to the upstairs and listens from the hallway to the clatter of the men's voices spilling into the kitchen a few minutes later. She tells herself it's best not to overwhelm Sam with a mass welcome, but she knows that isn't the real reason she stays away—and she suspects Whit does too. Suddenly she isn't quite as indignant about having so much space. Maybe this behemoth isn't big *enough*.

She calls Rachel, knowing her old friend is of the opinion that no amount of gold is worth opening old wounds, and is disappointed to get her voice mail. So she unpacks and takes a bath in the suite's enormous tub, sinking as deep as she can under a froth of lavender bubbles. When she hears the telltale sounds of food being prepared, chairs and tables dragged across floors and music blaring on the deck, she knows the bacchanalia of dinner is under way. A perfect time to make her entrance, she decides, toweling off and dressing in a pair of ivory shorts and a peasant blouse. All the activity will serve as smoke, cloaking any tension that might exist when she and Sam greet each other. Passing a mirror in the hall, she sees a faint blush on her cheeks and stops, feeling a strange pinch of guilt. It's just the heat of the day, she tells herself. Just the residual flush from the excitement of finding the bell.

Coming downstairs, she glimpses Whit outside at the grill, the crew flocked around him, shouting over Van Morrison. But where is Sam?

In the den, she finds him scanning the home's wall of books.

He has a beard.

This is her first thought when she sees him. He has buzzed his wavy brown hair military-style, shorter than she's ever seen it. Against the high shelves, he seems taller, tauter. He's always been lean, but now his body possesses a remarkable tightness, machinelike.

She lets her hands fall to her sides, not sure what to do with them. "Hi, Sam."

He closes his book and smiles. "Hey, Liv."

To hug or not to hug. Whether to even touch. Uncertainty overwhelms her. Liv slows her advance and Sam remains at his post, the decision made for them.

"I was starting to think you were hiding from me," he says, sliding the book back onto the shelf. "It wouldn't be hard to do here. This place should come with a map."

"You said that about the last place Whit found for us."

"Did I?"

Just the mention of that first weekend together thirteen years earlier and the enormous room fills with memories, charged and electric like the air before a summer storm. Liv feels herself sinking and forces her thoughts to stay afloat. In the present, where they belong.

She gestures to his jaw. "It's different."

"It's easy." He rubs at his beard. "I've gotten lazy in my old age."

"I find that hard to believe." She smiles. "I like it. It suits you."

His eyes flicker over her face. "You look good, Liv."

"God, not really." She pushes at the limp knot of her hair. "I feel about as toned as a roasted marshmallow. You're the one who looks like you could swim the English Channel."

"That's kind of you."

"I'm anxious to get back in the water. This project will probably be my last time diving. At least that's what I've promised my doctor."

His eyes widen briefly.

"You look surprised," Liv says.

"I am. I can't believe you're still diving."

"You couldn't believe I ever started." She regrets the comment as soon as it's out. The air, once fresh and unblemished, feels heavy now, the weight of their old argument landing between them like a dropped stone. She wants to repair her mistake.

"Can I get you a glass of wine?" she asks.

"No, thanks. I don't drink anymore."

She blinks at him. Sam, not drink?

He smiles wryly. "Now who looks surprised?"

"I'm sorry," she says. "I wasn't expecting . . ."

"It's okay—I get that reaction all the time. It's like telling people I've quit showering. They're horrified."

She laughs, maybe too loudly. She wonders if something happened to make Sam stop drinking completely.

"I *would* take some coffee, if you have it."

"Of course."

A purpose. Thank God. She leads him to the kitchen and

crosses to the still-warm carafe, finding some coffee remains. She pours, grateful for the crackle of the liquid rising to fill the quiet, hopeful her hands will hold without trembling when she delivers him the cup. She doesn't bother to offer him cream or sugar—he always took his black. To pretend she doesn't remember seems insincere. As he takes several long sips, she notices the strands of red in his short beard, reminded of the ones she was so shocked to find farther down his body when they'd first slept together. Copper and gold threads. In those early days, everything had reminded her of treasure.

She rubs her bare arms. "Thank you for rescuing us, Sam. I wasn't sure you'd be able to. Or want to, for that matter."

"So asking me was your idea?"

Liv meets his eyes. There's no point in lying; Sam would never have believed the suggestion came from Whit.

She moves to the sliders and looks out, not sure what she's searching for, or whom. It's dark enough that she can see Sam in the reflection. He's watching her as he drinks.

She turns back but remains against the glass, the cool surface startling on her neck.

"I was surprised to see you back in the charter business," she says. "I assumed when you left for law school, you'd eventually practice."

"I did. For a while. But after my dad died, I got out. He left me some money and I figured a boat was as good an investment as any."

"Your dad?" Sympathy washes over her. "I'm so sorry. When did he die?"

"Five years ago."

"God, I'm sorry," she says again, not sure what else to say. She'd never felt close to Robert Felder—he'd made sure she didn't—but Sam had been devoted. The loss must have been impossible for him. "So you're a dive captain again?"

He smiles. "Life doesn't always turn out the way we plan."

A flutter of nerves dances down her spine. The frankness of his comment dangles between them. She looks toward the window.

"What about you?" he asks. "Still writing?"

"Some. Mostly papers for journals. Lectures when I can. Whit keeps me pretty busy."

"I'll bet." The edge of insinuation is unmistakable.

Liv gestures to the island, covered with food. "It's gross, isn't it? You'd think he meant to invite all of Topsail."

"Knowing Whit, he probably did." Sam takes a slow sip of coffee. "I heard he bought back the *Phoenix*."

"He did. He changed the name. She's *Theo's Wish* now."

"I was always told it was bad luck to change the name of a boat."

She smiles. "That's Whit for you. Tempting fate every chance he gets."

Sam's eyes flicker, as if she's sparked a long-forgotten memory. "So you and Whit have kept up the hunt, then."

"We try." She shrugs. "Life keeps getting in the way, though."

"You've done well for yourselves. The *Bella Donna* was quite a find. I heard two million in coins?"

"Two point five, actually. And almost thirty feet of gold chain. It was incredible."

"Good for you. From what I hear, it's getting harder and harder to secure a license to bring up a barrel of bottles, let alone gold."

"It's been a challenge getting a recovery mission under way. Which is why we were so terrified of losing this one. Did Whit tell you he found the bell? At least, we're fairly certain it's the bell."

"I heard that," Sam says.

Liv can't help wondering if Sam has heard other things too: the string of missions Whit has lost or sabotaged in the years since their success with the *Bella Donna,* the crew members he's pissed off trying to circumvent red tape and cut corners.

What does it matter? Sam's here, isn't he?

"Whit's sure there's even more money on the *Siren,*" she says.

"So he tells me." Sam's eyes narrow slightly, signaling doubt.

"You don't believe it," she says.

"Blockade runners rarely carried gold. It would be unusual."

"And yet you came." She considers him. "So you must think there's at least a good chance of finding *something.*"

Sam smiles. "I think there's a very good chance."

His eyes meet hers and hold, gently probing. Liv has the feeling he wants to tell her something else. Maybe something that has nothing to do with treasure or diving, that he has someone special in his life, that he's fallen in love, that he's married. She knows she isn't entitled to this information, and maybe that's best. She's not sure she wants to know.

"Hallelujah!" Whit blows into the room, startling them both. One glance at his crooked grin and Liv knows that he's amply drunk. "In case you're wondering," he says, flinging open the fridge hard enough to rattle the beer bottles lined along the door, "it takes four crew members and one thickheaded project leader to figure out how to turn on a five-thousand-dollar grill." He reaches in and begins tossing packages of meat onto the counter. "Hope you're as hungry as that fire."

"None for me, thanks," says Sam. "I ate on the road."

"Really?" Liv can hear the disappointment in her voice.

"Damn," Whit says. "I was hoping we could all break bread together. Maybe even drag some wood down to the beach and get a fire going, for old times' sake."

"I'm pretty sure they'd fine us now," Sam says, looking at Liv. "See you all bright and early." He raises his mug to her before setting it down. "Thanks for the coffee."

She nods, feeling traitorous and not even sure why, when Sam excuses himself with a short wave.

She can feel Whit's eyes trying to catch hers as she takes Sam's mug to the double sink and rinses it.

He comes behind her. "Told you he's not over it."

"I think it went fine," she says, more defensively than she intended.

Whit smiles against her ear. "Liar." He kisses her neck and disappears out the slider. She watches him reunite with the men at the grill, letting the tangle of emotions pass through her. It's just the first night, she tells herself. The first time the three of them have been in the same room together after so many years. Of course it's awkward. Things will surely improve in the days ahead. They'll find their way to friendship.

They had once before, hadn't they? Three strangers with nothing in common but a passion for treasure and the mysteries of the sea.

Even though it seems another lifetime to her now, they came together once upon a time.

3

GREENVILLE, NORTH CAROLINA
Thirteen years earlier

Liv fell into her seat in the fourth row and tried to catch her breath, just grateful she'd arrived before they'd closed the auditorium's double doors. Above the stage, the screen glowed with the title slide: *The Hunt for the Patriot—Separating Mystery from Myth.* Of all the lectures to be late to! It hadn't helped, of course, that her father had followed her around the house with reports of flash floods and thunderstorm warnings, pleading with her to stay home. She hugged her bag against her chest, hoping to quiet her thundering heart. Her hair, she suspected, was a lost cause—its once-tight knot sagging at the base of her neck after her run through the rain. She tugged her red waves free and gave them a hard ruffling.

She saw a few familiar faces in the audience. Dozens of these lectures under her belt, she recognized many of the maritime studies students—and envied every one. What she wouldn't have given to be registered in the underwater archaeology program. Instead she came to the department's evening lectures, a landlubbing junior majoring in English lit, and pretended to be one of their kind for two precious hours, cloaked in the darkness of slide presentations, and asking questions during the Q&A sessions as if she were an expert in the field.

Her gaze landed on a group of three men several seats below hers—but it was the one sitting farthest away whom her eyes fixed on and held, watching him rake his hand absently through his dark hair as he and his comrades bent heads in conversation. She'd seen him a few times when she visited the archives. Finding it quieter than the student union, and far more interesting, Liv spent most of her free hours between classes sequestered in the archive's tomblike corridors. She'd heard him called Sam. On occasion, he came in with the same two male students who joined him tonight. He had serious brown eyes and a swimmer's lean body. She hadn't had this sort of crush since high school.

The bang of the auditorium doors shook her from her study. She glanced back as the latecomer fell into his seat and sprawled out, propping his feet on the chair in front of him. His mop of dark blond hair was as rumpled as his shirt.

At least she wasn't the tardiest one tonight.

She turned back to face the stage and did a casual tally of attendance. Barely thirty seats filled. Pathetic, considering the presenter. Dr. Harold Warner was a renowned marine archaeologist here to share his search for the elusive *Patriot*, a schooner that disappeared en route from South Carolina to New York in 1813, the ship and her passengers never found. What made this mystery all the more enduring was that the ship had been carrying the twenty-nine-year-old daughter of Vice President Aaron Burr, whose infamous duel with Secretary of the Treasury Alexander Hamilton had resulted in Hamilton's death and Burr's eventual disgrace. Theodosia's devotion to her erratic father was as legendary as her remarkable academic accomplishments.

Liv had learned of the mystery at ten, when her mother took her out of school to visit a shipwreck exhibit two hours away. She and Liv had pored over nautical books together, dreaming of the day Liv would start her own search for the lost schooner and end the mystery that no one in nearly two hundred years had managed to solve.

Not for lack of trying, of course. Theories abounded—and Liv had memorized them all. Everything from the ship being swept up in a hurricane to pirates commandeering the *Patriot* and her passengers—the latter theory the one Liv and her mother had subscribed to, Liv even hoping that Theodosia had managed to break free of her captors and escape to shore, as many local legends had supported. Dr. Warner's team, however, had gathered more leads that heavily supported the ship's sinking in rough waters near Hatteras—and there was even a rumor that he'd recently located wreckage he believed might be the remains of the *Patriot*. Liv knew Warner believed a hurricane had done the schooner in—not pirates—and Warner's intolerance of legend and lore was almost as rabid as Liv's own father's. She looked forward to a lively debate during the Q&A afterward.

"Good evening."

Warner's voice crackled through the microphone. Sam and his friends drew apart. The overheads dimmed and the screen above Warner's buzzed ivory hair lit up. At last all rumbles ceased and the room settled into the lecture.

Liv sank back into her seat and descended happily with the divers on the screen, the closest she and her fragile lungs would ever get to being underwater.

It is a common misconception that when a ship sinks, its wreck is frozen at the bottom of the ocean, forever locked in silt and sand—actually it's quite the opposite. When a ship settles on the seafloor, it is still in motion. Despite the anchor of bed and darkness, it continues to move throughout its new life of decay. The sea lives and breathes around it, shifting the wreckage, changing it. Sometimes the currents are gentle; others, like surges from storms, are vicious, blowing hard enough to scatter artifacts across miles, or bury entire debris fields in a single afternoon, hiding secrets from those who seek to uncover them. When she was younger and feeling trapped by her father's overprotective moods, Liv thought about that simple fact and it gave her hope. That even something stuck was still capable of motion, of change, maybe even escape.

For thirty blissful minutes, she swam with Warner's crew,

diving through the slides that charted their treasure hunts, nautical charts, and maps, until the lights came up, bringing her back, grudgingly, to the surface.

When the student moderator informed the audience there was time for a few questions, Liv's hand shot up with several others. The first three questions focused on speculation of Warner's upcoming and well-guarded mission off Hatteras.

Then he pointed at her.

She stood. "What is your opinion on the theory that the *Patriot* and her passengers were captured by the Carolina Bankers and eventually brought to shore?"

Warner stepped out from behind the podium and offered her a placating smile. "My opinion is that it's bunk." A few chortles rumbled through the audience; Warner smiled at the reaction and nodded to the moderator to move them on to a new question.

But Liv wasn't finished.

"Then what about the Nags Head portrait hanging in the Lewis Walpole Library?" she called out.

Warner turned back to her, his smirk fading. "What about it?"

"Many believe it's a portrait of Theodosia—specifically one she brought with her on the ship to give to her father as a gift. If it *is* the same one, wouldn't it prove that the *Patriot*—and possibly Theodosia—had made it to shore?"

"There's no proof that the portrait is Theodosia, let alone that it came from the ship."

"That's not true," Liv said, on a roll now and thoroughly uncaring that the chatter and murmuring had grown around her. "Frank Burdick claimed, just before his death in 1848, that he'd seen a portrait of Theodosia in the *Patriot*'s cabin after his shipmates had captured the schooner."

Warner squinted up at her. "Deathbed confessions don't make reliable testimony. Especially when they come from pirates who sailed with Jean Lafitte."

Liv knew she should have let the mistake go, that she'd already pressed her luck asking so many questions when there were other hands raised and waiting, but she couldn't resist.

"Actually, Dr. Warner, I think you mean Dominique You. Burdick didn't sail with Lafitte."

The whispers quieted. Warner's tight smile slipped briefly, then resurrected itself. He cleared his throat and glowered at the moderator. "Next question."

Ten minutes and a round of applause later, Dr. Harold Warner exited the stage with an attentive blond woman young enough to be his daughter—though Liv suspected she wasn't—and the audience rose to leave.

Liv gathered her bag and slipped into her raincoat.

"That was some volley." She looked up and a flash of heat stained her forehead. Sam stood in front of her, his windbreaker hanging open, revealing a faded University of Chicago T-shirt. "Let me guess," he said. "You did your dissertation on the *Patriot,* right?"

"Oh God, hardly." Pleasure coiled in her stomach at his suggestion. "I'm an English major. Shipwrecks are a hobby of mine. I just like to come to these things and pretend I know what I'm talking about."

But his warm brown eyes continued to radiate admiration. "You might want to consider changing your major." He extended his hand. "Sam Felder."

"Liv Connelly." She gave him hers, trying to ignore that the skin under the collar of her sweater was ripening to scarlet. She gestured to the emptying seats to rescue herself. "I would have thought there'd be a bigger crowd for him."

"Maybe the rain kept people away."

In the back row, the latecomer climbed to his feet. He had to be well over six feet. He wore a white collared shirt, most of it untucked. Despite his looking as if he'd just rolled out of bed, Liv had to admit he was handsome in a rugged kind of way.

"There's a party across campus," Sam said, pointing to his friends coming up the aisle. "Maybe you want to join us?"

Liv couldn't think of anything she might like more.

The clock above the stage read seven fifteen—possibility pounded in her chest. Even if she stayed a half hour, she'd have plenty of time to get home and cook dinner. The pork chops were already defrosted, the potatoes already boiled. And there was always that box of frozen lasagna she kept in case of emergencies.

Which, she thought as she met Sam Felder's expectant eyes, this most certainly was.

When she emerged from the auditorium, the heavy rain had thinned to a fine drizzle, leaving the air thick with the smell of warm, wet concrete. Sam stood by himself at the bottom of the steps, hands stuffed in his jeans pockets. He saw her and tugged one free to wave her down. "My friends went on ahead. I hope that's okay."

"Fine." Butterflies of delight took flight, fluttering up from her stomach, warming her skin. Just the two of them.

They walked through the mist, taking turns glancing at each other.

"English major, huh? Do you want to write books?"

"Hopefully."

"But you love shipwrecks."

"It's not the ships themselves as much as their stories," Liv said. "The people, the pieces of their lives left behind. Like a time capsule."

"Think you could get published?"

"Maybe. My father actually published a book once."

"Anything I would have read?"

"Not unless you like to read about calculus." The path narrowed as Sam steered them through an alley of crepe myrtles, forcing their bodies closer. "He's a mathematician. He helped write the definitive textbook on calculus when I was a kid. They still use it all over colleges."

"He must be pretty famous, then?"

"In certain circles, I guess."

"Does he do the lecture circuit like Warner?"

"Not anymore."

"He must think it's great you want to get published too."

Liv rolled her lips together, measuring her answer. "He would rather I write about something real. Numbers are his thing. Facts. He's not much for fiction."

"What about your mom?"

She pulled her coat tighter across her chest. "She died when I was thirteen."

Sam slowed. She could feel his eyes on her, the careful, wary stare of sympathy. "Jesus, I'm sorry," he said. "We don't have to talk about it."

"It's okay." Still Liv felt the familiar lump of tears crawl up her throat. "My mother's the reason I come to these lectures. She loved shipwrecks, loved all the legends, all the mysteries. We loved them together. Especially the *Patriot*. It was our thing. We were going to figure out what happened to that ship. What happened to Theodosia Burr . . ." She glanced at him. "We just felt so badly for her. I mean, it was awful. Theo had just lost her son to malaria. And then she disappears on her way to see her father, who was always—"

"Theo?"

Liv smiled sheepishly. "It was her nickname."

He pointed them to the left. "You still could, you know."

"Could what?"

"Be the one to solve the mystery."

Another flutter of possibility flickered in her stomach. "Not if Warner gets there first. Do you think he's really found the wreck of the *Patriot*?"

Sam shrugged. "I think if there's anything left of that ship, it's long gone."

"Then you think she sank?"

"Don't hate me, but I'm kind of in Warner's camp. I think it was a hurricane." He looked over at her. "You think it was pirates, don't you?"

Liv knew how ridiculous the theory sounded when someone said it out loud.

She smiled. "Everyone's entitled to their opinion."

The party came into view, the hum of its music and conversation audible even before they crossed the street. The two-story house was lit up, its porch packed with guests. Sam skirted them past the clusters of students who flanked the entrance, spilling in and out.

They walked into a cloud of moist air, ripe with the smells of body heat and warm beer. Sam touched her arm and leaned in close to make sure she could hear him over the noise. "See if you can find us a place to sit—I'll get us a couple beers." He smelled good beneath the thick layer of sweat and damp. Sandy and warm, as if he'd just climbed out of the sea.

Liv slipped through the crowd, just looking for space, and found herself in the kitchen. Three women moved around a cluttered island, filling bowls with potato chips. How quickly this had all happened—one minute she was sitting behind Sam Felder in a lecture hall, lost in fantasy, and an hour later, she was joining him at a party. Prickles of possibility skittered across her skin. She felt as wildly hopeful as a child about to launch into her Christmas stocking. Who knew what treasures she'd pull out?

"You look thirsty."

When the red cup appeared in front of her, Liv expected Sam Felder to be holding it. She drew back, finding the giant from the back row instead. His shaggy blond hair glistened, damp. He stepped close, smelling like hot pavement after a sudden summer storm.

She put up her hand to wave the cup away. "Thanks, but I'm here with someone."

"What was that?" He bowed his head to hear her better, sprinkling her lightly with rain.

She reared up on her tiptoes and shouted into his ear, "I said I'm here with someone!"

He straightened but didn't step back—not that he could have. The kitchen had grown crowded. Liv could feel bodies behind her where none had been before, the gentle pressure of strange hips and elbows.

"Well," he said, "if he left you alone for even a minute, he can't be worth your time."

"He left to get me a beer, actually."

"Oh." He smiled, looking only briefly repentant before he held the cup out again. "Take it anyway. Anyone who can make the Great and Powerful Warner squirm in his Top-Siders deserves a beer—not to mention my undying respect."

"I didn't make him squirm," Liv said, still not taking the beer. The room was steamy and she'd worn too many layers. She wanted to abandon her coat but didn't dare put it down.

"Shit, don't be modest. Warner couldn't get off that stage fast enough after you took a bite out of him, the know-it-all prick." He shoved out his hand. "Whit Crosby."

She accepted his shake, his big palm damp from his cup. "Liv."

"Just Liv, huh?" His mouth slid into a teasing grin. "What, like Cher or Madonna?"

"Exactly like that." Where was Sam?

Whit Crosby leaned back to study her. "I've seen you in the archives, haven't I?"

Had he? She'd never seen him there. "I've been a few times."

"But you're not a grad student."

"So what?" She bristled at the accusation. "The archives are open to anyone, not just—"

"Hey, relax. I'm not here to bust your chops. I'm impressed."

Liv pulled at her collar to cool herself—why had she worn such a thick sweater? She shifted, searching for Sam through the crowd behind Whit. "I should go look for my friend."

She hoped Whit Crosby might take the hint and step aside to let her pass, but he leaned against the wall, blocking her in. "Are you free this weekend?"

"Excuse me?"

"How'd you like to come to Hatteras and dive Warner's top secret site with me?"

"Sorry for the wait." Sam arrived with a red cup in each hand and cast a dubious look at Whit. "They had to tap a new keg."

"Hope it's better than this one," Whit said, scowling down at his cup, then looking back at Sam. "We're in class together. Whit Crosby."

"Sam Felder." He returned a quick shake, then gave Liv an apologetic smile. "We should go into the next room. There's a bunch of seats in there no one's claimed."

They managed to lose Whit Crosby in the doorway when a blonde with pouty scarlet lips grabbed his sleeve and pulled him down for a kiss, nearly spilling his beer.

Sam pointed them to an empty love seat. "Figures you'd get cornered by that guy," he said as they settled in.

"Do you know him?"

"Not really. He's in my conservation lab—and I know he's a total pain in the ass. Half the time he comes to class and won't shut the hell up. The other half he sits in the back and sleeps— Oh crap."

Whit reappeared and swung around a folding chair to join them. He leaned forward and looked right at Liv, his eyes fierce and breathtakingly blue. A crescent of red lipstick stained his jaw. "So you're coming, right?"

"Coming where?" Sam asked.

Whit took a swig of beer. "Livy and I are going to Hatteras this weekend to check out Warner's wreck site."

"What? No!" She stared at him, then at Sam, seeing his eyes darken with apprehension. "I never said that."

Whit looked genuinely surprised. "I figured with everything you knew about the *Patriot,* you'd want a peek to see if Warner actually found her, that's all."

Of course she did—but did Whit Crosby honestly think she would just run off with him for the weekend?

Sam broke in before she could answer. "You have no idea where the site is," he said to Whit. "No one does."

"The guy who took Warner out there first does, and he said he'd show me."

"Yeah, but even if you find the site, you can't dive it. Warner obviously has the license."

Liv might not have been a maritime studies student, but she knew enough about the politics of treasure hunting in North Carolina. So long as the wrecks were at least three miles from shore, treasure hunters could apply for licenses to salvage them, though they'd still have to give a percentage of their yield to the state. But once a license was secured, the claim belonged solely to the salvage group or the individual salvor.

Whit, however, appeared unfazed by the point. "It doesn't mean I can't take a look."

"And what do you plan to say if you actually find something?" Sam asked.

"That I was messing around with a friend's boat and came on it."

"You're a grad student in the maritime studies program. No one would believe you weren't there on purpose."

Whit sat back. "All explorers face risk."

"That's not risk," said Sam. "That's career suicide."

"You think guys like Warner got to where they are playing by the rules?"

"Maybe not, but I plan to."

Whit raised his cup in a mock toast. "Then I'll be sure to leave you out of the acknowledgments of my first bestseller."

Sam scowled. "You do that."

Liv looked between the two men, feeling like a referee at a tennis match. So much for thinking they were friends.

"Are you even sure you can trust this guy in Hatteras?" she asked.

Whit grinned. "I thought you didn't want to come."

"I'm just curious, that's all."

"He's an old friend of my dad's," said Whit. "They go way back."

"Way back, huh?" Sam glanced at Liv and she met his

eyes. Was she imagining the sparkle of interest in them? She didn't know him at all—was he agreeable to these kinds of plans? To doing something risky? He'd just admonished Whit for possibly trespassing on a claimed site—and yet Sam was a marine archaeology student too. There was no question the chance to see Warner's wreck up close was a remarkable opportunity.

"Of course," Sam said, "we'd need a place to stay up there."

"What do you mean, *we*?" Whit frowned at him. "I didn't invite you."

"Then you *don't* have a place."

"Of course I have a place," said Whit. "A huge place, as a matter of fact."

"So you have plenty of room."

"That's not the point. I don't know you from Adam, man."

"But you know *her*?" Sam pointed his beer at Liv.

"No," Whit said, then grinned at Liv. "But she's a hell of a lot better looking than you."

"Stop, please." Liv raised her hands. "I appreciate the offer—I really do—but I can't go."

Whit tugged his chair closer. "Oh, come on—don't let this guy scare you. I'm a total Boy Scout. I promise."

"It's not that," said Liv. "There wouldn't be any point." She glanced between them, savoring one final moment of this ridiculous fantasy. She sighed. "I can't dive."

"It's not a big deal to learn," said Whit. "I could teach you in an hour."

"No, I mean, I *can't*. I have asthma."

Sam's eyes darkened with concern.

"I know guys who have respiratory problems and dive all the time," said Whit. "It's not a problem."

"My doctor wouldn't agree," Liv said.

"Then you need to find yourself a new doctor."

Easy for him to say. Five minutes with Whit Crosby and a person could see that he clearly breezed through life without a care in the world. He obviously didn't have a father who monitored his every move like—

Oh shit. Liv pushed back her coat sleeve to find her watch. Eight fifty!

She grabbed her bag. "I have to go."

"But we just got here," said Sam. "And you haven't finished your beer."

"I'm meeting someone."

"Double-booked." Whit winked at her. "Busy girl, aren't you, Red?"

Red? She shot him a peevish look as she stood. Was he serious?

"Wait." From his coat, Whit pulled out a pen and a crumpled receipt, flattened it on his knee, and scrawled down a phone number. He handed it to her. "In case you change your mind about this weekend."

She took it, only to avoid any further delays.

Sam stood and pulled on his windbreaker. "At least let me walk you back to your car."

She met his eyes, warm with understanding and possibility, but still the weight of disappointment sank in her stomach. So much for her dream date.

"It's okay," she said. "I don't want you to leave on my account."

But Sam was insistent. "It's too crowded. I don't mind taking off."

"Me either." Whit tugged a pack of cigarettes from his pocket and shook one out. "I need a smoke anyway."

Change, damn you, change.

Liv glared up at the unmoving traffic signal, her fingers tight on the wheel. Was there some kind of citywide conspiracy in Greenville tonight? Since racing out of the campus parking lot ten minutes earlier, she'd managed to hit every red light.

It was her own fault for cutting it so close—but being with Sam Felder, and even Whit Crosby and his exhausting sales pitches, had been worth whatever path her father was likely burning into the carpet in front of their bay window waiting for her to pull into the driveway. They'd welcomed her into their conversation, their circle—was it any wonder she'd lingered too long?

"Finally."

The light flashed green and Liv sank the accelerator.

For as long as she could remember, Liv was always racing home to her father. From grocery stores or school dances, the post office or the beach. It seemed the one constant in her life, that charge of panic knowing she was going to be late—late for dinner, late for lunch, late to empty the dishwasher, late to fill it. Even before she had been the one behind the wheel. She remembered how fast her mother drove them home from the aquarium, not wanting Liv's father to know she'd taken Liv out of elementary school to visit a shipwreck exhibit he'd prohibited them from traveling to see.

"It's two hours away, Liza. On terrible roads. And for what? To fill her hungry brain with ghost stories and superstitious nonsense."

"It's hardly nonsense, Francis," her mother had argued. "It's history."

"If you're so bent on taking her to a museum, take her to Raleigh. There's a new exhibit on the feud between Newton and Leibniz."

"She doesn't care about Newton and Leibniz."

"She should. They're important."

"Not to her."

"And whose fault is that?"

So they'd gone anyway. Just two days after the argument, when Liv was deep and woefully lost in a fractions test, she'd looked up to see her mother in the doorway of her classroom. "A doctor's appointment," Liza Connelly had said to Liv's teacher, Mrs. Wilson, without blinking. "She's been fighting this very stubborn cough lately and I'm worried." Liv offered up a small hack, loud enough that Mrs. Wilson blinked with alarm. As she followed her mother back out to the parking lot, Liv's heart had raced, terrified they might be caught and dragged back. When they reached the flagpole, her mother's steady march had turned into a playful sprint. She'd hurried them inside the station wagon like escaped convicts. Revving the engine, she'd turned to Liv and winked. "That cough at the end was a nice touch, sweetie."

They'd stayed at the aquarium for nearly three hours. Poring over every display, every recovered artifact, every map, and every chart. They'd found the portrait of a dark-haired woman in white at the end of the exhibit and Liv was riveted by the woman's deep-set eyes. She'd scanned the label beside it, trying to pronounce her name. "Theo . . . Theodo . . ."

"Theodosia." Her mother had arrived beside her. "It says she was on the *Patriot* when it disappeared. We read about that one, remember? The ship that was on its way to New York and never arrived?" She had leaned in closer and kept reading. "It says Theodosia lost her son to malaria when he was ten. The age you are now," she had said, giving Liv's hand a squeeze. "No wonder she looks so sad."

Liv wasn't sure she saw despair in her expression. Despite the faint smile on her face, the woman's eyes were hard, almost distrustful. As if she watched the artist as carefully as he watched her. But there had been another quality to her dark gaze.

Haunted, Liv had decided. The young woman had looked haunted.

"It says she was headed to New York to see her father after years apart. Apparently they were extremely close."

"What about her mom?" Liv had asked.

"It says she died when Theodosia was a girl."

"She doesn't look very old."

"She wasn't," Liza had said. "She was just twenty-nine when she boarded the *Patriot*."

"And no one knows what happened to her?"

"No one knows what happened to any of them. Their ship was never found."

Never found. The news had crackled under Liv's skin like a rash, begging to be scratched.

Stopping in the gift shop on their way out, her mother had bought them a chart of the Outer Banks, a smaller version of the enormous map they'd lingered over in the exhibit. Back home before her father had returned from the college, they'd sat in Liv's room and made marks on the map with colored pencils, charting where the *Patriot* might have foundered, and where Theodosia had allegedly been spotted in the years following the ship's disappearance. Then they'd hung the chart beside Liv's bed and admired it for a long time before Liv had stored it safely in her bookshelf, hiding the evidence of their excursion.

Liv had been so sure they'd sailed through their day of delicious deceit, until after dinner, when she was dressing for bed. Her father's voice growing downstairs, the unmistakable volume of his disapproval. He'd received a call from Mrs. Wilson, making sure that Liv was feeling better. When her mother had come in to kiss her good night, Liv could still see the shimmer of leftover tears coating her eyes.

"It's not fair," Liv had whispered.

"It's not his fault, sweetie. People aren't always who you think they are. Sometimes they pretend to be someone else when you meet them, because they think you won't love them otherwise." Liza had brushed back Liv's bangs, her eyes filling. "But I'm not sorry we ran away today. Not even a little."

Was that what they'd done? Liv had thought they'd taken a trip—her mother had imagined it as so much more.

Then Liza had pressed her forehead against Liv's and kept it there. "We can't call ourselves explorers if we never go anywhere, can we?"

All explorers face risk. . . .

Lost in memory, Liv took several seconds to realize that the watery splash of blue twinkling in the leftover moisture on her windshield was parked outside her father's house, and blood rushed to her scalp. There were two cruisers, one in the driveway, another against the curb. Liv parked and dashed up the stairs, the sweat of panic already coating her upper lip. *God, let him be okay.*

A middle-aged policeman, ruddy-faced and compact, marched out of the front door, palms up to slow her advance.

"I live here. Is my father—?"

"He's fine." A second officer appeared, tall and fair-haired and brushing rain off his sleeves. "He thought he heard someone in the house. We checked around, didn't see any sign of entry."

Liv swallowed hard to catch her breath. Between their shoulders, she could see her neighbor Mrs. Carlin poking out her front door and wearing a condemning frown. She'd be over the next morning, the nosy crow—Liv would put money on it—pretending to give a damn when all she wanted was gossip to share with the Vendells next door.

She waited until both cruisers had pulled out before she went inside. The sink light was on in the kitchen. The air smelled of lemon disinfectant. She walked carefully into the den and found her father sitting in the dark, staring out the window onto the street.

She took a seat at the end of the couch and waited for him to speak. The rain had started again, drops clicking on the roof like tapping nails.

His eyes remained fixed on the glass. "I left you five messages."

She closed her eyes. "I was in the library and I had to mute my—"

"What's the point of having a phone if you won't answer it?"

She rose, not wanting this battle tonight. "I'll make you something to eat."

"Don't bother. I had a granola bar. It was the only way I could take my pills."

"You didn't have to do that, Poppy. There was a box of frozen lasagna."

"The plastic wrap had a small hole," he said. "I couldn't take the chance."

Of course not.

"There've been break-ins on this street, Livy."

One, six months ago, four blocks away. Kids had opened an unlocked car and stolen two cases of Diet Coke out of the backseat. Liv might have pointed this out if she'd thought there might be any use in it. For a man so enamored of facts—and with such distaste for fantasy—her father confounded her with his twisted logic. Scared her.

She moved for the stairs.

"You reek of smoke."

She stopped in the doorway, the flush of embarrassment burning her cheeks. "There were people smoking in the car next to mine in the parking lot."

"Didn't you tell them you have asthma?"

"It's fine, Poppy."

"You should have told them. You should have taken out your inhaler and used it then and there. Made them feel a little bit lousy. Selfish jerks."

She sighed quietly. "I'm sorry I wasn't here."

When he didn't answer, she walked to the stairs and began to climb.

Liv undressed and slid under her sheets, raising the hem of her nightgown enough to let the cool cotton slide over her thighs and stomach. In the tree outside her window, a bird fluttered in the branches, rustling with alarm. Maybe she wasn't the only one in this suffocating night who searched for flight.

Her heart knocked around her chest like loose change. She closed her eyes, letting memories of the evening return. Losing herself in all those slides. Standing up in the auditorium, debating with Dr. Harold Warner, feeling so smart and fierce in that safe, quiet dark. Then the way Sam Felder had looked at her when the lights came up, the admiration in his warm brown eyes. He believed she was outspoken, freethinking. Maybe even bold when she wanted to be. What would he have thought if he'd seen her creep into her father's house like a scared fourteen-year-old girl who'd missed curfew, not a twenty-one-year-old woman who should have been free to stay out for as long as she wanted, with whomever she wanted?

She rolled onto her back and stared up at the unmoving fan blades, shame washing over her.

At the party, she'd watched students drink and laugh and flirt without any concern for clocks or schedules. God, what was that like? Just the other day she'd met a junior named Amy who'd boasted of overnights at her boyfriend's off-campus apartment and the diner down the block where they regularly gorged on pumpkin pancakes at three in the morning.

Three in the morning.

Just the thought of it had made Liv's heart flood with envy.

She turned onto her side and listened to the familiar creaks of her father finally leaving his window post and climbing the stairs, the soft click of his door closing, then the hush of nothingness. Through her screen, the night crackled suddenly with sound, somehow louder now. She wasn't tired. Not even a little. Her pulse raced beneath her skin. Everywhere she touched, her neck, her hip, her knee, she could feel her heartbeat.

"All explorers face risk. . . ."

She could say she was going away with her class, that it was required for a grade. Yes, it was last minute, but she wouldn't be far and she'd have her phone with her, in case of emergencies. She could say whatever she needed to say to get away. Her father could manage for two days without her. Surely he could.

Yes. Yes, he could.

We can't call ourselves explorers if we never go anywhere, can we?

"No, we can't," Liv whispered into the darkness.

When she'd come out of the party, she'd squinted into the misty night and felt the knot of dread twist behind her ribs not to see Sam and Whit right away, sure they'd changed their minds at the last minute and abandoned her, that this was what she got for pretending to be someone she wasn't.

Then she'd seen them, two figures just beyond the edge of the streetlight, and her fisted heart had unfurled. Sam Felder stepping inside the bright globe and waving to signal her, solid and sure. And behind him, Whit, a tall mass of black except for the tiny orange dot of a cigarette tip, glowing and fading with each drag. Blinking like a lighthouse beacon, Liv had thought. But God help the woman who steered her boat toward Whit Crosby's rocky shore.

4

TOPSAIL ISLAND, NORTH CAROLINA
Wednesday

The remnants of overnight clouds stretch across the dawn sky, wispy and thinning like strands of cotton candy, and Whit is glad to see them.

He's slept poorly, but it's always this way the night before a dive. Excitement and anticipation race through his head like sugared-up kids stuck inside on a rainy day; his brain won't shut off. But it's not just his head that's hyperactive—his heart won't slow either.

He stops his pacing to rest awhile in the window seat. Across the enormous bedroom, he searches the darkness for their bed. It takes his eyes a while to adjust, but he can make out Liv's sleeping form, or maybe it's just memory filling in the blanks.

The first night he ever spent with her, he watched her like this, nursing a drink in the cramped blue-black of the berth, considering the beauty of her face, the slope of her body, parts covered and uncovered. He was in love with her even before that first day they met after the lecture when she'd corrected that asshole Warner, so much longer than she'll ever know. It had killed him to watch her and Sam grow close in Hatteras, knowing Sam Felder had already won her heart before Whit had even had a turn at bat. Finally getting to sleep with her had been like a dream you never wanted to wake up from.

Now here he is again, eight years later, afraid to fall asleep, afraid he might wake to find her gone. Just a dream.

A damp wind blows through the casement windows that box in the bedroom, tinged now with the heat of daybreak and the taste of salt. Even this far away, he can smell the soft vanilla of her skin. She hasn't moved much—is she having a good dream? Is he in it? Is Sam?

When Liv decided not to welcome Sam right away, Whit was relieved. Hell, he was thrilled. Then he interrupted their reunion in the kitchen and felt that confidence leak out. The way she looked at him when he blew in, the panic in her eyes that he might ruin this mission before they even got out on the water. Her lack of faith crushed him—but what did he expect? He hasn't always kept his promises.

She's out there and we'll find her.

He climbs to his feet, restless again, and walks to the stretch of windows that look out onto the water. They've got a good crew. He's worked with the older guys before—the others came recommended. One is very young, just twenty, and he'll make a good deckhand. Whit saw the agreeable way he smiled at everything the other guys said at dinner, how loudly he laughed at their terrible jokes, how quickly he offered to get more beers, more food.

Whit rubs his face, his jaw. He just wants to get to the site, start bringing everything up so there can be no contention, no doubt. He just wants it to be six already. But no matter how many times he cuts his gaze to the sky, that one damn streak of pink seems frozen, determined to sit on dawn's rise for as long as possible. The surf keeps curling over the shore and retreating, the ticktock of its rhythm. He turns back to watch Liv as the even sound of her breathing matches it.

And in the seconds of quiet between the rise and crash of every wave, Whit swears he can already hear the gentle crack of her heart breaking.

A flock of terns plunges to the water, their capped heads descending in unison, purple in the muted dawn light. Sam watches them from his seat on the sand, admiring their order and grace. He's always the first one up. He and the birds. His dreams were strange and chaotic, but what else would they be after seeing Liv and Whit again after so long? Liv *with* Whit. It doesn't make sense. *They* don't make sense. Not the way he and Liv had—that's for sure.

He wipes sweat off his neck with his T-shirt sleeve. Even after a hard run on the beach, he still feels amped up. He blames the house. All this space. A huge bed in a huge room. He's grown used to small quarters, come to crave them, frankly.

Too much wide-open space isn't good for a person—too much empty air needing to be filled with useless thoughts. Like his physical belongings, he believes in limiting his footprint too. But not Whit.

Typical Crosby, getting them something so outrageous.

He squints out at the water. They'll have a good day out there. No wind, no chop. They certainly celebrated well enough the night before. Sam remembers the wasteland of trash he passed on the deck as he left for the beach, empty bottles and crumpled napkins, paper plates still soggy with barbecue sauce and shrimp tails. Good to know Whit still leaves his messes for other people to clean up.

He should get coffee, get ready to go. Climbing the walkway back to the house, he sees a few of the crew wandering the deck with mugs. The house is waking. And somewhere up there Liv and Whit are also coming to—or maybe they've been awake for a while, restless as he is.

Sam had been so close to telling Liv about the diary last night. Looking into those mossy green eyes of hers, he'd felt the knot of his patience tugged hard, teased to the point where one smile, however small or short, and the rope he'd so carefully tied would have come undone in an instant.

Then Whit had crashed in—in that classic, infuriating Everybody-look-at-me way he always did, and the moment was gone.

Maybe it was better that he hadn't told her. Too fast, too soon. Too much.

He has time. After all, Whit will do something to blow this. Screwups are in Whit Crosby's DNA. Sam has no doubt this mission won't last. Despite his claims to Liv, Sam doesn't give much of a damn anymore about treasure. He knows there's nothing of value in that blockade runner Whit's brought them all here to strip bare. But Sam isn't here for fortune.

His eyes drift to the second floor, to the tall bank of windows that belong to the other master suite, and an unwelcome cramp of envy twists his gut.

One good thing about so much space: He won't have to hear them screw.

"Hey, Sleeping Beauty."

Liv wakes to the delicious sensation of a soft breeze on her bare skin—or maybe fingertips. She isn't sure which until she opens her eyes and sees Whit, dressing on the other side of the room, pulling on a T-shirt. The curtains float and fall with the air off the water.

She sits up and pushes hair out of her face. "Did you sleep?"

He grins. "Shit, do I look that bad?"

"Don't joke. You don't dive well when you don't sleep."

She's nagging him—as if they were an old married couple. Is that how Sam sees them?

Sam. A flurry of apprehension snakes in her stomach. Sam is in the house with them this morning—Sam. Here. Back. So many years later, they are all roommates again—only this time, she is Whit's wife.

She hugs her knees to her chest, baring her spine to the breeze. "Whit?"

He stops in the doorway, turns to her, and the fluttering wings of her heartbeat settle. Maybe it's where he's standing, directly in the path of the early sun, his hair and jaw catching the boldest streaks of gold and apricot, or maybe it's the warm, oddly sweet breeze that passes between them—but she's filled with longing for him. The sort she used to feel when they'd be left alone, a dangerous possibility that he might be the one to allow her the escape she craved, the approval to seize her own needs without apology. He may have foundered, may have sent them spinning for a bit, but he's fixed it. He's righted their ship and put them back on course. And for the first time in weeks, she thinks: *We'll be okay.*

"I love you," she says.

He grabs his shirt above his heart, grips it hard, and smiles. "I love you more."

Idling engines rumble in the driveway, doors slam, feet stomp up and down stairs. Departure. Liv loves every second. The energy of the first day on the water, the crackle of possibility that trails behind them all like a dog, tags jingling and tail whirling, who knows he is about to go for his walk.

But there is a calm to their frenzy too. No racing to the marina as they did their first go-round. Now the boat waits for them. Just a cup of coffee and Liv will be ready. There's some left in the pot, enough to get her started, and she empties it into a mug, then opens the fridge for cream. As she hunts, she hears movement in the foyer, the rush of air of the door opening and someone marching in. Whit, no doubt—having forgotten something.

She smiles as she turns. "What did you—? Oh."

"Morning." Sam motions behind her. "I just came back for waters."

"Of course." She steps aside to let him at the fridge. A memory flashes—their old apartment, making cappuccino on lazy Sunday mornings that were seconds away from becoming afternoons, the cloud of foam he could always coax from the machine for her, whipped and slightly shiny like meringue. How she'd loved the sound of the growing froth, hollow and even.

He nods toward the window and the view of supper's carnage. "I bet you're hoping the cleaning fairies will come and get rid of all that while we're gone, huh?"

"How did you know?"

"Wild guess."

He's pulling at that part of her that used to crave order, that cleaned and neatened obsessively. When she and Sam lived together, she never went to bed with dishes in the sink. Now she wakes to a house in chaos.

Sam grabs a pair of tall bottles, wedges them under his arm, and smiles. "At least this time we won't be late."

By seven, they are on the water, speeding out into the Atlantic in the taxi boat to where the *Aqua Blue* waits for them. Whit seems unusually restless, Liv thinks as she watches him pace the crowded deck. It isn't like him. This part of the mission is usually when her husband shines brightest, infecting the crew with his fierce optimism, like a football coach rallying his team in the locker room before the big game. Instead Whit seems distracted, detached. She wonders if Sam has noticed.

The *Aqua Blue* is an older boat, spacious and a little creaky, but still Liv swears her pulse syncs itself with the rhythm of her engines, the hum of her propellers, when they finally board. Their captain is a wiry man in his fifties named JT who wants to give them an orientation tour as soon as they are settled. They chartered a much larger salvage vessel when they excavated the *Bella Donna*, but Liv prefers this scale. Too big scares her. Not unlike the house Whit has rented for them.

They convene in the cockpit, where Whit is preparing the map they will use to chart the debris field, cataloging where they find artifacts. Sam suggests they dig first before sending divers down, but Whit is adamant they all get to the bottom right away. The current is already kicking, he says.

Following the safety briefing, they suit up. They'll go in two groups, Sam decides, and begin to map the site by setting grid lines around the wreck, marking north, south, east, and west. Once the ropes are set, the survey can begin. He tells Liv that she will go in the second group, a plan that fills her with much-needed calm. As confident as she is in her diving, she likes knowing Whit will be below if anything should happen. Not that anything *will* happen.

Her wet suit on, she goes to find Whit. He's alone outside the bridge, slugging coffee as if it's last call at the pub.

"What's wrong?" she says.

Whit turns and looks startled, as if he's been found sleep-walking. "We should have been down a half hour ago," he says. "I don't like wasting time."

"Safety checks aren't wasting time."

"I'm not talking about safety checks."

"What, then?" But she knows. "This is why we asked Sam, Whit. Because he does things the way they should be done—"

"By the book. I know, I know." He bites his lip and stares hard at the men on deck. "Don't let Chuck use the metal detector," he says. "I want Dennis. He's better with it."

She studies him. "Are you sure you're okay?"

"I'm fine, baby. Fine." He flashes an unconvincing smile and leans in to kiss her. "Just ready to get into the old girl's pants, that's all."

"You always did have a way with words, Crosby." Sam appears, suited up. Liv can't help remembering the first time she saw them together in their wet suits and gear, how her breath had caught at the sight of them.

It does again.

"Are we good to go?" Whit asks.

"Not quite," Sam says. "Dennis thinks he's bringing down the metal detector on our initial dive."

"That's the plan," says Whit.

"Well, I don't want one down there until the grid lines are set."

Here we go, Liv thinks. She shoots Whit an imploring look, pleading for him to back off and let Sam do his job.

Liv can see it takes all of Whit's control—which has never been much to begin with—to grit his teeth and agree. He gives her hand a quick squeeze and heads for the deck.

Sam comes closer. "He seems unusually wound up."

"He didn't sleep well."

She's making excuses for him—as Sam used to accuse her of doing—but now she has every right.

"Maybe he shouldn't dive, then," says Sam.

"You try telling him that."

Sam smiles. "You sure you don't mind going with the second group?"

"No," Liv says. "But I can't help wondering if you're still trying to keep me topside."

She means it as a joke, only to tease him, but his eyes flash with something so close to hurt that she adds, "I'm glad to go second, actually. I like to know there's a welcoming party waiting for me."

His smile returns but only partially. "That was always the idea, Liv."

Whit, Sam, and two of the crew go down first. Liv watches them descend, her heart racing with a mix of hope and dread. She just hopes they can all survive down there. She's let Whit make so many decisions about this mission—even the ones usually left in her hands: securing the license and filling out all the necessary paperwork—and now it's making her nervous.

She distracts herself by double-checking her straps, her tank, her regulator, hoses where they need to be, belts tight.

She needs to relax. They're here, on the water. They've made it.

Now they just have to find the start of the treasure trail. And it is a perfect day, she decides when she looks out at the water.

And just like that, the thrum of excitement begins to build behind her ribs. She thinks she will never recapture that first time on a salvage boat, that first taste of treasure and the possibility of what lies beneath the waves, and somehow she always does.

5

GREENVILLE, NORTH CAROLINA

Thirteen years earlier

Liv told herself she would wait two days before she called the number Whit Crosby had scrawled on the gas receipt he'd pulled from his pocket at the party.

She barely waited one.

"I knew you'd change your mind," Whit said when he picked up the phone, winded as if he'd just come off a sprint.

"Is this a bad time?" she said. "You sound like you're trying to catch your breath."

"Or maybe you leave me breathless, Red."

"If I go with you this weekend, you need to stop calling me that. Is Sam coming too?"

"Him and his truck," Whit said. "Turns out I needed a new muffler. "

She smiled against the receiver, this news squelching the ever-growing bloom of regret that continued to bubble up the longer she stayed on the phone.

"We should leave around noon," Whit said. "Have time to get settled. We can pick you up. What's your address?"

Panic charged down her arms. "I live a ways from campus," she said, trying to keep her voice calm. "Why don't I meet you at the library instead?"

To her relief, Whit agreed. She spent the next four days in a fog of equal parts excitement and terror, appeasing her growing guilt by spending as much time at home with her father as she could, filling the freezer with pasta dinners and whole pies. The lie she crafted to explain her departure was a sound one. A literary tour of North Carolina, and only the top students were invited to participate. She wasn't sure if she'd get a chance to call much but she'd try. Assuming there was cell service, assuming he wanted her to take valuable time away from her studies.

When Saturday arrived, Liv was sure the cloudless blue sky was the universe's blessing, or maybe even forgiveness, for her charade. She climbed into Sam's truck, wedging herself between him and Whit Crosby, and watched the landscape shift as they traveled the Albemarle Highway, dotted with crumbling old barns and swaths of cotton fields. She'd been to the Outer Banks twice before, but it looked different to her this trip. The bridge over the Alligator River seemed longer; the wall of sand dunes that flanked their truck just outside Avon seemed taller, smoother. When they passed through Buxton and Frisco, Liv began to wonder if Whit meant to drive them to the very tip of Hatteras. Then, just before the road split from the lane to the Ocracoke Island ferry, Whit directed them to the last stretch of homes that faced the Atlantic.

"Welcome to the end of the world," he said.

"Jesus," Sam whispered, squinting up at the enormous house they'd arrived at. "I hope it comes with a map."

"Not too shabby, huh? The owner's son and I are old friends."

"And they don't mind us staying here?" Liv asked.

"It's off-season. No one's around."

She scanned the row of equally giant homes to their left, their driveways empty, their porches bare of furniture, their enormous squares of glass dark. Liv thought of the bags of groceries they'd bought on their way, the baby red potatoes and littleneck clams, the sticks of butter softening in the bed.

"Just give me a sec to turn off the alarm." Whit took the front steps two at a time, disappearing around the porch.

Liv had seen pictures of interiors like the one they stepped into, on television and in magazines. Windows two stories high, living rooms that looked like hotel lobbies, and ceiling fans with blades as wide as ship propellers. The kitchen was as big as her father's whole house.

Her father. A wave of doubt slowed her quick steps through the downstairs, but she tamped it down. For two precious days she would be every bit as free as any of the students she shared classes with, students who took their independence for granted, who never had to suffer the third degree if they wanted to drive to the store for a new shampoo, but couldn't because there was a pileup on the freeway, or a prediction of rain . . .

Liv closed her eyes, a flush of shame blooming at her throat.

Glancing back to find Sam and Whit still touring the first floor, she clapped her palm reflexively to her neck to hide the color, her excitement waning, twisting to regret. Who was she fooling? She didn't belong here. Sam and Whit were real treasure hunters. They were gold coins—she was a dull penny. They'd clearly been raised to believe in wonder, to demand joy and possibility. They'd never known how quickly life's glory could be pinched out, like a candlewick between two fingers. Snuffed.

They couldn't know how good it felt to run away. Even for a day.

Waiting outside for Whit to find the keys, she'd stolen a look at her cell phone and felt a mix of guilt and relief to see there was no signal this far out. She couldn't have called her father even if she wanted to—which, God forgive her, she didn't.

She walked across the living room to the deck door and used both hands to open the heavy slider, allowing in a sliver of cool, malty air. The ocean roared beyond the whiskers of dune grass, building its strength and curling before it crashed against the sand, exploding in sizzling foam.

Prickles of gooseflesh erupted along the back of her neck. The beauty and violence of the sea always gave her chills.

Welcome to the end of the world.

Yes.

Now if only she could stay forever.

An hour later, the fragrance of chopped garlic and rosemary filled the downstairs.

Waiting for the rice to cook, Liv watched Whit take down

a pair of faded seascape paintings from the wall beside the stone fireplace and lean them against a chair.

"What are you doing?" she asked.

"Making room," he said.

"For what?"

"This." He unpacked a long cardboard tube and dumped out the contents, unrolling a massive map over the couch. "Give me a hand, will you?" She gave him thumbtacks and he secured the corners. It was a nautical chart, a larger version of the one her mother had bought from the aquarium. Liv recognized the familiar curves of the North Carolina coastline and the even polka-dot pattern of soundings showing water depth. It was just strange to see one so big and so clean.

She scanned the area Whit had already outlined, near treacherous Diamond Shoals, where he claimed Warner's team had been searching.

Sam, back from a run on the beach, joined them. "Where did you get that?"

"I borrowed it from the department office," Whit said, driving in the last tack and stepping back. "We'll use it to keep track of where we dive tomorrow and what we find." He marched to the kitchen for a bottle of wine and opened it, cracking the cork in his impatience. "This calls for a toast." He filled three glasses and handed them out, chunks of cork bobbing merrily on the surface of each one. "To the *Patriot*—and to the Outer Banks' newest band of treasure hunters," he said, knocking his wineglass against Liv's and then Sam's, hard enough to send liquid sloshing up the side.

Liv turned her glass to Sam and smiled. "Cheers."

"And to new friends," Sam added, tipping his wine to hers.

Friends. Liv looked between them as she took a sip, feeling deliciously conspiratorial as the wine slid over her tongue, as if she were part of some clandestine plot that could change lives.

Sam surveyed the plates of food they'd already produced. "If we eat all this, we won't need our weight belts to keep us down tomorrow."

"You'd think this was our last meal on earth," Liv teased.

Whit ambled over. "For all we know, it is."

Liv frowned. "Don't say things like that. It's bad luck."

Whit split a littleneck shell and popped its tender meat into his mouth with a relishing grin. "Only for the clams, Red."

They took over one end of a twelve-person trestle table that looked out onto the dunes, and feasted while daylight melted down the sky, the only noises in the high-ceilinged room the clinks of their empty shells tossed into the trash bowl, the crackle of a torn baguette.

First to finish, Sam pushed his plate aside and leaned forward for his wineglass. "We should talk about tomorrow."

"What's to talk about?" Whit reached between them for the last piece of bread. Liv watched him gut the end of the baguette with his thumbs and drag it through the leftover broth puddled at the bottom of his plate. "We meet Lou at the marina at dawn, suit up, go down."

"First we need to set some ground rules," said Sam.

Whit folded the sopping bread into his mouth and mumbled around it, "Here we go. . . ."

"I'm serious. We have to agree not to disturb the site."

Whit looked at Liv. "You agree with Saint Felder here, Red?"

Liv put up her hands. "I'm not diving, so I don't have any opinion on all this. I'm just happy to be here."

Whit lunged forward, his blue eyes flashing playfully. "Come down with us."

"She can't dive," said Sam. "Don't harass her. And don't change the subject."

"Who's harassing? I'm just saying I've known divers with asthma. They don't go as deep, but they still dive." Whit drained his wine and poured himself more, adding some to Liv's and Sam's glasses. She marveled at the speed of his drinking. Did he really mean to dive tomorrow after so much wine? But they were all growing warm from the wine, she saw, all of their faces—cheeks, foreheads, noses—flushed in the dusky rose of sunset and the glow of candlelight.

Liv leaned over to collect their plates. "We should clean up."

"Leave it for later," said Whit, climbing to his feet. "Let's take the rest of the wine down to the beach and light a bonfire like good drunk sailors."

"I'm not sure you can have fires on the beach anymore," Sam said.

"Maybe not, but look around," Whit said, gesturing to the darkened homes. "Who's here to rat us out?"

Sam cast a quick look at Liv.

"He has a point," she said.

• • •

Armed with blankets and the last bottle of wine, the three abandoned their shoes at the top of the boardwalk and followed the path of weathered wood through the fluttering sea grass to the water.

The sand felt cold and hard underfoot and the air was crisp with a cool breeze. Liv was sure if she raised her arms, she'd take flight. They collected driftwood, enough for Whit to get a fire started. He blew hard on the smoking embers until they caught and crackled loudly over the smashing surf.

They dropped to the sand and sat around the growing blaze. Above them, the sky sparkled with stars and three quarters of a buttercream moon.

"All we're missing is a good ghost story," Sam said. He smiled at Liv. "Know any?"

She smiled back. "Maybe a few."

"I'll bet there are ghosts all along this beach," Whit said, swinging the bottle toward the water. "The hundreds of wrecks out there? I bet it's a real party some nights. All that ghost rum." He took a swig of wine and handed the bottle to Sam.

Liv hugged her knees to her chest. "People near Bald Head Island say they've seen the ghost of Theodosia running through the dunes in a white dress, chased by a headless pirate."

"That'd be something to see," said Whit.

"No, thanks." Sam took his turn with the bottle and handed it off to Liv. "You don't believe in all that, do you?"

"Which part?" she asked.

"Ghosts."

She shrugged. "Even if I did, I refuse to believe Theodosia is spending eternity outrunning a headless pirate."

"Personally," Whit said, "I think this night calls for something a little saltier than ghost stories."

She sipped, meeting Sam's gaze as she swallowed. Crescents of firelight reflected in his dark eyes.

"What about truth or dare?" he said.

Whit grinned. "I like how you think, Felder."

Sam took the wine and Liv watched him drink, ripples of anticipation fluttering. The thought of his confessions thrilled her. The thought of him craving hers thrilled her even more.

Now all she had to do was make some up.

Sam handed her back the bottle. "I'll even go first."

"A volunteer. Good man." Whit retrieved a crumpled pack of cigarettes from his pocket and pointed them at Liv. "Will it bother you if I smoke?"

She shook her head. She'd be fine out here.

Whit knocked out a cigarette and tossed his pack on the sand. "Truth or dare—pick your poison," he said to Sam.

Sam looked at Liv. "Truth."

"Truth, huh?" Whit squinted as he lit up and exhaled over his shoulder. "Okay, Felder. How old were you the first time you had sex?"

Sam winced. "Going right for the jugular, aren't we?"

"Jugular is asking the first time you had *anal* sex, my friend. Missionary's completely PG." He grinned. "I'm going easy on you to avoid embarrassing our pure little undergraduate here."

"And what makes you think I'm so pure?" Liv asked. The smooth heat of the alcohol was winding its way through her, teasing her thoughts, loosening her inhibitions, making the night seem closer, warmer. Even Whit Crosby's bluster was growing on her. He had an undeniably gorgeous mouth. Lips in constant motion, framed by two deep dimples. He was probably a voracious kisser. One of those men who grabbed your face and inhaled you.

"I was fourteen," Sam announced.

Liv was certain her awe was bald on her face.

"Fourteen?" Whit snorted. "Amateur."

Sam scooped up a fistful of sand and pitched it at Whit, smiling as he reached over to snatch the bottle from his hand. "How the hell old were *you*, asshole?"

"Sorry, not my question." Whit leaned back on his hands. "I've never been very good at truth, so I pick dare." He grinned at Liv. "Got one for me, Red?"

She needed something shocking. She wanted them to think she knew far more about the world of sex and men than she really did. She, who'd only had a handful of dates in her life—none of them lasting long enough to turn into relationships. Boys who'd complimented her looks, who'd called her irresistible and then managed to resist her just fine when her father's constant supervision grew unbearable. There'd been one or two suitors, boys she'd met in high school, who'd tried to stick it out, sure she could be worn down, lured away from her father with passionate kisses and promises of devotion, like biscuits held out to soothe a skittish dog. She'd slept with only two of them, hoping the act would empower her in some way, shrink her father's hold, but all it did was leave her feeling more alone and fragile.

But not this, not now.

In this moment, she'd never felt more included, or more daring, in her whole life.

The crash of waves rumbled behind them in the darkness, building her courage like cheering fans at a ball game.

"Look, Red, if this is too hard—"

"I dare you to jump in," she said.

Whit took a swig of wine and scoffed. "If you want me to get in the water, at least dare me to do something impressive, like swim to Ocracoke and back with steaks strapped to my legs."

Why did she believe he just might if she suggested it?

Sam reached out and snatched the bottle from Whit's hand. "Points deducted for stalling."

"All right, all right." Whit climbed to his feet, unsteady in the sand. He flicked his cigarette into the fire and began to free his shirt buttons. "Personally I think Red just wants to see my junk."

"Don't flatter yourself," she said. Still she felt a blush burn across both cheeks, her skin already pink from the fire. "Besides, I didn't mean for you to skinny-dip. The water's freezing."

"Too late." Whit unbuckled his belt and snapped it out like a whip. "Don't write checks you can't cash, lass. You're playing with a pro here."

"Oh, you're a pro all right," Sam said with a snicker.

"Listen to sour grapes." Whit yanked his shirt over his

head and chucked it at Sam. "It's not my fault you were too much of an old lady to take a dare."

"And it's not my fault when you miss a week of classes because of pneumonia."

Sam caught her eyes and she smiled.

Whit was down to his boxers now, and the definition of his body surprised her. The solidness of his muscles, a trail of copper down that disappeared below his navel. He puffed out his chest. "Now, if only I had some chum to take out with me—make it a man's dare."

"Jesus, are you going in or not?" Sam said.

"Watch my fire. I may need it to find my way back." Hands fisted and arms out, Whit charged toward the surf. It was fully dark now; Liv could see him for several seconds before the night swallowed him up.

"I can't believe he's really going in," she said.

"Can't you? Ten bucks says he was the kid on the playground who ate worms because someone dared him to."

She laughed. In the next instant, Whit's yell rose from the surf.

Sam smiled. "I think he's in."

The fire sparked and hissed. Sam tossed on another log and prodded it with a piece of driftwood. Liv watched his profile in the flare of light, admiring the places where his cropped brown hair clung to his neck. She wondered if it curled the same way down his stomach, and if it was the same leathery brown. Craving burned through her, suffocating her fears—fears that she'd let her father down, fears that he would think poorly of her for lying to him, for choosing this night over him.

But now that she had done so, she wouldn't waste it. There was no going back. Tonight, she could be whoever she wanted. Out of range, out of sight. Pancakes at three in the morning, as many as she could eat. The possibilities made her dizzier than the wine.

She raised her face to the moon. The sky and water blended into one giant inky pool, shapeless and forever. She felt the weight of vertigo land in her ankles, like someone yanking her back from the edge just in time.

"That's what I like to imagine it looks like underwater," she said, searching the roof of twinkling velvet. "Vast and silent. Floating free in all that nothingness." She turned to Sam. "Is it?"

"It can be." Sam took a swig and handed her the bottle. "Some days the water is as clear as a bath. Other days you can't see your hand in front of you."

She sipped, grateful for the heat of the alcohol, and gave the wine back to him. The sound of splashing was growing farther away. A prickle of concern pierced her thoughts. "You don't really think he means to swim to Ocracoke, do you? He's been drinking. Quite a bit."

"He's a big guy. I think he can handle it." Sam tipped the bottle to his lips and considered her as he swallowed. "Are you seeing anyone?"

Heat bloomed across her face. That he'd asked, just like that. "No." She smiled. "Are you?"

"I was." His eyes fell to her mouth and rested there. "Not anymore."

Someone in his program? Someone from home, wherever that was? Suddenly Liv wanted to know everything about him.

"You look cold." He snapped open one of the folded blankets and draped it around her. So close, she caught a whiff of him rising from the gap in his jacket collar, the heady smell of body heat and damp denim. She wondered what it would be like to take a shower with him, to have him press her against one of the home's huge marble stalls and wash off all her worries.

Splashing grew in the distance, then a loud hoot. Liv scanned the darkness, waiting for Whit to appear. When he did, he gleamed with seawater, his boxers plastered to his body like a second skin.

"Jesus, that's freezing." He dropped beside them, a cold steam floating off him. Water dripped from his hair and jaw. He grabbed the other blanket and pulled it around his shoulders.

"So how was Ocracoke?" said Sam.

"Far." Whit reached his hands to the fire, palms out. Sam handed him the wine. "Thanks," said Whit, swinging it high and draining it. He screwed the empty bottle into the sand and lay down, grinning as he tugged the blanket tighter around his chest. "I say we sleep out here. Under the stars like shipwrecked pirates."

"Be my guest, Blackbeard—but I prefer sheets and a mattress," said Sam, rising. He brushed sand off his seat and reached out his hand to Liv. "Ready to go back up?"

"Don't jump ship yet," Whit said. "The night's young. And Red hasn't had her turn yet."

"She's cold," Sam said.

"So get closer to the fire."

Liv stood. "We'll see you back at the house, okay, Whit?"

He turned his face to the sky and closed his eyes. "Fine, then, you lousy mutineers. Go."

"Come on," said Sam, taking her hand and steering her back up the sand toward the house, the maze of the first floor lit up, blazing like the fire she could still hear crackling in their wake.

"It is a cool chart. I'll give him that."

Crossing through the living room, they slowed to admire the massive map Whit had hung earlier.

"My mom and I had one like it once," Liv said. "Just not nearly as big. We used it to figure out what might have happened to Theodosia. We scribbled all over it, places where people had claimed to see her, where the Bankers might have taken her captive after they seized the *Patriot*. Everything."

"What happened to it?"

"I don't know," she said, which wasn't entirely true. She'd looked for it after her mother died and not been able to find it where she'd always kept it in her bookshelf. She suspected her father had found it and thrown it away—not that she planned to tell Sam that. Not that she planned to tell him anything more about her father than she already had done.

She walked to the chart and drew her index finger wistfully along the coastline, recalling all the notes she and her mother had crammed into their miniature version. How tiny she'd had to make her letters to fit.

Possibility tore through her, a spark of defiance with it, not so unlike the confidence she'd felt in the lecture hall, raising her hand, then her voice.

She glanced over her shoulder to find Sam watching her expectantly.

She smiled at him. "I don't suppose you have something to write with?"

She made her first mark near Nags Head, the yellowed paper releasing a dry, powdery smell as she pressed the tip of the pencil against it. PORTRAIT, for where the painting of the woman in white believed to be Theodosia was found in an old woman's cottage, then another PORTRAIT for where the old woman's suitor had supposedly stolen the painting off a ship that had washed ashore.

Other labels returned quickly:

DETAINED, for the place where the British fleet had allegedly stopped the *Patriot* for inspection before allowing her to continue to New York.

BANKERS, for where the pirates were believed to have lured the *Patriot* into the shoals to her doom.

CAPTURE, where Burdick had claimed on his deathbed to have taken part in the seizure of the ship, and her passengers—adding a star beside the word, just as she and her mother had done years earlier.

When everything was labeled as she remembered, Liv stepped back to survey her work.

She glanced at Sam, pleasure rippling through her at the serious way he scanned the path of her marks.

She smiled sheepishly. "I told you I was obsessed."

"Not obsessed—passionate. Passion's good."

Did he really think so? The salty, buttery smells of their meal still hung in the air—Liv was ravenous again. Could he see how much she wanted him to kiss her, to wipe her mind free of worries for just one night, to put his hands on her body and never take them off?

"I know a grad student over in art history," he said. "Beth Henson. She volunteers at the Maritime Museum. Maybe she could help us find more clues."

Us. Liv searched his face, hoping the interest she saw there wasn't only from the wine. "I'd like that."

They turned back to the chart and considered the spread of her notes, the intersecting lines and labels.

"I suppose I have to erase it all now, don't I?" she said.

"Why? It's not like Crosby ever intended to give it back." Sam took the pencil from her hand and set it on the table. He stepped closer.

She swallowed. "Did you know Theodosia lost her mother when she was young too?"

Sam threaded his fingers through her hair. "I didn't know that."

"And that her father made her his whole world afterward?"

He searched her eyes. "God, you're beautiful."

"Not really."

"Yes, really."

She caught another whiff of his skin, warmer now. Her pulse hastened.

"I'm not who you think I am," she whispered.

He took her hand and squeezed hard. "No one is."

• • •

They wandered in and out of the bedrooms like prospective home buyers, turning on lights and opening closets.

In the farthest bedroom, its tall walls a satiny blue, Liv tested a canopy bed with a cloud of comforters and a wall of pillows two deep. "I feel like Goldilocks."

Sam flung open windows, letting in the roar of the surf and the wet smell of the tide. She closed her eyes and spread her arms out like a child making snow angels. She thought about her phone in her coat, useless and blessedly quiet. She thought of all she hadn't confessed to Sam Felder—the truth of her father's demands, how deeply she wanted to break free of him, but how scared she was that to do so would devastate him, that the guilt of abandoning him would devastate her even more.

A gust of wind pushed at the sheers, snapping them wildly.

She remembered Whit Crosby, still out there on that lonely sand.

"Are you sure he's all right? It'll get cold later."

"He's fine," Sam said. "He's probably already on his way back by now." He came beside the bed and looked down at her. "You're tired."

"I'm not," she said.

"There are plenty of beds. If this is too soon."

If he knew how long she'd waited for freedom like this, he'd know it wasn't soon enough.

"Stay," she said, reaching out for him. "Just for a little while."

When he came over her and spread her out, unrolling her

like a tightly wound map, Liv felt her body sink. His mouth was warm and sure, guiding hers. He bared her neck and marked a trail of kisses from her chin to the hollow of her throat, his lips and tongue doing as her pencil had done, connecting one place of significance to another, flesh to more flesh. When his hair brushed the tops of her breasts through her shirt, she thought fleetingly of Whit Crosby again, the several times she'd caught him staring at her during dinner; then she squeezed her eyes shut and willed her mind to empty. She felt as unsteady as a dinghy tossed in a swell, so she wrapped herself around Sam and held on, afraid of falling off this perfect mountaintop, wanting Sam Felder to carry her far away to a place not on any chart, a land impossible to pierce with a tack.

"Hey, wake up. We overslept."

Whit's voice, grainy and rough, pricked Liv's dream like a needle. She blinked against a wall of sun. Sam stirred behind her, the weight of his arm still around her waist. She rolled over, meeting his bleary eyes and warm smile.

"We fell asleep," she said.

"So we did."

He unearthed them from their cozy cocoon and disappeared into the bathroom. Liv sat up and rubbed her eyes, her whole body pinched and swollen from sleeping in her clothes. Daylight streaked across the bed, undulating like a school of spooked fish. The air was cold. They'd never closed the windows.

The sound of water spraying from the bathroom faucet broke through the quiet.

Then the sound of a door slammed unnecessarily hard down the hall.

They guzzled black coffee and piled into the truck. An old man with skin as sunbaked as the bill of his faded ball cap waved to them from the upper deck of a boat called the *Moonracer*.

"Fashionably late as always, kid." Their captain navigated the ladder with the confidence and speed of someone three times younger, and gave Whit a hug and a hard slap on the back. "Good to see ya, Whitty."

Whit made the introductions. "Lou, this is Sam and Livy."

"And this is Andy, my mate." Another man, younger by several decades, emerged from the compressor room and gave them a sharp nod before disappearing around the side. The smell of fuel and rust was everywhere. Liv felt foolish in her tidy clothes, her pale freckled skin.

"You kids are good luck," Lou said. "Gonna be unseasonably warm today. At least on the boat." He nodded to the shuttered hatch to the cabin. "You can change down there."

Whit motioned for Sam to follow him belowdecks.

"What about you?" Lou's crinkled face neared hers. Liv drew back.

"She's staying topside," Whit answered before she could. "So be nice to her, Lou."

While the men suited up, Liv stood on the deck and looked out, soaking in the sea the only way she could.

"It's just swimming, Francis."

"It's not safe, Liza."

"You can't keep her out of the water completely."

"Can't I?"

"You're sure you'll be okay up here by yourself?" Sam returned, his perfect body gleaming in his wet suit, slick as a seal. Behind him, Whit arrived, a few inches taller. Their collective beauty stole her breath.

"She'll be fine," Whit said, checking his straps. "Won't you, Red?"

Fine.

His smile gave her confidence—but it was fleeting.

Take me with you, she wanted to say. *Never mind my traitorous lungs—just don't leave me behind.*

But the plea remained safe in her throat as she walked with them to the swim platform. She squinted against the sun so she could make sure to see them take their giant strides—as Sam had called their exaggerated steps off—to land in the water. They gave Lou the thumbs-up sign and Liv watched them sink, thinking how glorious it must be to escape to that kind of peace, envy rising in her like a fever, so quickly she swore she saw stars when she finally blinked.

The wait up top was interminable.

Liv remained at her post on the deck, staring at the place where Sam and Whit had descended, her heart racing with expectation. What if at that very moment they were swimming over the hull of the *Patriot*? Or maybe digging out something precious and small from the seafloor—a hand mirror, a toothbrush? All the times Liv had stood in front of museum displays, studying artifacts stored behind glass, her fingers itching to touch. What if today there was no glass partition? What if today she got to hold something of Theodosia's, something no one since Theodosia herself had touched? Maybe a collar button Theodosia had secured when the wind grew too harsh, or a bottle that had once held medicine she had taken to soothe her hurting heart?

"You know what they say about watched pots."

Lou's voice startled her. She turned to find the captain approaching with a wide grin, wiry gray hair springing out in points from under his cap. "I have something you might find more interesting to look at it," he said, pointing her to the bench. She followed him and sat down, watching as he picked up a bucket and set it between them. Liv peered in, the sour smell of rusted metal and old seawater blowing up at her. It appeared to be a collection of chunks of concrete, but Liv suspected it was much more.

"This is like my loose change jar. Just crap I've brought up here and there. They look like big rocks, but there's actually stuff stuck in 'em." He reached into the bucket and pulled out a hunk the size of a baseball, tossing it into the air a few times. "A little salvor lesson for you. When metal hangs around on the ocean floor, the shells and sand and all the other stuff binds it together, forms a kind of hard coating like concrete, clumps everything into what they call—"

"A concretion."

Lou slapped his sunburned thigh and leaned back. "Well, now, I didn't take you for a treasure hunter like those two."

"I'm not officially. I've just read a lot."

"So how come you're not down there with them? Scared of the water?" He dropped his voice. "You worried about sharks?"

"Sharks?" She smiled. "No."

"Good. You'll have better luck up here anyway." Lou popped off his cap and gave his forehead a hard scratch. "Between you and me, I give them thirty minutes before they surface. There's nothing to see down there."

Disappointment flared. She'd been so very excited. "You don't think Warner found the *Patriot*?"

The old man snorted. "Shit, not even close. I knew it when I took that tightwad out here the first time—my boys went down with him; they said the same thing—but Warner comes up all sure of himself, telling me what's what. What the hell do I know, right? I just drive the boat."

"Then where *do* you think she is?"

Lou squinted out at the water. "All over, probably. If the pirates took her, they dragged her to shore and tore her apart. Looters took the rest. Pieces and parts. Probably salvaged her boards for houses and God knows what else."

"And if she sank in the storm?" Liv asked.

"Then the sea's spread her ashes real good by now."

He handed her the chunk in his hand. Liv rubbed her thumb thoughtfully over an exposed sliver of metal. "Do you think there could have been any survivors?"

"If the Bankers got them, then I sure hope not." He pointed to the rock. "See the ridge right there, that strip of greenish gold peeking out? I bet you money there's something in there."

"Like a coin?"

"Could be. Have your boyfriend take it to that fancy college lab and dig it out for you."

Liv looked at the concretion, then back at him. "I couldn't take this. Not if you think it's worth something."

"Take it. Your first treasure." Lou turned toward the water. "So, which one's yours?"

"What do you mean?"

His milky eyes narrowed, pleating the loose skin at their edges like tiny folded fans. "You haven't decided yet, huh?" Understanding bloomed quickly; he meant Sam and Whit. "Smart girl." He nudged her shoulder. "Keep 'em guessing. We fellas hate to win a woman too quick."

Andy swung around the side. "They're coming up."

Liv closed her hands around the concretion and followed Lou back to the platform.

Sam and Whit broke the surface together, rearing up like mermen, their masks catching the sun. Liv rushed to the edge, stepping back as they flung their fins onto the deck. They climbed the ladder, first Sam, then Whit, both winded and glossy.

"There were a few ribs," Sam said, trying to catch his breath. "They might be old enough, but they're way too small for a schooner. Warner's got a grid line set up, but there's not much inside it."

Whit tore off his mask and tossed it onto the bench, spraying seawater. "It's something, all right, but it's not the *Patriot*. I'm not really sure what Warner's smoking that he thinks it is."

Behind them Liv saw Lou back at the bridge. He gave her an I-told-you-so smile before motioning for his first mate to pull up anchor, the boat shuddering back to life.

They returned to the marina ahead of a small chop. Liv waited for Sam to emerge from the cabin, eager to hear more of what he'd found. Eager too to hear what he thought about the night before. They'd shared a bed, fully clothed—a small intimacy in the pantheon of college debauchery—but his kisses had been deep and insistent. Had his affection been a minor thing for him, a fleeting opportunity when he'd had nothing better to do, not so unlike getting to view the wreck itself? No, she needed to believe a man like Sam Felder wasn't the whimsical sort, someone prone to mercurial lusts. That, she suspected, was Whit Crosby's forte.

Dressed again in his T-shirt and shorts, Sam joined her at the bow and came close, nearly touching, the smell of the sea still fresh on his skin. Her nervous heart stilled. She'd been so afraid he might want to pretend last night had never happened, that he might claim amnesia, when she could recall every moment.

She moved her hand closer to his, waiting to see if he'd slide his fingers toward hers, possibly thread them together as he had the night before.

"You do understand we can't talk about this, right?" he said low. "We can't tell anyone what we did."

Hurt blew through her. She jerked her hand away from his. "I never assumed last night made us something more than just—I mean, I don't have any expectations, if that's what you're worried about."

Sam cast a strange look at her. "Expectations for what?" Then his strained features loosened with understanding. "I was talking about the wreck, about not telling anyone in the department that we did this. Not . . . Did you think I meant *us*? No," he said. "Last night meant a great deal to me."

She glanced over her shoulder to make sure they were still alone. "You don't have to say that."

"Why do you think I came on this trip in the first place? Sure, I was curious about the wreck, but I barely know Crosby—and what I *do* know I find annoying as hell."

She smiled. "You don't know me either."

"True." He spread out his long fingers, reaching the edge of her hand. "I'm hoping that's all going to change now." He felt the clump in her hand. "What's this?"

"Lou gave it to me."

Sam took the concretion and studied it.

"He thinks it could be something valuable," she said.

"Valuable, huh?" Sam smiled, but his eyes narrowed skeptically. "Then why give it away?"

Before she could answer, Whit burst out of the cabin, carrying sodas, and handed them each a can. "If this were my boat, these would be cold beers." He snapped one open and raised it.

"I don't feel right toasting when I didn't go down," said Liv.

Sam tapped her can. "You didn't miss much."

"Next time," Whit said, knocking his can against hers.

She smiled, grateful for his optimism, but as the harbor

appeared on the horizon, Liv felt as if her beating heart were a ticking clock, counting down her remaining minutes of freedom. She wanted to draw out the string of this adventure for as long as she could.

"We could stop somewhere for dinner on the way home," she suggested. "Maybe get some clam strips?"

"I need to get back," said Sam. "I've got a paper due I haven't even started yet."

"And I've got a date with a girl named Greta," said Whit. "Don't be jealous, Red."

She rolled her eyes. She could just imagine what kind of woman turned Whit Crosby's head.

The ride back to Greenville seemed far quieter than the trip there. When they neared the campus, Sam stopped at a gas station to fill up. Whit climbed out to grab a Coke.

Alone in the truck, Liv pulled her phone from her bag. As wonderful as it had been avoiding her responsibilities for the last twenty-four hours, it was time to return to real life. With a steeling breath, she turned on her phone and waited for the screen to light up.

Her stomach dropped.

Forty-five missed calls.

Fingers trembling, she scrolled through the call log, sure her heart would beat itself right out of her chest.

The calls weren't only from her father—though most were. There was another number, and they'd left several messages.

"Miss Connelly, this is campus security. Your car was broken into overnight. One of the students reported it this morning. We put a call in to your father and he's—"

Oh God. Liv looked up and searched the store window. Sam and Whit were still at the counter. She reached behind the bench to grab her bag and yanked it free, her heart pounding. If she left out of the driver's side, they wouldn't see her go. She could run around the corner and hail a taxi down the block.

They'd worry, but she could leave a note.

And say what?

That on the other side of town, disaster was waiting to swallow her whole—that she'd had such a glorious twenty-four hours being able to use her hands for something other than holding up her father's whole world?

Through the glass, she could see Sam and Whit moving toward the door.

It was now or never.

She tugged a piece of scrap paper from her bag, scribbled a sorry lie, and slipped her note into the cup holder.

"I thought you'd been abducted, Livy. I thought you'd been *murdered*."

Her father was standing in the kitchen, ready to spring like a champagne cork, when Liv opened the door an hour later.

She walked calmly into her room and set her bag down on her bed, hearing her father's steps behind her. He stood in the doorway while she unpacked. Maybe there was still a chance he didn't know about Hatteras, didn't know that she'd made the whole thing up.

"I called the school about the trip, Livy."

Her hands slowed. She closed her eyes.

"They said they had nothing like that scheduled this weekend. What was I supposed to do?"

She spun to face him. *"Wait,"* she said. "You were supposed to wait for me to come home. Did you think I wasn't coming back?"

"How do I know what to think?" He came toward her, looking utterly stricken, his hazel eyes huge and sad behind his glasses. "You lied to me about who you were going with, where you were going. Someone broke into your car and campus police called me when you didn't answer."

He sat down on the bed and slouched forward, his hands between his knees. He pushed up his glasses and swiped his eyes with his thumb.

His voice was thin with defeat. "Sometimes people don't come back, Livy. Sometimes you've had a fight about something and they go out for milk and you don't bother to tell them you're sorry or that you can't live without them because you're so sure they'll be right back."

She sat beside him, the mattress rolling forward with their weight. "I'll always come back, Poppy."

"You can't be sure. That's the worst part, really." His hand slid toward hers, his fingers damp. "But you're home now. And it's good."

• • •

Morning arrived with a cold rain. Relentless sheets slid down the windows, darkening the kitchen as if someone had closed the shades, but Liv couldn't bear to turn on the lights. What did she need to see anyway? She knew the prison of this house and all the routines she'd tried—and failed—to escape. Making coffee, she heard the rumble of tires in the driveway and assumed it was someone visiting Mrs. Carlin. Then she saw the streak of mustard yellow through the curtain of rain, and panic exploded behind her ribs.

Sam.

For a moment, she thought she could just stay hidden and not answer. Then a terrible fear—that Sam would ring the doorbell and alert her father.

She rushed for the door and stepped out before he had reached the top of the stairs. He took them two at a time.

"Sam, what are you doing here?"

"Making sure you're okay—what do you think?" Rain dripped from the edge of his hood. He pushed it off his head, his dark eyes fraught. "I came back out and you were gone. We just figured you'd gone to the bathroom. We'd waited almost a half hour before Whit saw your note."

Remorse coiled in her stomach. "How did you find me?"

"I have a friend who has a work-study job in the registrar's office. She looked your address up for me." He sighed. "I don't even have your damn number."

"I'm sorry."

"But you're okay? Everything's okay?"

How to answer that?

Sam glanced over her shoulder. "Can I come in?"

"It's not a good idea. My father's . . . resting."

"Is he sick?"

She shook her head. Where to even begin? The entire ride home from Hatteras, she'd imagined all the gentle ways she could frame her story to Sam without scaring him off or showing him what a fraud she was. That her father suffered from anxiety, and that sometimes he worried too much, that he wasn't a bad man, just desperately lonely and demanding. But no explanation seemed soft enough, reasonable enough. So she'd simply avoided the whole conversation.

Now, despite all her efforts to hide her truths from him, Sam Felder was here, on the threshold of her entire world, seeking to enter, and having no idea what he was about to step into.

Sam's eyes flicked past her again. "Does he need a doctor? Because we can call someone. I can take him to the hospital if it's bad."

"It's not that kind of sick. He just gets . . . difficult."

"Difficult?" Sam frowned. "I don't understand."

She looked up at him. The rain had darkened his hair to a glossy chestnut. She wanted to be in that enormous bed with him again, close and warm and far, far away from here.

She sighed. "I told you I wasn't who you thought I was."

"I remember," he said. "And I told you I didn't care."

"No—you said none of us are."

He shrugged. "Same thing." He shifted on his heels. "Have dinner with me tonight."

Liv searched his earnest eyes, sure she would see a flash of teasing in them, but the deep brown pools remained even and sincere.

"Everyone's family is screwed up, Liv. Even mine."

Somehow she doubted it. Still she was grateful to him for pretending otherwise.

"Dinner?" he asked again. "And this time, I'm not leaving without your number."

6

OFF THE COAST OF TOPSAIL ISLAND, NORTH CAROLINA
Wednesday

"Un-*fucking*-believable!"

Liv is sure the exclamation is born of joy when she hears Chuck's yell from across the deck, and she feels her heart soar, sure it's the bell, that they've recovered it already. Then she sees the older man rip off his mask and the pink of fury that covers his face like a rash. Seconds later, Sam climbs the ladder, then Whit, then Dennis, and they are all shouting at once, hurling fins and masks. Chuck lunges for Whit, and Sam and Dennis struggle to keep the two men apart.

Liv quickens her pace to reach the melee, dread rushing through her. What was she thinking? She should never have asked Sam to join them. They haven't even been in the water a half hour and already there's a fight. Whit has said something stupid and hurtful and Sam has changed his mind and wants to leave—but then why are Dennis and Chuck angry too?

As she nears, Sam slips out of the group and catches her by the arm to stop her approach. He steers her away to the quiet of the lounge belowdecks.

His eyes are grim. "There's a grid line," he says, low. "And two holes. Big ones." He waits, maybe because he wants to make sure she's still breathing before he confirms it: "The wreck's already being recovered, Liv."

She grips the top of the closest chair, sure her knees will give out if she doesn't hold on to something.

Oh no. No, no, no.

Above them, voices explode. Chuck and the younger crewmen march past, angry voices colliding. They want to talk to Sam and the moblike level of their rage scares Liv enough that she skirts around Sam to avoid them when they spill into the lounge. She needs to find Whit, but when she climbs the stairs, he is already there, coming toward her, wild-eyed and soaking.

"I don't understand," she says. "How could they give you a license on a claimed site?" She is sure, so sure, this has just been a simple misunderstanding. But when Whit takes her by the arm to still her, her breath catches. She knows that metallic shade of blue his eyes turn when he's foundered.

The roughness of his voice leaves no doubt. "Warner told me I could have half of whatever we brought up."

She jerks back, yanks herself out of his grip as if he has shaken her.

He knew it was someone else's site?

How long has he known?

"But—but the scans," she says, frantic now. "The ones you took."

"Warner took those, not me. He let me have copies."

"Oh God . . ." She swallows, the coppery taste of dread lining her throat. No wonder he hadn't wanted her help with the paperwork—he'd never filed for any of it! How could he, when it wasn't free to claim? He had to know the men would find out he'd lied as soon as they dived—was he honestly so delusional that he thought he could talk his way out of it once they did?

Liv rolls against the side of the ship, her head swimming with understanding. The fight at the bar. He'd ruined it with Edwards on purpose. He knew this project was doomed and he'd gotten cold feet, so he'd tried to sabotage it at the last minute.

"What choice did I have, Red? We can't recover with scraps—we need a mother lode and Warner has one. You and I know it's almost impossible to get a license on a decent wreck anymore. We were desperate."

"Not so desperate we had to break the law!"

"That's not what we're doing."

"Isn't it? We have no paperwork, no permits. We've brought all these men out here on a lie."

"Not a lie, Red—a misunderstanding. There's a difference."

God, he really is delusional.

She darts around him, but he blocks her escape, both hands on her now, as if she's a wriggly fish he's trying to free from a hook. "I can fix this, Red. I'm taking the taxi boat with Dennis. I've got another boat on its way for the rest of you, but, baby, you have to convince the guys to go back to the house and wait for me to make this right. You can't let them leave."

She stares at him. *The crew?* That's who he's worried about leaving?

"It's too late," she says tightly.

"Warner's just down the road in Southport—I can be there in two hours and I won't leave until he sees me and puts our deal in writing. I just need a few days to work this out. It's not too late."

"I'm not talking about the project, Whit."

Comprehension and hurt blink back at her. He knows what she means and for a second, she thinks he might admit it—that he really might lose her, that she might finally have had enough of his cut corners and broken promises—but he just pulls her in for a kiss and says, "I'll be back tonight."

"I won't be here," she calls after him.

She isn't sure if he hasn't heard her, or if he merely refuses to believe her—but in a matter of minutes, he's on the taxi boat and speeding away, leaving her in the storm of his mess.

On their way back to the marina, the uproar subsides. Maybe it is because Whit is gone, and the men have no one to rage at, but there's no relief in the silence. If anything, Liv finds the quiet more disconcerting than the cacophony of their anger. Everywhere she goes on the boat, she can feel the persistent hum of simmering fury, and it undoes her. She wants to find a solitary corner somewhere and hide, but she can't bear to sit still. Instead she goes down to one of the forward staterooms and is relieved to find it empty. She walks to the bunk and falls into it, the smell of crisp sheets so sweet she wants to cry. This wasn't how it was supposed to be.

"I thought I'd find you here."

Sam appears in the doorway with two cups. Liv sits up and gathers her hair into a twist. He takes a seat on the facing bunk and hands her a cup. Coffee. Clumps of powdered creamer float on the top. She normally can't bear anything but real cream, but today she has to keep herself from draining the cup in one sip, hoping the heat of the liquid will stop her incessant shivering. She's not even cold, dammit. Just angry. Just crushed.

"I was hoping to find you something a little stronger than coffee," he says, and she can hear the faint smile in his voice, but she can't bear to meet his eyes. She knows how angry he must be that Whit has dragged them all out here on a fool's bargain.

She glances up at the ceiling. "It's so quiet."

"I think I managed to calm the waters for now."

Liv doesn't blame the men for being so enraged. Working under the policy of "no cure, no pay" means the crew's compensation will come from whatever treasure they find and not a daily wage. If the project was a bust, they'd have no income. Never mind that they weren't told they'd have to split whatever they brought up with another salvor, on top of what part of their haul the state is due.

She manages a small smile. "Thank you, Sam."

"It's okay."

"No, it's not. I don't know what to say. I'm so incredibly embarrassed right now."

He frowns. "Embarrassed about what?"

He has to ask? "For this. For—for everything." She gestures lamely around them. "For bringing you all the way down here falsely. For making you uproot your whole life. I'm so sorry."

She stops a moment to study his face, waiting for anger to show in his eyes, the amber to darken to a deep brown, the space between his eyebrows to knit together. Unlike with Whit, Sam's emotions have always lived far below the surface of his features. Reading him isn't so unlike searching an ocean floor for buried treasure. Surely he's furious? After all, he's given up his work to help them, and this is what he gets? She doesn't understand how he can be so calm.

Even his voice is smooth, virtually untouched.

"It's not your fault, Liv."

"Of course it is," she says. "I never should have let Whit do all the paperwork. He insisted he had it all under control and now I know why he didn't want my help. I should have pressed him, but I was just so relieved that we finally had something real. I can't believe he went to Harold Warner, of all people."

"Neither can I."

A thunder of footsteps grows loud down the corridor.

Liv wants to curl up like a pill bug and roll away.

"Everybody but Chuck agreed to stick it out for a few more days," Sam says. "I told them the house was paid for, the fridge stocked—so why waste it all? That seemed to settle them down a bit."

"I assume you'll leave, though?"

"I told Whit I would."

She nods, drawing up her cup and taking a long sip.

"Are you familiar with the Outer Banks Shipwreck Museum?" he asks.

She looks up at him, confused by the question. "The one that just opened in Nags Head?"

Sam nods. "Do you remember Beth Henson from ECU?"

"Of course."

"She's the director there now. She e-mailed me a few weeks ago about a diary they've acquired, a diary written by Theodosia in the months after the *Patriot* disappeared."

A ribbon of gooseflesh snakes down her spine. Her fingers tighten on the cup. "Are you serious?"

"Beth's offering me the chance to go through the entries before the museum makes an announcement to the public. I was planning to go while I'm here." He looks at her squarely. "I was hoping you'd come with me."

Liv stares at him, startled by the information, his invitation, and most of all the way her heart wants to burst out of her chest. Then she realizes it isn't just the news of a diary that has her heart racing—it's that now she understands why he has been so calm, why his anger has never surfaced.

Why he agreed to excavate a blockade runner when he knew they rarely contained gold.

Heat burns a path up her neck.

Joining this mission never had anything to do with the *Siren*. It was about the *Patriot*, about Theodosia. About bringing this news to her.

Liv swallows. They look at each other, the truth settling between them softly, like dust.

Sam leans forward. "We could go as soon as we get back to the house."

"But Nags Head is four hours away."

"Three and a half," he says. "We could even take the ferry from Ocracoke on our way back. You always said you wanted to."

That he would remember.

She shakes her head, slowly at first, then more fiercely. "I can't."

"Why not?"

"Because I've put all that away."

"Or maybe you've just had to because Whit couldn't keep his end of the bargain?"

"It's not that simple." She stands and walks across the cabin, a bolt of loyalty charging through her. "You don't know what's gone on, Sam."

"I know Whit promised you one last mission and he screwed that up. I know he's great at making promises, just not so great at keeping them. . . ."

Liv can feel Sam's eyes on her.

"Should I keep going?"

She turns to find Sam's followed her—too close. The warm, sandy smell of him is too familiar. She knows she should step back, but she can't.

He lowers his voice, the way he used to when they'd pore over charts in bed. "I'm not asking you to shake up your whole life. Just one day, one ride up the coast. We wouldn't even have to stay the night."

Above them, she can hear the bang and clatter of equipment being moved, tanks being returned to their racks. Despite Whit's oversight—a kind word for it—she is as much a part of this project as he is. Her reputation and Whit's are woven together. Sam is free to leave if he wants to, but she has an obligation to these men.

"I can't go now," she says. "If the crew is willing to stay, I want to at least make amends for as long as they'll wait."

"You want to make amends?" Sam asks. "Then let these guys have the run of the house for a while. Let them drink all of Whit's single malt. Let the younger guys pick up a few pretty girls in town and bring them back and impress the hell out of them."

She laughs and reaches up to test the knot of her hair. "I don't know, Sam."

"Stay here. I want to show you something." He disappears and returns a few minutes later with his bag. He sets it on the bunk and pulls out a folded poster—at least, she thinks it's a poster. Until he opens it up—and her breath catches. She doesn't know how it's possible, but the paper has the same dry, malty scent. She remembers writing notes on it that night in Hatteras as if it were just yesterday, how her hand shook knowing Sam was watching her work, how she'd hoped he'd kiss her deeply before the night was over.

Then a flash of hurt cuts through, as she is reminded of how it came to be in his possession.

She looks at him. "I never understood why you took it when you left."

"I wanted a piece of you. Of *us*." He rubs his beard. "I meant to send it back to you a hundred times—I *wanted* to, but I couldn't."

"I don't even recognize my own writing," she says—but

that's not true. She's just afraid to look too closely. She knows if she starts to read her old notes, if she follows the bread crumb trail back to this shared past of theirs, the mystery will rise again, as high and green as a forgotten bulb, demanding to be plucked from the soil and sniffed deeply. She won't be able to put it back in the ground.

Sam lays his hands over hers and Liv feels the room fall away.

"One day, Liv," he says. "That's all."

But it's not all, and they both know it.

A sudden gust of air blows through the cabin door and flutters a corner of the map. As if the universe is trying to snap them out of a trance.

7

TOPSAIL ISLAND, NORTH CAROLINA
Wednesday

Two hours later, Liv is standing in the enormous kitchen they don't need and most certainly can't afford, stacking sliced cheddar and smoked ham into sandwiches as carefully as a mason building a brick wall, just grateful for the distraction while Sam tells the crew their plans to go to Nags Head. While she cleans up, the men wander in and out. She was worried that they might blame her for Whit's blunder, but their faces are pleasant as they retrieve sodas and cold cuts, almost pitying. Perhaps they understand that she's been as bamboozled as the rest of them. By one, Sam decides they are ready to leave.

She climbs into his truck, so much bigger than the yellow

pickup he used to own, but still as tidy. She marvels at the shiny dashboard, the empty cup holders. Whit's are forever stuffed with crumpled gas receipts and pens. Drives her crazy. She always wants to put down her coffee somewhere and never can.

For the first half hour of the drive, they say little, letting the air in the cab fill instead with music. Liv has to admit it felt good to flee that giant house; it feels good now to be moving forward, away from the wreck Whit has made of their mission, of everything, it seems.

The sun bakes the front seat. Liv makes a high knot of her hair to let the breeze at her neck, drawing in a breath of the deep, rich smell of hot leather.

Sam glances over. "I can turn on the AC if you're warm."

"I'm fine." She slips out of her sandals and pushes her bare feet into the cool rubber ridges of the floor mat, wiggling her toes until her heartbeat calms.

"I've been meaning to ask you about your dad," Sam says. It's not the subject she hoped he'd suggest, but it's safer than others. "Is he still . . . ?"

"He is. Although he doesn't recognize much anymore. And he thinks the staff is poisoning him. He's sure that the powdered creamer is really anthrax because it has no smell. He'll only eat what I bring from the outside. I keep extra containers and if I'm pressed for time, I'll swing by the cafeteria and get them to dump their food into them so he won't know." She glances guiltily at Sam. "Sad, isn't it?"

His eyes pool with sympathy.

Liv draws in a long breath, anxious to change the subject. "How's Michael?"

"Married with two kids and designing software in Vegas."

Liv blinks at him. "*Your brother,* Michael?"

Sam grins. "Yeah, I know. It blows my mind too."

She thinks about one of the last times she was in a truck with Sam, driving home from the restaurant after he announced he wanted to go back to Chicago for law school.

She never expected to see him again.

And now here they are, driving back to the Outer Banks to see Theo's diary.

Theo's diary.

Liv still can't believe it.

"What do you know about the entries?" she asks.

Sam leans back in the seat, lowers his hand to the bottom of the wheel. "Beth didn't say much. Just that all the entries are dated right after the *Patriot* disappeared and that they were definitely written by Theodosia."

Liv tucks a bare foot under her rear and smiles.

"What?" Sam asks.

"Beth obviously wants to make sure you'll come. If she shows all her cards, you won't need to."

He frowns over at her.

"Oh, come on," Liv says. "You know Beth Henson always had a thing for you."

Sam snorts. "You're kidding."

Was *he*? Exotic Beth Henson and her hammered-silver cuffs, her crisp black Bettie Page bob, bangs that might have been cut with a level.

"She's not going to be happy to see me show up with you now that you're finally single."

"How do you know she's single?" Sam says.

A fair point.

"And for that matter, how do you know I am?" he asks without taking his eyes off the road.

Liv's cheeks warm; she is sure he'll confirm or deny his status, but he doesn't.

They advance on a station wagon, a golden retriever sticking its coppery head out the window. Sam steers them around the car. The dog's jowls are white-tipped and loose in the wind. Liv waves as they pass.

"I never pegged Whit for the marrying type," Sam says. "But then he always did like a party."

"Actually there wasn't any party. There weren't any guests. It was sort of a spur-of-the-moment thing."

The cab warms again with the uncomfortable heat of truth and Liv regrets her confession. There were so many wonderful things about that frenetic, glorious day at the courthouse. She wants to tell Sam how Whit got them the last room at the hotel and insisted on carrying her up ten flights of stairs instead of taking the elevator. How he snuck them up to the rooftop pool after it had closed and stripped down to his boxers for a game of Marco Polo. How they made love in seven different positions—one for every year they'd known each other. How he ordered a whole cheesecake from room service and fashioned a bride and groom for the top out of toilet paper rolls and a Sharpie.

"Did *you* marry?"

Sam shakes his head.

"Did you ever get close?"

"Just once." He casts a look at her that makes her flush,

because she knows he is referring to her and she feels foolish for the question, that he'll suspect she's set him up. Then he rescues them both by adding, "Twice, actually."

"What happened?" she asks blithely, as if she's just being polite, as if she hasn't wondered this for years.

Sam shrugs. "She wanted to get married. I didn't."

"You make it sound so simple."

"Believe me, it wasn't."

Katie Easterday. Liv would bet money that's who he's talking about, and a long-lost spark of jealousy flares for a moment, then fades. She wants to ask, to let him know their past isn't so far away that she doesn't remember the people who mattered to him, who came before her, but the chime of her cell sounds from her feet where she has stashed her purse, startling them both. She turns to the window, needing the air. It seems as if the rings will never stop.

"He'll just keep calling, you know," Sam says.

"He might call you too."

"He won't." Sam glances at her. "I told him I was going back to the cape, remember?"

Guilt squeezes her ribs. Whit would never have left her alone with Sam willingly.

"He still lives in a world where he thinks it's better to ask forgiveness than permission," she says, her voice so low she wonders if she even means to have Sam hear her.

"Nothing changes."

"But he *has* changed, Sam. He's not the same Whit you knew."

"I don't know, Liv. He seems exactly like the same Whit to me."

She worries the hem of her shirt. "It's been a tough few years. We were on firm ground for a while, and then we started running out of money, and licenses became harder to get, and everything just seemed to . . ." She sighs. "I don't know."

"People don't change, Liv."

Liv considers his profile. "I like to think I've changed. Haven't you?"

"I don't know—you tell me. Have I?"

She frowns at him. "I always hated when you answered my question with a question."

"I did that?"

"*Do*. Present tense."

He smiles. "Then there you are: Apparently I haven't changed either."

Oh, but he has. Liv studies his profile, noticing details she didn't want to see before but closer now, she can't deny: the lines in his forehead, the fine threads of silver in his short beard.

The backs of her legs are damp with sweat—she shifts to let the air at them.

She feels like a ripe piece of fruit that needs peeling.

"You've definitely changed," he says. "You're more . . ." He squints quickly at her. "*Unbridled*. It's like you've let go of things. Things that used to matter to you."

"Like what?"

"Don't get defensive; I didn't mean it as a criticism." He smiles. "I like it."

She turns her gaze back to the road, but his description of her lingers in the quiet. Unbridled. Like a wild horse. And here they are, driving toward the Outer Banks and the famous wild horses of Currituck. He's right. Their lives together were so ordered—a structure she'd understood. She moved from her father's rules to Sam's, folded herself gently into his safe routines; then she lived alone for a year and discovered that maybe she didn't need so many rules after all. Then Whit had come back into her life, blown in the way he always did, and for the first time she understood that home could be a person, not a place. Living with Whit has forced her to surface from that fearful sea, to shake off years of dreading the slightest crack in a wall, in a plan. Whit's whole world is a collection of chipped dishes, of chairs with loose legs, forever in danger of collapsing. It occurs to her how much of their marriage she has spent being the glue.

She wonders again if Sam is probing, trying to unbutton her heart enough that he can see inside, or hold out his hand in case something should happen to fall out.

As they cross the New River, the breeze picks up, stirring the silence, blowing hard enough that she hopes the subject will exit with it, but then Sam says, "I don't know about Beth, but I am, by the way."

"You are what?"

He glances over at her. "Single."

She's not entirely sure what she's supposed to say, but when she turns her face back to the wind and closes her eyes, a ripple of possibility charges through her, then a flash of remorse.

The sandwiches she made so carefully. She forgot them in the fridge.

• • •

Whit wished he could follow the Jeep driver who had flashed his lights a half mile back; he'd buy him a beer and maybe even dinner for saving him a speeding ticket. Otherwise Whit would never have noticed the cruiser wedged in the thicket of bay trees off the highway and would have sailed past at eighty-five miles an hour. The same speed he's probably clocked since he left Topsail. But how else is he supposed to get to Little River in less than two hours?

Now he's ten minutes from the yacht club. He knows they won't let him in wearing shorts and a ratty T-shirt. As if he was going to waste time changing? He hasn't driven all this way to sip an overpriced, watered-down gin and tonic in the Officers' Club. He's here to find Warner and get him to sign off on this deal. Officially. The way Whit knows he should have done in the first place.

It's too late, Whit.

Liv's face flashes back at him whenever he blinks, the look of heartbreak he swore never to cause her again.

I'm not talking about the project . . .

He doesn't blame her for being angry—he's angry too. Angry that he trusted Warner to keep his word. Now instead of being on the water bringing up treasure, he's flying down 133 in his board shorts, damp as a wet dog. When he swings into the club, he pulls over as close as he can to the marina, not caring it's a loading zone and that he'll probably return to find a ticket stuck under his wiper. Put it on his tab. As much money as he's pissing away on this mission, a parking ticket is a drop in the bucket. He scans the collection of floating docks. So many boats—he forgot how big this marina was. How the hell will he find Warner's? He stops the first person he sees, a kid in a Southport Marina polo shirt, and the young man points him to the harbormaster's office, but Whit won't need him. Beyond the young man's buzz-top head, Whit spots Chowder Lewis slinging towlines into his boat and a flash of hope, fleeting but welcome, settles his racing heart. After twenty years on these waters, Whit knows someone in every port.

Chowder waves him down to the slip and Whit sprints the whole way there, thinking his luck might finally be turning. Chowder crewed for Harold Warner for years. He'll know where he's at.

"Whit Crosby—holy shit!" Chowder is forty-one, just two years older than Whit, but you'd never guess it. Sun, sea, and two packs a day have aged Chowder so much he could pass for twice his age. His shaved head is still as shiny as a newly painted buoy and Whit swears he could kiss it like the damn Blarney Stone, he's so relieved right now. "Don't tell me you're docked here?"

"I'm looking for Warner, Chowdy. Do know you where he is?"

"What do you want with that asshole?"

"You don't want to know." Whit scans the marina. "Is he here?"

Chowder nods to the water. "You just missed him. He took off early this morning with his girlfriend, the lucky old bastard. Headed down to the Caymans, I think."

The fat, beautiful balloon of relief Whit has been floating on pops. He rakes both hands through his salt-crusted hair and stares hard at the horizon, willing a new plan to arrive, but nothing comes.

Chowder puts a hand on his arm. "Why are you looking for him?"

"He promised me dibs on a steamer he claimed but never excavated off Topsail."

"You don't mean the *Siren*? I heard he tried to dig her up a few months ago but didn't find squat and gave up. You must be talking about another ship?"

"Nope, that's her." Whit blows out a weary breath. Hell, he might as well confess it all. "Warner said if I could pull together a crew, that I could excavate her, and that whatever we brought up, I could keep half. He said she was loaded. He'd taken some scans, but he swore he hadn't touched the site so the crew wouldn't have to know it wasn't all ours, but I got down there this morning and there was a grid line, holes, the whole thing. My crew went nuts."

"Can you blame 'em?" Chowder's green eyes pool with sympathy. "You know you can't trust that jerk."

"I figured it was a sure thing. I was going to do all the work and all he had to do was collect!"

"What happened to all that money you brought up near Marathon?"

"It went a lot faster than I expected."

"It always does." Chowder winces. "How deep you in for?"

"Deep as it gets. I need a lead."

Chowder runs his palm over the top of his head. "I haven't

heard about anything. Nobody's finding so much as a beer can around here."

"It doesn't have to be local. It could be Wilmington. Hell, I'd go to the Outer Banks if I had to. My crew'll cut bait if I don't come back with something. *Anything*."

Chowder's eyes are bright but pitying and Whit knows how he sounds, how strung out he must look—wild-haired, stinking of seawater and sweat. He's a junkie looking for a score. A gambler frantic for the biggest payout of his career. Whit's sunk everything into this mission. His savings. His marriage.

Red.

"Go home, Whit. Get drunk, get laid. Jesus Christ, man. You used to be the luckiest son of a bitch treasure hunter from the cape to the keys. Since when do you need me to throw you scraps?"

"I have to make this right, Chowdy. I can't lose her."

Chowder digs out cigarettes from his pocket. "Sounds like you already have—but if it makes you feel any better, there wasn't much in her to lose."

Whit opens his mouth to contest, then realizes Chowder is talking about the *Siren*—and Whit is talking about Liv.

"Smoke?" Chowder shoves the opened pack at him.

Whit stares hungrily at the perfect white rounds that peek out from the nest of foil, his tongue prickling. Eight years away and he can still recall the flavor of a fresh filter and that first drag, pure and sweet.

He swallows hard and shakes his head. "I quit."

"No shit?" Chowder says, chuckling as he snaps his lighter to life. "Me too."

• • •

Outside Washington, Liv's stomach rumbles, loud enough that she swears she can hear it over the din of air rushing through the truck's cab. She still can't believe she forgot their lunch. When was the last time she ate? She can't recall, but her head aches with hunger.

"Maybe we could stop for a quick bite," she says.

"How about there?" Sam points to a stand-alone restaurant in a nearing strip mall: Lucky's Grill. Liv's not crazy about the name, but it's just a name, isn't it? Surely there's nothing prophetic in a diner sign.

Sam pulls into the parking lot. The planters along the diner's railing overflow with zinnias. Liv thinks briefly of her plants back in Florida, how she'd meant to move them to a shadier spot under the awning but forgot, too distracted. Her frail jade, just recovering from root rot. It needs her care now more than ever, and she's abandoned it.

The restaurant is bright but mostly empty when they step inside, hot and thick with the smells of fried fish and ketchup. They slide into a booth and pluck menus from behind the table's napkin dispenser. While Sam scans his, Liv looks around and can't help smiling. She feels young and reckless again, the way she did that first trip to the Outer Banks. The three of them: spontaneous musketeers, hell-bent on trumping Warner's great discovery; her, Sam, and Whit.

Whit.

"Coffee," Sam says when the waitress arrives. "And a tuna on rye. Salad instead of fries."

"That's a dollar more," the woman says, turning her blue-shadowed eyes to Liv. "For you, hon?"

"Oyster sandwich and a Coke with lemon, please."

When the woman leaves, Liv gives Sam a teasing grin. "Who comes to a diner and exchanges fries for a salad? No wonder they charge you extra. It's a shaming fee."

Sam laughs. "And since when do you eat oysters?"

"I always ate oysters."

"*Whit* ate oysters," Sam says, pushing one of the rolled napkin sets toward her.

Liv watches Sam's fingers arrange the utensils on either side of an imaginary plate, memories spilling everywhere, his hands spreading open the map, spreading her.

The waitress returns with his coffee and her Coke. Liv stares at Sam as he takes several long sips. "What?" he asks.

"I'm just thinking how crazy this is. That just this morning we were on the water, all suited up—and now we're here. That this was your idea."

He casts a wounded look at her.

"Come on, Sam," she says. "You know this isn't like you. Being spontaneous this way. It's something . . ." She smiles sheepishly. "Never mind."

"It's something Whit would do, right?" he finishes for her.

A swell of warmth fills her, an appreciation of a past life. "I liked your rules, Sam. They used to make me feel safe."

"Maybe I don't play by the rules anymore."

Whatever threat he kept from his voice burns unmistakably in his eyes, startling her. She's not sure what rules he's referring to.

"I was thinking," says Sam, rubbing the handle of his mug with his thumb, "maybe on the way back we could drive by the place in Hatteras. For old times' sake."

Welcome to the end of the world.

She frees her fork and knife and sets them down, grounded suddenly by the reminder of what they've run from. "You know, if Whit fixes things with Warner . . ."

"There's nothing to fix, Liv."

"But suppose he *could*."

"Do you want him to?" Sam says.

She meets his eyes. "I want one more deep dive." But that's not what he's asking, not really, and they both know it. No matter what comes of this trip, she will have to decide whether or not to forgive Whit, to give him another chance.

Sam shrugs. "Maybe you just need a little space. A little time away."

"Maybe."

"You could always come back with me to the cape," he says, then adds quickly, "I don't mean for good. Just for a week or two, clear your head. I could use an extra hand on the charter. You could put your first mate cap back on again. If that's what you decide to do. Take a break, I mean."

"Isn't that what this is?"

He leans forward. "We're not doing anything wrong, Liv."

Not yet. The words blink back at her, sharply enough that she is sure Sam can read the guilt in her expression.

"I've taken off to the Outer Banks without telling my husband," she says matter-of-factly.

"You're researching a diary with an old friend."

She meets his eyes. "You're more than that, and you know it."

"You have every right to be here."

"He'll worry, Sam."

"So let him worry. It'll do him good to think of someone besides himself for once." Their food arrives and Sam waits for their waitress to depart before he says, "Think of it like old times—when it was just the two of us, and Whit would never give us a minute alone."

Loyalty surges again. "He just wanted to be part of us."

"No," Sam says. "He just wanted to be part of *you*."

Had he? Liv doesn't remember it that way. At least not in the beginning. After their return from Hatteras, and Sam's unexpected appearance at her front door, she and Sam had grown close, weathering January together when winter blanketed the campus with the occasional varnish of ice, Sam's affections—and the concretion Lou gave her that she kept in her backpack—the only reminder of their trip to the sea.

Their courtship wasn't always a smooth one—her father's demands of her time seemed to increase and in the wake of the Hatteras lie, Liv had allowed her guilt to indulge his wishes. Sam's patience was remarkable. She'd promised him she would try to move into a place of her own by the end of March. He'd told her there was no rush.

As promised, he'd also partnered in her continuing research of what might have happened to Theodosia and the *Patriot*, joining Liv on day trips to local historical societies that held collections of journals and nautical archives.

As for Whit Crosby, the trio that he'd been so certain would turn into something grand and world-changing had drifted away like a loose dory upon their return to Greenville. She never saw Whit on campus and Sam never spoke of his antics in their shared classes. Which was why when Liv stepped into the Student Union on a gray Wednesday morning and spotted a familiar head of rumpled hair and long legs sprawled out on a corner couch fast asleep, she couldn't resist making her way over and giving his knee a quick tap.

"Morning."

Whit woke with a start. "Hey! What are you doing here?"

"I go here, remember?"

"English. Right." He pushed himself upright and rubbed his face hard. "I only meant to close my eyes for a second. What time is it?"

"Ten thirty."

"Shit." He propped his elbows on his knees and groaned. "I'll give you fifty dollars for a sip of your coffee."

"The first sip's free."

He took several. It seemed a year since she'd last seen him, fleeing Sam's truck to get home to her father. Memories of their game of truth or dare on the beach flashed, how high the fire had grown, how hot; how careless she'd felt out there under that roof of stars, swigging wine and sharing secrets. Whit had seemed larger than life to her that weekend, roguish and daring. It was oddly pleasant to find him quiet and sluggish, charmingly out of sorts. Maybe she'd been wrong to think he couldn't ever be still, be thoughtful. Just *be*.

His hair was tousled with sleep, thick and wavy. Sam's

hair was always so smooth and tight against his scalp. She wondered what it would be like to push her fingers through Whit's, how different it might feel.

"I was hoping to see you at Warner's lecture last week," Whit said. "I was sure you'd be there ready to bust his chops about something." He grinned. "I was really looking forward to it."

"I'll bet." She smiled. "I meant to go, but I had to finish a paper."

"You ever see Sam around?"

"We're dating, actually."

"No kidding?" He looked surprised, though she didn't see how he could be after finding them in bed together. Or maybe it just surprised him that something had come of that one night. Liv suspected Whit Crosby wasn't the sort to seek out long-term relationships. Not that she had any proof. Not that she cared either way.

"I'll have to congratulate him when I see him in lab this afternoon," Whit said. "Lucky guy."

She felt the heat of a blush bloom at her chin. "Lucky *girl*," she said, hiding her color behind a sip of coffee. "I really did have a wonderful time that weekend. I'm sorry if I didn't ever thank you before I . . ."

"Before you took off like Cinderella?" His smile was forgiving. "You ask your doctor about diving yet?"

"No."

"Tell me when you do. I'll teach you myself."

She took another sip, a flutter of possibility sliding down her throat with her coffee. "I read that Warner's still insisting that site might be connected to the *Patriot*."

"He's getting all kinds of attention for it—why quit? But I know I plan to keep looking for her. How about you?"

"Absolutely. Actually Sam and I are planning to go out to Kitty Hawk to see a man with an antique shop—I've got the name right here. . . ." She tugged her calendar from her backpack and flipped through, finding the page. "Barnacles and Brass Antiques," she said. "Goofy name, but he specializes in old letters. He says he has some from as far back as 1805. You never know."

"Sounds like fun." Whit's eyes flashed. Was he fishing for an invitation? "Do you still think the pirates got her?"

She nodded. "I haven't had much luck convincing Sam, though. He still thinks she sank in a storm."

"Well, don't let him change your mind, whatever you do," Whit said. "You and I both know it was the pirates."

"You think so too?"

"Aye." He winked. "It's *always* the pirates, *lass*."

She laughed and reached down to close up her backpack. "I should go," she said, rising. "I'm meeting Sam at the library at one."

Whit climbed to his feet. "I'll walk with you."

On their way out, Liv slowed at the bulletin board outside the double doors and scanned the layers of announcements and advertisements.

"Looking for something?" he asked.

"A room," she said.

"There's a girl in Greta's hall who just dropped out last week. Kate, I think. Some kind of family thing. Her room's empty."

Greta. Wasn't she the girl he was going to take out the night they returned from Hatteras? Maybe Liv was wrong to think he didn't want attachments.

"I bet if you stopped off at Student Affairs, you could get her room," he said.

A dangerous hope rose in her stomach. Her own room meant she and Sam could spend the night together, like real couples. She'd never have to worry about time or bad weather or what sort of new excuse she'd come up with to explain her late-night return. Hadn't she lately worried that Sam was growing tired of her curfews, when there were so many willing women who didn't have to check their watches or phones, whose carriages wouldn't shrink back to pumpkins at midnight?

A week later, she was loading her books and clothes into the bed of Sam's truck and vacillating between tears of joy and knots of guilt. After cooking dinner for her father and sitting with him while he pushed slices of chicken around his plate and complained of a headache, Liv returned to her new room to find Sam waiting for her with a sausage pizza and a celebratory bottle of merlot. They feasted cross-legged on her bare mattress, too hungry to make the bed.

When only a single slice remained, Liv lowered the box to the floor and climbed into Sam's lap, kissing him deeply.

He put his hands on her waist and gently eased her back. "I brought you something."

"Better than pizza?"

"Much better."

Liv watched as he pulled a poster from his bag and handed it to her. "Think of it as a room-warming gift."

Even before she unrolled the thick paper and saw the familiar curls of her handwriting, she knew what it was.

"Whit wanted to chuck it when we got back, so I rescued it," said Sam. "Come on, I'll help you put it up."

Soon the huge chart was on the wall, tall and wide and filling the small room with the deliciously dusty scent of old books. Liv stared at it, thinking of all the leads they'd acquired in the weeks since she first put her pencil to it in Hatteras. "We have so much to add," she said.

Sam took the wine from her hand. "Later."

Afterward, the sheet around their tangled legs, they stared up at the map. Moonlight swam across the ivory paper, flickering hypnotically, pulling her toward sleep.

Sam traced her hipbone with his thumb. "What would you do if you solved the mystery?"

"Don't you mean *when*?" She turned her head, finding the perfect line of his nose in the velvety dark, warm ripples of longing stirring.

"You'll never guess who I got partnered with for my conservation lab project."

Liv nestled against him and smiled. "Whit Crosby."

"He said you told him we were going out to Kitty Hawk to look at those letters. He asked if he could come with us."

She rose on her elbows. "What did you say?"

"I said it was more of a two-person expedition. I think he took the hint."

"He does know a lot about ships and wrecks. He might surprise you, you know."

"That's what I'm afraid of."

Liv settled back against the heat of his hard chest. "Speaking of conservation lab, I can't find that concretion Lou gave me on the boat. Have you seen it?"

"No," said Sam, dropping a kiss on her temple. "But I wouldn't be too broken up about it. It didn't look like much to me."

After that, well. Maybe Liv would have to concede that Whit did try to insert himself into their world at every chance. Despite his reservations, Sam did grow to appreciate Whit Crosby's expertise in the field of marine archaeology. Just as Liv had predicted, Sam had to admit that Whit made an excellent lab partner, after several weeks on the project, his feverish intensity and spontaneity a perfect balance to Sam's methodical organization. When their project was awarded the highest grade in the class, Whit decided they should celebrate at Zephyr's, the most expensive restaurant in town. "My treat," he said. "Greta and I can meet you there at seven."

Thanks in part to traffic, and an emergency stop at her father's to assure him his thermostat wasn't in fact smoking, they arrived closer to eight. The restaurant was crowded and loud. Several groups waited in the entry for tables. Stalled at the hostess station, Liv spotted Greta's waves of shiny blond hair at a booth in the back.

Her bright red lips were as tight as her arms across her chest.

"Hey," said Sam. "Where's Whit?"

"Your guess is as good as mine." Greta's brown eyes flared. "He said he had to pick something up and that he'd meet me here at six thirty. That was ninety fucking minutes ago. I've called four times. He won't answer. And I'm sure as hell not ordering food if he thinks he's sticking me with the bill for this place."

"Maybe he had car trouble," Liv said.

"Car trouble? Are you kidding?" Greta rolled her eyes as she stood and smoothed the sides of her leather skirt. "I'm sure the only thing he had to *pick up* was a round of scotches at Tuck's." She pulled on a fringed suede coat, freeing the caught ribbons of her blond hair and shaking them out down her back. "If he does show up, feel free to tell him I'm breaking up with him—and that I really mean it this time."

"Do you need a lift back to the dorms?" Sam asked.

"I'll be fine." The tight line of her lips softened briefly. "Thanks, though."

When Greta had marched out the front, Sam muttered something under his breath and took Liv's hand to exit too.

She pulled gently to stall him. "We're leaving?"

"Of course we're leaving. I'm not buying dinner here. Whit's obviously blown us off."

Liv waited until they were back in his truck and Sam had twisted the heater to full blast before she continued to protest. "What if something really did happen to him? Maybe he got into an accident."

"Going a half mile down the road?"

"Should we call him?"

"You heard Greta—she tried."

"Maybe he lost his phone."

Sam lowered his hands from the wheel and turned to her. "Why are you making excuses for him?"

"I'm not. I'm just saying since we don't know for sure, maybe we shouldn't take off so quickly."

Sam reached over and threw open her door, a burst of cold air stinging her bare calves. "Then feel free to stay here and wait for him, Mother Teresa."

She slammed the door closed. "You're a jerk."

"*I'm* a jerk?"

She glared out at the street, willing the chilly air coming out of the vents to grow hot.

"Liv, I'm not the one who invited his friends and his girlfriend out to dinner and then stood them all up without so much as a phone call."

"I'm not saying it wasn't a shitty thing to do—"

"Then what are you saying?"

She tugged on her seat belt, feeling at turns admonished and furious, and not sure which was worse. A group of students walked in front of the truck, laughing loudly. Dressing for dinner, she'd felt glamorous and sexy. Free and full of promise. She couldn't remember the last time she'd spent so long fixing her damn hair.

Now all she wanted was to get back to her room and tear off this too-tight skirt, unravel this ridiculous twist she'd glued to her head with a million bobby pins.

But mostly she wanted to crawl under her flannel sheets with Sam, to stare up at their chart until they drifted to sleep, this night, and all of Whit's foolishness, fading with them.

But when they reached her dorm, Sam didn't turn off the truck.

She stared at him. "Aren't you coming up?"

"I have Waters's paper that I haven't even started. I should really go back to my place."

"Makes sense." But disappointment bloomed.

"I'll call you tomorrow," he said.

"Sure."

"Liv?"

Halfway out, she stopped and looked back at him.

"It is what it is, okay?"

She nodded and he pulled away, but she wasn't sure what *it* he meant.

She wrestled with sleep for far too long before her body—and brain—finally surrendered. Her dreams—nightmares—were vivid and horrible. Visions of her father falling off the side of a large ship, slipping under black waves, and somehow still breathing when she looked over the railing to see him staring up at her, his mouth moving like a fish's, eyes huge and unblinking. Another dream of him wandering around an empty house as an old man, just as Aaron Burr had done at the end of his life, destitute and alone.

When she heard the pounding, she searched for her clock and frowned at the time—two forty-three? *Sam*. Relief washed over her. Of course it was Sam. He'd felt badly for their fight and had come over to make up. She rushed from the bed to let him in, but when she swung open the door, it was Whit Crosby there instead, leaning against the jamb, his hair wilder than usual, his shirt untucked, one sleeve shoved up past his elbow, the other undone. He smelled of smoke and sweet liquor.

"Not exactly the tooth fairy, huh?"

Liv squinted against the harsh hall fluorescents. "What happened to you? You look terrible."

"Gee, tell me how you really feel." He raked both hands through his hair, trying to guide the thick waves into some kind of order.

As he did, Liv made out a streak of scarlet just below his lip. "Oh my God—is that blood?"

He touched his mouth and marveled at the stain on his fingertips. "Definitely not ketchup."

She pulled him inside and closed the door behind him, snatching a bath towel from her dresser and shoving it against his split lip.

"Ouch. Easy, Red."

"Serves you right," she said. "What were you thinking?"

"Shh—don't want to wake Sammy."

"He's not here." She turned on her desk lamp and pointed him to her bed. "Keep pressing that towel to stop the bleeding. I have aspirin somewhere. What you really need is ice."

"Why? Do you have bourbon?"

She rushed to the other side of the room and dropped down to the floor to dig through her toiletry bucket until she found her pill jar. Walking back, she felt her breasts swing loose under her T-shirt. If Whit noticed that she wasn't wearing a bra, he was enough of a gentleman not to stare.

"What happened to you tonight?" she asked, snatching a bottle of seltzer off her desk. "We went to the restaurant. Greta waited for you for over an hour."

"It was just supposed to be a few hands, a half hour tops," Whit said, watching her shake out three aspirins with drowsy eyes. He chased the pills with a swig of seltzer, grimacing as he swallowed.

"We thought you'd been in an accident. Well—" Liv frowned. "*I* thought that. Sam and Greta were sure you were getting shit-faced at a bar somewhere. Don't I feel like an idiot?"

"I don't know what happened. Hold'em's usually my game."

"What the heck is Hold'em?"

"Poker. Cards, Red."

"You stood us up for a poker game?"

"How the hell else was I going to buy dinner at Zephyr's?"

She stared at him, understanding washing over her. "Are you saying that's how you make money? Playing poker? Is that how you've been paying for *school*?"

"Of course not. I pay for school with high-interest student loans. Poker's how I pay for everything else."

He chuckled at his own joke, but Liv didn't feel like laughing. All these months she'd thought he was privileged, loaded.

"How long have you been doing this?" she asked.

"If you want to start from the beginning . . ." Whit's eyes turned wistful. "My dad taught me to count cards when I was seven, then how to box when I was eight—in case they ever caught me counting. Eight years old and I'm walking around school with this fat eye, looking like a puffer fish. You think I look bad tonight—you should have seen me then." He sighed. "I really wanted to show everyone a good time tonight, Red. That's all I wanted."

"The house in Hatteras?" she asked carefully.

"I don't know the owners—I know the girl who cleans it. I worked on a fishing boat in Frisco last summer and this guy was getting rough with her on the dock so I laid him out and took her home. She said anytime I wanted to stay on the beach in the off-season to let her know and she'd hook me up." Whit dragged his gaze around the room. "So where *is* Sammy?"

"He stayed at his place." She was eager to steer them back to his story. "Are you telling me your mom never said anything when you'd show up with a black eye?"

He tested his split lip with the tip of his tongue and winced. "My mom took off when I was five. My dad and I moved in with my uncle and his girlfriend."

"Didn't *they* ever say anything?"

"It wasn't always him, Red. I used to pick fights at school all the time. Pick fights and kiss girls. And when I couldn't, I made up stories, because I couldn't show up empty-handed. I'd come home and my dad would be there in the kitchen with a beer, wanting to know what kind of man I'd been that day. Some kids' parents want to know what they got on their math tests, their history papers—not mine."

Liv looked down, embarrassed at how wrong she'd been about him. She'd thought he was so untouchable, so lucky. Meanwhile, he was just as much a fraud as she'd been. She knew she should have been hurt, even angry, but all she felt was the strangest, surest thread of connection to him. The urge to relieve him of all his secrets overcame her. Just the two of them in the warm hush of her tiny room. It was dreamlike, and she believed for one splendid second that he was being more real with her than he'd ever been with anyone else in his life, and the possibility thrilled her in a wholly unexpected way. She wanted to be that real too. That free. Both of them with fathers who demanded too much—they had so much more in common than she'd ever imagined.

"It's hard when you can't be yourself for someone," she said. "When you always worry that you're letting someone down, and all you want to do is break away. Believe me, I know."

Whit squinted at her. "What do you know, Red? You're beautiful and smart and you tell it like it is."

"Not always," she admitted quietly, feeling the warmth of his compliment at the back of her neck.

"You *do* have lousy taste in men, but other than that . . ." He grinned at her. "You seem pretty damn perfect to me."

She smiled. "Then your definition of *perfect* must be very strange. Trust me, if you ever met my father, you'd understand."

"I'd like to meet him."

"Don't be so sure," she said.

"I'm sure about everything I want, Red. Everything, and everyone."

His voice deepened on the last word. She met his eyes, thinking he looked suddenly sober, and almost as if he wanted to, just maybe, *kiss her* . . .

Out in the hall, a door slammed, breaking their connection.

Whit swung his eyes to the chart on the wall and grinned. "It looks good there."

"I can't believe you wanted to throw it away," Liv said.

Whit glanced at her and chuckled faintly.

She frowned, confused. "What?"

"Sam told me we forgot it at the house."

"He said that?"

Whit waved his hand. "It doesn't matter."

"Yes, it does," Liv said. "You should have it back."

"I want you to have it, Red. It's the least I can do for ruining your towel."

"It's just a towel."

"It's just a map." He lowered himself carefully down to her mattress, resting his head on her pillow. "I promise not to bleed on your sheets. I just want to close my eyes for a second, okay? Just a second . . ."

She rescued the seltzer from his hand as the bottle began to tip and capped it. She could sleep on the couch in the common room. Covered with one of her clean sheets, she'd never have to touch any of the sticky residue of late-night cram sessions, the stains of pizza grease and spilled beer. She reached carefully past his head for an extra pillow and paused briefly, her hand suspended over his temple, and a stretch of thick, wild waves. Her fingers trembled as they dropped, sinking briefly into his hair and sliding upward, deep enough that she could feel the heat of his scalp against her fingertips. When he stirred, she straightened, deciding she'd go without a pillow and take a blanket from her shelf instead. At the door, she stopped and turned back, finding him fast asleep, one leg falling off the side of her bed. A swell of tenderness and something else—something charged and hopeful—rose inside her. A longing she couldn't quite grasp.

She hugged the blanket to her chest and whispered, "Good night, Whit."

Then, flicking off the light, she stepped out into the glare and soft silence of the hall and shut the door.

She woke to the nutty smell of coffee and then the brief weight of Sam's mouth on hers, teasing her lips awake. Disoriented, she blinked until the common room came into view beyond his shoulder, looking dusty and unpleasant in the piercing light of morning.

She sat up and pulled at her twisted shirt.

"A peace offering." He held out a to-go cup with a curl of steam.

She eyed it, then him. "A cup of coffee? That's your peace offering?"

"I'm sorry about last night. I was pissed at Whit and I took it out on you by not spending the night." He smiled. "How'd you like to come to Chicago with me for winter break?"

Ripples of excitement shuddered behind her ribs. "Are you kidding? Of course!"

"I know you can't leave your dad for the whole time, but at least part of it."

Her father. Right.

A student lumbered in and grunted something as he retrieved

a textbook off the coffee table. She and Sam came apart, sharing a sheepish smile.

"Is there a reason we're not having this conversation in your room?" he whispered.

Whit.

Walking down the hallway, Liv grappled with how to prepare Sam for the strange news that Whit Crosby had invaded her room in the middle of the night, that he'd arrived in a stupor and that she'd let him in. How could she, when their truce was still fresh, as tacky as a new coat of paint, and she was about to smudge it all to hell when she opened that door?

"Sam, last night—"

But he'd already opened her door for her, already stepped in, and when she did after him, Liv felt a rush of relief leave her throat. Her bed was empty and crudely made up, the towel she'd let Whit use hanging off the back of her chair, speckled with constellations of dried blood. She darted toward it, hoping to hide it, but Sam reached for the towel first.

"Is this blood?" he asked.

"It's nothing—I cut myself on that stupid plastic packaging they put everything in these days," she lied.

"Jesus, are you okay?"

"I'm fine."

"Look, there's even some on your shirt," he said, sliding his thumb over her sleeve.

"Oh God, really?" She looked down in a panic, startled to see drops of dark brown below her shoulder.

"Better get this in the wash," he said, already hooking his

hands under the hem and sliding the fabric up her body. She lifted her arms and let him ease the shirt over her head, let him slip it through her hair and away.

His eyes held hers, darkening with desire. "You started to say something about last night?"

She rolled her lips together, panic surging. This was it. If she told him Whit had spent the night, if she said it now, it would be easily washed off, maybe even laughed about—*that screwup Crosby*—but to say it later, even ten minutes later, after they'd made love and wound their flushed bodies together, would make it something secret, something shameful. People only lied when they felt guilty. What did she have to feel guilty for?

Her eyes flicked toward the chart as she remembered Whit's claim, Sam's lie. She'd bring it up later—she'd have to. But then Sam coaxed her underwear down, covering her bare skin with the curve of his palms and digging his fingers possessively into her flesh. When his hands slid between her legs, Liv told herself there was nothing to confess. Just friends being friends. Stealing a sliver of the night together. For all she knew, for all it mattered, she might have just dreamed it all. Whit in her doorway, his stream of confessions. Blood on a towel, an empty bottle of seltzer in her wastebasket.

And just like that, the guilt was gone—and Sam was inside her, rolling her over sheets that smelled faintly of old smoke.

It was only when he slipped out to use the bathroom afterward that she saw the small package on her desk, an unfamiliar crumple of newspaper that fell away when she turned it over in her hands to reveal a key, the kind used to open old padlocks, spots of leftover sediment dotting the thick shaft.

The concretion. Had Sam uncovered it to surprise her?

She turned the key under her lamp, running her fingertips lightly over the prickly brass, and then her eyes caught on a slip of lined notebook paper that must have fallen out.

Red:

You dropped this in the Student Union, so I took the liberty of cleaning it off for you. Hope that's okay. Amazing what treasure you can find when you scrape off years of crud, isn't it?

WC

8

OUTER BANKS, NORTH CAROLINA
Wednesday

There's so much she's forgotten. Crossing over the Alligator River, passing the seagull sentries along Warner Bridge, Liv can't believe she's back on the Outer Banks again. And it's Sam beside her. Sam, taking her to what might be the answer she has been searching for all these years.

We'll find her . . . I promise . . .

Not Whit. Sam.

She has forgotten too how built up Nags Head has become, the many chain stores and restaurants that line the North Croatan Highway when they veer left after crossing the sound, away from Hatteras and the untouched stretch of the National Seashore. She longs to be steered toward Beach Road, but the museum is on the main drag, on the edge of Kill Devil Hills;

the name, so deliciously sinister, used to fill her with possibility. She is pleased to find it does still.

The Outer Banks Shipwreck Museum is a stark, modern building—long and square and chalk white. The parking lot is empty but for two cars, and Sam pulls the truck between them. The sign at the head of the tidy gravel path claims the museum closes at five, but Sam assures her Beth has stayed late for them, and indeed the wide glass door surrenders when he pulls on it. The slick, soapy scent of fresh paint and recently polished floors blows at Liv the moment they step inside. It is a huge space, bright and clean and new. All around her, artifacts and photographs, the malty odor of history and secrets, all born of the sea. Realization shudders through her again, knocking her slightly sideways: *Theodosia*. Memories swirl and collide—at the aquarium with her mother, walking the beach with Sam, waking up on *Theo's Wish* with Whit . . .

She's back in the swell of this wave, maybe finally about to crest. And it is as if she's never been gone.

Sam touches her arm, steadying her, bringing her back.

He smiles. "I'll go find Beth."

The receptionist must be a college student, Sam thinks as he approaches the rounded information desk and sees her bright, wide face. Maybe not much older than Liv was when Sam first met her. The young woman offers to call Beth, and Sam steps to the side while she does so, admiring a row of black-and-white photographs: portraits of lighthouse keepers, from Cape Hatteras and Bodie Island, the creases in their weathered faces in sharp contrast to the unblemished taupe wall they hang from. They all look desperately haunted. Even the ones trying to hold a faint smile. He's spent plenty of time visiting lighthouses and studying the stories of their devoted keepers; he knows the loneliness behind their unblinking eyes. It's not a job for the faint of heart, certainly wasn't then. A few times in his life, Sam considered such a post for himself, but the position is changed now—no more cathartic marches up and down stairs to trim wicks and lower blinds. Everything is automated.

He doesn't regret being here with Liv; he's not sorry he encouraged her to come. Not even a little sorry he let Whit think he meant to leave. All those years Sam forgave Whit his lies. So he changed his mind and decided to stay—so what? It wasn't a lie, certainly not of Whit's caliber. As he paces up and down the exhibit, hands deep in his pockets, Sam wonders if Liv has stolen around a corner to call Whit. Once Whit had the power to talk her out of things, to confuse her good sense with his crazed antilogic, but Sam isn't so sure anymore. He knows it isn't even about being here with him, Sam, but it's about Theodosia. Sam would like to see Whit convince Liv to leave this opportunity, like to hear him try.

"Thanks, Jenny."

Beth's voice sails across the floor and Sam glances over to find her at the reception desk. The life of a museum director suits her. She looks crisp and modern, even sexy, in slacks and a fitted top, and for a moment the nearness of her overwhelms him, the strangeness of this reunion. After so many years away from that life, that he should find himself reunited with Liv, and now Beth Henson.

When they are close enough, she reaches for him, the unmistakable gesture of invitation, and Sam receives her hug, taking in a whiff of her citrus perfume. When she steps back, her eyes are shiny.

"How many years has it been?" she asks.

"Too many."

She smiles. "You look great."

"You too." He gestures to the displays. "This is quite a place."

"We're still in the process of raising funds to complete the permanent exhibitions," Beth says. "The diary will bring in some much-needed exposure and donations. We're quite excited."

"You should be. It was nice of you to let me know."

"Like I said, you popped right into my head as soon as we received the journal." When Beth turns to steer them away from the desk, her gaze slows and Sam sees she has spotted Liv across the floor, circling a glassed-in model of the *Priscilla*. "Is that . . . ?"

"Liv Connelly," Sam says. "Do you remember her?" Beth's smile drops the tiniest bit; Sam catches the shift before she repairs it. "Liv and I are working together on a salvage project just down the coast."

"Together? But I thought you and she had . . . ?"

"We did." He meets her eyes, nearly as dark as his own. "She married Whit Crosby."

"Oh." Beth's smile resurrects itself, higher now. She steps closer and another gust of perfume drifts toward him.

Liv has seen them and starts walking, waving as she nears.

Beth has let her hair grow. It falls to her shoulders now and her bangs are gone. She looks softer, Liv thinks. Or maybe it's just that they've all softened with age. Liv rubs her palms down the front of her shorts as she walks behind Sam and Beth, feeling as wrinkled and incidental as a used fast food wrapper.

Beth leads them into the conference room and closes the door behind them. The diary is the only thing on a long table that fills most of the room, the cover olive green under the fluorescents. Liv can practically feel the soft leather under her fingertips, practically smell the nutty, salty paper beneath. A box of white gloves sits beside it. Waiting for Sam to find Beth, she'd felt unglued, unmoored, unsure of what she was doing here. Now, as she is staring down at the journal, any doubt has vanished. Her ribs tighten with anticipation; her hands tingle.

In an instant, the stretch of years devoid of this obsession folds in like a fan. It's as if she never stopped hunting.

Liv advances on the book first, fastest, slowed by the pair of chairs that sit in front of it like a gentle fence. Beth joins her and remains close, as if Liv is a child in the glassware section of a department store. Liv has to remind herself not to take it personally. This is, after all, Beth's work. To allow them this viewing must have required special allowances from the museum board. Or maybe Beth hasn't told them.

Liv wants to assure her that she won't scoop the book up and run out the door with it—maybe ten years ago she might have seriously considered it—but when Liv turns to Beth, Beth's attention is focused solely, fiercely, on Sam.

"You understand, I'll have to stay in the room with you," Beth says. "As much as I'd like to let you have time alone with it, let you turn the pages yourself, I just can't—"

"No need to explain," Sam says. "We know the drill."

Liv frowns down at the journal, marveling at its length. She recognizes its distinctive shape. "It's a logbook."

"Correct," Beth says. "The first half of the entries were made by a lightkeeper. We suspect that's why no one noticed it before. A person has to wade through a great deal of weather reports and repair notes. Theodosia used the blank pages in the back."

"But where would she have gotten a lightkeeper's logbook?" Liv asks.

Beth smiles. "You'll see when you read it. Or would you rather I just give you an overview first?"

Not on your life, Liv thinks. Two decades of study and searching and waiting—no one will spoil this ending for her.

When she looks over to meet Sam's eyes, they darken in agreement.

Beth tugs out a pair of gloves and pulls them on. "I thought I might stand and turn the pages from here," she says, moving to the other side of the table.

Sam gestures for Liv to take a seat first. A warm, woody smell rises when Beth eases back the cover, despite the plastic sheet that encapsulates it. Beth has marked the beginning of Theodosia's entries and opens to the exact spot, carefully removing the tissue sheet so they can begin.

Liv presses her hands into her lap, needing to keep her fingers occupied for fear she might reach out and fondle the page Beth has just bared to them. How badly she wants to slide the faded paper between her thumb and forefinger, as if Theodosia's pulse still remained in the fibers, the delicate edges scalloped with age and wear, stained the pale brown of an egg.

When she swallows, the sour-sweet flavor of anticipation coats her tongue, then the quickest blast of bitterness.

Forgive me for not waiting, Whit.

Sam reaches for her hand and gives it a reassuring squeeze, as if they are pilots taking their first flight.

They lean forward together, and Liv has to remind herself to breathe.

January 6, 1813

Papa, there is so much I want to tell you, and yet I know not where to begin. Or how.

It is now seven days since the Patriot left Georgetown, seven days since I took to the sea carrying the promise of our reunion like a shiny coin in my purse, the sole glimmer of hope left in my sorrowful heart.

Now I sit in a bare and drafty room, watching a giant man with wild red hair march up and down the stretch of beach beyond my prison's only window. I know not what he waits for, or perhaps who, any more than I know if I've been delivered to an island or simply a bleak finger of shore still connected to land.

We arrived here together three days ago, he and I, though not by choice—at least, not for me. As for his preference in this crude arrangement, I can't be certain. What I am certain of is that in a few hours, he will cease his relentless watch and climb the dunes to this cottage as he has done the previous evenings. I will hear the door below give with a groan and then his boots will fall hard on the crooked steps to my room. He won't bother to knock and I won't bother to grant him entrance. He will set a bowl of watered cornmeal just inside the door frame and leave me with it, and I will do my best to pretend it doesn't exist for several hours until my hunger wins out and I lick the bowl clean. Then I will take to my bed—a term I use loosely, as would you, Papa, were you to witness the sour, stained mattress I have been provided—and I will wait for sleep to come.

Aren't I the sharp one? you are thinking, Papa. Seven days and she's learned the routine of her prison! But then, there is so little to it. After all the years I organized your household, Papa, keeping the clockworks of our estate's rigorous schedules in constant order and polish. Now I have only the responsibilities of swallowing gruel and staring at a man who stares at the sea. What a pair we are.

If not for this logbook I found, and the blessed empty pages it contained, I would not have the company of my words, and a record I will keep of this horrific journey only to preserve my history in the event that I forget it, if such a blessing is possible, not because I fear it will be my legacy. For I am sure that any day now, Papa, you will submit their ransom and I will be free to come to you at last.

January 7, 1813

I have solved the mystery, Papa. My captor waits for a boat.

Shortly after dawn, a rowboat slid into the inlet and a man unloaded several baskets to the flame-haired giant (would that he might tell me his name). It did not occur to me to feel dread or fear, only hope. Surely he came with news of my release? The man in the boat pushed off as soon as she was emptied and I waited for my captor to make his way to my room, sure he meant to inform me that you had supplied the ransom and that we are to be reunited. But there was no announcement with my evening's rations. Before my captor took his leave, he cast a wary look at my book and I fell upon it, clutching it close. He asked what I write and I told him plainly, my Last Will and Testament, of course, and that he is due to become a very rich man indeed. Fine worn shoes and this waste-stained dress. Won't he be the envy of all his pirate friends?

I demanded to know his name, but he did not acknowledge me. I told him I shall have no choice but to give him one of my own choosing, that I cannot bear to call him "You" as he is so fond of calling me. He tells me to do as I wish, that he couldn't care less, and though I feel disgust toward him, I do not blame him for the charade, any more than I suspect you might, Papa. We can none of us be who we are just now.

January 8, 1813

Today I saw spring.

The lavender bursts of redbud trees, the milky perfection of bloodroots clinging to wooded hills, the limy white of dogwood blossoms. Then I opened my eyes and saw only the bleakness of winter's bite on this barren slip of sand. Colorless and gray, cold and damp. The view from my imagination is far superior to the one that looms beyond this window. In my dreams, rare as they are now, I have visions of jasmine blooms, so sharp and clear I can practically smell their sweet petals on my skin when I wake. If you knew the horrors I carry in my memories of the night we were captured, Papa, you would understand my desire to rinse them with fantasy. I know that tale is one you and my husband will be eager to hear, and one I must confess, if only to rid myself of even a piece of its torturous grip. But I fear I am not yet strong enough to revisit it.

Soon.

January 9, 1813

The boat arrived again and I made another mark in my book, sure there will be a pattern to these deliveries that I can measure. You know how I cannot bear a lack of routine, Papa. Any more than I can bear silence. Without my beloved boy, my home has been drained of life and laughter, emptied as a pitcher poured dry. If my captors mean to make me suffer, they need not deny me food or shelter. Instead starve me of conversation, of the sound of voices, if they truly mean to break my spirit. My contention grew so today that when my captor arrived, I told him I would trade my bowl of mush for ten words. Ten simple words of his choosing, be they ugly or kind, I cared not. I only wished to hear a voice other than my own.

He considered me harshly for a long moment, again leading me to believe he might not speak English, but then he scooped up my bowl and said, More for me, then.

You owe me six more, I yelled as he left, knowing I wouldn't receive my due.

Still my victory, tiny as it was, was immeasurable.

January 10, 1813

I grow bolder. Who can blame me?

Tonight I offered him the same bargain of ten words—but I was careful to take up my bowl before he could reply. As I did, I noticed it wasn't the same cornmeal mud he'd been delivering to me for the past six days but a curious stew, bearing chunks of what I thought had to be crabmeat. Surely I was having visions?

I could feel his eyes on me as I stared at my allowance. Did I dare risk losing something that smelled so sweet?

Father, you know me better than that.

Thirty, I said. A feast like this is worth far more than a bowl of mush.

When he lunged to take it from me, I drew back. The words first, I said. Then you get the bowl.

Anything I want? he asked.

Three, gone. I nodded.

He said, How do you know I haven't poisoned it?

Eight more. I don't, I said. Perhaps I only hope you have. The sooner I leave this prison, the better. I raised my chin and said, Nineteen more please.

Aren't you afraid of me?

No more so than I am of this stew. Fourteen.

His black eyes narrowed. I've nothing else to say to you.

Haven't you? Then this stew must not taste nearly as good as it smells. Perhaps I was wrong to think it merited such high praise.

Stains of fury bloomed above the crescent of his beard. It's the best you'll ever find. Better than you deserve, you ungrateful snit. I'll not sully your fancy tongue again!

When he snatched it from my hands, I did not try to hold on to it, though I did contain the victorious smile on my face until he'd marched from the room.

Thirteen extra.

I'm still your clever girl, Papa.

January 11, 1813

My boldness has taken its toll. Two days with meager conversation but without food and I am quite weak indeed. I arrived here already so diminished, Papa. I do not wish to worry you, but I am newly concerned for my health.

Tonight when my captor entered, I found myself too weak to rise for his delivery or proposition him for precious words.

No more games, he said. Eat.

When he set down my bowl this time, I did not argue.

January 12, 1813

My strength returns and with it, my ire.

It has been a fitful day for me. Clouds have sealed off the sun, blanketing the world in gray, and I've felt the fiercest agitation at my predicament. When my captor arrived tonight, my frustration could not be contained. I demanded again to know his name, and when he would not relinquish it, I finally cast my choice. Be grateful you did not have to hear it, Papa, for the woman of honor and grace you know so well has taken leave of this cell. My captor certainly appeared shocked at my selection—I drew a laugh from him. A laugh! Can you imagine it? After days of his skulking around me, practically growling, the sound of mirth rose from his throat and filled this dark and miserable room. I might have hated him more had the sound not been so remarkably pleasant that I too felt my tight lips betray me a moment and dance upwards before I had the good sense to force them down.

Too late, perhaps. On his way out, he said to me over his shoulder:

Simon. But I've been called all that too, miss.

January 13, 1813

I have been in this room for ten days now. I do not understand why I am kept in a room at all! Even if I escaped the confines of this house, I would have no means of flight from this island.

Today my mind drowns in thoughts of you and Joseph. All the many questions you must have, so much anguish and unknown. When our ship didn't arrive as scheduled, when the sea yielded no hope, how long did you have to wait before you received word of my capture? Have you comfort in knowing I am still alive, or does worry for my continued safety drown any relief?

I wonder too how the toll of this war continues to ravage my husband's heart and soul. I beg for news of the world outside this prison, but receive none. I wonder too if you and Joseph have continued to correspond. I like to think you have. Or is it too painful to see each other? Does it only make my absence more acute? When we lost Aaron, Joseph and I struggled for months to hold each other's gaze for any length of time. It was as if all we could see in each other's eyes was our sweet boy.

I look through my room's windows and think instead on your words, the ones you delivered to me in the interminable days after Mama's death: Every dawn is a finger without a print.

Surely my captivity will end soon, and then we can put this nightmare behind us.

January 14, 1813

Tonight I asked for fifty words.

I stopped counting at two hundred and four.

January 15, 1813

It appears Simon is an artist! When I scanned the horizon to find him at his usual post, I saw him instead sitting in the grass at the base of the house with a canvas. I can only assume it came with one of the deliveries. I strained my eyes to decipher the subject, but what else might he paint beside the endless sea?

January 16, 1813

Simon wishes to paint me. I was startled at the request, then overjoyed. He sat with me nearly all morning, and though he wishes my portrait to be a somber one, I cannot bear to keep silent long enough for him to accurately paint my mouth—a concession I feel is a worthwhile one, though I am not the artist.

We spoke of you. He is not familiar with you or your history, Papa, which is lovely. Because I have no need to defend or argue, only to enlighten. He said that my husband must grow jealous of you, for I spoke of you far more than I did of Joseph, and I assured him he did not. But truth be told, Papa, I am not sure I have ever considered the prospect.

Simon's eyes are not nearly as black as I'd first believed. Without his beard and perhaps with a trim of all that tangled hair, he could be quite handsome. I asked him to paint me in my favorite ivory dress, as if I am reading in the conservatory, as if I have taken tea in the parlor.

As if I am anywhere but here.

January 17, 1813

Tonight, smoked meat and cheese. Bread. A feast.

A thinking person might fear she'd been delivered her last supper. But I try to do as little of that as possible now, Papa. Think, I mean. Or fear.

January 18, 1813

Heaven today. A walk on the beach. Cold and damp as the sand was, I relieved myself of my shoes to let my bare soles feel it, to let the glorious chill of it seep into my skin and then deeper into my bones. I have been so sure that my nerves have gone as dead as my heart, and yet feeling surges, alive and primed. A ways up the shore, we arrived at the remains of a sandstone structure and understanding tore through me. Papa, I feel so foolish. Why else had I found a logbook if not because a lighthouse and its keeper once lived here? Walking back, Simon spotted the boat nearing the inlet and hurried me into the grass, pointing me back to the house. I obliged his command without hesitation and took the path quickly. Upstairs, I confined myself, hopeful that the captain of the boat did not witness my freedom. I do not blame Simon for sending me back to my prison. I am not so full of hope that I don't believe my kidnapper's would make both of us suffer for our strange new arrangement.

I have endured this lonely life too long now to risk escaping it, Papa.

January 19, 1813

Tonight Simon asked me to join him downstairs for my meal. He spoke of his child, Nicholas, and a woman named Lucy who I assume is the child's mother, though possibly not Simon's bride? I didn't inquire. I barely took in breaths, let alone spoke, fearful of breaking the spell of our curious confessional.

I understand now what it means to be haunted, Papa. To be pursued by ghosts and regrets. How I wish you had shared your anguish in the wake of that terrible mistake with Hamilton. Surely you wish you'd never challenged him to the duel. Was there a moment, however fleeting, before you took aim when you considered retracting? What had transpired to make you take such drastic action? There were terrible things said, things I couldn't bear to believe. Speculation that Hamilton's weapon wouldn't fire but you shot him anyway. I know that couldn't be, Papa. In my heart, I know it. How often I wanted to ask you these things, how often I kept them buried. It would have done your soul—and mine—such good to share the pain and remorse. Why did you not?

I only hope you will when I return.

This mortal coil is too short to waste in silence.

January 20, 1813

A rainy day, and the flat gray sky sinks my spirit, leaving me melancholy.

Simon's words linger with me—and though I know I shouldn't take to heart the opinion of a stranger, especially one aligned with thieves and madmen, I can't help thinking on our lives together, Papa, and a strange worry overwhelms me. Do you suppose we have depended too much on each other? Worse, have I neglected my obligations as a wife in my need to be a good daughter?

In better news, Simon is making great progress on my portrait—embellished as it is. His efforts have become my singular joy in this world. Fourteen days now and still no news of my release. The boat arrives with supplies and then leaves. There is never news and lately I dread making inquiries. Fears of all sorts plague me. Perhaps they have taken their ransom from you and do not mean to keep their word? Perhaps at any moment Simon will draw a blade or a pistol and put an end to me? Perhaps a storm has detained word of my ransom to you and the silence has left my captors believing you won't meet their demands? Perhaps—the most vile of all words.

These worries spin through my thoughts with such fierce speed and frequency that I am seized with coughing fits, as if my lungs are trying to force the fear from my body.

January 21, 1813

More storms. Great, unending sheets of them have blanketed my two windows. I cannot seem to slow this terrible cough. Even Simon looks at me with alarm when we are together, which is nearly all the time now. He assures me a doctor can be brought across the water as easily as a bag of cornmeal and I believe him. I am worth nothing to my kidnappers dead, though lately I feel sure I'm not worth much to anyone alive either.

Except you, Papa. And, of course, Joseph, though I am not certain we have been the best of soldiers in the battle of grief, he and I. How can a marriage survive, never mind thrive, in the wake of losing a child? I am not certain it can.

January 22, 1813

The boat never came today. Simon assures me the weather is to blame, rough seas, an impending storm. He tells me we have sufficient supplies for several days if the weather does not improve and for reasons I cannot explain, I believe him.

Trust is a curious knot, Papa, but it is all that keeps my fragile soul aloft, so I dare not untangle it, or sink.

January 23, 1813

Another day and again, no delivery of supplies. The storm has reached us, twisting the surf and pelting the shore. Streaks of lightning break across the sky for hours. Thunder too, shaking the ground almost as much as I do when I fall into one of my coughing fits. I think Simon is scared too, but I am not sure of what. And perhaps that scares me most of all.

Twice I was certain I saw my sweet Aaron tumbling in the shallow surf, the way he did the first time Joseph and I brought him to the water's edge. I wept uncontrollably, just grateful Simon wasn't near. The mind can be so terribly cruel. Does it mean to hearten me with these visions—or drive me further into despair?

January 24, 1813

Visions of my capture return to me often now, relentless in their clarity. I wish to purge them, Papa. I can no longer carry them alone.

I should never forget the noise of that night, the screams of my fellow passengers, the shattering of our ship as she was swept into flames. But it was the crack of her steadfast bones as she surrendered to the sea, wood and flesh drowning as one, that I will never erase from my memory.

I can still see the flash of light on the horizon, blinking like a star just above the black swells of the sea.

If it occurred to any of us on deck that the glare might be false, that it might not be a lighthouse beacon at all but a hobbled horse forced to march up and down the beach with a lantern around its poor neck, no one dared to say. Our ship battered, our bodies drenched and shivering—when death is so close you swear you can feel its breath warming your icy cheek, hope is far too precious to squander. When we were faced with drowning, the threat of trickery by pirates may have seemed an enviable alternative to most of us.

No, not until our ship foundered on the shoals and we saw the first advancing Bankers' boat charging toward us through the pelting rain did we want to believe anything but that we'd been spared the wrath of the storm. By then, there was no time for escape. Some of us scurried below—where we should have remained in the first place, according to our weathered captain—but I refused to hide. If there has been one blessing from losing my child, it is that I have no fear of death or dying—it is the threat of survival that scares me most of all. And though I know it will break your heart, dear Papa, to read this, in that black and sopping night, I may have prayed for the pirates to end my interminable mourning for my son.

But in the frantic minutes of their plunder, I was spared. Simon plucked me from the melee and dragged me into one of their boats. After I'd been shoved to my seat, there was a terrible roar, and I looked up to see the Patriot burst into fire, the reach of the furious flames nearly engulfing our tiny boat as we were steered away.

It is the pieces of what happened next that I fight my memory to retrieve. There was darkness, and unbearable noise: deafening howls and grunts that belong to animals but came from the mouths of men. The fetid smell of old clothes and dirty hair, the choking stink of smoke, the char of things meant to burn and those unholy. I am not sure I will ever rinse those horrific tastes from my throat so long as I live. Nor will I ever be truly warm again. The air that bit at our skin as we crawled toward shore was deeper than cold. I will not lie—many times in that tiny, rocking boat, I considered how easy it would have been to tilt my body toward the edge and allow the water's churn to send me over the side. It would have been only moments before the frigid water had silenced my heart. But the same bitter chill that would have ended my suffering kept my muscles frozen, and I could barely blink, let alone rise.

And so I watched the land grow closer and closer, seeing with sickening clarity that the flash of light we had minutes earlier believed salvation was the deceitful flicker of a lantern, no more remarkable than any of the dozens that were now blazing across the sand to mark our arrival.

In the next instant, something damp and rough covered my eyes—hands?—but then came the squeeze at the back of my head, the knot of my blindfold being tightened, and fear bloomed fresh and deep. The boat lurched, hard enough to send me crashing into whoever—whatever—sat beside me on the thwart, and I could hear the scratch of the boat's bottom being dragged over the sand and slid back into the sea. Two men whispered, their voices raspy. I twisted my head, trying to glean their words, but all I could hear was my heart thundering.

I do not know for how long we crossed the water, or in what direction our tiny, miserable vessel charged. I may have lost consciousness—I know for certain it was not anything as peaceful as sleep—but what my eyes could not see, my mind observed keenly. The creak of the rowlocks as they turned with each stroke, the slap of the oar paddles breaking through the whitecaps.

Then a slowing, and a change in the wind. The smell of low tide, the salty, metallic flavor of mud and clay filled my throat, and I knew we'd returned to shore.

When I felt the weight of hands on my head, I recoiled so fiercely that I nearly capsized and a pair of panicked voices collided. A quick tug and the canvas around my eyes loosened, then fell away. I squinted against the shock of daylight and saw first what I still see now through my room's only window. Simon, and a crooked shack atop the rise.

Now you know everything, Papa. That I have waited, that I have held hope. That no matter what, I love you always.

January 25, 1813

I will be brief today. These coughing spells exhaust me and I fear losing control of my pen when one comes on. Still no news. I have lately seen worry on Simon's face—and I cannot be certain which of us he worries for most. He tells me he will send word with the boat captain to bring back a doctor when he comes with the next delivery and the news helps me sleep a bit. Or maybe it is just the whiskey he gives me. Did it come with the last delivery?

He tells me when I am feeling better, we should take another walk down to the beach, even longer than before. He tells me I am lovely. He tells me I am kind. I feel the slightest bloom of hope, of pleasure, and I allow myself to savor it. I believe you and Joseph would not begrudge me this reprieve, that there is no crime or disloyalty in it.

I send this wish to whoever needs it most: Please hurry.

January 26, 1813

There is no ransom. There is no doctor coming. There will be no boat ever again.

There is no rescue but that of God's will and his delivery of me to my son, and one day, to you and Joseph, Papa. I understand all of this now and I am at peace.

Simon understands this too and I feel sorry for him. He has a child he will never see again. A woman he might have loved deeply. Like me, he was delivered to this island falsely. We are both castaways now, abandoned to end our days at a forgotten lighthouse that once offered rescue. We have only each other.

There is just enough cornmeal left for a small pair of cakes, both of which Simon insists I eat, though we both know my countenance is too far from repair.

Should he ever escape this island, I have asked him to deliver his painting of me to you, Papa. He promises me he will. Along with it he promises to bring this brief record of my life here, so that you may know I was cared for, and that I left this world without fear. I cannot bear to think on the horrors you and Joseph have imagined for my fate. May this record provide you with some comfort, and most of all, the proof that I must surely be gone, for otherwise we would be together, Papa. No earthly binds could keep us apart.

I think Simon will be sad to lose me. Perhaps it was my imagination, or wicked tricks of my feverish brain, but today I swore I saw moisture in his eyes, Papa.

I am just glad one of us still has tears to shed.

"This can't be all of it."

Liv isn't even aware that she's blurted this out loud, or that her fingers have lunged for the journal, until Sam puts a hand over hers to slow her advance.

"Liv." His voice is gentle but firm.

She blinks up at him as if he's yanked her out of a deep sleep, but his intervention isn't needed. Beth has already moved the book out of reach and closed it. She plucks off her white gloves, finger by finger. "Incredible, isn't it?"

Is that the word? Surely there must be another, Liv thinks. All the years she's spent on this search, the piles of theories she's built up. *Incredible* seems hardly grand enough a word. Yet it's not only awe she feels—something else she can't quite land on. Uncertainty. Tiny but strong. A hangnail of doubt that she can already feel herself begin to tug on. She wants to read the entire book again. She's missed something. But Beth picks up the journal and holds it possessively against her chest, the plastic slipcover catching the ceiling fluorescents.

Liv looks at Sam, hoping he will request more time—surely he can't be satisfied with just one read?—but he's standing now too, and his expression is even, comfortable. Content.

Ripples of panic flutter through her, driving her to her feet. "There were a few passages I wanted to look over again," she says. "I still have a few questions—"

Beth cuts her off with a tired laugh. "We all do, believe me," she says, coming around the table. She gives the book a fond pat. "But I'm afraid I have to get this to our curator. I've scheduled a press conference for tomorrow morning." Beth glances warmly at Sam. "We can't wait any longer." She returns the book to the safe behind her desk. Liv watches the journal disappear, feeling another swell of regret; then she reminds herself that Beth didn't even have to share this with them, that just a peek was beyond generous. Still a small rustle of suspicion stirs behind her gratitude. "Are you all right?" Beth asks her. "You look positively pale."

"She's in shock," Sam says. "I know I am. I never gave any credence to the Bankers theory."

"Neither did I," says Beth. "But there's no disputing this

proof. I got goose bumps the first time I read it. Absolute chills. I'm sure you did too, Liv."

No, Liv thinks to herself. She didn't. How is that possible? That she would be reading Theodosia's words, the answers she'd been searching for, and not feel the prickles of their weight?

"It's strange," Liv whispers, not even sure she means to be heard.

"What's strange?" There's an edge of impatience in Sam's voice. When she glances over at him, he's frowning.

She'd been so sure he'd be the first to point it out.

"The windows," she says.

"What windows?"

"The windows in the journal. In one entry, Theo refers to her room having a single window, and in others, several windows. You didn't pick up on that?"

Sam smiles but it's a small smile, a placating smile. "Liv, I only read it once."

"So did I," she says, not sure what his point is. "It's a glaring inconsistency, Sam. Really, it's huge." She shifts her gaze to Beth, sure she will agree, but Beth simply shrugs.

"I'm sure the team's taken note of any discrepancies," Beth says.

Team. The word makes Liv's teeth hurt, as if Theodosia is a medical experiment requiring clinical observation.

"Theodosia was obviously under great strain," Beth continues. "All the trauma she'd been through and her failing health. It's more than likely she might have had hallucinations. That she would have misunderstood her surroundings."

Liv bristles. "I know what kind of strain she was under.

But everything I've ever read showed Theo to have possessed a sturdy mind in the midst of great challenge. Her father's political ruin, losing her son. It seems surprising that someone so lucid in the face of stress would misrepresent such a simple detail as windows."

Sam takes a step toward her. "We should get going," he says to Beth. "We need to let you prepare for tomorrow."

"Oh, don't rush off just yet." Beth's polite smile softens. "I actually packed us a little snack. I thought we could take it down to the beach, catch the sunset. I feel like we've hardly had a chance to catch up." She moves behind her desk, leans down, and reappears with a basket, which she carries to the table and sets down.

She opens the lid of the basket, and the peppery smell of summer sausage rises. On top, a bottle of Prosecco—and two wine goblets.

An uncomfortable quiet settles in the room.

Beth smiles tightly. "I'll find us a third glass."

The air is soft with evening. The sun slides down the sky, a honey-colored lozenge about to be swallowed by the horizon. Liv tries to keep pace with Sam and Beth, but their long legs carry them farther faster and the sandy path is really only wide enough for two, or maybe this is what Liv tells herself so she can hang back in silence and tie off her dangling thoughts. Sam's resignation, his lack of doubt, confounds her, enhances her own doubt. Has no one else found the entries curiously uneven? Beth called the details discrepancies, as if they were a few missed pennies in an accountant's books. Liv wishes she could see it that way too. She'd been so sure after reading the journal, the mystery solved, she'd feel the shawl of relief and understanding draped over her, would know how warm and cozy it would feel at last to know the truth.

But then, so much of this moment isn't as she imagined it.

At the top of the beach, they leave their shoes in a pile and pick a spot to sit. While Sam scans the water, Liv helps Beth unpack the basket. Smoked meats and blocks of cheese. Grapes and figs. A container of strawberries, plump and shiny. A flush of embarrassment courses through her as Liv sets down each carefully wrapped item. This is a feast for lovers. The flavors of seduction. How very disappointed Beth must be to have to share it.

Sam joins them. "This is quite a spread."

"It was nothing, really." Beth sweeps the dark curtain of her hair behind her ear. "I never asked you where you're staying."

Sam glances at Liv. "We're not."

"I don't understand." Beth looks startled. "You're driving back to Topsail *tonight*?"

"It's not a bad drive," says Sam.

"But it's almost seven," Beth says.

"We have to get back."

Liv looks up to meet Sam's eyes, seeing a curious flash of question in them. Is he waiting for her to disagree and give them permission to stay on?

"If you're driving, then I suppose you won't want any of this," Beth says, returning the bottle of Prosecco to the basket.

"Don't bury it on my account," Sam says, looking at Liv. "Not all of us are driving."

Liv concedes. "Maybe a little."

Beth hands Sam the bottle and he tears off the foil and points the Prosecco toward the water. The cork gives with a fat pop. Beth holds up the glasses and Sam fills them. The sparkling wine is the same copper as the melting sun.

Beth raises her glass. "To Theodosia, may she finally rest in peace. . . ." She turns to Sam, her eyes warm. "And to old friends."

Liv takes a full sip, the carbonation prickling her tongue.

"It won't be long before the hunt for the wreckage starts up again, now that there's proof where she went down," Sam says.

Of course, the ship. Liv's focus has always been on Theodosia, but this information will provide answers about the final resting place of the *Patriot* too. Assuming it's all true.

There she goes again. Questioning their findings. She saw the book with her own eyes, read the words herself—why can't she simply accept them? God knows how long she's waited for the truth.

"When the news releases, everyone with a boat will be looking, I'm sure," Beth says.

Sam smiles at Liv. "I guess we don't need our map anymore."

Beth looks between them. "Map?"

"Liv and I kept all our notes on a chart. Filled it up over the years with all our theories, all our clues."

Until you took it, Liv wants to add but doesn't. Of course he'd leave out that part for Beth's benefit. She is visibly excited by his confession.

"I wish I could see it," she says.

"You can," says Sam. "It's in the truck."

"You brought it?"

Liv looks at Sam, but this time his gaze doesn't shift her way.

He stands and brushes sand off his shorts. "Why don't I go get it?"

When he disappears over the dune, Liv scans the water, hoping a breeze will blow away the uncomfortable silence between her and Beth. Or maybe Liv is just imagining it. Maybe it's just her own guilt at being here with Sam, that Beth knows their history and doesn't approve. Like Liv's friend Rachel. What Liv wouldn't give to talk to her right now.

"It's amazing to me," says Beth.

Liv turns to her. "What?"

"That you should pick up on that about the windows after only one reading."

"I pay attention to details."

Beth fingers the stem of her glass. "Sam tells me you and he and Whit are in the middle of a salvage project. I hadn't heard about it. A blockade runner, he said."

"Whit's had his eye on her for a few years. He's sure there's a great deal of gold to be brought up."

Beth frowns. "That would be unusual. Most blockade runners carried supplies, not gold."

Just as Sam had pointed out. Liv knows this too—it's one

of the reasons she was apprehensive about the mission, even before Whit's mess. Which Liv can't bring herself to admit to Beth, and why should she? It's none of her business.

Beth reaches for her earring, gently twisting the thin hoop. "Can I be honest about something?"

"Of course."

"I never understood why so many women fell for Whit in school. I mean, yes, he was ridiculously charming and handsome, but he was so *manic*."

"He still is."

"Handsome or manic?"

Liv smiles. "Both."

She sees her purse where she left it a few feet up the beach and wonders how many more calls from Whit she has missed. Avoided. Maybe he's back at the house by now. Maybe he knows where she is.

Beth offers her more Prosecco and takes some for herself. "It shocked me when I heard that you'd left Sam for him."

Liv blinks at Beth. "I didn't leave Sam for Whit."

"Didn't you?" Beth looks genuinely confused. "I just assumed when Sam said . . . My mistake." She smiles sheepishly behind her glass as they both see that Sam has reappeared with the chart under his arm.

He spreads the map out over the sand, using bowls to hold down the corners.

"Good Lord." Beth scans it. "It must have taken you years to write all this."

"It did," Liv admits, feeling an unexpected swell of pride.

"And look." Beth lands her finger on the stretch of writing

near Hatteras where Liv wrote BANKERS in big letters. "You even put a star beside this one," she says, her eyes bright with awe. "It seems you knew even then which theory was right."

Did she? Liv scans the rest of the pencil marks, memories of the house in Hatteras flooding her again. How little she understood about anything then. Not just about Theodosia, but about Sam. Whit. Herself. What it meant to crave someone so much you couldn't take a bite of food without wondering what his tongue might think of the flavor.

"How long have you had this?" Beth asks.

"Since grad school," Sam says.

"And you've kept it all these years."

Liv feels a strange blush of discomfort and glances up to find Sam staring at her. *I meant to send it back to you a hundred times. . . .*

"Would you be willing to lend it to the museum for the exhibit?" Beth asks. "I think it would make a fascinating display. We'd credit you both, of course."

"And Whit," Liv says. Sam's dark eyes burn on her, quizzical.

Beth smiles politely. "Think about it. There's no rush."

The wind picks up, fluttering the edge of the map. Beth closes the top of the basket and sits back.

"So, what have you been able to find out about Simon?" Liv asks.

"Nothing yet," Beth says. "There's no record of anyone named Simon having sailed with known pirates You or Payne, though it's possible, probable even, that Simon wasn't his real name. We've only really started to dig." She sweeps sand off her slacks. "As you can imagine, the diary presents as many questions as answers."

"Like if her father ever received it, as Theo had hoped," Liv says.

Beth nods. "Obviously the diary made it off the island eventually, but not likely into Burr's hands. There was never any mention of the journal in any of his papers or letters—and one has to imagine he would have shared the news in some way, even if only in his personal diary. The portrait, of course, survived too. The director of the Lewis Walpole Library was quite stunned by our discovery. This revelation is monumental news for them as well."

The portrait. Liv has nearly forgotten. Memories of her long-ago debate over the painting's origin with Harold Warner at his lecture, his dogged insistence that the famous Nags Head portrait held no significance in the *Patriot* mystery, how unlikely that it was even Theodosia, let alone that it offered proof of her fate. A tremor of satisfaction moves through Liv, only to be quickly buried under a cloud of regret. After Whit's fiasco, she has no business being so smug.

"All the stories that claimed the portrait came off the ship, that it came with Theodosia from Georgetown," Beth says. "It's amazing how little we got right."

"Assuming what she wrote is what actually happened," Liv says.

An awkward silence lands over the blanket like a dropped glass. Beth takes up her drink, her eyes flashing warily. "I thought you'd be more pleased than anyone, Liv. The diary proves everything you'd believed all along about what happened to Theodosia."

Liv glances at Sam. "It does."

"Then why are you trying to discredit it?"

"I'm not trying to discredit it," Liv says.

Sam frowns. "Aren't you?"

Beth smiles patiently. "Liv, I know it must be hard for you to accept. Knowing how long you've searched, how hard. If it makes you feel any better, I'm a little sad myself that it's over."

Liv forces a polite smile to match the one Beth and Sam share, but her thoughts continue to spin with doubt. Beth is wrong: This feeling of inaccuracy that she can't shake has nothing to do with an inability to accept this proof. It's not the violence of the story; Liv had been prepared for Theo to have endured much worse at the hands of the Bankers. Something in the entries seemed . . . *inauthentic*.

Liv can't think of another word, and it circles her mind like a noisy gull.

It is nearly dark when they walk back up the path to Sam's truck, the sand cool under their bare feet without the sun's heat. Back at the museum, Liv asks to use the bathroom. Sam and Beth walk toward the wall of windows that look out onto the road.

"Are you sure I can't convince you to stay the night?" Beth asks him. "I've got a guest room. And the couch pulls out if . . ." She swallows the rest of the thought, her pale skin flushing noticeably.

"Thanks," he says, "but we should get back."

"Of course. Whit's waiting."

Sam nods, even as a fierce knot of frustration fists in his stomach. He has purposefully avoided Whit's name all night to pretend he isn't part of this, to keep Whit Crosby at bay, maybe even because he hopes the exclusion will cause Liv to forget her husband even exists. Sam knows Beth doesn't mean to do any kind of damage by mentioning him, but still Sam resents it. Or maybe it's Liv he resents: her inability to simply take the truth of the diary and move on. It should have been enough that he brought her to the answer, the proof she'd wanted for so long, the truth Whit had promised her and never delivered. It never occurred to him she'd find suspicion in the diary—maybe it should have, knowing how deeply she once cared for the search. Or maybe her doubt has nothing to do with the diary and everything to do with her own conscience.

When he glances back at Beth, she brushes her hair from her face, the movement oddly erotic. "Or maybe you and Liv aren't so anxious to get back to him, after all," she says. Her voice is clipped with uncertainty, but her eyes flash with expectation. He watches her play with her bracelet, twisting the thick silver cuff back and forth as if it's a screw she's trying to loosen.

Outside, the traffic speeds by. Across the road, a restaurant's wraparound deck teems with diners.

She lets her hands drop to her sides. "I feel foolish," she whispers. "When you said you were coming to see the diary, I just assumed you wanted . . . I thought maybe . . ."

He lays his hand on the back of her neck, not even sure why he does, but the instant his palm covers her skin, her eyes close and her head falls back. He finds the top of her spine with his thumb and makes even circles around the small rise, growing in pressure until her hands drift upward to rest against the glass. He knows his gesture has filled her with expectation, but he doesn't know what to do about that. Nothing about this moment, this day, has been safe or well thought out, which is the way he's always liked it. From the moment he heard Whit's voice crackle back at him on that message three weeks ago, Sam has known his ordered life would be thrust into disarray and he has embraced that fact. Beth's shoulders drop back. Sam can see down the front of her shirt, the thin fabric pulsing with her rapid breathing, her collar yawning and closing like a mouth. Thoughts of undressing Liv have crashed in and out of his brain all day—he hasn't tried to drive them away or even push them down—and his own craving has become nearly unmanageable, so he draws his hand slowly down Beth's spine and watches gooseflesh rise along her neck.

"I'm glad I came," he says, low.

He releases his hand from the middle of her back, and a faint sound slips from her lips, his name, he thinks. Or something close to it.

Now what?

The question floats in the truck the instant Liv climbs inside beside Sam and watches him start the ignition. Out the passenger window, Liv sees Beth in the foyer of the museum, waiting for them to pull out of the parking lot, her silhouette against a tall window. Liv is sure she will wave, but Beth turns to go, disappearing back into the museum. Sam's gaze is fixed on the road, both hands on the wheel.

The silence in the cab is startling. Liv was so sure the minute she and Sam were alone again, the excitement of the diary would spill out of them like an overfilled tub. Instead the air is choked with uncertainty. Liv rolls down her window, desperate for a rush of wind to stir it, but there's hardly a breeze. It seems the whole earth is determined to be quiet.

Sam turns to her. "Are you okay?"

She pulls in a deep breath and lets it out. "My heart's beating a mile a minute." She smiles. "Maybe it's the Prosecco."

"Or maybe it's the company."

Liv is sure Sam is teasing, but his gaze is hooded and heavy. A weight lands in her stomach.

She turns to the view and swallows. "I keep waiting for it to sink in. To be real."

"It is real, Liv. It's done. We know the truth now. You and me. Like we always wanted."

"Then why don't I feel like it's really over?"

"Maybe because you don't want it to be."

"It's more than that," she says. "Something in that diary felt . . . I don't know . . . false."

"Just because she miscounted a few windows?"

"I know what my gut is telling me, Sam."

"You heard what Beth said. It's Theodosia's book."

"Then why didn't I get goose bumps too?"

"What?"

She holds out her arm. "Every single inch of skin on my body should have erupted in gooseflesh, Sam, but it didn't—"

"Liv—"

"—and the only explanation I can think of as to why is that the entries weren't—"

"Weren't what?" Before she can respond, he turns them off the road to the shoulder and shoves the truck into park, hard enough to lock the strap of her seat belt and snap her back. "First you tell me you've given up on all this, and now suddenly you're all in again? Which is it?"

The harshness of his voice startles her. "Why are you so angry? I'm just being honest with you. I'm just telling you I don't feel in my heart that it's—"

"In your heart?"

"Yes, my heart. I thought you of all people would understand." She looks out the window, feeling tears mount.

Sam releases a heavy breath and flexes his hands on the wheel. "I'm sorry. This is a lot to take in. And we're both exhausted. Maybe we shouldn't try to get back tonight," he says. "It's been a long, crazy day. There are plenty of places we could stay."

"At the height of the season? We'll never find a room."

"It can't hurt to look, can it? Besides, there's not much point in driving to Hatteras in the dark."

The Hatteras house? Is that the excuse he wants to use to stop for the night?

Flutters of uncertainty push against her ribs. When she glances back at him, his eyes are soft. "I know why you're doing this, Liv."

"Doing what?"

"Making excuses about the diary, about why it's not real

or true. Trying to find the red herring so you don't have to believe it's really over."

She opens her mouth but can't decide what to say.

Sam's smile is tender now, all impatience gone. "I know Whit wanted it to be the two of you solving this, but it wasn't—and I'm not going to apologize for that. And you shouldn't either. You've spent too long searching for answers. You're entitled to celebrate this. We both are. It's not like this wasn't a huge part of my life too, you know."

She nods. "I know. But, Sam—"

"No buts." He reaches across the seat and lays his hand on her knee, the heat of his palm burning up her leg. "Let's just celebrate this, okay?"

His hand remains, heavier now, his fingers gently pressing. Possibility swims through the cab, charging the space between them like the air seconds before a savage summer downpour brought on after too many days of unrelenting heat. So many hours on the road, maybe this heat too has to break. She hasn't wanted to think about this fact—or any of the other facts she's been blissfully ignoring, like her phone humming again, the vibration thrumming against her thigh through her purse. The fact that Whit thinks Sam has left. The fact that her skin hasn't cooled to its normal temperature since she stepped across the threshold and saw Sam standing in front of the bookshelves yesterday.

Now he's telling her they need to get a hotel room. That in the morning they can drive by the house in Hatteras, just to see.

You're entitled to celebrate this.

We both are.

"It *is* late," she says.

And that is true.

Sam lifts his hand from her bare thigh, peels it off slowly as if he's applied a temporary tattoo to her skin and wants to be sure it will take. Then he settles his fingers over the gear-shift, tugs hard, and turns them around.

Crossing into Wilmington, Whit picks up his cell and taps the screen for Liv's number. He wedges the phone under his jaw so he can turn down the radio. This will be his sixth message; he's been keeping count. He's made a dozen calls but only left half that many messages.

He's going to tell Liv he's on his way home with news. Forget the *Siren*. After stalking every pub, every dock, every fish fry shack in Little River, he's got a lead that could be worth twice as much as the *Bella Donna*. Gold coins off Oak Island. Okay, so it's not exactly on their doorstep, but it's not the moon either, right? Sure, it'll take some work relocating the team, finding them new housing, a new boat—but he's made magic in less time before. He's not worried.

The rings continue. He stares hard at the road. "Pick up, Red. Pick up. . . ."

"Hi, you've reached Liv Connelly. I'm not here right now, but if you—"

He hangs up—deciding he's near enough that he'll just save his good news for when he sees her, when he scoops her up into his arms and kisses the breath out of her.

He glances at the dashboard clock. He's making good

time. If the roads stay clear, he should be back at the house by nine. He'll stop at Wharton's and pick up a bottle of champagne. He and Liv will take it down to the water and drain it under the stars. Then they'll screw like teenagers. Sam will be long gone and they'll start fresh—make believe Sam was never there. He'll scrub the place clean of all traces of Felder. Make it theirs alone. Make it all right. And when this is over, when they're home and flush, they'll get back to their search for the *Patriot*. He'll find Theodosia for her. He'll keep his promise, dammit. Because it's the only one that really matters.

So close now, he'll do whatever it takes.

There are many motels, so many more than Liv even recalls from her last visit to Nags Head. Sam drives them slowly down Beach Road so they can read the signs, as if there might be something telling in their descriptions, when they all offer the same things: free Wi-Fi, ocean views, cable TV.

Sam points. "That one has rooms."

The Sundowner is a classic seaside motel: faded brick with white plastic Adirondack chairs flanking each door. The Vacancy sign blinks invitingly, the first one they've seen for several blocks. Liv can already imagine the interiors as they park: the thin bedspreads, the thin walls, the grit of leftover beach sand in the tub. The man at the front desk is young, so young that Liv isn't even sure he has ever grown out a full beard. The stubble around his chin is faint and uneven, reminding her of the feathers on a baby bird. A TV plays local news in the lobby. There's been a boating accident in Avon. One person still missing.

"How much for a room?" Sam asks.

When the attendant answers, Liv isn't sure if it's the high price or Sam's request for a room—*one*—that makes her heartbeat hasten. He glances at her expectantly. She knows what he's thinking: that at this time of year they are lucky to find even one room available, and that if they are fortunate enough to find two, it would be a sinful amount of money to waste.

"It's not like we haven't shared a room before," Sam says with a smile. "But it's your choice."

Her choice.

"We'll need two," she says. "If you have two."

"Got three if you want three," the clerk says.

Sam's smile is tight. "Two's plenty."

Liv searches the small rack of toiletries that sits behind the desk, remembering that they have nothing with them. "And one of those travel toothbrush packs, please."

"Better make that two," Sam says, pulling out his wallet.

When they have their key cards and are back outside, Liv feels a rush of regret, and the overwhelming need to explain. "I just thought—"

"It's fine." His smile is patient. "It's the right thing."

The right thing. Everything always came down to that for him, didn't it? So why had he tempted her to do the wrong?

Maybe I don't play by the rules anymore. . . .

"This is you." He stops them at room number seven. His is farther down.

"Why don't you get settled and we can meet back outside?" he says. "It's a beautiful night. Be a shame to waste a room on the water without a walk on the beach."

He's right. The air is smooth and warm and teasing, and her mind is racing—the last thing she needs is to sit inside a motel room and stare at the walls.

"Fifteen minutes enough?" he says.

"Plenty."

The back side of the motel sits right on the sand. Liv looks down the long stretch of deck and finds Sam waiting for her, shirtless and barefoot, leaning against one of the posts that flank the steps to the beach. His body is as trim and fit as she remembers, maybe even more so.

"I thought I might go for a swim," he says. "It's so warm."

I dare you to jump in. . . .

Liv rubs her arms, cold suddenly.

"Do you want to put on something else?" he asks.

"No. It's fine." And it is, really. The chill isn't from the air. The breeze is tepid, muggy.

I got goose bumps the first time I read it. Absolute chills. I'm sure you did too, Liv. . . .

They walk toward the sound of the surf, unable to see its curl and strength, only able to hear it. Liv draws in a quick breath, startled by the volume and the power. The sand feels silky under her feet, pressed beneath her toes. And then they are at the edge of the waves, and with the next crash, a foamy curtain stretches out and slides up her ankles, frothy and soft, before it retreats.

"Loud, isn't it?" Sam says.

"I'd forgotten how strong the surf is here, how hard it hits the sand. The canal is always so still, so calm." Even in the dark, she can feel Sam staring at her. She lifts her face and searches the stars. "Even the sky seems bigger out here. It always did."

"I remember when you said you thought being underwater would look like the night sky. Floating in all that nothingness." He smiles. "So, did it?"

"In a way," she says. "Everything feels so far away when I dive. Like another universe. And I feel truly free."

"You know I never meant to make you feel any other way, Liv."

"I never said you did."

He sweeps his foot through the surf. "I look back and wonder when we first started to fall away from each other."

"We didn't fall away, Sam. You left."

"You stayed."

"It's not that easy. . . ."

"I think it is."

She doesn't know what they're doing and she can't blame the Prosecco—its winding buzz has long left her. Her thoughts are sharp now, too sharp.

The waves crash again, hard enough to make her jump. She feels the tide in her bones.

She turns back to the motel, the strip of porch lights like Christmas tree bulbs, and all she can think of is Theodosia, standing on the deck of the *Patriot,* seeing the glow of those false Banker lanterns, and how her heart must have soared, so certain she was going to be saved.

Was that really how it ended for her? That bleak, that hopeless?

A gust of fear swallows her. Liv shivers.

"We should go back," she says.

Sam comes closer, his voice a husky whisper. "How far?"

9

Thirteen years earlier

When the plane touched down, Sam reached across the seat for Liv's hand and squeezed it almost as hard as she'd been squeezing the armrest.

"Relax," he said. "My folks are going to love you."

"I hope so." And God, she did. While she'd never seen pictures of Sam's family, she'd gathered they were every bit the traditional, all-American unit. What would they think of her fractured home life, her overly dependent and controlling father? Would they pity her, judge her? Sam assured her that he'd already laid the groundwork of her history over the phone—her mother's accident, her father's challenges (Sam's word, not hers)—and that she didn't need to feel self-conscious.

Easier said than done.

It had taken Liv three weeks—from the time of Sam's invitation almost to the exact moment she climbed into the shuttle for the airport—to convince her father that he could manage one long weekend without her near. She'd almost not told him about the plane, sure that news would seal her fate—airline crashes were on the rise; did she need him to read her the terrifying statistics?—but with only four days to travel, even she couldn't spin a road trip convincingly. Even though she was only going for part of their long break, she'd promised to keep her cell phone with her at all times, just in case, and to call him the minute she landed, which would have been right then, she realized as she looked around, aware suddenly of how desperately quiet the cabin had become.

Around her, mumbles of the delayed arrival circulated. Liv felt sure she'd jump out of her skin if she didn't exit soon.

"We're late," she said. "I feel bad if we've kept everyone waiting."

"Don't. Michael always runs late for everything."

His younger brother. Liv had heard little about him—only that he'd flunked out of his second college and was back home again.

The door opened and the line of passengers lunged forward. Slipping into the aisle at last and following the stream, Liv felt a strange charge of panic, as if her father had somehow followed her, as if he might be waiting to bring her home before she could have a chance to enjoy her freedom. Sam's hand folded around hers, but still she scanned the expectant faces that waited outside the doors when they emerged from the carpeted corridor; still she feared seeing her father's among the crowd.

• • •

"Miracle of miracles." Sam pointed her to a blue Volvo on the other side of the arrival lane where a rangy, dark-haired man leaned against the back of the car with his hands shoved up under his arms, squinting against the wind. Michael. Liv reached up with her free hand to hold her coat collar closed, the brisk air needling her bare throat.

"Don't tell him we were delayed," Sam muttered. "I want to keep him on the hook awhile. He needs it."

"Welcome home, bro." Michael peeled himself off the car. "This Liz?"

"Liv," Sam corrected tightly, opening the back and flinging their luggage inside.

Michael pried one of his hands free and gave her a half-hearted handshake. "Hey."

"Hi," she said back, glad when Sam steered her to the door.

"Watch that shit on the seat," Michael called as they climbed in. "I had to pick up the old man's dry cleaning."

"Glad to see he put you to work," Sam said.

"You're a fucking riot." Michael swung them out into traffic before Liv even had a chance to buckle up, and accelerated into the passing lane, abruptly enough that the driver behind them honked.

"Slow down," Sam said. "Jesus."

"I just figured you lovebirds would be champing at the bit to get home, sweet home." Michael cut Liv a look in the rear-view mirror and wiggled his eyebrows suggestively.

She flushed and turned toward the window. Small patches of snow speckled with dirt dotted the side of the highway.

"I can't believe Dad let you drive Mom's car," Sam said.

"It's not hers anymore," said Michael. "She gave it to me. He bought her a Benz. You still driving that P.O.S. truck?"

"Until someone hands me a new car on a silver platter."

"She didn't hand it to me. She was trading up."

"So you did her a favor taking it for free, right?"

"Screw you." Michael jerked them around a slow sedan; Liv gripped the door to steady herself. "I told Dad I have an interview at Home Depot tonight, so if he says anything, just go along with it, okay? Marcus and the guys are meeting at Pup's to watch the game. Dad would just give me shit. Oh, hey—guess who I saw Friday night at Lucky's." There was a teasing crackle in Michael's voice. Liv looked at Sam.

"How should I know?" he said testily.

Michael grinned. "Annie Newcomb. She asked about you."

Liv leaned forward. "Who's Annie Newcomb?"

"No one," Sam said.

When Michael turned them—slung them—into a cul-de-sac of stately brick Colonials with multicar garages and deep swaths of flawless lawns a few minutes later, Liv felt a shiver of surprise. Sam had always led her to believe his childhood home was modest, working-class—just like hers—and the irony startled her. While Whit had overblown his upbringing to hide his meager roots, Sam had done the exact opposite to downplay all his privilege.

A pretty middle-aged woman with a neat twist of auburn

hair waved to them from the front door, holding a wineglass in her other hand.

Michael snorted. "Fifty and still perfecting her Miss America wave." When Sam reached for the door, Michael grabbed his arm. "Remember: I've got an interview."

Sam shook him off. "I'm not lying for you."

"I'm not asking you to lie. Just don't get weird about it."

"Don't forget his dry cleaning," Sam said, pushing open the door.

Liv was sure the woman would walk the tidy curl of pavers to meet them at the car, but she remained at her post, smiling and waving eagerly, like a pet who knows better than to press the boundaries of her invisible fence.

"Penny put you in my old room," Sam said, leading Liv up a set of wide carpeted stairs.

"Who's Penny?"

"Our maid."

Sam's family had a maid? Liv followed him down a corridor flanked with framed photographs. She wanted to slow to study each one, but Sam's pace was relentless. Already he'd rushed her through introductions with his mother in the home's high-ceilinged foyer.

It was a nice room, she thought, stepping inside. Tidy and homey. She glanced around, charmed by the curtains that matched the navy blue wallpaper, the bed's smooth quilted cover. When Sam opened the closet to show her hangers in case she wanted them, the scent of fresh cedar rushed out.

A real house, she thought. *This smells like a real house.*

"Is your father here?" she asked.

"Still at the firm, probably. He'll show up for dinner."

She toured the room, slowing at a shelf of sport trophies. Sam's name etched in fine letters, year after year. Champion. First place. Most Valuable Player. She picked up a statue of a bronze runner holding a flag and admired it.

"It didn't look like this when it was my room," Sam said, coming in behind her. "I didn't keep these up here."

"Why not? They're impressive."

"They're dusty." He dragged his index finger over a gilded basketball and wiped it clean on his shirt.

Michael passed the doorway wearing earphones, tapping out a drumbeat on his hips.

"Sorry about my brother. My mother keeps bailing him out and my father keeps threatening to send him into the service. It's what he needs."

Liv closed her eyes and let her head fall back against his chin. She almost didn't dare keep them shut, afraid she'd open them to find herself back at the table with her father, her hard-earned recess only a dream. The scent of roasting meat drifted toward her, faint but sweet.

"Your mother's very pretty."

"She'd appreciate you saying that—she works hard at it. She doesn't eat." The disdain in his voice surprised her. "She drinks wine like it's water, but she never actually *eats*. She spends her whole meal pushing food around her plate to make it look like she's eaten. Watch her at dinner. You'll see."

Liv moved to the bed and stretched out. She smiled up at the ceiling fan, its long blades still. "I can picture you lying here," she said. "Staring up, night after night . . ." She turned her head toward him. "Ever have sex in here?"

He grinned. "You mean with someone other than myself?"

"Very funny." She rolled onto her side, meeting his level stare. "So, who's Annie Newcomb?"

"Just a girl."

"I figured that part out on my own, thanks. Did you date her?"

"No. She was just a friend."

"A good friend?"

"Not as good as you—how's that?" Sam leaned down and kissed her on the mouth. "Get unpacked, okay? I'll meet you downstairs."

Robert Felder was seated at the head of the heavy oak table when Liv followed Sam into the dining room at six thirty. His resemblance to Sam startled her. Both men shared the same dark, serious eyes, the same crisp features.

Liv glanced at Sam's mother, who was scanning the table. "Everything smells delicious," she said.

"It does, doesn't it?" Faye Felder motioned to the middle-aged woman who emerged from the kitchen with a basket of rolls. "Penny is our angel."

Footsteps thundered down the stairs and Michael blew into the room, earphones slung around his neck.

"You're late," Robert Felder said sharply.

"Actually I am." Michael dropped a kiss on his mother's cheek and reached over her shoulder for a roll from the basket, tossing it up like a baseball. "Later."

Faye blinked at him. "You're not eating with us?"

"Can't," Michael said. "Got that interview at Home Depot, remember? Save me some, will you, Penny? I'll eat when I get home."

Mr. Felder's eyes rose. "Strange time for a job interview."

"Yeah, well. It's a tough job market." Michael's gaze slid to Sam's and flashed with warning as he strolled out of the room. "Wish me luck."

"Good luck, sweetheart," his mother called after him.

"I suppose I should just be grateful he's even interviewing," his father said.

Sam shoved a cube of steak into his mouth and chewed roughly.

Faye Felder swirled her wine. "You have any brothers or sisters, Liv?"

"No, ma'am. Just me."

"And your mother, is it?"

"Her father, Mom." Sam shot his mother a disapproving look. "I told you all this, remember?"

"Oh, I'm sorry. You did." She smiled wearily at Liv. "He did, dear." She cut off a few tidy cubes of steak and arranged them around her salad.

Robert Felder speared a slice of butter and spread it evenly over his roll. "Where are you from, Liv?"

"North Carolina. I was born in Raleigh."

"A Southern belle." He slid his eyes to Sam. "That's a first for you, isn't it, son?"

Liv's cheeks flushed hot. She looked at Sam, waiting for him to say something, but he just reached for his wine and took a long sip.

"You don't have an accent," Faye Felder said, tilting her head back and forth as if Liv were one of those find-the-hidden-picture puzzles. "There's a lady in our women's league from South Carolina—I forget where exactly—but she says *y'all* this and *y'all* that. I just get such a kick out of her."

Liv forced a polite smile.

"Before I forget—" Robert Felder pointed his fork at his son. "I told Bob Newcomb you'd have lunch with him tomorrow. He's excited to introduce you to the new associate."

Flickers of alarm scurried up her spine. They were planning to go to the Field Museum tomorrow.

Sam snapped open his napkin. "We'll see, Dad. Liv's only here for two days."

"Who's Bob Newcomb?" Liv asked.

Mr. Felder glanced up at her and frowned, as if he'd forgotten she was there.

"He's a lawyer in my dad's firm," Sam said. "He practices maritime law."

"And makes a heck of a lot more money than ninety-nine percent of the treasure hunters he represents too," said Mr. Felder.

Liv grinned. "But probably only has one percent of the fun."

She expected to earn an agreeable laugh, but Sam's expression turned startlingly stony. She glanced around the table, finding his father and mother equally unamused.

"Is that what you're majoring in, Liv?" Robert Felder asked coolly. *"Fun?"*

His tone was just cutting enough to remind her of Harold Warner when he'd tried to belittle her line of questions at his lecture.

Feeling Sam's pointed gaze, she said, "I don't think there's anything wrong with choosing a career you enjoy."

"Said every broke would-be artist working the drive-through." Sam's father snapped his fingers for the rolls. "Hand me those, Faye."

After dinner, Liv followed Sam down the hall into the den. He poured them two splashes of whiskey and led her to a stiff leather couch in front of the stone fireplace, the gas flames lavender and steady behind the square of glass.

A pair of mounted bass hung above the mantel, their bodies shellacked, their wide mouths gaping.

Liv pointed at them. "Is that where you plan to mount your very first Southern belle too?"

Sam groaned. "I'm sorry about all that."

"You could have said something, you know."

"It's just how my dad is. He's hard on people. Women, especially."

"And that's supposed to make it okay?"

"I'm not defending him, Liv." Sam sipped his drink, his eyes on the fire.

"Is it because of that crack I made about having fun?"

"He doesn't want me getting that degree. He wants me to go into maritime law. The only reason he agreed to the program at ECU was that I said I'd consider law school afterward."

"You never told me you wanted to be a lawyer."

"Because I don't." Sam set down his glass on the coffee table and motioned to the door. "Let's go out and get a beer. I need some fresh air."

"Then we're still going to the museum tomorrow?"

"Absolutely," Sam said, helping her into her coat. He opened the front door and led her out into a cold rain.

But Sam's heavy expression at breakfast the next morning was all Liv needed to see to know they weren't going. She did her best to hide her disappointment for the benefit of his mother when Faye came to join them for coffee and eggs, but when they were alone upstairs in his room, Liv fell against him.

"I'm only here two days, Sam."

"I know that." He stroked her hair. "But this is my father, Liv. You of all people should understand that sometimes you have to make sacrifices for your parents."

She understood—of course she did. How many times had Sam patiently tolerated her need to cut short their evening to help her father change a lightbulb or spray for imagined bugs?

Regret pushed at her ribs. She smiled up at him, comforted that he needed her patience for once.

"It'll just be an hour," he said. "Two, tops. And when I get back, we'll still have plenty of time to get to the museum. Just make yourself at home while I'm gone, okay?"

She promised she would, and when he left, she tried, venturing into the vaulted sunroom and settling into a wicker armchair to watch a flock of sparrows descend on a hanging feeder in the backyard, but when Sam's mother came in on her phone, Liv felt desperately intrusive and rose to leave, her discomfort only confirmed when Faye Felder failed to insist Liv stay put. The deck, tidy and sheltered, would have been fine had the rain not resumed its chilly descent within minutes of her stepping out, so Liv returned to Sam's room and hunkered down on his bed with a book Whit had recommended on the history of wooden ships. But every few pages, she checked the time, eager for Sam's return, feeling like a dutiful house pet, and hating herself for it. Had it never occurred to her that she could go to the museum without him?

When she heard movement in the hallway shortly before three, she glanced at the doorway, sure it was Sam, and started to find Michael slouched there instead, midyawn, his black hair standing up on one side. Had he only now just gotten up?

He made his eyes into slits. "You're not Sam."

"He isn't here," she said.

"Probably still slugging back G and Ts with Big Bob at the country club." He cupped his hand and tipped it toward his open mouth.

Liv turned back to her book, sure he'd move on, but he came into the room and dropped on the other end of the bed, hard enough to bounce her. He smelled stale, like old sheets.

"So, what do you want to know?" he said.

"About what?"

"About Sam, obviously."

She scooted farther up the bed, uncomfortable at how close he sat, his hand so near to her bare feet.

"I'm all set, thanks," she said.

"Bullshit. Sam never tells any of his girlfriends anything. They all come to me for the dirt."

Liv bristled. *All* of his girlfriends? How many had there been?

Michael leaned back on his elbows. "So, how long have you two been seeing each other?"

Liv closed her book. "Awhile."

Michael snorted. "Not very long if you still think he's so perfect."

"I never said I thought he was perfect," she said. "I don't think anyone's perfect."

"Well, he's *definitely* not. Trust me."

Liv opened her book again, determined not to bite whatever bait Michael was dangling.

"He didn't tell you about Annie, did he?"

He was trying to rattle her and she wouldn't be rattled, dammit. She answered without lifting her eyes from the page. "He told me she was a friend."

"Is that what he called her? Damn, that's cold."

Now Liv felt a ball of dread bounce in her stomach.

"So you're saying he dated her?" she asked carefully.

"No," Michael said. "He dated Katie Easterday. He *cheated* with Annie Newcomb."

Cheated. The word landed against Liv like a glass door

she'd walked into. She felt actual pain from it. As if Michael had smacked her with his palm.

Sam might have been a lot of things, but he wasn't a cheater. Absolutely not.

"But hey, you didn't hear that from me." Michael bounced off the bed and lumbered to the door. "Enjoy your book."

Liv called to him, "Why did you tell me that?"

He stopped and turned. "Because I just found out my father knew I wasn't at an interview last night, that's why."

By the time Sam returned, it was almost five.

When he came upstairs, Liv rushed into his arms as if she could force Michael's words out of her heart if she pressed against him hard enough.

"I'm sorry about our day," Sam said. "Next time. I promise. Make it up to you with some pizza?"

But their last night together suffered a similar fate as their afternoon. Instead of enjoying dinner alone at Sam's favorite pizza parlor, they were invited—ordered, to Liv's ear—to a neighbor's anniversary party. A formal affair, Liv was informed by Sam's mother. Surely she'd brought something suitably dressy?

Liv stared down at her opened luggage and scanned her meager collection of clothes.

"You could always borrow something of my mother's," Sam said.

Liv looked at him. Was he serious? She decided on a wool skirt and a turtleneck sweater, and pulled her hair into a tight bun. "When I get back, we'll go out for real," he said as they walked through a pair of high oak doors into a sea of older faces.

Watching Sam at the fireplace, laughing with a couple in their mid-sixties, one hand in his pocket, the other gesturing with his cocktail, Liv felt tremors of uncertainty. She'd been so eager to visit Chicago, to meet his family and see where he came from—now she longed to get Sam away, get him back to the home they'd made together in Greenville. She didn't know who he was here.

Did he?

Rain followed her home. From Chicago to Charlotte to Greenville, a persistent shower doused everything in her path, returning her to her father's porch damp and chilled and edgy.

"How was your visit with the boy?" Francis worked his way through a stack of white meat. She'd picked up dinner on the way back from the airport, in no mood to cook.

Liv reached for her Coke. "His name is Sam, Poppy. And he's twenty-six."

"He's not the rude one, is he? The one who curses like a sailor?"

"Whit's not rude." She couldn't argue with his second point.

Her father took up his fork and pushed it through his potato salad with renewed intent. "It's good you came home early. There's bad weather moving into Chicago tomorrow. I'd hate to think of you flying home in a storm. I'd be a wreck." He smiled tightly. "I thought we could go through the old albums tomorrow."

Liv kept her eyes on her plate. "I'm actually going to see Dr. Sinclair tomorrow."

Her father set down his fork. "Is something wrong?"

"Just a checkup."

"Do you have an appointment?"

No, but she would, she thought as she pierced a cherry tomato and swallowed it whole. If she had to wait in his office all day, she'd have one.

"I can't guarantee the doctor will be able to see you today," the receptionist said when Liv stepped up to the desk the next morning.

"I'll wait," she said. "It's important."

So she did. Nearly three hours, before a lean, blond nurse stuck her head out the exam doors. "Liv Connelly?"

Dr. Sinclair always reminded her of her father. Same thick glasses, same piercing black eyes, same receding hairline. But, unlike her father, he laughed.

Usually.

"Now, Liv . . ." He took a seat on a wheeled stool and gave her a hard look. He put down her folder, flattened his palms on his thighs, and rolled closer, bringing the fresh smell of spearmint with him. "What is it you want me to say here? You want my approval—is that it? I'm your doctor. I'm well aware of your health issues. Surely you don't expect me to recommend you start scuba diving."

"All I'm asking, Doctor, is have you had patients with asthma who've dived?"

"Of course." He folded his arms. "I've also had patients who smoked three packs a day. I didn't condone that either."

Then, just as he had done when she was diagnosed with asthma at nine, Dr. Sinclair brought out X-rays and charts to review why deep diving was hazardous, and Liv listened just as she had back then too. But this time when she walked out of the office's broad glass door, she wasn't holding back tears.

This time when she lifted her face to the sun, she held back a smile.

Liv had never been to Whit Crosby's apartment, and the only reason she knew how to find it was that he'd lent Sam an archaeology journal with his address printed on it. He rented part of an old brick bungalow on a historic tree-lined street in the West End. Crossing to the sidewalk, Liv looked up to see a leggy blonde in an oversize turtleneck sweater and velvet pants scooting down the stairs of his house, sliding on sunglasses as she passed Liv.

The name on the buzzer was faint but readable.

After a few minutes, Whit arrived at the door, shirtless and smelling of soap.

It was clear at once that he was expecting her to be someone else, but he rescued himself admirably. "Come on in."

Stepping inside, she thought it was a surprisingly lovely apartment, bright and spacious with high ceilings and a kitchen with a cutout to the living room. The windows were all open, the fresh air helping to diffuse the smell of old smoke.

"I was just about to make some coffee," he said, tugging on a T-shirt. "Want some?"

"Sure." She wandered into the living room, which consisted of an uncomfortable-looking couch and a wagon wheel coffee table cluttered with empty beer bottles and overflowing ashtrays.

She grimaced. "You do know you can empty ashtrays, right?" she called out.

"What was that?" Whit yelled back.

She smiled and shook her head, advancing toward a curious pile of timbers resting against his fireplace. She counted seven, each one at least six inches thick. "What's with all the wood?"

"My buddy Wes found those in the Keys last year. He thinks they're from a tobacco ship. I keep meaning to take them over to the lab. Hey, I don't have any milk."

"Black's fine." She ran her fingers over the end of one timber, the splintered wood sharp and gritty. "So, who's the blonde?"

Whit leaned back to meet her gaze through the cutout. "You met Lona?"

Lona. Liv had decided having an exotic name was a prerequisite for dating Whit Crosby. "We didn't officially *meet*. She came out just as I walked up. What happened to Jocelyn?"

"She transferred."

"Oh." Whit came in with two mugs and handed her one. The coffee was flavorful and strong. "Lona's lovely."

"Yeah, she is." He squinted at her. "But you didn't come all this way to rate my dates and tell me to empty my ashtrays, did you, Red?"

"No." She grinned, suddenly feeling as if she might explode with the news. "I went to my doctor."

His eyes flashed over his coffee. "And?"

"And I need you to teach me to dive," she said, "before I lose my damn nerve."

"The first thing you should know is that Curtis talks a big game, but he's really a teddy bear. Buck, on the other hand, is one hundred percent bastard. He's especially not kind to new people, so whatever you do, don't take it personally—but don't let him get under your skin either. Ignore him. Drives him nuts."

Whit gave Liv his lecture when they'd pulled into the marina an hour later and walked briskly down the dock toward a black-and-white boat with the name *Phoenix* painted in fat orange letters on the hull.

"What if they have customers?" Liv asked.

"They won't. It's the quiet season. That's why Curtis brings her up here. Normally they charter out of Wilmington. She used to be a shrimp boat. Curtis found her being sold for scrap and retrofitted her as a dive boat—that's how she got the name *Phoenix*—but unfortunately she still runs as slow as a shrimp boat."

"You better not be knocking my old lady!" A man with bushy brown hair, wide-shouldered and compact, leaned over the rail and cackled as they approached.

Whit's face lit up. "Permission to come aboard, Captain?"

"As if you'd keep out if I said no?"

"Livy, this is Curtis," said Whit. "I stowed away on one of his trips to the cape when I was fifteen and he didn't make me walk the plank."

"Just made him eat Dickie's food—same difference." Curtis took her hand and shook it roughly. "Whit always gets the pretty girls. Only reason we let him on the boat. God knows he can't steer for shit." He gave her a gentle tug. "Come aboard, Pretty Livy, before you get your senses back and run screaming from us hooligans."

No chance, Liv thought, stepping onto the cluttered boat. It would be getting her to leave that would take convincing.

Underneath her sneakers, the boat growled to life and Liv felt the delicious sensation of movement as the crew steered them away from the dock and out into the open water.

When the boat was at a good clip, Curtis waved them toward the cabin. "Come on down. Buck's got us chasing a little sparkle today."

A heavyset man with a gray ponytail and a matching goatee was hunched over a chart. He glanced up and scowled at Whit. "Definitely keep the mermaid, but throw the other one back."

Curtis pointed behind them. "You and Pretty Livy help yourselves to a cold one, Whitty."

"Thought you'd never offer." Whit reached down to flip up

the top of the cooler and tugged out a pair of cans. He handed her one. "When in Rome, Red."

She took a quick sip, then a longer one, the blast of cold carbonation startling and delicious.

Whit leaned in to see the map the two men were scanning. "What's on the hook today?"

"Coins," Curtis said, sliding his index finger up and down a stretch of the chart. "Spanish. We pulled up a few yesterday."

"Merchant ship?" Whit asked.

Curtis shrugged. "Could be a galleon. Hard to say. Figured we'd come back with the metal detector and take another look before we start sending up flares."

Liv had read plenty about galleons, the many Spanish merchant ships that had sailed—and sometimes wrecked—along the Carolina coast, their holds flush with unimaginable treasure.

The power was cut and the boat quieted.

Curtis elbowed Whit. "You game for a peek down below?"

"You know it." Whit winked at Liv. "But first the mermaid needs her fins."

Liv had never realized how long it actually took to get ready to dive. Watching Sam and Whit suit up, she'd sworn their equipment checks had taken just minutes, but it seemed as if Whit had been checking her gear for an eternity—and not gently either. Between all the yanking and tightening and pulling, she was amazed her teeth remained in her gums.

"Now I know how a roaster feels," she said.

Whit grinned. "Some women actually enjoy getting poked and prodded by me, you know." He came behind her and gave the straps on her buoyancy compensator vest a last, hard tug. "Does that feel tight enough?"

"That depends—am I supposed to be able to breathe?"

Her mask fitting came next. Satisfied with the grip, he handed her a pair of fins. "Don't put them on until we're almost in or you'll face-plant."

"Thanks for the tip."

"A few other things you should know. Things are magnified underwater. Something about light transmission—hell if I know—but it's freaky if you aren't used to it."

Her impatience was building behind her ribs like an engine warming up. Was there a reason he wasn't telling her all this *in* the water?

"Everything's bigger," she said. "Got it."

"And it'll be loud, but only at first."

"Loud. Right."

"And watch for the hand signals I showed you—they're important."

"When exactly are we going in the water?"

"Christ, I thought I was impatient." He directed her to put on her mask. "Don't forget to rub a little spit in there first, keep it from fogging up." He secured his own and gave her a hard look through the lens. "Where's your inhaler?"

"It's in my bag." The high, pinched sound of her voice from the pressure of the mask on her nose made her want to laugh. "Now who's stalling?" she teased.

"Come on," he said, pointing them to the ladder. "We'll climb down."

Disappointment burned under her wet suit. Climb down like some terrified child who has to take the steps into the deep end of the pool?

"No way," she said. "I want to take my giant stride off the platform, like everyone else."

"Red . . ."

"Either you come with me or I go by myself. But I've dreamed of this moment for too long and I am going off that platform, dammit."

A chuckle came from behind them. "Attagirl," said Curtis, coiling rope into a pile. "About time you found a woman who could stand up to you, Whitty."

Whit sighed. "Fine," he said. "But don't get too far away from me once we're in."

As if she could. No sooner had she landed in a startling froth of cold and salt, and sprung back to the surface, than his big hands were around her vest and drawing her close to him. They practiced using her regulator so her body wouldn't balk at the unnatural effort of breathing underwater. Only after Whit was certain she'd practiced enough, they descended.

Liv had been underwater before, had let herself sink in pools and lakes as a child, but this stillness was larger than any she'd ever experienced. The muffled sound of her breath was instant and otherworldly, womblike. The water was silty, not as clear as she'd always imagined, but she could see Whit clearly enough through the necklace of bubbles that spilled out of her breathing apparatus. She reached out her arm, sure he was just in front of her, but her fingers didn't touch. She smiled around her regulator. Magnification. Just as he'd warned.

Whit had told her to expect volume, a lack of quiet, and yet there was a tremendous peace in all the strange sounds. The even rhythm of air in, bubbles out. She'd been worried she'd feel afraid, unsure, but suspended in the filmy water, she felt a startling calm. No one could find her here, could need her. Not her father. Not even Sam, wherever he was in Chicago. She floated, weightless, willing her thoughts to follow. The current pulled her gently and she let it. The bottom was a whirl of shapes beneath her, the distance equally blurry. She kicked toward it.

Entering the water in a wet suit had felt strange at first, the protection sparing her from that initial burst of cold, but now the temperature was starting to reach her skin. What if a person was cast out in this water without a barrier? How long could someone last?

Was this what it had been like for Theodosia? If she had been cast into the water, had she had time to put on anything substantial, or, as some of the legends claimed, had she gone in wearing nothing but a thin nightshirt? If she'd been made to walk the plank and drop into the depths in just a layer of cotton, the shock would have been unimaginable. A thousand needles piercing her skin. Winter sea. Her skirt growing heavy with it. Pulling her down. The chill below, the slap of the bitter air above. Which agony would have been worse?

And as Theo's mind had been seized with panic and the freezing ocean, had she tried to wait out the waves or had she found the strength to swim? Had she time to think of her father waiting for her? Her husband? That they might never know where she'd gone.

"I can't lose you too, Livy."

Liv pointed her fins to find the bottom, and alarm scampered up her spine. Her feet couldn't touch. How far out had she drifted? Turning, she sought the shape of Whit in the murky water, but the window of her mask was so small. She looked up, sure the surface was right there, but when she began to climb, it only moved farther away. Was it her weight belts? Was she supposed to abandon them to rise?

Think. Think.

Ice plowed through her veins. What if the current had pulled her too far out? She spun around, her heartbeat louder than her breathing. She couldn't see anything. Not Whit, not the anchor line, not even the hull of the boat.

Don't panic. Whatever you do, don't panic!

She touched her mask, resisting the urge to bite down harder on her regulator. Were there supposed to be so many bubbles? Once the stream had been a thing of grace and beauty. Now the ribbon of bubbles was a dangerous screen; she could barely see beyond them. As she waved her hands to clear her view, her hand caught her regulator and knocked it from her mouth. She flailed her arms, churning the water, praying Whit was close enough to see her struggle. But even as water filled her mask, her brain screamed for her to slow, to calm. Then she felt hands close around her waist and tug her hard, tug her up. She felt air on her face, the heat of the sun, her legs banging against metal rungs, and then her body lowered to the wet, grimy deck.

Whit's voice. Her chest tightening with a familiar squeeze.

Don't panic, don't panic.

"Hold on, Red!"

She could hear him yelling for her bag, hear the rush of feet nearing, the clatter of knees and equipment landing beside her. She blinked up into the sun, the shine of wet rubber. Then she felt the familiar round of her inhaler shoved into her mouth and Whit's hand guiding hers around it, pressing hard until she managed to depress the top, and then—

Air.

Air.

Air . . .

As the calm of her breath returned, she let her gaze drift over the crowd that had gathered around her.

Whit's face came over hers, drops of water sliding down his nose, dripping from the ends of his hair. Her mouth open, she caught several drops, seawater startling against her dry lips.

Whit's eyes. Silver-blue pools. Beautiful. She blinked up at them, finding her anchor.

"Easy, Red." He smoothed her hair from her forehead. "Easy . . ."

The coppery taste of blood sizzled against her cheeks. "It was like I was in her head, Whit," she whispered. "Like I was her and I got confused and then I panicked—"

"Shh. Just relax."

"What if she drowned? What if she didn't get away?"

Whit bent closer, the slick, warm wetness of his jaw brushing her cheek. "Don't talk. Just breathe."

She closed her eyes and swallowed, needing moisture.

Her thoughts swam toward silence, closing in. Then a single spark of dread.

Sam.

She couldn't tell Sam.

"I'm going to regret this, aren't I?"

Sam cast a wary look at Liv over the top of the tumbler Whit had just handed him. It was late April, and they were on Whit's porch—"the poop deck," as Whit was fond of calling it—braving an unusually sultry Sunday morning to toast the midpoint of the semester. It had been a cold, wet spring, but summer was finally in sight. Crepe myrtles were blooming and daffodils were stubbornly poking up out of still-brown grass. To celebrate, Whit had made—*burned*—a stack of pancakes and an obscene amount of bacon—also burned—which they'd eaten with their fingers while Whit disappeared to concoct his purportedly infamous Bloody Whits. He'd emerged with a trio of tumblers, stuffed with leafy stalks of celery and gnarled pepper strips.

Sam winced as he swallowed and set down the glass. "Jesus, that's awful."

"I think it's delicious," Liv said, taking another spicy sip.

Whit pointed his glass at her and raised it. "Now, there's a woman who knows a real drink."

She smiled and lifted hers in return, overcome with a sense of calm and joy. Maybe it was the day, bright and steamy and spread out wide in front of them. Sam wanted to take her to the movies, but Whit had his heart set on a road trip to the waterfront where a team was examining Castle Harbor for submerged wrecks. He had promised crab legs on the dock. Whit always promised something, Sam pointed out.

Whit drained his glass. "Who wants seconds?"

Sam balked. "One of us needs to drive to Washington."

"Fine by me—so long as I don't have to steer the boat. And this time, Red, you can teach *me* to dive."

Even outside with the generous breeze, Liv felt certain all the air in the universe had come to a complete standstill.

Sam stared at her. "You dived?"

Whit looked between her and Sam for several long seconds, confused. "You didn't tell him?"

Liv could feel Sam's eyes on her as surely as heat from the sun. She turned to him slowly. "It was just a quick trip, Sam. A friend of Whit's had a boat—"

"When?" Hurt twisted his features.

"While you were in Chicago. It wasn't deep. And it wasn't even for very long."

"Unfortunately," Whit said. "Or fortunately, really."

Liv cast a warning look at Whit to plead for him to shut up, but Sam had already caught on.

"Something happened?" Sam's eyes darted between them. "What happened?"

"I was fine—I *am* fine," Liv said, just wishing Sam would stop looking at her as if she'd burned down someone's house.

"I let the current pull me out too far, that's all, and I got scared and I had a little . . ."

"A little what?"

"An attack," she said. "But I had my inhaler right there. Really, it wasn't a big deal."

"Jesus Christ." Sam's face flushed. He set down his drink and pushed past her for the steps, taking them hard enough to rattle the railing's loose spindles. Liv shot Whit a worried look, then hurried after Sam.

"Sam, wait!"

When he wouldn't, she rushed around him, forcing him to stop.

"You said you couldn't dive, Liv."

"Because that's what I'd always been told," she said.

"By people who know better." He cast an accusing look toward the porch, but Whit had gone inside. "It was his idea, wasn't it? He bullied you into going, didn't he?"

"No! I asked *him*."

"Why didn't you wait for me?"

"Because I knew you'd try to talk me out of it."

"Which, clearly, would have been a bad idea, right?"

She took his hand. "Let's go back inside."

"Absolutely not." He pulled free. "I'm not going back in there. Honestly I need a break from Crosby. We both do."

Back in the truck, Sam snapped on the radio, filling the cab with sound. Liv knew the music was a mask to cloak his anger, albeit short-lived. As soon as they were back at his apartment, the silence simmered with it. For the rest of the day, Liv caught Sam studying her strangely.

By dinner, she was ready to jump out of her skin.

"Please stop looking at me like that," she said.

"How am I looking at you?"

"Like you don't know who I am."

He speared a stack of spinach leaves. "It just makes me wonder, that's all."

"Wonder what?"

His eyes bored into hers. "What else you might be keeping from me."

Spring's drab rusts and olives gave way to summer blooms. Their temporary break from Whit slipped into something far more permanent. Despite Liv's hope that the passage of the seasons might mellow Sam's grudge, three weeks before his and Whit's graduation, Sam still remained determined to keep Whit Crosby out of their lives.

"You can't ignore him forever," Liv said as they lay in bed on a Sunday morning. Rain had come through overnight, shrouding everything in a veil of mist.

Sam rolled her against him. "Can't I?"

"I'm the one who took the risk, and he's the one you keep blaming."

"You'd rather I blame you too?"

Liv lifted her head to deliver him a weary look. "So your plan is to pretend he doesn't exist?"

He sighed. "I graduate in three weeks, Liv."

"So does Whit."

"Your point?"

"It's a small pond, Sam. It's not like you and he won't have to keep dealing with each other in the field."

"You honestly think Crosby will make a go of it in the real world?"

"He's not Michael, Sam."

Sam rose on his elbows, the line between his brows deepening. "What does my brother have to do with anything?"

Liv tilted her head pointedly. Was he honestly going to deny the unspoken comparison he made between his brother and Whit?

Sam motioned to the chart. "I thought you were going to add that theory about the ship being commandeered to the Bahamas."

He was changing the subject, but it happened to be a subject she liked.

"I did," she said, pointing to the note she'd added earlier that week. With the exception of Sam, the chart was the first thing she saw when she woke and the last thing before she drifted to sleep. If Sam was her compass, the chart was her Bible. But lately it was hard not to look at it and feel prickles of disappointment. For all of her and Sam's—and Whit's—efforts, she was no closer to solving the mystery of the *Patriot*—or Theodosia's fate—than she'd been before she met them.

Sam threw back the sheet and sat up on the edge of the bed. She marveled at the firm expanse of his back, the even shade of bronze he'd managed to keep all winter.

"Did that guy at the marina get back to you?" she asked.

"No." Sam took his dive watch off her nightstand and tightened it around his wrist. She'd seen the application for law school on his desk earlier in the week, and been immeasurably relieved to find the forms inside still blank.

"He will," she said, reaching out to touch the hollow at the base of his spine.

Sam stood and walked to where he'd left his clothes. "I can't flip burgers at Skipper's waiting for an opportunity, Liv."

She smiled weakly. "Can't you?"

Dressed, he returned to the bed and patted her exposed hip. "Come on. I'll buy you breakfast."

But her appetite had been missing for weeks. "Nothing for me."

"It's all this rain." Sam leaned across the bed to squint out the window. "It's depressing as hell. Wish for some sun."

Liv nodded, but she had no intention of doing as he asked. Her wish list was already full—her wishes spent on a job that would keep him close to her, or bring her closer to him. The clock was ticking; the days were passing. She didn't have time or space to spare for weather.

It would turn out she didn't have to.

Four days later, Liv sprinted through an evening shower to find Whit in front of Sam's apartment building, thoroughly soaked and wielding a bottle of tequila. They escaped together into the entry's tiled vestibule.

She surveyed his tousled, dripping hair, his drenched shirt, nearly opaque with rain. "Don't you own a raincoat?"

He smiled ruefully. "It wasn't raining when I got here an hour ago."

"You've been outside an *hour*?"

Whit glanced toward the stairs. "Is he here? I didn't see the truck outside."

"He stopped to pick up a pizza," she said. "He's just a few minutes behind me."

"Dare to be alone with me until he gets back?"

Whit followed her up the stairs and inside Sam's apartment, taking a seat on the couch, not unlike the way he'd dropped in on her months earlier. She slipped into the bathroom and snatched a towel from behind the door, flushed with a piercing sense of déjà vu as she returned to hand it to him.

"Thanks," he said, wiping his wet hair roughly with it. "At least I'm not bleeding this time, right? No, wait. I take that back—" He opened his calloused palm and stretched out his thumb. "I got a paper cut opening my water bill this morning—damn thing won't close on me."

She gave in to a laugh. An appreciative smile spread across his face.

"How have you been, Whit?"

"I've been okay. Trying to finish up my damn thesis without turning into a boring old bastard."

She smiled. "You could never be boring."

"Thanks. I think." He squinted up at her. "You know, I'm still not exactly sure why I've been in the doghouse this whole time with him. It's not like I dragged you out there that day."

Liv sighed. "I've told him that. A hundred times."

Behind them, the door clicked and opened. Sam stopped on the threshold holding the pizza box in one hand. He kicked the door closed with his heel and walked past them.

"Don't blame her," Whit said, following Sam into the kitchen. "I barged my way in."

Sam snapped open the box and motioned to the bottle of tequila. "Where did that come from?"

"It's a peace offering," said Whit.

"Well, there's not enough pizza for three."

"I didn't come over here to eat your food." Whit glanced at Liv before adding, "I came with news."

Sam took out a pair of plates from the dish drainer and cast a wary look at Liv before sliding his hard eyes back to Whit. "Whatever it is, I'm not interested."

"You know Curtis and Buck, the guys I told you about who run the treasure-hunting charters out of Wilmington with their boat, the *Phoenix*?"

It was dangerous, but Liv knew how to jog Sam's memory. "Where Whit taught me how to dive."

Sam glowered at Whit. "Is that what you were doing?"

The air, already pinched with tension, tightened further, but Whit seemed determined to move them forward. "Curtis is retiring," he said, "and he and Buck asked if I wanted to take over the business. Not just the *Phoenix,* but the whole treasure tour."

Sam handed a plate to Liv and reached in for a piece of pizza.

Whit moved closer. "The only problem is I need a partner, someone I can trust. Someone who knows what the hell they're doing."

Liv's pulse hastened. She met Whit's eyes, imploring him to just say it.

"Be my partner, Felder."

Sam's eyes snapped up to Whit, his hand still on the slice he meant to tear from the pie.

"I can't run the business alone," Whit said. "And I think we'd make a great team. Best of all, it's turnkey. All we have to do is switch over the permits, make a few updates to the boat, and we could start up as soon as we want."

Liv looked between them, feverish blooms of hope spreading across her cheeks. She spun toward Sam to champion all the reasons this offer could be his salvation—*their* salvation—but before her excitement could spill out, he said, "I can't—I'm going back to Chicago to law school."

Shock and hurt knotted in her stomach; he'd assured her he wouldn't send in his application without telling her.

"Congratulations, then," Whit said, gesturing to the bottle. "You can use that to celebrate. Thanks for the towel, Red."

She blinked at Whit as he moved for the door. He was going, just like that?

She wanted to rush after him, to fling herself across the door as a barricade so he couldn't give up so quickly—since when had Whit Crosby surrendered without getting his way?—but Sam's hand came over hers.

The door clicked shut, sending the room into silence.

Liv looked up at him. "You promised you'd tell me before you applied."

"I didn't apply," Sam admitted. "I just wanted to shut Whit down as soon as possible."

Relief fluttered through her—but only briefly.

"But you still plan to?" she said.

He moved the slice closer to her. "You should eat."

She pushed the plate away. "You didn't answer my question."

"Liv . . ." He leaned back against the counter and dragged his hands down his face. "Jesus, we've been over this. If nothing else comes up, then yes, I'm going to law school."

"But something else *has* come up."

"I mean something real."

"What's not real about a charter business? I've been on the boat, Sam. It's an amazing operation they've got." She could hear the desperation rising in her voice. "You said you don't want to go to law school, that you don't even want to be a lawyer. Was that a lie?"

"Of course not," he said. "But you do realize the only reason Whit put this out there was that he thinks I'll get my father to bankroll it—which he won't."

"That's not the only reason and you know it," said Liv.

"We'd have to take out loans. Huge ones."

"People do it, Sam."

"If I did start my own business, I'd be crazy to go in on it with someone like Crosby."

"Then what about with me?"

He stared at her. "You still have another year of school."

"I'll defer."

"What about your father? Wilmington's three hours away."

"Then I'll move him down there too. The truth is he needs to sell the house. It's too much for him. He needs something smaller." She fixed her mouth in a resigned line. They could go on this way all night. Sam could keep throwing up obstacles—she'd keep knocking them down.

He sighed. "Liv . . ."

She threw her arms around his neck and linked her fingers, determined not to let go until he agreed. "It's perfect, Sam. Really, it's a miracle."

He rolled his eyes. "I wouldn't go *that* far. . . ."

"Well, I would," she said. "Think about it: We could be together, doing what we want to do. Exploring wrecks, not just reading about them. The two of us."

"Three."

"Not all the time. Not when it really mattered. And we could keep searching for the *Patriot,* for Theo. Just think how much ground we could cover if we had our own boat, our own equipment. And I'm so close to getting my scuba certification. . . ." She searched his eyes for a spark of agreement. "Say something, Sam."

He frowned. "Something, Sam."

A joke. She'd take it. She raised her body higher, bringing her lips close to his. For a moment, he refused to dip his chin to grant her a kiss, but when he finally did and she closed her eyes, Liv saw only a blur of blue-gray, the color of the sea, calm and undisturbed.

10

OUTER BANKS, NORTH CAROLINA
Wednesday

"You were always hard to say no to, Liv," Sam tells her as they walk back up the beach to the glow of the Sundowner.

"Because I knew we'd make a great team. All of us. And we did."

"I suppose. In some crazy way."

She smiles. "Not so crazy."

They take the sandy steps slowly and pause at the top. Her room to the right, his to the left. Two doors down, a man in his twenties steps out with a beer, barefooted and shirtless. He glances at them and offers a weak peace sign before shuffling down the deck. The smell of pot drifts toward them in his wake.

Sam grins. "Happening place. Don't say I never take you anywhere."

Liv laughs, inexplicably grateful for the interruption, the chance to smile, to joke, as Sam runs a hand over his head, fluttering the short hairs. Liv wonders if they feel prickly or smooth like moss. What about his beard? Flashes of memory spark in and out: sitting on the beach at Hatteras, studying the places where those chestnut curls he's buzzed off once hugged his neck. Not even an hour later, feeling them brush against her throat.

The air swells suddenly, as if someone's opened an oven door and let a burst of heat fill the space around them. She feels a string of sweat trickle down her spine, another between her breasts. She turns her face to the breeze, needing it to cool her, to blow away dangerous thoughts, but the air's too soft to dry her damp skin.

She smiles out at the darkness, hearing the yawn of the surf in the distance. "I keep thinking I'm going to wake up tomorrow and this will all be a dream."

"Which part?"

Good question. Some of the day's events she would gladly find having occurred only in her imagination. Other parts . . . not necessarily.

"It's not a dream, Liv. We did it." Sam's moved closer and now he's studying her face as if he were planning to sketch her, lingering on certain features. Her eyebrows, her nose, her lips. He's tracing her with his eyes. "I never wanted to give up on this, Liv."

He's not talking about the mystery anymore. Liv knows this, just as she knows she should step back, far, far back, because in the next instant, his palm circles her head and his mouth covers hers, his lips and fingers firm and insistent, the strange prickle of his beard startling but his warm breath tasting so familiar.

Before she can respond, he releases her and pulls back. His eyes are as dark as she's ever seen them, almost black. She searches them fervently in the heavy heat of the night, but she can't find any regret in them at all.

He smiles. "That time was *my* choice."

The beach house looks like a bonfire when Whit pulls up to it. He could swear every room is lit up, and the noise—Jesus! There must be a half dozen cars parked in the driveway—only two of which he recognizes. Sam's truck is gone—thank Christ for that. Whit swings the van under a palm and takes the steps to the entrance two at a time. Who the hell left the front door wide-open?

As he storms inside, the music is so loud he can't tell where it's coming from. Women in bikinis wander past him with wineglasses and cast him curious glances as if he's the interloper. Where is Liv? Beyond the slider, he can see the ponytailed kid—Lance, he remembers his name now—slugging a beer and chatting up a great-looking blonde, and his anger surges. Whit feels like a father coming home from out of town to find his sons throwing a party without his permission. He wants to grab someone by the ear and toss them out the front door. He knows he should just be grateful the men are still here, but instead he feels parental—he feels *old*—and he doesn't like it.

Liv must be upstairs. She's not one for this kind of scene, this level of noise. Maybe she's in the bathtub, maybe reading in some quiet corner somewhere? Is she still so angry at him that she is letting them trash this place out of spite?

"Livy?" He stops at the bottom of the stairs and shouts up, "Red!" He scours the house, easily at first, and then his pace increases. There is a spark of hope when he thinks that maybe she has taken a walk on the beach—the beach!—and maybe he should take a shower first, at least change out of his—

"What's the story? You get it or not?"

Whit whips around to find Dennis in the doorway, the older man's cloud of white hair windblown, his equally white and unkempt eyebrows meeting in a fierce point.

"Have you seen Livy?"

"She left. She and Felder took off this afternoon. So, are we going back down, or what, man? 'Cause I've gotta line up something else if this isn't going to fly. . . ."

Whit is sure someone cut the lights in the adjoining rooms—his peripheral vision suddenly goes dark. Jesus, it can't be true. Felder said he was leaving—Whit never would have left them alone otherwise, never would have been so stupid. And now Sam's taken Liv? No, Whit doesn't believe it. Liv wouldn't—couldn't—do that to him. Leave with Felder?

His heart pounds, hard enough that he claps a hand over his chest, genuinely afraid his ribs might split from the pressure. "Where did they go?"

"Some new shipwreck museum in Nags Head," Dennis says. "A woman he went to school with runs it, he said; something about a diary—hell if I know. So are we good to go now, or not?" But Whit isn't listening anymore. He tells Dennis he's sorry, that God, he's sorry as hell and he'll make it up to him, but right now he has to go. Whit can't care that people he doesn't know are spilling wine on rugs he can't afford to replace, and tripping up the stairs, hand in hand, to screw on beds he's paid for with money he doesn't have.

He ransacks his memory as he climbs back into the van—a woman Sam went to school with. Law school or grad school? Nags Head. There is a new museum there; Liv told him about it recently, didn't she? He punches the search into his phone and scrolls down the Outer Banks Shipwreck Museum Web site as the engine churns. The director, Beth Henson. He thinks he remembers someone with that name.

He can't take the ferries—he's sure they don't run overnight—but it's fine. This late, the roads will be empty—he can make it to Nags Head in three hours.

In the rearview mirror, the blazing house shrinks to a fiery cube. Let them have the house, he thinks. Let them have everything. All he wants—all he's ever wanted—is with Sam Felder. Again.

Liv lets the hot water spill down her shoulders, the faint smell of chlorine rising in the steam. She's washed her hair twice now, and emptied the tiny bottle of shampoo, but still she can't bear to step out of the shower's cloak. She scrubs her underwear with soap and squeezes out the lather, hoping it will dry by morning. Unwrapping the little bar felt decadent, defiant. On road trips after her mother had died, her father would always forbid Liv to use the complimentary toiletries, rushing into their motel room to sweep the space free of possible contaminants. Surfaces were wiped down, pillows covered with towels. Her father always insisted they sleep fully clothed, not wanting any skin exposed to the sheets. Once she found a welcome mint that had escaped his search and chewed it quickly while he used the bathroom.

Back in her T-shirt, she climbs onto the bed and clicks through the channels, not caring what's on, just needing noise. A door slams several rooms down and the light on the nightstand shudders. She reaches over to turn it off and the television screen glows, bathing the faded blue bedspread in flashes of Technicolor. She won't peel the blanket back, won't inspect the sheets for bedbugs' telltale red dots, won't lay a towel over her pillow. Whit has broken her of these crippling habits, her father's obsessive training, and she is grateful to her husband for it. So why is she so nervous?

Liv can't remember the last time she was in a motel by herself. At home, she finds herself sleeping alone sometimes—Whit on the water, Whit staying out late—but a motel alone is different. A night in a motel is purposeful, intentional. Looking around at the pine-paneled walls, a warm, creamy shade of butterscotch, she thinks of the lake camp her father's stepbrother had offered them after her mother's funeral, a place to escape, a reprieve cut short by her father's discovery of something unsafe—a leaky boat that might sink them a mile from shore, ancient wiring that might combust and burn them to cinders in their sleep. "It's just us now, Livy," he said to her, driving home, and she nodded numbly as she fingered the hot metal of her seat belt and quietly released it, not sure why it felt so good when the strap loosened over her lap.

Guilt swims through her again. Throughout the day she's had the urge to call Whit and share the news of the diary with him, but still she hasn't. She unearthed her phone to charge it the hour before but refrained from checking her messages. The missed call icon is proof enough of her newly tangled life, considerations she didn't have twenty-four hours earlier. She can't sleep—she won't even dare try. Her mind is at a rolling boil and Sam's kiss sits in the very center. *That time was my choice*. When he walked off afterward, waved to her as if kissing her good night had been the most natural thing, she'd felt as if her feet were glued to the concrete. She reaches up to the wall to test the sheet of pine, the layers of shellac perhaps as thick as the wood itself, and presses her palm against the panel, as if feeling for a pulse. It would take nothing to step back outside, walk four doors down, and knock—but it would take everything to walk in. Is Sam lying as she is, wondering if she will come to him? Is he debating going to her?

She hears a creak and her gaze snaps to the door, sure it is Sam on the other side, sure he's choosing again, and her breath catches while she waits for the knock. It doesn't come.

She looks down at her phone in her hand. Her father never sleeps before two a.m. If she calls now, he'll be watching TV. He might even be calm enough to talk to. Maybe, just maybe, she'll catch him in a sliver of lucidity and he'll call her Livy. But when the phone is answered on the tenth ring, she knows it won't be her father on the other end.

"Francis Connelly's room." His nurse, Mary, a saint, and fifty-year-old grandmother of three.

"Mary, this is Liv. How was he today?"

"Not so good. Tomorrow'll be better."

God bless Mary and her dogged optimism. Liv closes her eyes, feeling the swell of tears.

"I wanted to tell him good night." *And that I'm in a motel. That I've used the shampoo. That I'm sleeping without a towel but I'm still a little afraid.*

"He's fine, sugar. Don't worry about him. How are *you*?"

"I'm okay."

"No, you're not."

No, I'm not.

"What's the matter?"

It was supposed to be with Whit. Not Sam.

"I'm just tired," Liv lies.

"How's the treasure hunting going?"

"It's . . . it's fine," Liv says, because she knows even to scratch the surface would cause her whole heart to break apart and she'd never get it closed again.

"Finding anything yet?"

The biggest treasure of all, Liv wants to say. The only one that ever mattered. So why does she wish she could give it back to the sea?

"Remember that man of yours promised me a gold necklace for my trouble," Mary says. "But you tell him I'll take silver—I'm not picky." Then she gives in to a big, deep cackle and Liv can't help smiling, even as tears leak out.

"Anything you want me to tell him, sugar?"

Liv smiles. "Tell him I used the shampoo," she whispers.

"Used the what, baby?"

She closes her eyes. "Just tell him I love him. And that I'll be back soon."

When she hangs up, she sets the phone down on the nightstand and stares at it a long moment before she picks it up again.

Let him worry. It'll do him good to think of someone besides himself for once.

She taps the screen and waits, so sure Whit will pick up.

When the voice mail message comes on, the sound of his voice makes her want to cry again.

"It's me," she whispers. "I took a little road trip to the Outer Banks to follow a lead. Mostly I just need some time away. Maybe we both do, Whit. All I know is it's very strange being here without you. And I can't decide what that means." She pulls at a loose thread in the blanket's hem and it gives easily. "I love you, but I don't know if it's enough anymore and . . ." She stops, releasing the thread before the whole length of edging comes loose. "Good night, love."

In the dark, she draws the sheet around her and waits for the call back, but the phone remains silent. Eventually sleep comes, even as a single thought drifts in and out of her early dreams:

She meant what she said to Sam tonight. The three of them had made a good team.

For a while, the best.

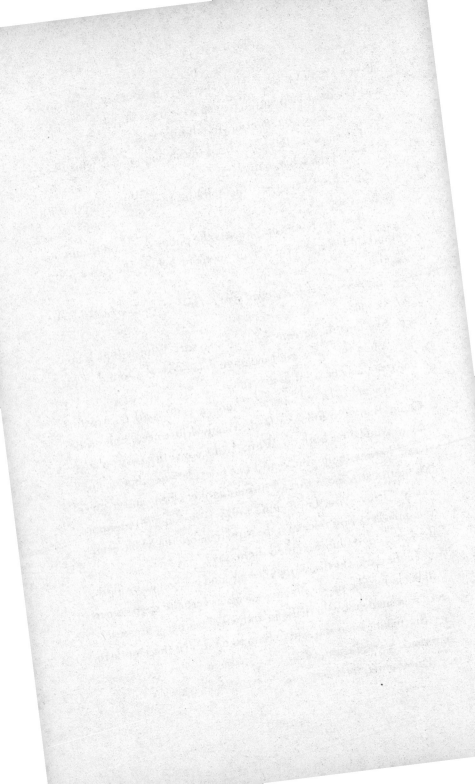

11

Twelve years earlier

"So, what do you think?"

Whit's eyes were wide with expectation while Liv and Sam surveyed the stretch of canvas that flapped wildly in the breeze, its four corners tethered to the boat's rail. The old-timey lettering was fitting for the name they'd settled on: FCC Treasure Tours, the initials to represent their last names.

"I thought we agreed no goofy decorations," Sam said, pointing to the four skulls and crossbones that grinned horrifically from each corner of the banner.

Whit shrugged. "I told the guy when I placed the order to keep it simple, but you know how it goes."

Liv could see Sam wasn't convinced, but it was too late now to quibble about clip art. Their first charter was scheduled for the following day and their signage had been two weeks late, a delay that had been the norm for their efforts. They'd arrived in Wilmington a month earlier to find the *Phoenix* had needed far more updates than expected. For the next two weeks, Whit had overseen the repairs while Liv had secured the paperwork and Sam the financial details, which quickly taxed the well of their loan. To help cover costs, they all found extra work. Sam and Whit took odd jobs at the marina and Liv waited tables in town. They'd rented a two-bedroom apartment with terrible water pressure but decent natural light, though they didn't make the best of roommates. Sam turned in early and rose early—Whit was a notorious night owl who rarely wandered downstairs before noon on his days home. Liv, equally enchanted by moonlight swims and sunrise breakfasts, always found herself somewhere in between.

Fortunately they existed far more harmoniously on the water. On the *Phoenix*, their oppositional habits worked in the business's favor—just as Whit had insisted they would when he'd proposed the idea. Since Whit was a natural salesman, he would organize the tours and act as dive captain. Sam, an expert sailor, would manage the boat and run the bridge. Liv would pitch in wherever she could.

"Well, I love it," Liv decided. "I think the pirate theme will help business. Get people in the mood. Make it look like we know what we're doing."

"Who says we don't know what we're doing, Red? That's just nerves talking."

"They're actually *yelling*." Liv smiled at Sam.

"I bet a celebratory pitcher at the taproom would shut them up," Whit said.

"I should really check on my dad first."

"You should," Sam said. "I'll take you."

Windswept Estates was neither of its names—its false advertising offended Liv every time she pulled into her father's run-down condominium complex just outside Wilmington. But the rent had been priced right, even if the décor was all wrong—a point her father had made repeatedly the entire time they moved his belongings off the U-Haul and into the one-bedroom ground-floor apartment. But what choice did she have? The two-hour commute to Greenville would have been impossible to endure on a regular basis, and given her father's increasing anxiety attacks, regular would have meant almost daily. While the combined income from his disability and the royalties from his textbook offered him a comfortable budget, real estate by the water was three times what it had been inland. Liv had taken him to over two dozen apartments before finally finding one he agreed—albeit cantankerously—to move into. There was a grocery store and a library nearby. He had cable and a stove that was easy to keep clean—not that he ever used it for fear of burning down the unit.

"You don't have to come in," Liv said as Sam turned off the truck. "I'll be quick."

She found her father at the sink, staring out the window at the parking lot. "He's just going to sit there?"

"He offered to come in. I told him it was fine if he didn't."

"Are you ashamed of me?"

She pulled in a sigh. "Of course not, Poppy."

"The ants are back. Nothing I do seems to help."

She glanced at the empty counter where he'd claimed there'd been an infestation the week before. "I don't see any."

"Of course not. They hide when they hear noise. I just swept up a whole bunch. It's the lady who moved in upstairs. She's a slob. She empties her pans over the railing. I find grease drippings on my deck. I've told the maintenance people, but they won't do anything."

Liv turned away, rolling her eyes. "We have our first customers tomorrow, Poppy." She knew he didn't approve, but she hoped he might at least congratulate her.

"You could still go back, you know. Get your degree. Do something meaningful. Classes haven't even started."

With every visit came the same reminder. She knew leaving school had been a hard pill for her father to swallow. "I will go back," she said. "Eventually. But these charters are meaningful to me, Poppy. They're everything."

"Nothing can be everything." His gaze remained fixed on the window. "Does he plan to marry you?"

"We've been so busy. All the preparation. Getting a new business off the ground is a full-time job. It hardly leaves any time."

"How much time does it take to ask someone to marry him?"

She lowered her eyes, feeling her neck flush at his point. She didn't want to admit that anytime the subject of marriage came up, Sam changed it, a habit that was growing harder and harder to dismiss.

"Maybe I'm not sure I want to be married, Poppy."

"People need to be married, Livy. It's too scary alone."

"You're alone."

"No, I'm not. I have you, don't I?"

She nodded and helped her father lay down another set of ant traps along the backsplash, leaving him with a kiss.

FCC Treasure Tours' first charter—two couples, both celebrating their twenty-fifth anniversaries—proved a startling success, and resulted in very satisfied customers who'd promised to recommend the adventure to all their friends. To celebrate, Whit suggested a feast of crab legs and beer. It was all so reminiscent of their initial meal together that Liv was sure Whit would suggest truth or dare when they cleared their plates, but he skipped out for a date with a woman named Honor instead (Sam had said there was a joke in that somewhere), leaving Sam and Liv to round out the day's success together on the balcony under a star-prickled sky.

"Be right back," Sam said, and Liv settled into her chair, marveling at the night and her good fortune at no emergency calls from her father on such a special evening. She wondered where she and Sam would make love, having the whole apartment to themselves, no doubt until morning. Whit's dates usually lasted all night, which wasn't to say their duration was any level of his commitment. For a while Liv had tried to keep up with Whit's ever-changing roster of lovers, the cavalry of women he burned through like matches, strangely curious to see which ones lasted longer, but the exercise became impossible, and really, why did she care so much?

"I was hoping he'd leave us alone tonight." Sam returned with a pair of flutes in one hand and a bottle of champagne in the other.

As he took his seat Liv searched his dark eyes, realizing there was something else in his hand besides the glasses, a shape colored the same shade of navy blue as the night sky, catching no reflection until he held it out. A flutter of possibility tore through her. To think, just the day before her father had asked if Sam planned to marry her, and she'd wallowed silently in her own distress over the subject. Now he was about to propose. Flickers of excitement raced across her scalp.

He handed her the box. "To new beginnings."

She had already imagined the ring even before she pushed up the velvet lid—the shape of the diamond, nothing too big; the band fine and delicate; a straightforward, simple design, no-nonsense, just like Sam—so clearly that it took her brain a moment to fully process the small anchor charm that shimmered up at her instead, and the V of thin, lacy gold chain that held it.

Aware of her stunned silence, she fixed a smile quickly on her face. "It's beautiful," she said, freeing the necklace carefully from its tiny clamps. And it was.

"You look disappointed."

"I'm not," she said, grateful for the dark to hide the heat of shame crawling up her cheeks. "No, really. I love it."

He sighed and put his hand over hers, finding her eyes and holding them. "One thing at a time, Liv. Let's get this business more than floating," he said. "Let's get it sailing."

She turned to let him secure the clasp beneath her lifted

hair. He was right to wait. But still his presentation crushed her, his choice of language impossible to ignore. One thing at a time. *Thing.* It was as if he couldn't even say the word *marriage.*

The first few months of their charter business passed quickly, despite the predictably quiet winter season that Curtis had warned them about. After too many rows over dirty dishes and music after midnight, Whit decided to move onto the boat, which meant Liv and Sam could find a smaller apartment, which they did, closer to the marina. By June, they were back on the water almost daily. Today's wannabe salvors were coming from Virginia Beach, so they had requested a noon dive—a plan that had pleased everyone. After weeks of five a.m. alarms, Liv was grateful to wake to a sunlit house. She reached up and slid the curtain back to scan the sky. Flawless blue. Another perfect day for treasure-hunting. She rolled over to find Sam's side of the bed empty and already cool to the touch. He never could sleep in.

The rich, nutty smell of espresso pulled her down the cottage's narrow corridor to the kitchen. Stopping in the bathroom, she glared at the cowlick that had sprung up in the night like a middle finger, but what did she expect? It had been over a year since she'd had a proper cut, and the length and mass of her hair continued to startle her—she'd never let it get this long.

Sunshine spilled into the kitchen, spraying golden streaks on the peeling linoleum floor and warming her bare feet on her way to the fridge. She poured herself a glass of orange juice and carried it into the living room, where their chart resided on the only wall in the small house that was big enough to hold it. Liv scanned the map lazily as she sipped the tart, frosty juice, thinking with a rumble of regret that it had been months since they'd had any leads to add—not that she resented the fact. How could she? FCC Treasure Tours had finally taken flight—and she and Sam had little free time to continue their research, never mind time for each other. Days began early and finished late. But ten months on the *Phoenix* and Liv considered herself an able crew member topside and a strong diver up to fifty feet below.

The balcony slider opened and Sam stepped in, shirtless and smelling of sand. Almost two years after they'd moved in together, she still loved the sight of him in the morning.

"Make you a cappuccino?"

She stepped aside to let him at the espresso machine that occupied nearly half of the galley kitchen's short counter.

"So, what's the story with today's group?" she asked.

"Insurance reps here for a conference. Two guys and a woman." He shot her a knowing look as he snapped the filter into place. "One guess who Whit'll buddy up with."

Liv smiled. "We do what we can to keep him around."

Every few months, Whit would talk about leaving for far-flung seas, offers of jobs on giant salvage vessels headed for Australia and beyond, but his grand plans would always crumble at the last minute. "He's never pulling out," Sam would always say. "We'll leave this business before he does."

Not that they had any plans to do so. They'd made enough

money to hire two deckhands for larger groups, even taking on overnight trips. Liv almost always stayed behind, fearful of being away from her father, whose demands were growing increasingly impossible for her to manage. She'd grown used to the fits of paranoia—but lately he'd been forgetting things, finding himself disoriented, even in his apartment. His own father had suffered from Alzheimer's—it had never been far from her mind, nor had her promise to not put him in a home. But the other day, waiting for him at his doctor's appointment, she'd picked up a brochure on a nearby assisted-living facility called Sunset Hills and felt equal parts relief and guilt as she'd fingered the glossy pamphlet, the pictures of smiling residents waving over their flower boxes. The exhaustive list of activities: yoga, trivia, and, for the very ambitious, glass blowing! What would her father do with any of it?

She finished her cappuccino, wiping the side of the mug with her index finger to catch the last sweet streaks of foamed milk.

Sam leaned over and she fed him her catch. He sucked her finger clean.

"We better get to the boat," he said.

Their three clients were already there when Sam and Liv pulled into the marina's parking lot at eleven. The two men, Frank and Doug, looked to be in their forties, both well tanned but slightly soft. The woman, Shannon, at least ten years younger than her male partners, was trim and pretty, shiny brown hair melting down her back like hot fudge. No wonder Whit had been grinning like a clown when Liv boarded the boat.

While the customers suited up, Sam, Whit, and Liv gathered at the bridge and bent their heads over the chart.

"They want to go deep," Sam said, running his finger up and down one of their most popular channels.

"That stretch is pretty well picked over," said Whit, "but it's an easy dive. Thirty feet max."

"Which is why I think we should try here." Liv watched Sam's finger drift to the right, the sounding's depth well beneath her cutoff for safe diving.

She swallowed her disappointment.

"Next one, Liv," Sam said. "I promise."

A half hour later, they were anchored and taking their giant strides off the platform.

The only one to find anything worth bringing up was Shannon. Out of her wet suit and touring the boat in a turquoise bikini and sunglasses, she rushed to show off her treasure: a musket ball. "Is it valuable?"

Liv smiled, remembering when Lou had handed her the concretion on her first treasure hunt, the key Whit had unearthed for her, and that she still kept in her purse for luck.

Surely she'd worn that same hopeful expression too.

"Whit saw some timbers," Shannon said. "They looked big to me."

Headed back to the marina, Liv found Whit on the flybridge with a beer, his wet suit unzipped, the top wrapped around his waist, his tanned chest bare. Some days the golden color of his skin made her feel deeply self-conscious, as if she'd walked in on him in the shower or in bed.

Today was one of those days.

"How'd they do down there?" she asked cheerfully, feigning interest in a passing pelican.

"Not bad. A hell of a lot better than those investment bankers who came through last week."

"Shannon certainly enjoyed her time with you."

Whit grinned. "Don't be a troublemaker. You know I never mix business with pleasure."

"She said you found some ribs."

Whit's mouth slid into a knowing smile. "I knew you didn't come over to talk about our customers." Liv suspected the hope was bald on her face. Any mention of found timbers and her heart galloped with possibility that it might be the wreckage of the *Patriot*.

She stared expectantly at Whit, waiting for him to confirm her excitement as he took a long swig. "And?" she said.

He swallowed. "It's not her."

"How can you be sure? Ribs could mean—"

"They were small, Red. Too small."

"Oh." The bloom of hope in her belly deflated. She smiled ruefully. "You know Sam would freak if he saw you drinking that with clients on board."

"Then you better help me finish it so we can get rid of the evidence." He held out the can.

She came beside him and took a small sip. "She's still all I think about, you know. Every time we go down, every time we check a chart. My brain knows the ship probably didn't sink this far south, but my heart can't help thinking, What if?"

"Storms and currents have been known to spread wreckage out over tens of miles," Whit said. "But I know what you mean." He gave her thigh a tender pat. "I still want to find her too, Red."

The heat of his palm startled her. She handed the can back, so quickly it knocked against his arm and sprayed a few beads of beer on his wrist.

They looked out at the water a moment in silence.

"I heard you and Sam talking about moving your dad," Whit said.

"I don't know, Whit. I promised him I'd never put him in a place like that."

"We can't always keep our promises, Red. We do the best we can at the time. But you can't beat yourself up over something you can't control."

Couldn't she? Sunset Hills. God. Just the name evoked dreadful images. Herds of elderly people marching down life's final slope. Vultures circling.

She closed her eyes.

"It's not wrong of you to want to have a life." Whit leaned against her shoulder and gave her a gentle push. His bare skin was still cool from the water. A charge plunged deep down her stomach and she stood, feeling suddenly guilty, afraid Sam might find them there.

"I should check on the group," she said.

"Livy?"

On her way to the ladder, she stopped and turned, startled to hear him call her something other than his favorite nickname.

He grinned. "If it ever gets too bad, you can always run away with me."

"Very funny," she said.

Three hours later, home and showered, Liv made a twist of her wet hair and padded downstairs through a tangy cloud of ginger and lemon to find Sam at the counter mixing up a marinade with Jack Johnson's smooth, upbeat voice on the CD player.

She had just poured herself a glass of red when her cell rang.

"Ma'am, this is Officer Cook with the Greenville Police."

Liv set down her wine, watching Sam at the stove.

"We picked your father up in town and we're holding him here at the station."

She swallowed. "Of course," she said evenly, quickly. "I'll be right there."

"Everything okay?" Sam asked without turning, and Liv was grateful he couldn't see the panicked flush that had surely spread across her face.

"It was one of the maintenance guys from the condo," she said, already reaching for her purse. "They want to inspect the fuse box."

"At this hour?" Sam wiped his hands on a dish towel. "Give me a second to clean up and I'll come with you."

"No," she said, so forcefully that he looked startled. "Really, stay. My dad just wants some company. I'm sure it's nothing."

But it wasn't nothing, of course. And her legs felt boneless as she pushed her feet into her flip-flops and hurried out the door.

"Someone called from their car. He was walking up and down the median." A woman with a graying ponytail handed Liv a clipboard and a pen. "Sign on the *X*'s for me and you can take him home."

Liv forced her eyes off the man in the plastic chair long enough to scribble her name. It was like seeing a stranger. There was no way this person, head bent and body hunched under a blanket, was Francis Connelly. Her father.

"If you need help, there are people you can call." The woman returned with a packet of pamphlets and gave them to Liv. "It's not easy, hon. Don't be afraid to reach out." Her smile was patient and kind. How to explain that it wasn't the reaching out Liv feared. Only the ease with which she worried she would be able to do so.

The air in the car was stifling, choked with remorse and dread.

Liv sent her window down all the way, afraid she'd be sick if she didn't fill her lungs with something fresher.

Her father rubbed his knees, as if he were working out invisible stains. "I tried to explain to them that I just got confused, Livy. They changed the front of the store and it just got me all mixed up. Everyone gets turned around in the dark. I really don't see why they had to bring me in there. Had to bring *you* there. It was just so unnecessary."

She pulled into the parking lot of his condo and turned off the car. The terrible truth of what was coming next hung between them, the knowledge that the night's event had brought them to a place they could never go back from.

Her father released his seat belt but didn't move to get out.

He stared out the windshield at his front door. "I'm scared, Livy."

"Me too, Poppy."

She chewed the side of her cheek, trying to stem the tears that had been threatening since the woman with the clipboard gave her that motherly smile. Reaching across the seat, she found his hand still gripping his knee, his thin fingers bent and ice-cold.

She took the long way home, skirting the town limits for almost a half hour to let her red eyes return to their normal shade. She'd called Sam to say the maintenance men had been late getting there, and that she'd had to take her father to the grocery store. Telling him the truth, then or earlier, seemed too overwhelming. Confessions made things real, and there was still so much about her life with her father that she feared making real to Sam. If Whit had been there, she'd have spilled all her secrets from the start, cried herself dry and probably even managed to laugh somewhere in the middle of it all.

Maybe, she thought, she still could. She just needed a few more minutes to pull herself together, to spare Sam the burden of her messy life tonight before she had to expose him in the morning.

The marina was still with its usual evening hush as she swung into the parking lot and hurried down the steps to the dock, praying the wind off the water would soothe her swollen eyes. The *Phoenix* was silent as she climbed aboard. Maybe Whit had gone out? She hoped not. She needed his company just now, needed his carefree laughter to fortify her.

"If it ever gets too bad, you can always run away with me. . . ."

She toured the deck and found an opened bottle of wine on the hatch. She could use a swig, she thought, reaching down to pick up the bottle, but her hand slowed when she counted two glasses beside it. Stepping back, she stumbled and turned to see her obstruction: a strappy heel, its mate kicked off a few feet away.

The skin under her ponytail prickled, every hair snapping to attention.

When she heard the creak of movement below, she bolted. Tearing across the parking lot of the marina, she hoped Whit hadn't come up to search the deck for an intruder, prayed he didn't see her disappearing into her car when he didn't find one.

The house was dark when she finally climbed the steps, Sam already in bed. She undressed, letting her clothes fall to the floor, and crawled in beside him, rolling against his back. Her eyes closed, she tried to focus on the rhythm of his breathing, willing her thoughts to quiet, but her mind swam with fear and confusion, flashes of anguished images:

her father wandering the median like a lost dog. How it hurt to see him behind glass as if he were a suspect in a terrible crime. The knot in her stomach when she'd discovered Whit wasn't alone, shame that she'd gone to see him at all. Just that morning, her head and heart had been at peace; any complications in her life manageable, familiar. Now nothing made sense. She longed for sleep to wash it all away.

In the morning she'd explain everything to Sam, the awful truth that she would have to call Sunset Hills and hope they had room for her father right away, but for now she wanted just one more night to pretend that everything was as it was, as it should have been.

Everything and everyone.

Was that asking too much?

Apparently. After three interminable months of chased phone calls, canceled checks, and lost paperwork, Liv was finally able to secure a room at Sunset Hills. At the recommendation of the facility's caregivers, Liv took her father out for breakfast while Sam and Whit helped a pair of movers pack up his apartment. Watching her father inspect his fruit salad, checking every blueberry and every cube of cantaloupe for mold, Liv told herself that he had never liked living in Windswept Estates, that she was doing the best thing for him. That he'd be safe at Sunset Hills, and after all, wasn't that what mattered most?

But for all her preparation, delivering her father to his new home proved agonizing, though not in the way she'd imagined.

She'd expected his hostility, even steeled herself for violence—cursing, lashing out. But his surrender came without any fight at all. From the moment he stepped through the automated glass doors, Liv could feel his body shedding opposition like old skin. His shoulders rolled forward, his steps, once staccato and sure, slipped into whispering shuffles. He toured his room with dull eyes, saying nothing. Liv knew Sam was waiting for her in the parking lot, but she couldn't bear to leave him. Finally his nurse, a woman with a beautiful high knot of tiny black braids, took Liv's hand in hers and gently led her to the door. "Tomorrow will be better, sugar. Every day it gets better. You'll see."

Liv nodded, too afraid if she opened her mouth a sob would come out instead of words. She held back her tears all the way to the front doors, squeezing through them when they wouldn't part fast enough, gasping for air like someone nearly drowned.

"You did the right thing, Liv," Sam said to her a week later. They had come downtown to play tourists on their day off, walking the river and ordering overpriced drinks and oversize bowls of she-crab soup.

"Then why does it feel so awful?" she said, making lazy figure eights through the creamy broth with her spoon.

"Because sometimes the right things do. It's just how it is." He checked his watch. "We should get back to the marina and make sure everything's set for tomorrow."

Liv pushed her bowl to the side. "I want to dive with the group tomorrow."

Sam shook his head. "Absolutely not. It's going to be deep water."

"A hundred feet, I know. I have to push it eventually."

"Says who?"

"I want to challenge myself."

"This isn't learning the piano, Liv. There's challenge and then there's dumb risk. I know you're upset about your dad, but—"

"This has nothing to do with my father. I've been diving for almost two years now, and in all that time I haven't had a single episode. Not one."

"Because you've stayed shallow," Sam said.

"Whit thinks there's something down there."

"Ah." Sam sat back and folded his arms. "So that's what this is about."

"He didn't tell you?"

"He was too busy telling me all about Australia, the lucky son of a bitch." Sam took a beat while he wiped his mouth and tossed his napkin into his empty bowl.

Liv felt the unmistakable creep of dread. "Australia?"

"He took that job with Wes in Sydney. You didn't know?"

She swallowed. "But—when did this all happen?"

He shrugged. "You know Whit. One day he's in. Next day's he's out. You done?"

She nodded, giving him her trash, her movements stilted with shock. How could Sam be so calm about this? Liv knew he and Whit had never been best friends, but surely Sam felt something akin to remorse to be losing him?

There was something else underneath her surprise too. Hurt. Crisp and cutting and hard.

"He didn't say a word," she admitted quietly as they walked back outside.

"It's not the best timing, but we'll figure it out. I've already talked to Bo and Tony about coming on full-time."

The deckhands they'd recently hired. Liv forced her mind to focus on the logistics of this news—the impact to the business and not the impact to her heart. But the truth was undeniable, as impossible to swallow as the remainder of her meal. Three years since he'd first forced his way into their conversation at that party, Liv couldn't imagine their work, their *life,* without Whit Crosby.

All evening, she kept her phone close by her side, sure that Whit would call her himself to tell her his news, but he never did. When she arrived on the boat the next morning, she believed he'd confess his grand plan with mournful eyes and a heavy heart, but two hours into their tour—college roommates in town for their twentieth reunion—he'd barely said hello to her, let alone *I'm leaving.*

After bringing the customers a snack of granola bars and sodas, Liv found Whit alone on the upper deck, finishing his cigarette.

"Good dive, huh?" he said.

"Not bad."

"Sam said your dad's all settled in his new place."

Was that honestly what he wanted to talk about?

She nodded stiffly. "*Settled* is not exactly the right word. He's there. I'm not sure he'll ever be settled." She glanced at him. "But then you probably know all about that."

She hadn't meant her tone to be so sharp, so accusatory, but there it was.

Whit stared at her, his eyes flashing with confusion.

She threw out her hands. "Were you just going to leave in the night without a word? Was that your plan?"

"Of course not."

"What, then?"

"I just figured Sam would tell you."

"You didn't think I'd want to hear it from you?" She turned away from him before the tears could spill over. Dammit, she'd vowed not to cry.

"Red . . ." He reached for her arm, but she yanked it out of reach, wiping her eyes roughly on her sleeve.

"First my dad, now you—everything's changing too fast." She turned back to face him, her eyes filling again. "You could have at least waited a few more days so I didn't have to say good-bye to both of you in the same week, you know. Selfish jerk."

He smiled patiently. "It's just Australia, Red. Not Mars."

But it might as well have been another planet, and they both knew it.

Whit rubbed out his cigarette on the edge of a soda can and dropped it in.

"You really need to quit those," Liv said, sniffling.

"When the right woman comes along to quit smoking for, I will."

"You could quit for *yourself*, you know."

He grinned. "Then I'd have to quit today. If I wait for the right woman, I might never have to."

She rolled her eyes, but when he reached out to grab her a

second time, she didn't fight his capture. The smoky, salty scent of his wet suit and his skin beneath it were familiar and comforting.

"You still have that key I dug out for you?" he asked.

She nodded against his chest.

"Good, then you'll have something to remember me by."

"You're not exactly forgettable, you know," she said, slipping free to wipe her cheeks again.

He smiled. "I hope not."

"Can't you at least stay until the fall?" She looked up at him. "We're getting closer, I can feel it. I bet we find her in the next three months."

"It's not just that, Red."

"What, then?"

"I *have* to go."

"Why?"

He touched her cheek. "Because I'm not a good loser, that's why."

She watched him as he climbed down the ladder and disappeared under the bridge, her face hot where he'd brushed his fingers against her damp skin.

What did he mean, not a good loser? They hadn't lost anything yet.

Their last day on the water with Whit was sunny and cloudless. The three of them guided a newly married couple over a stretch of water with several sunken trawlers and put on a show of great admiration when the husband surfaced with a broken bottle neck that looked thick enough to be over a hundred years old.

Returning to the marina seemed to happen too quickly. Liv wished they might have chartered to a place farther out, maybe even run out of gas or gotten lost. She'd barely had time to soak up the sight of Whit one last time at the bridge, his rumpled hair caught in the wind, his crooked smile and equally crooked dimples, his exploding laugh. With just a two-person tour, there wasn't much cleanup to do. At the last minute, Liv decided the galley needed a thorough cleaning, despite its shining surfaces, its spotless fridge shelves. Anything to stave off the night's inevitable good-bye.

Sam suggested a toast at the taproom to send Whit off properly, but Whit declined, claiming he had far too much packing left to do, which Liv knew was an excuse to avoid a drawn-out farewell—Whit Crosby prided himself on being the sort of man whose entire life could be contained in a paper bag—and neither she nor Sam pressed him. "Be good," Whit whispered into Liv's ear just before he released her from an embrace and she nodded, unable to speak over the knot of tears in her throat.

Instead of going out, she and Sam stopped off at the store on their way home, bought a bottle of red, and drank it on their balcony. The night seemed especially still. Even the usual flutter of insects and rustling palm leaves was silent.

Everything, everywhere, would be so much quieter now.

Sam lifted his face to the sky, his forehead silvery in the night. Polished like stone. A fair comparison, she thought. Nearly three years with him and she still couldn't read his thoughts when she needed to most.

He turned his head toward her. "You okay?"

She smiled thinly. "I guess."

"You did the right thing moving him in there, Liv."

She frowned, startled. "I'm not thinking about my father."

"What, then?"

He had to ask?

"Whit," she said.

"I know. It's definitely going to be hard without a third person."

"That's not what I meant." She reached over and feathered her fingertips across his hand, hoping to soften his knitted brow. "Can't you admit you'll miss him?"

"It is what it is, Liv. People leave, life goes on." Sam took up their glasses and the bottle, not yet empty, and rose. "Coming in?"

"In a minute," she said, not sure her legs would hold if she were to stand just then. His lack of emotion alarmed her. It was as if Whit had been gone from their life for years and not just hours. His eyes had been so cold—chilly enough to send a flicker of fear across her neck. For a terrible instant, he'd been a stranger.

"People aren't always who you think they are, sweetie."

Her mother's words pierced the night—but Liv blinked them away, unwanted words that she was sure didn't apply. They couldn't possibly.

12

OUTER BANKS, NORTH CAROLINA

Thursday

When Whit was in seventh grade, nearly a foot taller than all the other boys in his class, and barely shorter than their gym teacher, Mr. Collins, he met Jimmy Parsons.

Before Jimmy Parsons, it had never occurred to Whit to envy a boy for having a father. He'd envied Ronald Crispin, whose father had left town with another woman when Ronald was three. And Joey Rogers, because his father was serving time for selling drugs. But to envy someone because his father had stuck around was unfamiliar territory. That Jimmy's father came to the table for dinner seemed unimaginable to Whit—that he came sober and agreeable was nothing short of miraculous. When Jimmy reported a poor grade on a test, Mr. Parsons chewed on the news quietly, then moved briskly to a different subject. When Whit joined Jimmy after school, Whit was stunned to see that it was possible for a boy to come inside and confess to a quiet day. That a boy could mount the front steps with visions of what he might do with the rest of his afternoon, not burdened with the panicked fabrication of adventures suited to gangsters, not twelve-year-old boys.

Most incredibly the Parsons told the truth. There was no shame in an unremarkable day. Honesty came with its own rewards.

Then there were Jimmy's four sisters. All older, they possessed an otherworldly beauty that Whit studied with an anthropologist's feverish devotion every chance he got. But it was Colleen—Collie—the middle daughter, who fascinated him most of all, with her quiet, confident beauty, her lack of interest in wild things. If the Parsonses preached the power of truth, he'd gladly join their flock. Pushed to the limit by his infatuation, he'd declared his love for Collie just minutes before Buddy Jones was due to pick her up for prom. She rewarded his honesty with a wet kiss, then flattened his heart when she climbed into Buddy's Mustang five minutes later. Two months afterward, Mr. Parsons took a new job in Birmingham and the family was gone in a week. Whit lost his virginity to a junior named Jennifer in her parents' game room a month later, three days after his fourteenth birthday. So much for honesty.

When Whit saw Liv Connelly twelve years later in the archives, the curtain of her red hair brushing the book in her lap, his heart had rumbled with interest. When he watched her stand up to take on Harold Warner with all the confidence and pluck of a rabbit staring down a wolf, he was sure someone had reached in and squeezed the air out of his lungs. Soon he was envisioning how he could win her, the million perfect ways he could impress her. She was nothing like the women he was used to pursuing—women accustomed to being adored, who spent too much time on their bodies and not nearly enough on their opinions of the world around them. Women who were interested in him for his looks and wild reputation, and because they were hoping to piss off their fathers—but they didn't know his heart, and they didn't care to.

But not Liv. Any woman who could go toe-to-toe with someone as insufferable as Harold Warner and come out smiling would make the world a worthwhile place, a better place, Whit was sure of it.

Liv became his measure of what made sense even before he knew her, proof that maybe he wasn't entirely undeserving of good things, of love. The unconditional and unfailing kind. The kind of love that wasn't a sport, that didn't require lies to be won.

And now here he is, digging himself out of a hole of lies.

He only wanted to get them back on track, only wanted to reassure her. And now—

"I love you, but I don't know if it's enough anymore."

He leans back in the driver's seat and rubs his forehead hard, Liv's voice mail on a constant loop. He must have listened to the message a dozen times.

Squinting through the windshield at the reddish brown town house that looks almost pink in the electric light of dawn, Whit double-checks the number on the door against the number he's found online, then takes another glance at the street sign to his left. The GPS says this is Beth Henson's place—so what is he waiting for? There's one car in the driveway—what if it belongs to a husband, a boyfriend? Someone who will threaten to call the police if he doesn't leave? A chance he has to take. The first threads of sunrise creep up the horizon. Soon the blue fog of dark will disperse, exposing him in this quiet development.

He catches himself in the rearview and winces at the deep crease gouged between his eyes. Jesus, when did he get so old?

Out of the van, he looks around as he crosses the visitors' parking lot, unnerved by the lack of movement around. The row of condominiums is so quiet he can hear the whir of an air-conditioning unit click to life, the crackle of night birds in the manicured bay trees that fence the path.

When he knocks on Beth Henson's door, the sound is like a gunshot. He hunches his shoulders and tries to step out of the light. The door opens a crack—a sleep-swollen eye and a sliver of creamy cheek peer back at him.

He leans in. "Beth, I don't know if you remember me. We went to school together at ECU. I'm Whit Cr—"

"I know who you are." The door opens a crack more, enough that he can see her sour expression. "You do realize what time it is, don't you?"

"I know—and I'm sorry."

"They're not here," she says flatly.

"But they were."

"I'm not getting involved, Whit." She considers him more harshly now, looks him up and down. "Are you drunk?"

"I wish." He can feel his smile waning. He leans against the jamb, too tired to support himself. "Can I talk to you?"

"I told you they're not here. I'll be at my office at the museum at nine. You can come by then."

She moves to close the door, but Whit puts his hand out. "Just five minutes—" He catches her eyes and holds them. "*Please.*"

After another long moment, she sighs and steps back to let him in. "Five minutes."

He scans the small foyer, his mind spinning away from him again. Everything he sees—the stairs, the white table with the basket of catalogues, the watercolor of a reclining woman—he wonders if Liv has seen too. He's just crazy and tired enough to imagine he could sniff hard, like a wild animal, and pick up her scent if he wanted to. And God, he wants to.

He's sure Beth will point them to the living room that he can see through the archway, but she shows no signs of moving them from this spot. He wonders why she even bothered letting him in.

"I don't suppose you have any coffee?" he asks.

She clutches her robe closed with folded arms. "I don't drink coffee."

"Beer's fine too." He waits for her steely expression to soften the tiniest bit, but it won't. "That was a joke," he says.

"What is it you want, Whit?"

How long does she have? He wants to fix everything he's ever screwed up in his whole damn life. He wants to find a time machine. He wants the do-over of all do-overs.

He wants his wife back. "I just really need to know where they went."

Beth looks at him coolly. He'll have to work on her. Like a shoe that has to be worn in to avoid getting blisters. "Maybe you should try calling her, then," she says.

"I have. She won't answer."

Beth glances at the clock on the entry table. Whit's sure his time is up, but he's not leaving yet. He drags a hand across the back of his neck, feeling the grit of sand and sweat. What he wouldn't give for a shower.

"Livy said she came here because you had a lead—a lead for what?" he says.

"She didn't tell you?"

Of course. He's an idiot. "It was about Theodosia, wasn't it?"

"We found a diary," Beth says. "An old logbook Theodosia used to write in while she was being held for ransom."

Ransom? "Jesus," Whit whispers. "Holy shit." He swallows hard, taking it all in. "Can I see it?"

"It's not here," Beth says. "It's at the museum."

"But I really need to read it."

"I'm afraid that's not possible. We're having a press conference in the morning to announce its acquisition."

"Then can you at least tell me what it said?"

Does she honestly think he drove three hours, on the heels of the four he already clocked today, to leave here without answers?

He moves toward her, abruptly enough to force her back a step.

"It was supposed to be me and her, Beth. It was our mystery, do you understand? Ours."

But she doesn't understand. And now Liv knows the truth, and he wasn't here.

Sam was.

Whit drops down to her stairs, laces his hands over his knees. "How did they seem?"

She squints at him, and for a moment Whit isn't sure she will indulge a question like this. And why should she? She's already told him she doesn't want to get involved. And yet, damp and hot and unholy smelling as he is, Whit can remember that she had liked Sam, maybe even still did. And maybe she's pissed at him, Whit, because if he hadn't blown it with Liv, then Sam might have come here alone. And maybe he'd even be up in her bed right now. And she'd be up there with him, instead of talking to a crazy old classmate at the foot of her stairs.

Beth sweeps her hair behind her ears. "He still has feelings for her, if that's what you're asking. It's painfully obvious."

Dread tumbles behind his ribs. "I know."

"You know, and yet you left them alone together?"

Whit glances up at her. "Sam told me he was leaving."

"I see."

Her assessment is without judgment, as if she too wishes she could turn back time for a while. Whit considers her as she looks at the clock. Daylight is coming faster now, slipping through the sidelights that flank the door and frosting everything in its path with silver, including Beth.

She's prettier than he remembered. Not so harsh and aloof.

She moves to the door and turns the knob. "You really have to go."

"You were hoping he was coming to see you, weren't you?" Whit says. "Not the diary—but you."

Beth turns to him.

"I know what it's like to want a second chance with someone," he says. "To tell them what you couldn't say the first time around."

"I don't see how my personal life is any of your business."

"It isn't," Whit says.

Her features slowly soften with surrender, and maybe even sympathy.

She sighs and closes the door. "I have digital files of the pages on my computer. I'll bring them up on the screen and you can read them that way, but only if you promise not to let anyone know what they say. We aren't sharing the entries with the press yet. We'll unveil them at an upcoming exhibit." She locks a hard look on him. "Can you give me your word?"

Whit considers her offer, and he imagines they are both thinking the same thing: that her request is a foolish one, that once, not so long ago, his word meant nothing.

But today he needs it to mean everything. "I promise," he says.

What Sam first imagined of his parents' marriage was probably no different than what any kid might. Their brief exchanges, short but consistent demonstrations of affection, division of labor and household responsibilities, all mirrored the structure of the other unions he observed around him. His neighbor Felix Cranston was the first person he knew to have his parents divorce, which seemed perplexing, considering that the Cranstons behaved just like Sam's parents, serving up the perfect cocktail of tolerance and indifference. "My dad said my mom got bored and stayed that way," was Felix's explanation when Sam raised the subject in the lunchroom. After that, Sam watched his own parents with fresh scrutiny, deciding that the comfort he'd observed previously between them was actually disdain. At parties, he began to notice his mother's fondness for wine, how she emptied glasses one after another while his father nursed a single splash of liquor for hours. Even the shoe salesman who fitted Sam and Michael for sneakers earned admiring glances. What did his mother have to be bored about? Sam would wonder. Didn't his father provide all she could need? Maybe if she ate more and drank less. Maybe if she didn't care so much about making the college boys at the supermarket laugh at her jokes when they bagged her groceries.

After watching an eager waiter whisper in his mother's ear while Sam's father was in the men's room, Sam considered blowing the whistle on the ride home. Michael pleaded with him not to. "You don't know what a tyrant he is to her. You think it's so easy to please him?" It was, Sam knew, having pleased his father from the time he was old enough to cast a fly rod expertly into a pond. Sam wasn't going to apologize for appreciating order and dependability, and he sure as hell wasn't going to excuse Michael or his mother's fervent need to ignore it. Rules may have been tedious and even boring, but they kept life certain and intact. Pretending otherwise was inviting a chaos wholly deserved.

Lying in the darkness now, Sam can't stop thinking about Liv. A few times tonight he's considered getting out of bed and walking to her door. He knows if he knocks, she'd invite him in. When he kissed her—something he'd been planning for some time—and felt her mouth melt under his, he knew. So why hasn't he thrown off this damp sheet and marched over there already?

Because he's patient. Something Whit never was.

Unlike Whit, Sam knows the value in control and endurance. Thanks to endurance, Sam has delivered Liv the answer she has waited most of her life for. Thanks to control, he kept his cool while all the rest of the crew flew off in a rage, while Whit himself tore off on the taxi boat, hell-bent to save his own skin. Just as he had done the night at Zephyr's when Whit promised them all a feast to celebrate and failed to deliver. It was Sam who'd calmly rerouted their evening, Sam who'd given Greta a way to sort out her hurt when he ran into her at the corner market after dropping off Liv. Leaning against the cooler, Greta told him she was tired of Whit's shit and Sam bought them a six-pack. They drained four cans in his truck before he walked her into her apartment. In the entryway, she swung around and looked at him, as if she worried there was still a chance he wasn't staying, as if he hadn't already made up his mind to take her to bed when he saw her in the store, tapping her lips as she considered the spread of liter bottles. "It just sucks that the good guys are always taken," she said; then he'd freed the last can from her hand, still dangling in its plastic necklace, and kissed her hard.

His phone chimes and Sam's sure it's Liv, but it's just a text from Michael, complaining about their mother and can he call the insurance agent about the roof?

Jesus.

Sam tosses his phone on the nightstand and falls back onto the mattress, training his eyes on the beams of headlights that slide across the ceiling every few minutes. So much traffic. Where is everyone going at this hour? Are they like him? Trying to turn back time, contemplating ruining marriages by dawn?

Tomorrow he will drive Liv to the house in Hatteras, the place where he first held her heart in his hands. He has no doubt that when she sees the cottage, whatever uncertainty she's been fighting since they left Topsail will float away and she'll surrender to him again. She'll confess what he's been hoping to hear: that she's sorry she chose Whit. That she misses the order of him, Sam, the boundaries of rules.

This certainty is what keeps him in this room—when every ounce of him wants to step out into the night and knock on her door, wants to break her down, break her apart, just to be the one to put her back together.

Every few hours, Liv wakes in the blackness, sure Whit is standing in the doorway, dripping wet, that he's found her, that he wants to crawl into bed with her like any other night, but when she scans the dark, the door is closed, the room is hushed, and she feels alternately swells of relief and deep disappointment. How she hates the uncertainty of night, how nothing makes sense in the dark—even things that light can easily assign logic to. After her mother died, Liv remembered her father coming into her bedroom and sitting at the foot of her bed for hours, leaning in to make sure she was breathing. Sometimes in her dreams she is still afraid her lungs will forget how to work.

The digital clock by the bed shines. Five thirty-five. No point in trying to get back to sleep now.

She tugs the blanket free from the bed, wraps it around herself, and steps outside. The concrete deck is damp and prickly with sand, so she settles into a plastic chair and draws her knees to her chest to cover her bare feet. Warm now, she can savor the faint chill in the air as she watches slivers of pink and copper cut through the horizon, slices of brilliant color signaling a day she has never known before, a day she can never get back.

Every dawn is a finger without a print.

The memory of the diary floods her, the shock and disappointment raw again. She'd been so sure in the morning she'd feel relief, closure. Absolution.

"You're entitled to celebrate this. We both are."

She glances down the row of doors, wondering who sleeps behind each one. Have they, like her, come here and unraveled in the night?

Sam kissed her.

The recollection returns with fresh shock. And she'd stood there, stunned and numb, as if she'd approved. Had she?

A tremor of guilt sends gooseflesh up her arms. She pulls the blanket tighter.

"Still worried it was all a dream?"

She turns to find Sam walking down the deck toward her, his dark eyes slightly puffy from sleep.

It takes her a second, but then she blinks at his bare face. "You shaved."

"So I did." He drags a hand along each side of his clean jaw, testing the smooth flesh.

The change unsettles her. Now he looks like the old Sam, the Sam she used to wake up next to, the Sam she used to love.

He takes the other plastic chair beside her door and drags it next to hers. "I know the mattresses are uncomfortable, but please tell me you didn't sleep out here."

She laughs. "No, but maybe I should have. Maybe I wouldn't have had such awful nightmares."

"Did you call Whit?" Sam asks.

"I tried. . . . I got his voice mail."

He leans back, the molded plastic creaking with his weight, and squints out at the horizon. "We can go back, Liv."

Back where? she wants to ask. *Back to my husband? Or back to the past?* She searches Sam's profile, seeking her answer, but his eyes just burn out at the view. Maybe he isn't sure which either.

And suddenly she's crying. The kind of tears that spring up too quickly to be swallowed or blinked away, and she is wholly unprepared for how to contain them, so she doesn't. What's the point? These tears have been patient—God knows how long she's made them wait to surface.

She stands and moves to the edge of the deck, tempted to rush down the steps, to run to the water and fling herself into those cold, unforgiving waves to snap herself out of whatever strange world she's fallen into.

"I'm sorry." She covers her face with her hands. "I just didn't expect this."

"Which part?"

"All of it. This mess with the *Siren*. Us back here together. And the diary. That I would ever find out the truth. I'd just given up and maybe that was better."

Sam's risen too; Liv can feel the heat of him behind her, closing in.

She wipes her eyes with her fingers. "And I know I'm supposed to feel this huge wave of relief because I finally know what happened to her, because it can be over and I can stop searching. But all I feel is lost."

Now he comes around to face her. His palm slides under her hair and cups her face, turning her toward him, and she doesn't resist.

"I don't know what I'm doing here," she says, meeting his eyes. "I don't know what I'm *doing*."

Sam makes two swipes with his thumb to dry her cheeks. "Then let me take you somewhere where you will."

13

Nine years earlier

Liv raised her coffee to her lips and scanned the view of the living room. The first time she'd entered this apartment, Sam assured her they'd be moved out in six months, a year at most. Three years later, it was home.

The wall chart looked noticeably fuller, new notes having been added through the winter, their continuing search efforts no longer shuffled to the back of their to-do list. They'd traveled north in February to New Jersey to visit the Hermitage Museum where Aaron Burr had married Theo's mother, Theodosia Prevost, in 1782, then to the New-York Historical Society, where they'd read through letters and deeds. Liv had returned with renewed confidence in their search. In all, it had been a productive winter, the low season in their business. Quieter months used for much-needed repairs and planning, filing paperwork that was always shelved in the swirl of their busy summer schedules—a sluggishness only tolerable thanks to Sam's added hours at the marina and Liv's at the restaurant.

But now summer was nearly here, and her bones shivered with excitement. Back to the water, back to the freedom of diving. The day's mail sat on the counter, fanned out where she'd left it, too thrilled to find one of Whit's postcards in the pile to bother with bills or bulletins. His hopeless handwriting scrawled across most of the blank space, bleeding over into the address box. It was always a miracle the cards ever arrived. They'd received the first one two months after Whit left for Australia, and then one every month after that. Liv had grown accustomed to the unspoken schedule, finding herself noting the passage of weeks between them and growing increasingly expectant of each new one, and the unofficial itinerary they revealed. Mexico, Italy, Greece.

This one had come from Scotland.

> *Sniffing around for gold and finding mostly glass. Be good. WC—which, by the way, is the abbreviation for* toilet *in these parts. Insert joke here.*

She heard the sputter and crunch of the truck pulling in as she diced an avocado for their salad. When Sam came inside, she pointed him toward the pile. "Postcard from Whit."

He scanned the card quickly and tossed it back on the counter. "I don't know why he bothers sending them. It's not like he ever leaves a return address where we can write him back."

"Maybe he just wants us to know how much he misses us."

"From the sound of those postcards, I'd say he wants us to know how much he *doesn't*."

He pulled a beer from the fridge and snapped the tab, releasing a loud hiss in the quiet.

"Your father called," she said. "He said you'd know what it was about."

Sam came behind her and offered her a sip.

"I really hate when he does that," she said. "Acts as if everything is code-red top secret. We've been together over four years now. He can feel free to stop treating me like some girl you got conned into taking to the prom."

She glanced up at Sam, waiting for him to agree, or even add his own words of outrage, but his gaze was elsewhere, weary. Days at the marina were grueling and relentless; she didn't doubt he was exhausted. She knew he craved returning to the sun and excitement of their charters as much as she did.

She tore open a bag of spring greens and emptied it into the salad bowl, then wiped her hands on her rear. "So what *is* it about?"

Sam considered his beer. "He's coming for a visit."

"When?"

"This weekend."

Prickles of dread raced down her spine. She skirted around him for the fridge and pulled out a tomato, determined to ignore her nerves. "Good," she said with a confidence she didn't feel. "We've got that group from Atlanta lined up. What better way to show him how well the business is doing?"

• • •

Robert Felder arrived an hour early and sat on the very edge of their couch as if he was expecting a fire drill. Liv had never seen anyone look so uncomfortable in her life. Years after their introductions, she still felt as edgy around Sam's father as she had that first dinner in Chicago. For Sam's sake, she'd tried her best to close the gap Robert Felder seemed determined to force between them—making sure to always have his favorite wine, to compliment his ties, even keeping up with Bears and Cubs standings—but his regard, never mind respect, remained elusive. She knew he blamed her for Sam's pursuit of treasure—for entering into the charter business in the first place—and she could live with that. Although she wasn't always sure Sam could.

"Want a beer, Dad?"

"No, thanks." His father glanced around. "I thought you were moving out of this place."

"We plan to. Eventually."

Liv hurried around the kitchen, glad to be out of sight but not out of earshot. She'd decided on a simple menu—lamb and potatoes—and was pleased with the results. Even the rosemary biscuits she'd been sure she'd ruined had emerged perfectly browned.

Robert Felder checked his watch and stood. "We should really get going."

Sam looked up at him. "Go where? Liv made dinner, Dad."

"And I made reservations."

• • •

To make sure they had time to show Sam's father their whole operation, Liv and Sam arrived at the marina at eight the next morning. Robert Felder rushed through the tour, saying little and wearing an expression of mild disdain.

When nine arrived and their clients still hadn't, Liv offered Sam an encouraging smile. "They're just running late," she said, loud enough that his father might hear.

By noon, they had to admit defeat.

"What a foolish way to run a business," his father muttered as they followed him back to his rented Cadillac. "No wonder you're drowning."

Later at dinner, coming back from the restroom, Liv overheard Sam and his father and slowed her approach to their table.

"And what about her father? Who's paying for his care?"

"He is," Liv heard Sam say. "He has savings. He gets royalties."

"Royalties from what?"

"A book he wrote. A textbook."

"He can't possibly live off that."

"Liv says he does."

"But for how long?" Sam's father demanded. "You do realize if you marry this girl, he's your problem too. You'll be responsible for paying for him. God only knows how long he could stick around. Son, do you honestly want that burden?"

Liv resumed her steps and swung around the corner, sure her fury blazed hot on her face as she took her seat.

As they were walking out, all she wanted was to sprint for the car, but Sam caught her by the elbow and slowed her pace. "I'm sorry," he said, coming beside her. "I didn't mean for you to hear that."

"That's why you're sorry—because I heard it? Not because he was a jerk for saying it?"

"He is who he is, Liv. I'm not apologizing for my father. Any more than I'd expect you to apologize for yours."

But my father can't help his actions, Liv wanted to say as she watched Robert Felder march across the parking lot and slip into his car. *It's not the same thing.*

A week later, nearly recovered from their guest—and feeling flush with two more charter reservations—Liv was boiling lasagna noodles in the kitchen when Sam came in and said, "Save those. I'm taking you out. I've got news."

The last time Sam had announced "news" he'd informed her the *Phoenix* needed a new propeller. Still Liv changed into a fresh linen sundress and tied her hair back into a low ponytail, hoping for something more romantic.

Only when they'd taken their seats and the waitress had left with Sam's order for a bottle of wine did Liv think his big news might be a proposal. She'd grown so tired of waiting for the words, she'd trained herself to quiet the possibility, but glancing over the top of her menu at Sam's expectant eyes, she felt a rumble of curiosity moving within her. His father's visit had been especially trying, but they'd survived it—and maybe doing so had allowed Sam the freedom to finally make the commitment she'd been waiting for. If not marriage, then what could tonight's news be?

A waiter passed, carrying a pair of dinner plates. The smell of sautéed onions floated in his wake. Liv couldn't remember ever being so hungry.

When she looked back at Sam, his expression was stony. Prickles of dread raced up her arms.

She hoped she might be wrong.

"So, what's this great news?" she asked cheerfully.

"I never said it was great." He blew out a hard breath and looked around the floor. "Maybe we should wait for the wine."

She swallowed. "Should I be worried?"

"*Are* you worried?"

"I hate when you answer my question with a question."

He sighed. "Liv, I've given this a lot of thought. I need you to know that—"

"Oh God, just say it," she pleaded. "Whatever it is, just say it."

He set his hands down on the edge of the table. "We need to close the business."

All the blood in her body sank to her ankles. Liv allowed herself to feel its awful weight for only a moment before she sprang into her argument. "But it's just the start of the season. It's always tough at first—you know that. You get discouraged and then suddenly we're so busy we can't keep up. We just had two new reservations!"

"It's different this time, Liv."

"Why?"

"Because I don't want to do this anymore."

She sat back, his admission like a flaring fire. Her cheeks burned with the heat of it.

Sam dragged his hands down his face. "I'm going to law school. My dad secured me a spot in the fall at the University of Chicago."

The waitress returned with their Zinfandel, offering Sam a small sip to approve before filling both of their glasses. Numb, Liv watched him offer her a pleased smile. He'd ordered a bottle of wine as if this were some kind of celebration. Was that what he thought this was?

"What exactly were you planning to toast?" she demanded when the waitress left. "Breaking my heart?"

Sam leaned in. "I told you when we started, Liv. We talked about this way back at school. If this charter business didn't work out—"

"But it *has* worked out!" She lunged forward, uncaring that her voice was rising, that eyes and chairs had turned her way. "We're just going through a rough patch right now."

"A rough patch? Liv, be real. We are underwater—and that's not a pun. That's the truth."

She knew they were sinking financially, of course she did, but was folding the only answer?

He reached across the table for her hand. "Come with me to Chicago."

"And do what? Be your maid?"

Now it was his turn to sit back, scorched by her words.

"My work is here, Sam. Everything I've worked for—everything *we've* worked for."

He took a hard sip of wine and set his glass down.

"And what about my father?" she said.

"He can come too. There are places we can put him."

"*Put him*? Sam, he's not a goldfish in a plastic bag. I can't just keep moving him around. And why do you have to go back to Chicago? There are law schools right here in Wilmington."

She watched a flicker of hesitation cross his tight features. Why had she bothered to ask a question she already knew the answer to? These were his father's terms. Robert Felder wouldn't pay for law school in Wilmington, only in Chicago.

The waitress arrived to take their orders. Liv shook her head. "I'm not hungry."

"We'll both have the snapper," Sam said, handing back their menus and watching the young woman leave. "This hasn't been an easy decision, Liv."

"What about the *Phoenix*?"

"We'll have to sell her, obviously."

"You have to tell Whit. He should have a right to buy her."

"He's halfway across the world."

"Still."

But she knew he wouldn't reach out. Then again, how could he? As Sam had pointed out just days earlier, Whit's spirited postcard greetings never included a return address.

Back home, they spent the rest of the evening on the couch, taking turns staring at each other and the stack of magazines on the coffee table between, as if waiting for a solution to blow in through the open screens. But there was none. Sam was determined to go, and Liv was determined to stay.

Just before two in the morning, they rose and made their way to bed, rolling toward each other in slow motion.

Unable to sleep, Liv watched the outline of Sam's back in the milky night, an ache swelling in her stomach, rattling her chest like a chill.

It was decided that Sam would stay for the rest of the month, that they'd need that time to untangle themselves from their partnership—both personal and professional, though Sam seemed to give more attention to the dissolving of the business end of things. To keep herself sane—and solvent—Liv took on extra shifts at the restaurant and filled out paperwork to enroll in classes at UNC Wilmington for the fall. The admissions officer felt confident she'd be able to apply all of her earlier credits and that she could complete her degree in just a year; Liv's fingers were crossed.

On the day Sam moved out, thin clouds stretched across the sky, wispy as spider silk. There were boxes already lining the hall when Liv stepped out of the bedroom into a weave of sunlight. Sam was in the kitchen, drinking coffee.

"I'll call you when I get to Chicago, okay?"

Tears burned up her throat. She didn't bother wiping at them anymore. She'd cried herself to sleep for weeks now. She'd grown accustomed to waking up looking as if she'd been stung by a swarm of bees.

When he set down his mug and moved to embrace her, she stepped away, shaking her head. "Please don't do that."

All around her, the sounds of their everyday lives singed the air like sparks, impossibly loud and fleeting—water gurgling through the pipes, the cardinal letting go his plea from his perch on the railing, the whir of a neighbor's lawn mower. She wanted to capture each moment, preserve them like lightning bugs in a jar. And meanwhile, Sam filled the back of his truck and came in one last time to say good-bye.

Only after she watched the truck swallowed behind the corner did she turn back to face the room, nearly containing all it had held the night before, and yet emptied of so much.

Her eyes caught on the wall between the kitchen and the living room, bare now. Shock and sadness tore through her. She thought for sure she was mistaken, that perhaps he'd only moved it, only hidden it, but there was no other explanation.

He'd taken their chart.

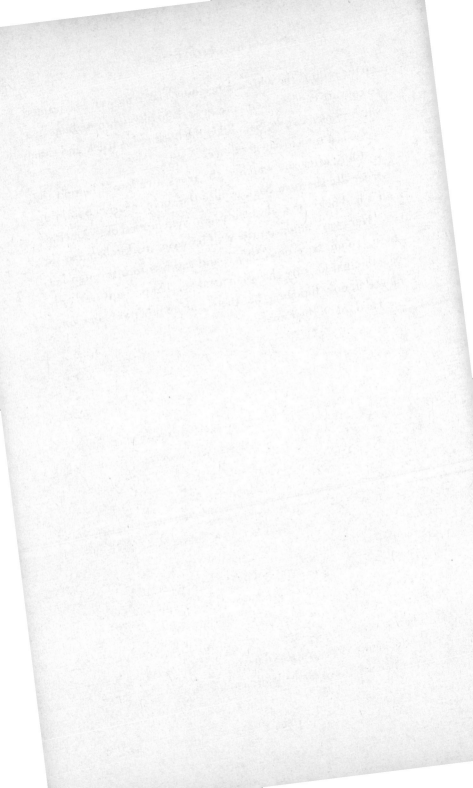

14

OUTER BANKS, NORTH CAROLINA

Thursday

How could Liv have worried she wouldn't recognize the house? It looks just as enormous and ostentatious as it did when the three of them pulled up to it thirteen years earlier. Only this visit, the homes that flank it are brimming with activity: crowded driveways, crowded decks, towels draped over railings, surfboards leaned against stairwells. No one would ever believe they'd arrived at the end of the world today. Their weekend of anonymity had been a rare gift.

Sam slows as they near the house. The breeze soothes her face as Liv studies the exterior, her eyes swollen from crying. They had spent only one night here, and yet she is certain she recalls tiny details of the place as if it were her childhood home—the smooth, cool curve of the railing under her fingers when she followed Sam back up the steps to the house, the salty smell of clam broth that hung in the air overnight, circling her arms over that satiny duvet.

"Look." Sam points to a Realtor sign stuck in the grass. "It's for sale."

"You should call—I'm sure we could afford it," Liv jokes.

Sam pulls out his phone and begins to tap in numbers.

Liv stares at him. "Sam, I was *kidding*."

He raises his cell to his ear and smiles as he waits. Liv lunges to take the phone from him, but he rears back, out of reach.

"We're on our way somewhere," she says. "We don't have time to—!"

Sam raises a finger to quiet her. "Hi, I'm calling about the property on South Beach Drive. Is it still available?" He stares at Liv as he listens, his dark eyes hooded with an unfamiliar mischief. "That's right . . . Uh-huh . . . We're here now, actually."

Is he out of his mind? Still her pulse races at the thought of what they're doing, the possibility of getting inside again, the lie he's constructing.

Sam, making up a story? It doesn't compute.

She whispers urgently, "What are we supposed to tell her?" but Sam won't be derailed.

"A half hour?" He grins at Liv. "Sure, we can wait."

Whit doesn't know how long he's been sitting in this empty parking lot, only that he can't wrap his head around the diary. That all the years he and Liv searched, in one sitting, thirty minutes, he knew everything.

It was pirates, just like we always believed. You and me, Red. We were right all along.

What had Liv thought of the truth? Had she found her legs wobbly when she tried to stand, had she cried, had she smiled? What?

And Simon. The man in the center of Theo's crumbling, strange world. All the years she'd put up with her father's demands and mania, and at the end of her days, she had finally found someone who made her his world.

Had Liv celebrated that news? Whit wonders. Or did she just mourn that Theodosia left this world much in the way she'd inhabited it? A captive, held for a different kind of ransom?

But she hadn't been alone. Because despite his crimes and his savage associates, Simon had been there for Theodosia, remaining at his post and protecting her when her captors had abandoned them. He'd made good on his vow to keep her safe, and free of fear or doubt. He'd never let her down, not even at the end.

The regret chokes Whit: Even a lawless pirate was a better man than he is.

He leans his head against the seat.

He should have been there when Liv read those entries, should have seen the sparkle of discovery in her eyes flashing back at him.

All she's ever wanted from him was his honesty. That night so many years ago when she let him crash on her bed, the night he nearly kissed her, bloody lip and all, she told him he was good enough as he was, worthy enough, so why has he never believed it? She is the only woman he's ever wanted to impress—and the irony bites down on his bones: To impress her, he had only to be himself. Could he have been so damn lucky all these years?

He squints out at the morning. The sun is hot and fierce and unforgiving. He knows how many hours behind the two of them he is, how futile this race has become. Sam isn't the reason he will lose her; Whit understands that now. Sam was never the danger. Not then, not now. Whit has been so busy blaming everyone else. All these miles up and down the coast, he's been chasing the ghost of his own mistakes—and there's just no catching up to that truth.

His lids hurt, the weight of fatigue too much for them. All they want to do is fall and stay shut. Jesus, he needs sleep. And a shower. All the windows down and he can still smell himself. He'd risk a quick nap right here, but there's a police car parked at the diner next door. He's not even sure he knows which direction he's going, not sure he even cares anymore. He pulls out and takes a right, through Kill Devil Hills and into Kitty Hawk. He could stop at the water for a while, if he can find a parking spot. He scans the road, looking for a place to turn, his tired eyes drifting over the stretches of strip malls, the stores and restaurants, all nautical-themed. Soundings' Café, Blackbeard's Books, the Porthole Pub, Barnacles and Brass Galleries—

Barnacles and Brass.

The name cuts through the thick fog of his tired brain. He lifts his foot off the gas reflexively. Why does it strike him as familiar?

Think, dammit.

Then it arrives.

"Sam and I are planning to go out to Kitty Hawk to see a man with an antique shop . . . Barnacles and Brass Antiques . . . Goofy name, but he specializes in old letters. . . ."

Whit spins the van into the first parking lot to turn himself around, so abruptly the SUV behind him shrieks out an angry horn. Sure, he's in Kitty Hawk, but so many years later, the chance that it's the same place, that it's any connection at all is slim. Still, he's just exhausted enough, just desperate enough, that he'll check to be sure. The Open sign hangs in the window above a pair of watercolors; big, bold paintings that belong in the big, bold homes that line the coast—homes like the one he snuck them into years earlier.

Even before he steps inside, Whit knows this is a foolish chase, but he's already in, and frankly he's grateful for the fresh, cool blast of air-conditioning. The woman at the counter is young and pretty, and he can see she is trying desperately hard not to appear disappointed when he arrives. He hardly looks the type to be making large purchases of art. When she smiles, he decides that if nothing else, he will buy something from her. He scans the wall and chooses a woodcut of terns. It doesn't matter how much it costs.

"I love this one too," she says, ringing him up. He smiles, thinking that she must be a student, that she's got so much ahead of her, and that she probably thinks it can't come soon enough. "Is this your first time visiting us?" she asks as she runs his credit card and hands it back to him.

"No, I just . . ." *What the hell?* he thinks. *Tell her*. "I was driving by and the name reminded me of a place I'd heard about a long time ago."

"This used to be an antique store. Maybe that's what you're thinking of?"

Whit's fingers slow as he takes the card from her and slips it back into his wallet. "I think so, yeah."

"That was my grandfather's store. My mom took it over when he died and she changed the last part of the name. He sold nautical memorabilia. Maps and letters. It wasn't really her thing."

"He specializes in old letters. You never know. . . ."

Don't quit now. "Cool," he says casually, conversationally, as if his heart isn't racing, as if his whole world doesn't hang on the answer to his next question. "So, what happened to it all?"

"The maps went to a collector, but there's still some boxes in the back with other stuff. My mom keeps meaning to call the Historical Society to get it all. She said she wouldn't feel right just chucking it. All that work he put into it, those years of history. It's important, you know?"

"Yeah," he says. "I know."

She hands him his purchase, and the tug of chance keeps him standing there, keeps the stupid grin plastered on his face. It's not as if he hasn't made an ass of himself already today, already asked the impossible and been given it.

"I don't suppose you kept any of the old letters he might have collected?"

"I could go back and check," the young woman says. "He labeled everything."

"I'm kind of a history buff. I'd love to get a look at them. I'd be glad to pay whatever you wanted."

The bell on the door jingles, signaling a new customer. A pair of older women wearing visors and Outer Banks T-shirts. They *ooh* and *aah* at a huge canvas of the Bodie Island Lighthouse.

The young woman's eyes return to him, flashing with hesitation. "I'm the only one in the store right now, so I have to stay up front," she says. "But my mom should be here in a half hour if you can wait."

Whit smiles, the best one he's got in his arsenal. The one he's been told makes his eyes turn a little turquoise, and his dimples sink all the way down his jaw.

At least, that's what Liv used to tell him.

"I can wait," he says.

"This must be Diane."

Sam points to the silver Mercedes that slides up into the driveway. A middle-aged blonde who looks only faintly like her glossy portrait on the sign steps out and waves to them where they have been waiting on the steps.

"I can't believe we're doing this," Liv whispers as the woman approaches. "She'll know we're not serious."

Sam slides his hand into hers and holds on. "Which is why I'll tell her we're a couple. It'll carry more weight."

Before Liv can argue, the woman arrives and extends her hand, a stack of gold bracelets colliding at her wrist.

"The property has only been on the market for a few weeks, but there's been a great deal of interest," Diane says as she opens the front door and ushers them in. "I'm surprised it's still available."

The smell is different—that's Liv's first thought as she follows Sam into the house. Cleaning spray. The grassy smell of new sisal rugs. And they've painted the taupe walls vivid shades of terra-cotta and mustard and teal.

"I'm not crazy about the palette," Diane says chummily, "but paint's an easy fix. Everything else is in great condition. It's move-in ready. And what a time of year to move in, right?" She steers them through the kitchen, pointing out the gourmet appliances she doesn't know they once used, the Sub-Zero fridge they once filled with far too much food, and they smile with appropriate awe. Liv glances at Sam, wondering if he's changed his mind about their charade.

"Wait until you see the view from the deck," Diane practically squeals. "It's worth the price alone."

When they are outside, Sam finally admits, "We stayed here once. A long time ago."

Diane turns to them, her blue eyes wide. "And here you are, back to possibly buy it." She passes a smile between them. "How romantic is that?"

Diane leads them back inside to the kitchen, stopping at the polished granite counter they piled their groceries on years earlier. It had seemed so much bigger to Liv then.

You'd think this was our last meal on earth.

"I just have to make a quick call," Diane says, holding up her phone, "but there's a master suite and four additional bedrooms upstairs. Feel free to go on up and look around. I won't be long."

They watch Diane exit onto the deck and wait until she's on her phone before they turn to each other.

"Told you she'd buy it," Sam says.

Because she hopes we will, Liv thinks as she circles the island.

"It looks the same, doesn't it?" he says.

"Not to me."

Sam comes around the counter to where she stands. "What's different?"

"I'm not sure exactly." A safe answer, she thinks. But Sam's gaze is level with hers and unrelenting.

"You heard Diane." He takes her hand. "We should see the bedrooms."

Walking up the stairs, Liv doesn't dare look down. It doesn't matter that the walls are newly painted, or the smell of clam broth is no longer thick in the air—doesn't matter that she insisted the space seemed different to her. In this moment, as she's following Sam to the second floor, time has turned back and everything is as it was that night.

And just like that night, they wander down the hall, in and out of rooms, until they reach the very last door.

Sam steps back to let Liv cross the threshold first. The bed is in a different place. No longer against the wall, it sits in the center of the room. Liv can't imagine why anyone would set it there. She moves to the window instead, wanting to be as far from the bed as she can, as if it is a mountain lion curled up but not asleep. It terrifies her. But not Sam. He circles it close, like the mattress is a roaring fire, offering heat on a cold night. She wishes he'd move away from it.

"We're back where we started, Liv."

She flattens herself against the windows. "Where we all started."

"I'm not talking about the three of us."

He comes toward her. The memory of his kiss invades her thoughts, flashes every time she blinks like a bulb stared at too long.

The last time they were in this room together, she'd pleaded with him not to go, not to leave her. Is he waiting for her to ask the same thing again? His gaze is level, even, familiar. *That's* the Sam she remembers. Controlled and calm. Not the Sam who concocts wild stories and fantasies for a Realtor—who is he?

She's sure he'll come beside her, but he slows several feet away, taking in the view. "He's not here, Liv."

"Yes, he is." Guilt and confusion flood her. Whit is as much a part of these walls and these floors as they are. No amount of moved beds and fresh paint can hide that. "If Whit knew we were here together," she whispers.

"He'd what?" Sam presses. "He'd be a different person?"

She spins away from him, unable to face his question, but Sam moves behind her.

"He'd die," she says simply.

"So where is he?" She steps away and Sam catches her hand, gently but insistently. "He had his chance, Liv. You said it yourself—he's broken your trust more times than you can count."

What can she say to that? In the quiet, she can hear the front door open and Diane enter the foyer, talking loudly on her phone.

Liv turns back to the sea, her nerves primed, so close to the surface of her skin she is almost afraid to touch anything, but she wants to put her hands somewhere to steady herself, so she flattens her palms against the glass. The surface is cool and she's grateful for it. Time stops and collects in a single rush of images, charting her history in this house. Sam's right: Everything began here. Their first kiss. Her pencil marks on that chart. Whit barging in the next morning, spilling sunlight everywhere, slamming a door down the hall. Why didn't she realize how much Whit loved her then?

Sam comes behind her and she doesn't dare turn to face him.

"Tell me what you want, Liv."

She closes her eyes and presses her fingertips harder against the window. When she exhales against the glass, cool air blows back at her. Why does he have to ask her this now? Doesn't he know her whole body is a propeller on a rubber-band plane, wound to its very tightest and waiting to be set free to spin?

"I just want to stop running away," she whispers.

"So stop." He reaches around to cover her hands with his, his fingers heavy and insistent. His breath is hot against her scalp, her neck. His body leans into hers.

"Sam," she whispers, then again, *"Sam."*

If she tips her head back, she knows exactly where she will land, just below his chin, where she always used to rest. And she'll stretch her neck; she'll tilt her head to bare her throat to his mouth, and he'll reach down and slide her underwear to one side, wordlessly, seamlessly, because that was always how they made love. Silently, and from behind, where she could never see his face. Whit needs to look into her eyes when he's inside her, needs to possess her in every way. Whit doesn't care that his whole face twists up, doesn't care that the craziest grunts and curses burst out of him when he comes. He lets her in, lets her know it's okay to lose control. And here she is, letting Sam's hands sweep up her body, and she is spinning, just like that propeller, but instead of flying, she feels sure she's drowning.

When his hands cup her breasts and squeeze hungrily, she slips from his grip and retreats to the other side of the room, leaving a wide berth between herself and the bed, swallowing to force moisture to her parched throat. "I can't do this now."

"Then we'll go somewhere else," Sam says, his voice husky.

"No, I mean I can't do this anywhere."

He falls back against the window and drags both hands through his short hair. Even from across the room, she can see the rigid weight she felt against the small of her back bulging stiffly beneath his zipper.

"I'm sorry, Sam."

"Jesus, stop saying that."

His harsh tone startles her.

"What do you expect from me?" she says. "You can't just show up after all these years and make it like it used to be."

"Hey, you came to *me*, remember?"

She claps her hands over her eyes. "I know," she says. When she lowers her fingers, Sam is near her again.

He touches her cheek. "A minute ago you were moaning

my name. An hour ago you were telling me you didn't know if you could go back to your husband."

Your husband. He says it as if Whit is someone he doesn't know, a stranger, a man he's never met.

Her heart pounds; she's sure he can feel her pulse through her skin, through his fingers.

Sam tips her chin to raise her eyes to his. "You and Whit don't make sense, Liv. *We* made sense."

Made. He's right to use the past tense, but he's wrong in every other way.

She and Whit make perfect sense. Why has she needed this trip to see that?

"My whole life was about boxes, Sam," she says. "About what I couldn't do, who I couldn't be. My father kept me in that box for as long as I can remember. Then I let you put me in another one, because I thought being safe would make me happy. But all I ever wanted, all I ever needed, was someone to tell me it was okay if I climbed out of that awful box. Even for a little while."

"Congratulations, you found him." He releases her.

So she had. Life with Whit might not have always been tidy or predictable, but unlike Sam, Whit has always known what he wants. What . . . and *who*.

And there it is, Liv realizes. The piece she couldn't make fit for so long. The only safety she ever really needed was Whit's love. It was uncontrolled, but it was unconditional. It was messy and manic and sometimes utterly devastating to be around, but it was pure, and it was steady. Maybe the only thing in Whit Crosby's life that ever would be.

For all of Sam's caution and protection, for all of his evenness and order, he'd never made her feel safe about his love for her. How many times had she hoped he would ask her to marry him, gently pressed him only to have him change the subject? She's not even sure she can count on one hand the times in four years he said he loved her.

"Why did you lie about the chart?"

He stares at her. "What?"

Her heart races, so fast she worries it will push through her ribs. "You said Whit didn't want it after we left this house—you said he wanted to throw it away."

"Jesus, what difference does that make now?"

Only all the difference in the world.

She takes a seat on the bed, its power suddenly gone. It's just a big, empty bed. In a big, empty house.

"This trip was never about the diary or me, was it?" she says. "You came back to punish Whit. To take me away from him, just to prove you could."

"I asked you to come to Chicago with me, Liv. You were the one who said no."

She shakes her head. "You knew I couldn't leave my father. You knew I had to stay. You could pretend all these years that it was me, that the reason we didn't work out was *me*, but it was you, Sam. You never wanted me to come with you. You never knew what you wanted. Only what you *didn't*." She watches him a moment, seeing him so clearly now, and a thread of sadness stitches its way up her throat. "I did love you, Sam."

Even now she can say it, and even now he still can't.

He folds his arms. "But you ran to Whit."

She smiles. "Not right away."

"Yes, right away. From the start, Liv."

And this time, Sam's right. Even when she'd been standing still and alone, she was running toward Whit Crosby. He'd been her beacon before she ever knew she needed one. She'd been so sure a heart as wild and big as his would sink her, would leave her to drown.

But all these years later, she understands Whit was never the one who'd needed saving.

Amazing what treasure you can find when you scrape off years of crud, isn't it?

The clack of heels grows louder and Diane appears in the doorway.

"So, lovebirds . . ." She looks between them, wearing an impish smile, her pink lipstick gleaming with a fresh thickness, shiny and sticky like hastily chewed bubble gum. "Will we be putting in an offer?"

15

Eight years earlier

Liv had vowed she wouldn't hunker down at the café for so long this time, wouldn't turn on her laptop, wouldn't spread out her papers, but here it was, almost noon, and she'd covered the round table so entirely that there was barely any sign of the lacquered wood underneath. Worst of all, in the three hours she'd been there, she'd nursed one damn cup of coffee and a blueberry muffin. If there was a minimum purchase requirement for hogging a table for four, she wasn't even close. When her friend Rachel had texted to invite her to the beach, Liv begged her to stop by and fill a chair for a good cause instead. Not that her offer of sand and sun wasn't a tempting one. It had been such a busy spring trying to complete her course work that Liv had barely been to the water at all in April or May.

Most days it just blew her mind that she'd graduated at all.

When she'd enrolled—or reenrolled, depending on how you looked at it—at UNC Wilmington, Liv had been so sure the bottom would drop out of her plan, that she'd be sitting in class and the teacher would point to her and tell her to leave, that there had been some dreadful mistake and her hope of finishing what she'd started had only been a dream.

Not that the first few weeks of school weren't without hiccups. Student loan paperwork had been held up, credits improperly transferred, add/drop deadlines missed.

But eleven months later, at twenty-six, she was finally a college graduate. There'd been barely enough time to think about what she'd do next before "next" had arrived. The lure of boat work remained—God knew she still had plenty of contacts at the marina and in the salvage world who would gladly have brought her back into that particular fold. But she'd promised her father—and maybe herself too—that she would at least try for a job with benefits and regular hours, a job that didn't leave her sun-kissed and salt-licked, her hair constantly thickened with sea spray and wind. Not that she had minded those unconventional perks. Truthfully she missed the chalky feeling of dried sea on her skin, her toes and fingernails always so clean from the water. Most of all, she missed the excitement of the hunt, of knowing that a shipwreck might be just beneath her, that a few seconds of hand-fanning could yield unimaginable treasure.

And she missed Sam. And she missed Whit. It had been so long since she was truly alone.

Not that she *was* alone, she had to remind herself. Her friend Rachel was proof of that. Liv had rarely had girlfriends growing up, rarely had friends of any kind—who could with such an overprotective father who feared the possible dangers of after-school playdates and sleepovers? Her years with Sam and Whit had been so deeply inclusive that she'd barely formed any relationships outside of their trio. But in the days following Sam's departure, the void had been unmistakable. Until she had returned to classes that fall and found herself seated next to a bubbly brunette with a nose ring and a great story about changing majors, Liv had genuinely feared she might not even know *how* to make friends, as ridiculous as that sounded. Two weeks later, she'd met Rachel in her seminar and they'd connected over a shared love of Michener's *Hawaii*. Like her, Rachel had recently ended a long relationship—hers with a high school boyfriend back home in Georgia—so the two had navigated the waters of singlehood together, and, with the exception of a few ill-advised affairs, painlessly.

It helped too that Liv had found herself a new coffee shop to haunt, a place with no ties to her life with Sam, no memories attached to its benches or wall hangings.

Rachel pushed through the door carrying her bike helmet. Liv waved her over.

"You didn't go as short this time—it's good," Rachel said, sliding into her seat and pointing to Liv's new bob.

"I missed being able to put it up," Liv said. "How was last night?"

"Terrible, but it's done, so that's a relief. I didn't want him coming with us to Wilson's opening anyway. You *are* coming, aren't you? Because I told Wilson you were and he lit up."

"Oh God, you didn't."

"He's adorable. What's the problem?"

"The problem is I'm not looking for anything serious."

"And you think Wilson *is*? By the way, Moondance is doing the catering."

"I said I'll think about it."

"And did I mention the open bar?"

Liv smiled. "Only ten times." Her phone hummed with a call, saving her. Just an automated message from her father's facility updating their new emergency notification system. A year after Sam had left, still a tiny part of her always imagined it might be him when she heard the chime. She'd called him several times, usually late at night, but he'd never answered. E-mail was his communication of choice. She'd received a few messages early on, most of which were to share news of revised loan repayment schedules from their folded business, another to tell her the *Phoenix* had been sold, which had sent her into a crying jag in the middle of the quad.

But oddly enough, it was Whit Crosby, not Sam, she most often believed she spotted in a crowd. Sometimes it was a laugh, loud and exploding; other times a flash of rumpled bronzed hair on someone unusually tall.

Not often, just sometimes. The way objects dance into the peripheral vision when a person has been looking straight ahead too long without blinking.

She had nothing chic to wear—that was her first excuse for not going to the gallery when Rachel called at seven. Parking would be impossible on a Friday night—excuse number two. And never mind that she had wanted to fill out that online application for the job at the Historical Society. And of course there was her father. . . .

No, not really. But years after she'd moved him into Sunset Hills, Liv still found herself unconsciously building his possible needs into her plans. What if he heard something outside and needed her to come over? What if the TV remote needed programming? The idea that he was being cared for, monitored—it had taken so much getting used to. It did still.

"Come over now," Rachel said. "Or I'm sending Wilson to pick you up."

Liv doubted he would leave his own opening, but she didn't care to risk it.

"Fine." She hung up, missing the satisfaction of heavy receivers that could be slammed down into cradles.

Crepe myrtles lined the street, at their ripeness peak in clusters of scarlet and pink blossoms. Liv found herself dusted with petals cutting through a hotel courtyard to reach Front Street. The gallery was busy and loud and hot. She managed to secure a square inch of peace on the second floor and looked down at the crowd. Somewhere in the soup was Rachel, who'd promised to wear her turquoise top to be easily spotted, but all Liv could see were shades of black and red.

This had been a terrible idea. The very worst. She'd put off finishing her online application for this. Not to mention now she remembered why she'd never worn these heels for any length of time. Admittedly they made her feel utterly statuesque, but no amount of added height was worth the pain to her littlest toes.

She scanned the floor again, deciding she would give the swarm one last search and if she still didn't see Rachel, she'd leave as she'd come in, unnoticed—

Her gaze snagged. The profile was right, but the hair was wrong. Too short. Still. It looked an awful lot like . . .

She drew closer to the railing. Her breath caught.

There was no way he would hear her over the roar of the crowd and the thunder of music, but she leaned over and yelled anyway. "Whit!"

To her shock, he looked up and around, and then saw her. His hand rose and he pointed at her. "Stay there!"

Whether it was his height or his powerful strides up the stairwell, somehow he cleared the space around them enough so that as soon as he was within range, she was able to fling herself into his open arms and lock her fingers behind his neck. He smelled different, she thought, something missing. When she let go, it hit her: no smoke.

She felt breathless, as if she were the one who'd sprinted up the steps. "What are you doing here?" she cried.

"I know one of the guys in the show."

"No, I mean *here*. In Wilmington."

"I came back to check on a few friends. What gives? I went by the old apartment, but there was some crabby guy living there."

She smiled. "I moved out when Sam left. I'm living near campus now."

"Holy shit . . ." He reached out and cupped a handful of her hair, fingering the short red curls that she'd tacked back with combs. "What the hell did you do with all of it?"

His touch sent sparks of heat circling her scalp. "Me? What about you? Did you really have to go all the way to Australia to get a proper haircut?"

"I fell asleep on the lid of a can of marine paint. Had to buzz it all off. I almost looked presentable for a while. You should have seen me."

Whit with a flattop? She couldn't imagine it.

"Damn." He took her in again, longer this time, his gaze so baldly admiring that she felt the urge to laugh. Or maybe it was to cover the irrepressible blush that crept up her neck. "How come you never wore this outfit on the boat?" he said.

"You know, I tried but I could never get my fins over the heels."

"I bet you have to beat the boys off with a stick."

She grinned. "A chopstick, maybe."

His teasing smile relaxed. "It's good to see you, Red."

God, how she'd missed that name. To think there had been a time she'd bristled at it, at *him*. Impossible. She couldn't remember ever being happier to see someone.

"Where are you staying?" she asked.

"A friend of Wes's lent me his place on the Riverwalk for a few days. Why don't you come over later when you're done here?"

She smiled. "I'm done now."

Over the years, they'd passed this stretch of apartments many times strolling along the Riverwalk after beers at the taproom or crab omelets for Sunday brunch. She'd wondered what it would be like to eat out on one of their balconies, how beautiful the river would look from above.

She followed Whit up the stairs and into a lushly lit apartment with gleaming wooden floors and a gas fireplace.

He went straight for the galley kitchen. "Are you hungry?"

"Starving," she said.

"I have some shrimp. I could make us a quick stir-fry."

Since when did Whit cook?

"Wine or beer?" he asked.

"Wine's good."

He poured her a glass of white and she carried it over to the French doors that looked out onto the Cape Fear River and the bustling boardwalk below. She stepped out of her heels, resisting the urge to fling them off the balcony, and padded back across the cool hardwood floor to the kitchen, her short self again but immeasurably comfortable. Or maybe her comfort wasn't just from being free of her shoes.

Whit leaned down to retrieve a wok and spun it easily before landing it on the range top.

"Okay, what gives?" Liv said. "Last time I saw you, you were reading the directions for microwave popcorn."

He laughed. "I learned some moves from the guys on the ship. They'd pull up this crazy-looking fish and we'd have to make it ingestible. It's amazing what enough lemon pepper and soy sauce can do."

She settled onto one of the barstools to watch him work. "So tell me everything."

"Not until we eat." Whit winked. "Patience, lass."

Liv eyed him dubiously. Since when did Whit Crosby know anything about *that*?

• • •

They ate on the balcony under a full moon. The shrimp was cooked perfectly, flavorful and moist. The wine tart and cold. Even the salad dressing was just the right balance of tangy and sweet. Liv couldn't stop marveling at each bite, each sip. Who was this man who cooked, who didn't smoke, who had reign over a sexy apartment on the Riverwalk and hadn't filled it with underwear models and vats of liquor?

Whit leaned back and stretched out his legs under the table, brushing Liv's bare feet.

"Wilmington must feel tiny to you now after being all over the world," she said.

"Not really. I missed it."

"Oh, please. Excavating ships that Caesar himself probably sailed on, and you missed our little steamers?"

"I didn't say I missed the wrecks."

A sparkle of affection flashed back at her, scalding her cheeks. She was suddenly aware of their bodies touching, the cool cotton of his khakis brushing against her ankle.

Whit reached for his wine. "So, now what, Graduate?"

"I've applied for a few things. There's a position with the Historical Society that sounds promising."

He frowned, looking skeptical. "Sounds like a desk job."

"What's wrong with desk jobs?"

"Nothing, except you have to do them *at desks*."

The wind kicked up, bringing with it the smoky smell of

river traffic. A group of women spilled out of the restaurant below and rushed loudly to the edge of the railing to wave at a passing tour boat. Liv watched them a moment, enjoying their mirth, before she said, "It could be a good thing. A way to combine my degree and my work on wrecks. It would make my dad happy. Before he forgets me completely."

Liv regretted the confession immediately and took a long sip of wine to wash it away.

"How's he doing?" Whit asked.

"He has good days and bad days."

"Don't we all?"

While Whit emptied the bottle between their glasses, Liv watched him, still grappling with his curious evolution. He looked like the same Whit who'd left her life three years earlier. Maybe he was a bit tanner, a bit leaner—he'd never be as slim as Sam—and his hair was shorter, but these were fine details. It was the differences below the skin that startled her.

"So bring me up to speed," he said.

"On?"

"The hunt, what else?" He tilted his head. "Don't tell me you stopped looking for her?"

Regret sent her shoulders back. "It's been hard with school. I've kind of lost track."

"I bet the old chart still has a few empty spots we could fill up."

"I wouldn't know. Sam actually took the chart with him."

"I'm surprised you gave it up."

"I didn't. He never asked me. He just took it when he left."

"Jesus, that was a lousy thing to do."

She shrugged. "I guess he wanted it more than I thought. It was as much his as mine, I suppose."

"Or maybe he was just being a jerk. . . ." Whit considered his wine before taking a sip and setting down his glass. "People don't always get it right when they have to say good-bye."

Liv raised her eyes to his and felt a charge of longing rise. She suspected he wasn't referring to Sam.

"Have you stayed in touch?" he asked.

She shook her head. "I tried calling him a few times, but he never called me back."

"That makes two of us."

She offered him a weak smile. "So what about you? I'm sure there's a trail of broken hearts from here to Australia and back."

"Not quite."

"I don't believe it."

"Well, there is this *one* lady I've been seeing a lot of lately. . . ." Whit flashed an all-too-familiar rakish grin. "Her name's Bella—and she's loaded."

And blond, and perfectly shaped, and fond of all-night parties, Liv would bet.

Prickles of disappointment nipped at her heart. So much for thinking him a changed man able to go one week without chasing a woman's affections.

She forced a halfhearted smile and feigned interest in her napkin. "So, where's lovely *Bella* now?"

"About fifteen feet down."

Liv glanced up to meet Whit's teasing grin.

"She's a *ship*, Livy."

Relief tore through her, so fast she hoped her cheeks didn't flush with it.

"Check this out." Whit leaned back to reach deep into his front pocket and tugged out a Spanish coin, a coveted piece of eight. "It's from the *Bella Donna*. No question. And her manifest says she was carrying gold, silver, *and* emeralds."

Liv leaned in to touch the coin, running her fingertips over the mottled surface, still warm from being so close to his skin. "Where?"

"The Keys."

The thrum of possibility began its frantic beat behind her ribs.

"Now all you need is a license and a generous investor." She smiled. "Oh, and a boat, of course."

"I have the boat."

"You do?"

He drained his wine and stood. "Come on."

"But we've been drinking," she said.

"It's okay." He took her hand. "We're walking."

Looking back, Liv might have known what boat was his. Even before Whit took them down the stairs to the Riverwalk, then snaked them through the chains of pedestrians enjoying a moonlit stroll. Regardless, by the time he stopped her at the right slip, her eyes had already filled.

She looked so much bigger, moored between two smaller boats.

"Sam never said *you* bought her."

"I didn't buy her from Sam," Whit said. "I heard she was for sale. The guy who bought her from Sam was a friend of Chowder's—you remember Chowdy, right? Anyway, he hunted me down to let me know and . . . Oh shit." He squinted at her. "Are you crying?"

She swiped at her eyes. "Of course I'm crying."

"That hurts, Red. You didn't even tear up when you saw *me*."

She laughed, though it came out so quick and loud that it sounded more like a bark. He always could make her laugh through the tears. But that had always been Whit's way, hadn't it? He was the yeast in every starter, the spark, the match.

"You'll be glad to know she's still the same, slow-as-wet-sand boat," he said. "Same cheap galley, same lumpy berth. The guys Sam sold it to didn't do a damn thing to fix her up. The only thing I changed was—well, see for yourself."

When he walked her around to the bow, her breath caught.

Theo's Wish.

"Whit." She looked up at him. "But I thought it was bad luck to rename a boat."

"Well, I'll find out, won't I?" He smiled. "So, you approve, or what?"

She opened her mouth to say that she did, to say *something*, but before any sound could come, he took her hand again and led her on board.

"It's true—they didn't do a thing," she whispered, looking around.

"I know, lousy bastards."

"No, I mean it's wonderful." She spun around in place,

taking it all in, the urge to tear up returning. "It's the same exact boat." Needing to revisit every inch, she walked the deck, the cockpit, then climbed to the flybridge and scanned the river before coming back down the ladder.

Whit waited for her at the bottom. He always looked so devastatingly handsome on a boat, the wind brushing the hair back from his forehead—she'd forgotten. He belonged on the water. Once, she'd thought she did too. But after nine months in fluorescents-baked classrooms and hushed libraries, and only seeing the ocean from the shore, her sea legs had turned soft. Her freckled skin, having adjusted to the relentless sun topside and turned a careful gold, was back to being fair.

Yet five minutes on the *Phoenix*—no, *Theo's Wish*—and her bones were absorbing the rippling water beneath them.

How could she have ever doubted where she belonged?

A burst of pedestrian traffic passed above them. Three women, all in black cocktail dresses, slowed their walk to admire the boat and her captain.

"Be careful," Liv said after they'd gone, "or you might find yourself back in the charter business before the night's through."

"I can think of worse things." He considered her face a moment, then said, "I'm going to recover the *Bella Donna*, Red."

"I assumed that."

"I want you to come with me."

"You're not serious."

"Aren't I?"

"You're not," she said again, smiling. "You're never serious about anything, remember?"

"Don't bet on it." He took a step toward her. "I mean it, Red. Come work with me. Come *be* with me."

She looked up at him, longing and fear colliding. "Don't say things you don't mean."

"I'm not."

As he came closer Liv watched him, filled with the dizzying sense of time-stopping, slowing, thinking to herself: *This is a moment I will remember, a moment I will look back on and say, Everything that meant anything was in this one perfect instant.*

And now it's here.

She searched Whit's eyes as they held hers. She'd never seen the circle of navy that hugged his pupils. Or the flecks of copper in his eyebrows. She'd never been this close before. All this time.

"What are you saying?" she whispered.

"When the right woman comes along to quit smoking for, I will."

He cupped her chin and tipped her face up to his. "Wait—suddenly you're not the smartest woman I know?"

But there wasn't time to answer, barely time to breathe. In the next instant, he kissed her. The only way Whit Crosby could ever kiss her, Liv would realize later—deeply and fiercely and with his whole heart. She let him explore her mouth, breathing in his breath, and burying her fingers in his hair, the way so many other women had done, women she'd envied desperately and never dared to think why.

"You're shaking," he said.

"I'm scared."

"You don't think I am?"

She couldn't take her eyes off his mouth. "Liar," she whispered. "Nothing scares you."

"Never seeing you again scared me. Terrified me." He covered her mouth with his again, pulling her so close and so tight that the hard rounds of his shirt buttons dug into her breasts.

She shifted her eyes to the dock. "We're kind of on display here."

"Good point." He moved to the closest towline and began unwinding it. "Then we better move."

He steered them through the channel until he found them an inlet to drift in. Not so long ago, they had worried that rangers would catch them building a fire on the beach—now they were tearing off each other's clothes in the middle of the Cape Fear River as if they'd been stranded on the moon. Whit, his familiar impatience resurrected, abandoned his efforts to strip Liv entirely and picked her up with her dress halfway down her hips, carrying her belowdecks to continue his unpeeling on the bunk, hitting his head in his zealousness. He wore her out, in every conceivable way, until the blankets lay on the floor, and all that remained was a damp fitted sheet that clung to the mattress with only two of its four corners. They rose from their stupor the way they'd ascended dives together: breathless and slick and euphoric.

"A break," she whispered, winded and dizzy.

"Maybe a short one," he conceded, wrapping them in a blanket and leading her out of the cabin. They made a new bed on the deck and lay down. Above them, the map of stars was endless.

Whit rolled her into his arms, folding her against his chest. "Cold?"

"No," she lied, the heat from his skin already burrowing into hers.

They didn't talk about Sam. Eventually they would have to, Liv knew that. But not tonight. They didn't talk about how curious it was that they had come together this way either; how shocking or surprising, because there was no surprise in it.

Instead they talked about the stars, and treasure. Because that, Whit said, was what salvors did at night on decks. "When they're done doing this," he said.

"What if we never know what happened to her?" Liv whispered. "What if no one ever does?"

"We will, Red. I don't care how long it takes, we'll find her together. We'll solve the mystery before anyone else."

Liv pressed her lips against his heart. "It can't be this simple."

"Why can't it? It's not like we just met, you know."

Before she could argue with his point, Whit climbed to his feet and stood in front of her. Buck naked. In the middle of the Cape Fear River.

"Now listen," he said, "because I'm only going to say this once: I'm not perfect—"

"This is news?"

"Will you let me finish?"

She rolled her lips inward, guaranteeing her silence.

"And I can't promise you I won't screw up from time to

time," he went on. "But what you see is what you get—and I swear there is no one, on land or sea, who will love you more than I will." He returned and came over her, kissing her deeply. "And Jesus, I love you."

"My turn." She searched his eyes. "I have this sinking feeling that I've loved you forever too."

"Sinking?" He grinned. "A little shipwreck humor, huh?"

"It seemed well placed."

"Speaking of well placed . . ." Whit rolled her on top of him and settled himself inside her. The sea swayed and shuddered; the sky burned and sparkled. Liv flattened her hands on his broad chest and closed her eyes, seeing only stars.

16

TOPSAIL ISLAND, NORTH CAROLINA
Thursday

Whit sees Sam's truck even before he pulls into the driveway. It can't be missed—the only vehicle in the entire turnaround. And just as he did a day earlier, Whit takes the front stairs two at a time, but today he's too tired to be combative, too sorry to be angry. He wants only to hold Liv, to find her and give her the letter he's carried from Kitty Hawk, folded in his pocket, warm from the heat of his heart. This time he enters quietly; he doesn't call out. Alone in all the polished wood and high walls, Whit has to remind himself how long he's been gone. Twenty-four hours? Twenty-four *days*? He scans the room, the wide, glossy stairs, remembering the chaos he left, the space then crowded and loud, a circus of strangers with plans to get drunk and get laid, and how he drifted through their party, no more impacting than a breeze. He steeled himself for mess and stink, and is shocked to find very little. Liv must have cleaned up. He hates that she came back to such a disaster, but then he remembers that she came back here with Sam, and he doesn't feel so apologetic. If they want to break his heart, the least they can do is clean the goddamn house first.

His mind races, but his steps are even, measured, for once in his life, *controlled*. If they are upstairs together, he thinks as he climbs the curved wooden treads, he won't blame her, he won't lose his shit—as if he has any left to lose?—but he won't relinquish her either. He came back to fight for her once before. But the bedrooms are empty—every last one. The whole house is empty. Whit comes back downstairs and pushes out the French doors to the deck, and there he is at the far end. Sam, reclining in an Adirondack chair, his sunglass-covered eyes lifted to the sky. Is he asleep? Whit isn't sure as he begins his approach. His heart slams against his ribs with every step. What is he going to say? Screw it. He's not a planner, why start now? The words will come, the right words, dammit. When Whit's just a few steps away, Sam finally stirs, rolling his head slowly toward him, unstartled.

Sam tugs off his sunglasses, his dark gaze level and unimpressed, as if Whit had only gone into the house a few minutes earlier for more beer, and now he's back.

Before Whit can begin, Sam says, "She's not here. I dropped her off in New Bern. She took a plane back to Miami."

Gone? Whit drops into the neighboring chair, letting the information sink with him.

A gull lands on the railing. Sam picks up a mug off the glass table between their chairs.

The only thing Whit can think to say is "The *Siren*'s a bust. Warner stripped her clean."

Sam looks at him just as Whit knows he deserves to be looked at—with confusion; like, *Jesus, is he kidding?* Of course it's a bust. The proof of this mission's swift and certain death is everywhere. The house is empty, the equipment packed up and gone. Even Liv is gone. Gone home.

Without Sam.

Possibility—hope—burns through Whit. He grips the arms of the chair and glances at Sam, reminded of his gripe, ancient as it seems now. "You told me you were leaving."

Sam calmly sips his coffee. "I did leave."

"Alone," Whit clarifies. *Smart-ass.* "I heard about the diary."

"We saw it," says Sam, staring out at the water. "We read the whole thing."

We.

Whit bites his lip to stop himself from saying more, not yet ready to confess how unglued he was that he chased Liv up and down the coast like a storm; that he rapped on Beth Henson's door at five a.m., stinking of salt water and sweat, and pleaded with her to show him the diary; that she did and he read it hungrily. He could tell Sam too about the letter in his pocket, the letter Whit believes might tell a different story about Theodosia and Simon the pirate, a different truth, but not until he tells Liv. It's a gift for her alone. Whit only hopes she'll accept it.

"There's more coffee," Sam says, as if it's any old day.

"I'd rather have a beer," says Whit.

"Then you're out of luck."

The gull moves toward them, inquisitive and bold.

Whit has always liked seagulls, always thought they got a bad rap for their moxie. "This is the part where I say friends don't do what you did."

"Give me a break," Sam says flatly. "We were never friends, we both know that. I'm pretty sure we didn't even like each other."

"We didn't." Whit smiles. "We liked Livy." And it's the truth. Liv was the piece that joined them, the cement that held them all together.

Is that a smile rising on Felder's mouth? Whit is sure his bleary eyes are playing tricks on him.

But still he confesses to Sam, to the seagull, to anyone who might hear, "I don't deserve her."

"Apparently you do." No tricks now. Sam smiles fully.

"You should know I'm not giving her up," Whit says.

"I know."

And in the silence, understanding settles between them, falls over the deck like flurries, sure and steady as the reach of pelican wings.

Key Largo, Florida

A final, interminable cab ride from Miami International and Liv is home. Not that she is even sure this is home anymore, but right now it feels as safe and certain as anywhere she's been in the past three days.

Three days.

She can't help calculating the changes—years' worth—

crammed into less than a week. The last time she stood in this house, she'd let Theodosia go. Now all the loose squares of fabric she's been collecting for so long have at last been sewn into their quilt.

And she is back, with her answer.

Alone.

Outside on the lanai, her lungs fill with the warm, mossy damp of early evening, the earth that cushions the slab under her feet soft and moist. *Theo's Wish* bobs gently, as if the boat is breathing during sleep. She feels an urge to board it, maybe even to set sail. But she's done enough running away for now. The dew of dusk glistens on every surface, the glass patio table, the fringes of the sago palm fronds. Tomorrow the sun will burn everything dry. She scans the empty chairs before she walks to the edge of the canal and peers down into the flat stretch of water, not sure what she expects to see. As she feared, the heat has ravaged her more tender plants, and yet, remarkably, the jade has survived her absence. Its thick, rounded leaves remain glossy and deep forest green. Just the sight of its continued health and Liv tears up, flushed with an unexpected burst of hope.

We are both castaways now, abandoned to a lighthouse that once offered rescue. We have only each other.

She checks her watch. It's late, but she still has time.

The carpeted halls of Sunset Hills smell of dish soap and warm plastic. Gold and green wreaths dangle from every patient's door—the mark of a new month, a singular change in an amber land of perfect preservation. Soon there will be displays of Indian corn and pumpkins in the lobby, strands of silk maple leaves draped around the reception desk, gourd centerpieces at every table in the dining hall. Liv anticipates the decorations—proof of how long her father has been living here. If this can be called living. She's still not entirely sure.

A new nurse, Tammy, is in her father's room when Liv steps inside. She's so young, her skin so smooth that even when she smiles, there are no creases.

"He's in the sitting room," Tammy says. "Want me to take you?"

Liv appreciates the young woman's kindness, but she knows the way. Her father blinks rapidly as she approaches, as if she's a bright bulb, or the sun. There's a streak of dried toothpaste on his chin. She drops beside him to wipe it off.

"Hi, Poppy."

He stares at her as if she might transform into someone else at any moment, his eyes filmy and hooded. Some days she thinks he's been crying, but mostly she thinks it's just the fog of old age. Today, though, she's not so sure. There's a pack of oyster crackers on his tray. His fingers shake as he tries to open it; she reaches over to help.

"I took a trip, Poppy. Did you miss me?"

He doesn't respond, but Liv doesn't expect him to. She watches as he inspects each cracker before he eats it, the dust of tiny crumbs raining down his pilled terry cloth robe, and her heart aches, heavy with love. Perhaps it is because of the glow of the reading lamp beside his head, but she can see the veins so clearly through the threads of gray and white. His head reminds her of a sparrow's egg, the shell of his scalp a bluish taupe speckled with brown spots. Longing rushes up, a flood of forgiveness. It wasn't his fault. He never meant to need her so, and now he's here. And maybe this time she needs him. Needs to know he can still remember, so she won't ever forget. She wasn't the only one who lost her way when Liza Connelly spun off that slick road. Her father lost his compass too. Liv found hers again—her father never did.

And in all the years she has tended to him, worried for him, resented him too—it is what she hasn't said that startles her.

She leans her head onto his lap and rubs her cheek against the creped skin of his hand.

"I'm sorry she left us, Poppy." She closes her eyes, feeling the warm trail of her tears slide down her nose, and knowing they must surely be landing on his fingers. "I'm so sorry."

For a moment, she thinks she feels his hand shift, as if he means to move it to her head and stroke her hair as he used to do when she slept. But it is only to tug out another oyster cracker.

Still she smiles.

Walking out, nearly past the reception desk, Liv hears her name. The new nurse is jogging toward her, waving a folder.

"I found this in your father's room last week when I was putting away his books." She hands Liv the folder. "He claimed he'd never seen it before, but I thought I'd ask you just to be sure."

When she opens to the map, Liv's eyes well before she can read the tiny words that hug the lines of the coast. But she doesn't need to. As she did that night in Hatteras, she could recite every word from memory all over again.

The nurse, still waiting, presses gently. "Do you recognize it?"

The plastic sheathing they've slid it into is a bit much, but Liv appreciates their effort. "It was lovely of you to protect it," she says.

"Oh, we didn't do that, ma'am. That's how we found it."

When a ship sinks and spills her hold, storms and currents can spread her bounty over miles of seafloor. But sometimes, in shallower waters, objects can corrode and concretions are formed, treasure bound into concretelike lumps, requiring tremendous care and effort from a marine conservator to separate their pieces, artifacts of another life tangled in the cement of sand and silt and always difficult to separate after being joined for so long.

Lying in bed, Liv holds up the old key and turns it in the path of light from her nightstand, wondering how it is that in all her years searching the ocean, she has never seen the obvious connection between wrecks and love.

The sheets still smell of Whit. The warm, metallic scent of his sweat, and hers somewhere underneath. She rolls over to his pillow and buries her nose in the center, drawing in what she can, the odor faint and growing fainter the deeper she inhales. She wants suddenly to empty his dresser, to surround herself with everything he's touched, everything he's ever put against his body, and drown in it.

When she hears movement on the boat, she bolts upright, panic prickling her bare skin. Someone is breaking into *Theo*—it's happened before, but never when Whit was gone. She'll call the police—if only she can find her phone. As she creeps down the dark hall, the banging grows louder, but she can see her cell on the kitchen counter. If she can sneak by the sliders unseen, she can make the call. Close enough, she darts past the tall doors of glass, but as soon as she draws up her phone, she lowers it.

Whit is on the flybridge. She can see the outline of his body in the glow of the dock lights.

He hears the slider cast down its track and spins to face her.

Her steps are slow, cautious. For a crazy second, she fears he is like a wild animal that will bolt if spooked.

But he doesn't move. Just smiles. And her lungs expand.

"I thought we could take her for a moonlight ride, Red."

"It's nearly dawn," she says.

He considers the sky and nods. "So it is."

Her heart. She swears if she doesn't cross her arms over her chest and squeeze, her ribs will burst from the pressure of its beating. All she wants to do is run to him, to curl up in his body and let him enfold her—but God, she's suddenly so scared he won't let her. Does he know that she's been with Sam for the last two days? That she's solved their mystery at last? Can he read the regret on her face?

She stops at the edge of the dock and looks up at him. "Permission to come aboard?"

"Permission granted."

As she steps onto the deck, he descends the ladder. Her arms want to reach for him, but she hugs herself instead.

"A lot's happened, Whit."

"I know, Red."

"I don't see how you could."

He scans her face. "Now, hold on. I don't get to be angry too? My wife takes off with her ex-boyfriend and doesn't tell me where, doesn't answer my calls?"

Liv looks away. She walks to the edge of the boat and searches the houses on the other side of the canal, dark and so far away.

"I know about the diary," Whit says. "And I know about Simon."

She spins back to face him. "Sam told you?"

The look of disappointment in his eyes crushes her.

She drops down to the bench and rocks forward. "I so wanted it to be us, Whit. It was supposed to be you and me."

"Maybe it still could be." He sits beside her and pulls out a folded piece of paper from his shirt pocket. She takes it. The bridge lights cast a strong beam. Liv knows from the ivory color that it must be old.

She unfolds it carefully, the thick paper soft from age and damp.

"I found it in Kitty Hawk," he says. "From the collection of the guy you and Sam saw that weekend about the letters. Barnacles and Brass, remember?"

"We never ended up going," she whispers as she lays the

page in her lap and smooths it gently with her fingertips. She looks up at him, suddenly so nervous she can barely swallow. "What is this, Whit?"

He shrugs. "Maybe nothing. Maybe everything." He nods to it. "Read for yourself."

February 3, 1813

Ivan,

By the time this letter reaches you, I will be gone.

Brother, you know I am not a foolish man. I have suffered too much heartbreak to entertain fancy of any kind, and yet, five weeks ago, I found myself bewitched by a love that cannot be, and yet cannot be denied either.

Maybe if she hadn't looked so out of place on that bustling dock, I might never have approached her, might never have asked how I could help. She claimed to have stepped off a ship, a schooner detained—so many are during this unstable time. When I asked why she did not get back on when the ship was cleared, she told me I wouldn't understand. When the weather turned, and she had nowhere to go, I offered her shelter. And perhaps even as I laid my coat over her trembling shoulders, I knew our paths were meant to cross. Twenty years on the water, a man is a fool not to heed its warnings. Tides and currents are the only true compasses we have in this world. Losing Lucy and Nicholas taught me that.

I have labored with grief for too long now, brother. To be given a seed with which to grow salvation and harvest joy, however impossible, is a gift I cannot refuse. I know in my heart you and Sally will not begrudge me this chance for happiness, wherever I may find it.

I should like to take my love away. I am telling you of my plans, dear brother, because I am sure there will be gossip of my departure, conjecture that I've done something drastic and perhaps even sinful. I would not wish for you to think it true. After all of your faithful counsel, I could not bear your scorn or disappointment.

I know of a spit of land, a strip of abandoned shore. I have heard there is still a structure there, bleak and needing care, but I think it could suffice. Love can compensate for many things.

Brother, forgive me but I ask that you and Sally make no mention of this letter, nor that you seek to find me. For reasons I cannot explain, my beloved too wishes to start over, to be freed from the anguish of loss and the burdens of duty, and so we hope to do so together.

Farewell, dearest brother. Let our arms embrace each other again in heaven and may our journeys be ever kind on the way.

Simon

Simon.

Liv raises her head slowly and finds Whit's eyes fixed on her.

It's not possible. That it could be the same Simon from the diary? The same Lucy and Nicholas? The odds that Whit had found something . . .

Looking down at the letter again, she feels her breath catch. On either side of the yellowed paper, her bare thighs are pebbly with gooseflesh.

"There's no way to prove it's the same Simon," she whispers. "Or that the woman is Theo."

"No. . . ." Whit smiles. "But there's no way to prove it *isn't*."

Liv stands and walks numbly to the edge of the canal, holding the letter against her chest. This would explain why the entries felt false, why Theodosia had miscounted the windows. She'd made up the story of her capture. But if Theodosia got off the *Patriot* when she was detained by British troops, then what happened to the ship?

And at this very moment, divers are heading out to search where they believe the *Patriot* sank.

Liv stares at the water. "But she loved her father more than anything."

Whit comes beside her. "Or maybe after all her heartbreak, after taking care of everyone else, she just wanted to be free. Like the letter says, to start over."

"But her guilt would have been unimaginable."

"Which is why she had to fake her death," Whit says. "Because she knew the only way she could live with the guilt of leaving her father and her husband was if they believed her dead."

May this record provide you with some comfort, and most of all, the proof that I must surely be gone, for otherwise we would be together, Papa . . .

Liv raises her eyes to Whit's and finds him smiling tenderly.

"You're not Theo, baby. You don't have to start over to be free."

Her eyes well. "I don't want to start over," she says. "I want to keep going just like this."

"So let's keep going," he says.

"How, Whit? We're broke."

"Aye, lass. Broke, but not broken."

She turns away from him and walks to the stern. Whit follows her.

"Livy, I know I can't make this right in a day—"

"No." She spins to cut him off. "You can't."

"But I can promise you I won't quit trying. Starting now." He pulls a napkin from his pants pocket, a few jagged, blurry pen lines. As scant as it is, she recognizes the curves. "Oak Island," he says. "It's a good lead, Red. A great one. I promised you one more dive, and I plan to keep that promise too." He searches her eyes. "You do want one more dive, don't you?"

She snatches the napkin out of his hand, crumples it up,

and casts it high into the air where it uncurls on its way down, floating to the canal like a feather.

She is crying as she says, "I don't want treasure and I don't want deep dives. I just want you, dammit. I want *us*."

He takes her face into his hands, planting the pads of his thumbs on either side of her lips and holding them there. She was right that night, to think he was the sort of man whose kiss—whose very heart—could swallow a woman whole.

"If it wasn't Sam who told you about Simon, then who?" she says. "The museum hasn't released the entries yet."

He grins as he searches her eyes. "It turns out Beth Henson doesn't hate me nearly as much as she used to."

Liv stares at him. Anyone else and she might have doubted the claim.

"I think even Felder's coming around," he says. "The only person I'm not sure about is my wife."

Tears sting the corners of her eyes. She swallows to stay them, but they rise and spill.

"I could never hate you," she whispers.

"But you tried, didn't you?"

"God, yes."

He smiles. "Good girl."

Then he leans in and inhales her at last, filling her mouth, maybe even her lungs, with his breath, because she has forgotten how to breathe for a moment, but it's only a moment, and there are so many more.

DIARY DISCOVERED IN BEACH HOUSE ATTIC SOLVES CENTURIES-OLD MYSTERY OF LOST SHIP

HATTERAS—Over two hundred years after the schooner *Patriot* disappeared without a trace on its way to New York, a diary written by her most famous passenger has been discovered in a Hatteras beach house. The entries, written by Theodosia Burr Alston, in the blank pages of a lightkeeper's logbook, detail the *Patriot*'s harrowing capture at the hands of infamous pirates, the "Carolina Bankers," and puts to rest over two centuries of speculation and local lore of what happened to the schooner when she left her port in Georgetown, South Carolina, on December 31, 1812.

"This is a monumental discovery," said Beth Henson, director of the Outer Banks Shipwreck Museum in Nags Head. "The disappearance of the *Patriot* has been one of the nation's most enduring nautical mysteries. This diary not only sheds light on the events of the ship's capture, but also provides tremendous insight into Theodosia Alston Burr. For historians and shipwreck enthusiasts, this is an exciting day."

The daughter of Vice President Aaron Burr, whose infamous duel with Alexander Hamilton resulted in Hamilton's death and Burr's subsequent trial, Theodosia was highly regarded for her academic and social accomplishments in an era when women were not allowed opportunities for advanced education. An unwavering champion of her father after the death of her mother when Theodosia was ten, Theodosia (often referred to as Theo) remained devoted to Burr even in the wake of his many scandals, and after the tragic loss of her only child, a son, Aaron, who died at ten from malaria. She was on her way to reunite with Burr after his return to the States when the schooner disappeared without a trace near the Outer Banks.

Details of the entries have not yet been released—the museum plans to display them in an upcoming exhibit—but Henson says, "The passages are expertly written and read with all the intrigue, suspense, and romance of any bestselling novel." She says also, "They prove once again that Theodosia lived her life in the face of peril as she did before her capture: with grace, wisdom, and an enduring devotion to her father."

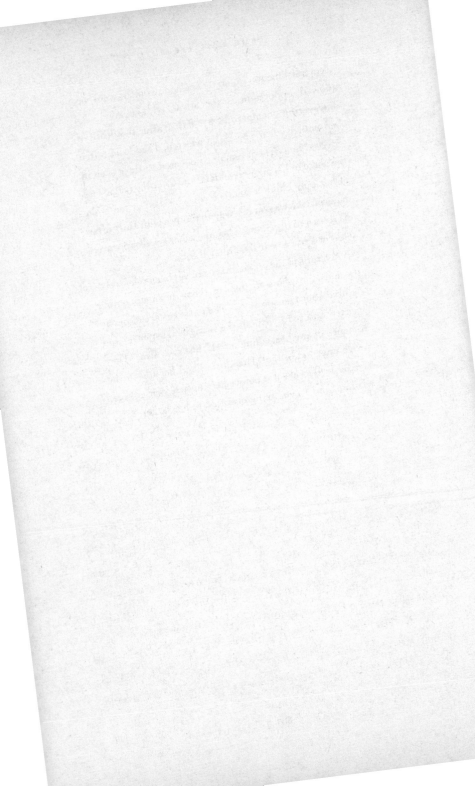

Author's Note

While there has been much recorded about Theodosia Burr Alston's life, there is little known about how she and the *Patriot* disappeared after they left Georgetown. The exact location of the schooner's wreckage, as well as the details of her demise, remains a mystery. But the theories and legends are boundless, and I made use of as much of the lore as I could in this novel. Some details are not myth. The "Nags Head" portrait, whether a portrait of Theodosia or not, is indeed a real painting that is in the collection of the Lewis Walpole Library in Farmington, Connecticut. I have also woven existing shipwrecks into the novel, such as the pirate ship *Whydah*, which lies off Cape Cod; others I have imagined for the sake of the story, such as the *Bella Donna*, which I modeled after galleons found and excavated off the Florida Keys. I found great insight and inspiration in the following sources: Bob Brooke's *Shipwrecks and Lost Treasures: Outer Banks: Legends and Lore, Pirates and More!*; Kevin P. Duffus's *Shipwrecks of the Outer Banks*; David Stick's *Graveyard of the Atlantic: Shipwrecks of the North Carolina*

Coast; and *Treasure Hunter: Diving for Gold on North America's Death Coast* by Robert MacKinnon with Dallas Murphy.

On the subject of maritime and salvage laws, I have endeavored to be as accurate as possible in this novel. However, the rules and regulations, especially state by state, change often—and for the sake of my story, I sometimes simplified aspects of the process.

Even though this novel presents a wholly fictionalized final chapter of Theodosia's life in my imagining of what might have happened to her on her journey to be reunited with her father, I wanted to be as true to Theodosia's character as possible in my conjecture. She was renowned for her great intellect and charm, as well as her scholarly accomplishments during a time when women weren't allowed, let alone encouraged, to seek proficiency in advanced studies. But my depiction is hardly exhaustive, so I very much hope that if you find Theodosia as compelling as I do, you'll research her history further.

Most of all, I hope that my work of fiction inspires a deep passion for the wonder and marvels of the sea. May her mysteries never cease to amaze and her beauty be protected for generations of treasure seekers to come. This story has been in my heart for many years, and I am grateful to have had the courtesy of your company while finally sharing it.

Acknowledgments

With each book I write, I am more and more indebted to the generosity and talents of so many others in helping my stories come to light. . . .

I am tremendously fortunate to work with such an amazing team at Penguin. Thank you to Sarah Blumenstock; to my publicist, Danielle Dill; to copy editor Dan Larsen; and to Sarah Oberrender for giving my novel such a breathtaking cover. To my editor, Danielle Perez, for her incredible insight once again in helping me dig deeper into characters I often loved too much to set truly free—this novel is so very much richer for your expertise. To my agent, Rebecca Gradinger, whose guidance and support strengthen everything I write—seven years in, I hope she knows how grateful I am for our partnership. To Veronica Goldstein, for her help and her cheer. To the members of the PB Literary Society, whose friendships are treasures to me. To Harrison Bell, who kindly and patiently gave of his vast knowledge of scuba diving—any errors or omissions on the subject are mine alone. To my little mermaids, my heart, Evie and Murray, you are all that is right and beautiful in this world. And to Ian, the steel to my magnet, the love of my life. The compass of us is everything.

CONVERSATION GUIDE

The *Last* Treasure

Erika Marks

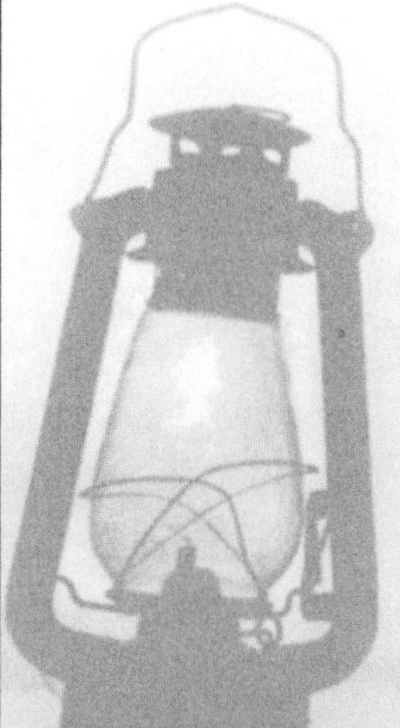

This Conversation Guide is intended to enrich the individual reading experience, as well as encourage us to explore these topics together—because books, and life, are meant for sharing.

A Conversation Between Erika Marks and Her Editor

Editor: What made you center a novel around a shipwreck? How did you come to use the story of Theodosia Burr Alston and the *Patriot* in this novel? Was it a part of the novel from the outset?

Erika: I have long been fascinated with shipwrecks. I grew up near the ocean, so sailing history and the legends of the many ships lost along Maine's rocky coastline buried themselves in my imagination from an early age. When I was researching lighthouses for *The Mermaid Collector,* I knew I would eventually thread a shipwreck into a later novel—the only question was how.

While I had always planned to have Liv, Whit, and Sam pursue a mysterious shipwreck, I assumed I would have to imagine one for the story. Then, as so often happens in writing, remarkable narrative roads intersected and provided me with something different. While doing research on the Outer Banks, I discovered the history of the *Patriot* and her most famous passenger, Theodosia Burr Alston, who, upon further investigation, proved as fascinating a subject as the ship she disappeared with. Curiously enough, Theodosia, like my present-day character Liv, had a complicated and deeply dependent relationship with her father, Aaron Burr. The parallels between the two women were too remarkable to ignore—so how could I not bring the *Patriot* and Theodosia into my story?

Editor: *The Last Treasure* features a love triangle—something you explored in previous novels, such as *Little Gale Gumbo* and *The Guest House*. What about this concept interests you?

Erika: I think there is something fundamentally exciting and fascinating about watching two men vie for a woman's love. I remember seeing a performance of *Camelot* when I was young and being fascinated by the dynamic of Arthur and Lancelot vying for the attention of Guenevere—not who would choose her, but who would *she* choose, and why? Whose love was right for her, and how did she balance that choice in her heart? And when the three people are all close friends, does that strain affect their unit as a whole? Love and desire change us at our core—and the ripples of our feelings spread far out into the pond of our lives. In *The Guest House*, Edie, who is a fiercely unconventional young woman, finds herself smitten with a charming summer visitor and yet also confused by her growing feelings for a man she has always considered a bossy, older-brother type. The reader follows her journey to discover which suitor is ultimately the one her heart craves, and the road getting there is, of course, bumpy and full of unexpected turns.

For *The Last Treasure*, I wanted to explore the dynamics of two very different men in one woman's heart. Whit and Sam came easily to me—especially Whit, whom I loved deeply from the very start. Despite his messiness and his reckless ways, his love for Liv is unwavering, and that level of unabashed desire and certainty is, to me, the sexiest quality in a leading man. So often the "bad boy" is patently unfaithful, his lothario ways somehow romanticized, which I think is a fatal flaw. I can forgive a man most anything in a novel, if his heart remains faithful to the woman he loves, and Whit's always does—even when his actions suggest he can't get out of his own way at times.

With Sam, I wanted to explore the man who *appears* to be the total package on the surface—attractive, responsible, faithful, dependable—but over time, he reveals himself to be someone very different. All of us grow through relationships—or hope to—and what we think makes sense in a partner isn't always right for us, and it can take a long time to understand that distinction. I wanted to explore Liv's evolution of listening to her heart, to see her finally breaking away from familiar patterns of her past—her father's control, her fears of taking risks and of being alone—to find her happiness.

I loved Liv's duplicity—sometimes she is fiercely defiant; other times she is terrifically fragile—and I wanted to watch how she would reveal herself in the company of men who spoke differently to those contrasting personality traits—and ultimately, which one would allow her to be her most honest self, which I think is the measure of true love.

When the novel opens, Liv is on the threshold of possibility—her marriage is strained to the breaking point and her old lover comes back into her life. What would a woman do when faced with that opportunity to revisit—and possibly rework—the past? Would she find her heart's mind changed by nostalgia or would it be a chance to be reminded of all that is right in her marriage? I knew Whit would have to work to win her back—and I wanted very much to see him succeed, but I also wanted the readers to be waiting for that mystery to be solved, just as they were for the mystery of the *Patriot*.

Editor: What intrigues you about writing stories that have a contemporary/present story as well as a past story? Why do you enjoy writing about people at various points/periods of their lives? What does that enable you to do as a writer with the story?

Erika: I love this question because I have often asked myself this when I begin a novel and find myself invariably drawn to the structure of moving back and forth in time with my characters. I myself tend to hyperanalyze most everything in my life (don't we all?), so I'm always drawn to characters who are at a place in their lives where they are facing a crisis of some kind that requires them to dig deep into their pasts in order to move toward their futures. So often we rewrite our histories to suit our emotional needs, which is all well and good—until someone enters that story and reminds us that maybe what we've been telling ourselves for so long isn't the reality.

In the case of Liv, when the reader meets her, she is vulnerable and torn. She loves Whit desperately but is forced to consider whether she can continue to stay married to him. During this, she is reunited with Sam—the ex-boyfriend who was once everything stable and safe in her life. How can she not reconsider the choice she made to leave their relationship?

Structuring the novel by moving between the present and the past allowed me to explore the evolution of these characters as individuals, as pairs, and as a trio. It also allowed me to show the reader the foundation that Liv's marriage—and her relationship with Sam—is built upon. Not only that, but looking back allows Liv the opportunity to revisit the truth of her history with both men—and to be honest with herself and her heart at a time when she might easily rewrite her past to suit her present.

It is that moment of indecision, that gripping flash of consideration, that intrigues me as a writer; a pivotal instant in a person's story that has been building up for years and years. In life, we rarely have the opportunity for leisurely reflection in the midst of emotional distress—in fiction, we can grant our characters that gift.

QUESTIONS FOR DISCUSSION

1. While the end of the novel indicates that the mystery of the *Patriot* was solved by the discovery of Theodosia's diary, Whit brings Liv possible proof of an alternate solution. Which do you believe is the real story? Do you believe Theodosia wished to have absolution by writing the diary to her father? Do you like to imagine the diary was eventually delivered to him?

2. Though they lived nearly two hundred years apart, in what ways are Liv and Theodosia similar? Why do you believe Liv is so devoted to solving the mystery of what happened to Theodosia, and why is she attached to the theory that Theodosia ultimately escaped from the ship? Do you think Liv sees herself in Theodosia? How?

3. At one point, Liv's mother claims that "People aren't always who you think they are" in reference to Liv's father. To whom else in the novel could this statement apply?

4. Throughout the novel, feeling at odds with her marriage, Liv is given the opportunity to revisit her past with both Sam and Whit—and possibly be given a chance to make a different choice in her present. Do you feel the choice she makes at the novel's end is the best for her? Was it the choice you'd hoped she'd make?

5. Sam claims he isn't sure why he took the chart when he broke up with Liv. Why do you think he did it?

6. The novel's nautical themes of "wrecks" and "salvage" could also relate to the emotional journey of each of the main characters, who all act in ways that derail their happiness at one point or another. Did you find yourself rooting for one character's redemption more than another's? Were you satisfied that each character grew through his or her mistakes by the end of the novel and emerged as more emotionally healthy people? Who did, and who didn't?

7. Just as Whit and Sam are two very different men, Liv acts differently around each one. Which man brings out her most authentic self? Which one ultimately gives her what she wants? What about what she *needs*?

8. The reader senses Whit's attraction to Liv (as does Sam) long before Liv will admit to it herself—why do you suppose that is? Do you believe her attraction to Whit was there all

along? If not, when do you think Liv first became aware she had feelings for Whit beyond friendship?

9. Did Sam's later confession regarding what happened after leaving Zephyr's Restaurant surprise or shock you? Why, or why not?

10. What did you think of the final scene between Whit and Sam? Do you believe the men came to a place of peace—or do you think that isn't in the cards for them?

Courtesy of the author

Erika Marks has worked as an illustrator, an art director, a cake decorator, and a carpenter. She currently lives in North Carolina, with her husband and their two daughters. This is her fifth novel, following *It Comes in Waves*, *The Guest House*, *The Mermaid Collector*, and *Little Gale Gumbo*.

CONNECT ONLINE

erikamarksauthor.com
facebook.com/erikamarksauthor
twitter.com/erikamarksauthr
instagram.com/erikamarkswriter